SMILEY'S RUN

D.E. OSBORNE

OEC PUBLISHING

ISBN: 0692494529
ISBN-13: 978-0692494523

Smiley's Run is dedicated to all the veterans I've known over the years, who have been my friends and family, and whose anonymity I respect.

ACKNOWLEDGMENTS

I wish to thank the people in my life who have made this book possible. First I want to thank my wife Dawn, without her tolerance I couldn't have done this. J R Lankford, author and teacher and mentor, has taught me more in offhand comments than any other teacher has through lectures and labs. Ms Lankford's writing group, Novel Pro, was instrumental in developing my writing and Smiley's Run, specifically Gloria Piper Manjarrez , Sudarshan Bharadwaj. Aimee Salter, Vanitha Sankaran , and Joyce Moore , each of whom is an accomplished author and generous teacher. I wish to thank the other members of Novel Pro who allowed me to learn the craft while offering suggestions on their manuscripts.

And at last I want to thank my daughter, Roseanne Osborne, who has been a sounding board, a truth teller, and a great graphic designer. Without her, I'm not sure I would have finished the book, not to mention publishing it.

1. DEAD MAN

The dead inhabit dark places in my dreams. The flash of explosions, the terror, the grief, the anger, faces contorted in the rigor of violent death, but without the sensations. Never the sound of the screams, nor the smells of cordite, camel shit, and death.

Death has an aroma. Not just the banal release of body fluids, or the metallic smell of blood, but the gases released when something living and breathing stops. The taste of death crawled into the back of my throat and pulled me up from the darkness.

I woke up shivering, next to a dead man.

His cold, still flesh pressed against my naked skin. Revolted by the intimate touch, I pulled away. I don't generally find myself with naked men, alive or dead. Two neat little holes perforated the back of his head. Brains had leaked out on the pillow.

I notice those sort of things. My name is Jason Smiley. I'm a detective.

And I was pretty sure something bad had happened last night.

I squinted against the sharp glare of sunlight. We were in the kind of motel room where you'd take someone else's wife; clean, with a bed, dresser, table, chair and not much else. Marks on the end table and a broken jack indicated where the room phone had been removed with violence.

The dead man——overweight, hairy, Italian——was Bruno Girodinelli, a low level mobster from Hollywood, and a client of mine. Before 9/11, the Army, two tours in Afghanistan and one in Iraq, I'd been a detective in the Chicago Police Department. Now I'm a private investigator, strictly insurance and divorce. That I don't do mob work is about the only principle I have left. Bruno became a client because he didn't want to dump his wife's body in the scrubland off the road to Bakersfield.

Why was he dead? Was it a mob hit? Or was he dead because he was my client?

I closed my eyes against the painful brightness. A hell of a way to wake up on the day you're supposed to save the world. My thoughts fragmented with no sense of urgency or dread, very like the after-effects of the anesthetics and pain meds they fed me in the hospital in Kandahar. But it wasn't the battlefield in Afghanistan that replayed on the inside of my eyelids.

Bruno, running toward me from an SUV. A scoped rifle pointing through the rolled down window of a passing car, a mustachioed man behind the gun. The surprised look on Bruno's face as he fell on me. Over Bruno's shoulder, Jack Nesmith watched, shock clear on his face.

I hadn't gone to meet Bruno. Jack, my battle buddy from my tour as an interrogator at Abu Ghraib, had called me Monday night - last night- making this Tuesday morning as a starting point. Subject to adjustment as I could determine the facts.

Jack and I hadn't spoken in the eight years I'd been back. I hadn't thought about him more than four or five times. Jackie-new-boy, freshly minted FBI agent from Quantico didn't mix well with an ex-

Chicago cop from the land of organized crime.

"Smiley, I need your help," he'd said. "I can't go into detail. They listen for keywords. But I need your help to save the world, or at least Chicago."

No matter where I live, Chicago is home.

So I'd caught a cab across town to a margarita bar on the East LA stroll at midnight. Bruno ran up to me in front of the bar and got whacked mob style. Gangster gets gunned down in the street. Nothing to do with me and Jack. Just a coincidence -- but there are no coincidences.

Time to leave. I sat up, placed both feet solidly on the floor and grabbed my head so it didn't fall off. My stomach clenched, I didn't care about Bruno or Jack until space stabilized.

I tested the tender spot on the back of my head, deciding it probably wasn't cracked. Bruno had died in motion, knocking me down. My memory gaps, and the bruised injection site on my shoulder, indicated I'd been drugged to keep me unconscious, but why kidnap me? I smelled of cheap soap and rotting Bruno. Someone had cleaned me up.

The coffee pot hissed from the bathroom with the promise of ambrosia suggesting my abductors had just left. But there were no clothes, no toiletries, nothing indicating who the room belonged to. The only thing out of place besides my own naked butt was Bruno on the bed staring back at me in full rigored surprise.

I wrapped a towel around my waist. Without a gun, I'd be better off half naked on the streets than in a motel room with a corpse. I strode toward the door.

Before I touched the knob, the electronic lock mechanism cycled.

I slammed the dead bolt home, locking my erstwhile abductor out, and myself in. Post-traumatic stress disorder is a wild animal just behind my eyes, clawing to get out. Trapping myself brought out its claws. Sweat beaded on my forehead even though the air conditioner had been turned up high.

The electronic lock cycled several times. Braving the sunlight, I pushed the drapes aside enough to see the lone woman burdened by several shopping bags fumbling with the door. The wild animal wanted to lash out at the tormentor. I fought to control my breathing. My brain felt like it had overheated. I needed action.

The towel might serve for basic modesty until I could get in touch with my office, but I was naked without a gun. If I opened the door at best I might snap at her with a towel. Dizzy and nauseous, I couldn't have won a fight against my grandmother, God rest her soul. I slammed the door with my hand until the windows rattled. The cycling of the lock and rattling of the latch stopped.

"Mr. Smiley? Are you all right?" the woman called out in a posh English accent.

"Go away." I sucked in a deep breath of the machine washed air and pressed my eye to the peep hole.

The security glass provided a contorted, fish-eye view of a woman in a yellow dress on the short side of thirty, with hair shimmering in a thousand hues from amber to cinnamon.

She tried to glamour me through the peephole with a cheery smile before she knocked on the door. "Mr. Smiley. I've got clean clothes for you."

"Leave them at the door. I'm not decent," I said with more indifference than I felt, like she'd brought the extra towels. I leaned my throbbing head against the door.

"Quite all right, actually. I helped fix you up last night." She smiled at the peephole and managed to convey a look of friendly frustration, no doubt for the benefit of any inquisitive neighbors.

Her voice stirred a bit more of my memory from last night. Somewhere in the darkness, I had been back in Afghanistan and the whole world had gone to hell. She'd been there. I'd been fighting for consciousness and she'd said, 'Take it easy, Mr. Smiley' in the same posh English, before I'd faded into blackness until this morning.

"You drugged me," I said, in flat accusation. It didn't matter how

4

she responded. I suddenly began to shake. Sweat trickled into my eyes.

"You were having a bad time. I thought it would help." The careful patina of patience and nonchalance in her voice sounded strained. Maybe with a little more effort I could get her so frustrated she would leave, otherwise I had to drag her through the door and knock her out. Given the choice, I won't hit a woman.

"Who are you?" When I was married I talked through doors a lot. Sarah, my ex, slammed doors in my face at least once a day.

"Mr. Smiley, let me in. I've got your breakfast. We can discuss what happened last night over the coffee." She shifted her awkward load of boxes and bags.

The smell of fresh brewed coffee from the other room cut through the memories. I needed coffee with lots of sugar. I shuffled to the bathroom to fix a cup. "I've got coffee."

I sipped the sweet, black drink and looked out the peephole again. "Did you bring me here last night?"

"Yes." She scanned the parking lot showing a good defensive posture. She knew I could be stalling her until backup arrived. Or maybe she expected her own backup.

"Alone?" I asked.

"No, of course not." She grimaced at me through the door.

"Where is your help, now?" A bead of sweat on her forehead, enlarged by the optics of the peephole showed the strain my recalcitrance caused her.

"Not here. Now let me in." She kicked the door in frustration.

"Who are you?" The sugar in the coffee began to kick in. I started hearing the theme from CSI playing in my head.

"A friend, Mr. Smiley. Now open the bloody door before we attract attention." Her voice slipped into a less cultured mode, reminiscent of docks and factories. She really wasn't a posh Brit.

"I prefer to meet people on more even ground." I watched her glare at the door. She looked like she regretted bringing me to the motel. Good. "If you intend to give me a change of clothes leave them by the door and walk to the parking lot directly away from the door. Otherwise you may leave and I'll make my own arrangements."

"That would be unwise, Mr. Smiley. Your companion might be a trifle difficult to explain." She smirked at the peephole.

"I've explained away many dead men in my time. One more won't mean much. Besides, I'm thinking what happens to Bruno matters to you. Or you'd have left him on the sidewalk." Time to up the ante. "I presume your employer wants something from me. I can't imagine what, since I don't do mob work."

"What makes you think this is mob work, Mr. Smiley?" Her attempt to maintain the posh accent, in spite of her increasing frustration, forced her words to sound clipped and brittle.

"Bruno was small-time mob. You used Bruno to find me so you could ask me to work for your employer. Therefore, it's mob work," I said as I drained the last of the sugar from the bottom of the plastic cup. The throbbing in my head started to subside. "And I don't do mob work——for any reason."

"There are ways, Mr. Smiley, to coerce the Bishop of Canterbury to kiss the devil's arse." She quickly suppressed the smile that quirked her lip. "But I don't have time or inclination. You ought to be glad I'm trying to help you."

"I was minding my own business when Bruno fell dead in my lap and you had someone stuff me in a trunk. I could use a lot less help like that. Put the packages by the door and we'll talk when I'm dressed." Knocking her out began to have a greater appeal. "Or you can leave and I'll take care of myself without your help."

The English lady emitted the most unladylike grunt and kicked the door harder. My ex-wife says I've got a gift for exasperating women. "All right. We don't have much time. Please hurry." In defeat, she dropped her packages and stalked out into the parking lot where she turned to face me, arms tight across her chest, yellow dress iridescent in the sun, breeze ruffling her hair. She had retreated but hadn't run.

Now I could either bolt down the street like a madman in a towel and see if she chased me, or get dressed and walk away from her like I didn't have a care in the world.

I undid the dead bolt and pulled the boxes inside. The bright sunlight felt like lasers beamed at my brain. I slapped the dead bolt home again and sat hard on the bed to recover from the pain. Whatever drug she used on me had a wicked light-sensitivity response. I wished for more coffee but the motel only provided a one-shot pot.

I undid the string around the biggest package. The first box contained expensive men's boxers, argyle socks, wingtip shoes, a shirt and silk tie. The second box held an Armani suit in light gray. Everything looked store new and none of the clothing was mine.

I took my time dressing. I'm not a big man, and whatever is on the racks seems to fit me just fine, but this suit felt custom tailored, with enough extra size in the chest to hide a shoulder holster. But none of the parcels had my guns and holsters. In a few minutes I was ready to meet the world. The bag held one last item, a gray fedora to match the suit. I dropped it on my head at a jaunty angle and checked myself in the mirror. The hat changed me from a nice looking guy in a pricey suit to a made-man of the old Chicago Outfit, Chicago's Mafia. I felt like a scruffy version of Jimmy Cagney from the movies about Old Chicago.

I wiped down every surface I might have touched, hoping I wouldn't be connected to Bruno's corpse if the crew that brought us here didn't clear up after I left. I winked at Bruno who just looked at the wall. The breast pocket of the suit coat contained a pair of Ray Ban sunglasses. I put these on and opened the door.

The English lady still waited in the middle of the parking lot with a greasy bag of take out. She stood maybe five foot seven with her long red hair tied back against the heat. She carried herself with a natural dignity even waiting in a morning-scorched parking lot.

"You do clean up well, Mr. Smiley." She crossed over to me, her

7

mask of professionalism slipped slightly as she examined her handiwork. "The gray suits you."

I returned her compliment with the ritual baring of teeth. "Thanks, lady."

She smiled back, but her sunglasses hid the telltale crow's feet that indicate a genuine smile. "Mr. Smiley. Let's start over. My name is Blankenship and I am here to facilitate a meeting. Were the furnishings satisfactory?"

"I like the suit. Much nicer than the jeans and leather jacket I had, but I'm missing a few personal items." I scanned the parking lot and buildings. Too many places for observers, and too easy to set up a snatch and dash. At the end of the parking lot a painted arrow pointed to the office. A call from the desk phone to Lucy Diamonds, my office manager, would get me extracted.

Blankenship ran faster in her heels than I expected. She caught up to me half way to the office. She huffed once, handed the bag of food to me and dug through her large shoulder purse. The smell of sausage and old grease turned my stomach so I set the bag on a trash can. I collected one of the cartons of coffee, hot with cream and lots of sugar, intended to combat the hangover. I gulped the hot coffee while she extracted my watch and my wallet, a Swiss Army knife I'd had since I was a Boy Scout and a package of chewing gum from her purse. I placed all the items in their correct locations and popped a piece of gum in my mouth. "Want some?"

She glared at me.

"I'm still missing my rigs." I normally carry a 10 mm Smith and Wesson Auto under my left arm, a .44 S&W short barrel revolver in a fanny pack, a Walther .380 auto as an ankle gun and a .38 Ruger snub in a crotch holster. I've been told the armory is a compensation mechanism but I feel naked without my guns.

She crossed her arms again, and leaned back like my third grade teacher did when I sassed her, except Lady Blankenship made it look sexy as all hell. "We don't have any more time for this. I've been asked to bring you to meet someone. He wants your help but he doesn't need any security problems. You'll get your guns after you meet with him."

"If your client wants to meet with me, have him call my office. I'm usually there between 10 and 6." I turned my back on her and walked away.

"We did call your office, or rather Bruno did." She clattered along beside me taking two steps for every one of mine.

"And now you've caught up with me and asked me to speak to your client. I decline, because I don't work for the people you work for." I gave her one more wistful look. An intelligent and independent woman would be a delightful change from the gold-digging bimbos and gigolos I'd followed for the last few years.

"I'm afraid you must come with me." Her pace increased as I widened my stride. Sweat beaded on her forehead. "If you come with me, your questions will be answered. All of them."

"I'm only curious when I'm paid to be," I lied. "You can call me when you have a legitimate job for me to do, like divorce or insurance fraud."

She caught my arm and dragged me to a stop. "I can't very well call when your cell phone is dead." She dug into her bag and produced the new iPhone I'd picked up the day before. She tossed the dead phone to me. "But, right now, you need to come with me."

I studied her just to remember the moment. The more her annoyance poked through her veneer of civility, the more attractive she became. The animal behind my eyes feared being trapped by her, drugged and caged. With a shrug and a sigh, I turned my back to her, again, and hoofed it out of the parking lot. If I could get in contact with Lucy, I could still catch up with Jack. Lucy had a talent for finding people.

I didn't recognize the section of LA we were in, but then I'd only been in town for three years. I didn't know all the ugly yet. Now, Chicago was my hometown. I knew ugly there.

I reached the street when Blankenship called out.

"Wait. You can't leave." Her voice didn't have the edge of panic in it her words implied.

I waved at her without looking and set out at an easy march in the most convenient direction away from the motel and poor dead Bruno. Even if she had a gun, I didn't think she would shoot me in the street because it might be messy. I walked away with my stomach knotted tight and an itch in middle of my back.

I kept close to the buildings so I only had to watch my front, back and left at the same time for the slow-moving box-vans favored by the snatch-and-dash artists. Kidnappers the world over favor the same style of van: boxy with no, or opaque windows and enough room to conceal a body or two. Since I'd been grabbed and drugged once, twice wasn't unlikely.

After about a block the heat, the sugar from the coffee, and the exercise had sweated the headache away. A ten-year-old, orange and white Cadillac Seville dressed in urban chic with twenty inch rims and low profile tires pulled up next to me. The tinted passenger window rolled down exposing Blankenship pointing a Lady Smith at my chest. "Open the door," she said, punctuating every word with a jab of the gun.

A woman with a sharp knife in her hands has been a threat ever since Lorena Bobbitt shortened her husband's manhood with the kitchen cutlery. Put a gun in an angry woman's hand and a person courted certain injury. I opened the door. She immediately dropped her aim. "Get in the car, please, or I'll put a bullet in your leg."

I shrugged. We were outside and away from Bruno, and the heat behind my eyes had disappeared. She might be a little melodramatic but I wasn't going to test her. I climbed in the car and shut the door. As kidnappings go, this was almost civilized. She dropped the locks and rolled the window up.

"You're a very stubborn man, Mr. Smiley." She poked at a package on the seat between us. "Please open the envelope. This is the man Bruno thought you could find."

The Caddy eased away from the curb and floated down the road. The air conditioner had been set on 'Freeze Meat' but I hardly noticed.

An elegant scrawl decorated the front of the envelope with the name 'Jackie New.'

Opening the envelope revealed a grainy surveillance picture of my old Army buddy, Jack Nesmith.

2. THE OFFER

The pimped-out Caddy's lowered suspension and ultra-low-profile tires transmitted every bump and rock in the road to the passenger compartment. The air-conditioning froze morning humidity to the windows but didn't touch the fire breathing animal behind my eyes.

The picture in my hand showed a different Jack Nesmith from the one I knew; thinner, scraggly chin beard, hair stuck up in the angry punk style and his full lips held in a sinister curl like a kid pretending to be a tough guy.

Jack working under cover.

A more dangerous Jack Nesmith than I worked with in Iraq, but I'd caught a glimpse of this character just before Bruno died. Definitely Jack in disguise. And the name, Jackie New? Dead giveaway. He'd earned the nick-name because he had to wait for the midnight mortar attack every night before he would go to bed.

I controlled my surprise. Blankenship didn't need to know I knew Jack. Whoever Blankenship worked for was more connected than Bruno.

Bruno belonged to the local LA mob. He worked for a boss named Sammy 'the Suit' Schwartz who monopolized vice on the Hollywood strip. The Chicago Outfit had a hook into the West Coast ever since Vincenzo "Vinnie T" Tortelli took over the Outfit, which connected Bruno through Sammy with the organized crime syndicate I'd fought before 9/11.

Jack had to be under deep cover as a 'wise-guy' in the Outfit. The Jackie New image easily obscured the mild-mannered desk-jockey Jack Nesmith I knew. He had never been good with people.

Maybe he couldn't hold himself together under cover. He shouldn't have called me. And how did saving Chicago tie in with the Outfit?

But, I trusted Jack. We were brothers from different parents. If he said we needed to save the world, then he meant it. If he couldn't call anyone but an old, discarded soldier for help, he was in deep trouble. Maybe too deep for me to get him out. I looked up at Blankenship. "So why was Bruno interested in this guy?"

"My client will explain." With the faintest trace of a frown on her face Blankenship eased the Caddy through early morning city traffic.

Not a satisfactory answer. We rode in silence for several minutes through an increasingly industrial area of warehouses and neglected buildings. I used to think each city possessed a unique underbelly, where the denizens scrawl their individuality on building walls in the same illegible style. But there're only so many ways garbage blown against chain link, or concrete block buildings can be left to decay in the elements. We weren't in any part of LA I knew, if we were in LA at all.

I felt a little jerk of dislocation. If we weren't in LA, where the hell were we?

What else didn't I know about the situation? I studied

Blankenship.

Little tendrils of her wonderful red hair escaped the loose bun. High cheek bones with just a touch of blush, full lips, a bit of cleavage, and nipples erect from the air conditioning. Where did she fit into Jack's problem? She acted like a 'fixer' for the mob, but the Italian boys are chauvinists, and not likely to listen to any woman except their mother. She didn't look like anyone's mother.

Since she wasn't inclined to answer important questions, I tried a simple one. "So, if we're not in LA, where are we?"

The silence continued until she stopped for a light, then she turned her Ray Bans toward me, showing me my own reflection. "We're in San Diego. Since Bruno's passing, Los Angeles has become unhealthy."

"Why is LA less healthy than S Dee? The cartel really doesn't like visitors."

She looked forward again and gunned the Caddy away from the light. Looked like I had exceeded my daily limit. A tire-chirping turn into an alley took us behind a strip club called Paradise Found.

Daylight is never kind to strip clubs. The cheap paint, cracked siding, and garbage piled in every corner are not erotic. I like strip clubs at night. All that neon and soft spot lights on naked girls makes a magical world. In the daylight, I've seen nicer crack houses.

When Blankenship stepped out of the car she released her hair and her entire attitude shifted. Her walk became a swagger and her head and shoulders squared back giving a tougher, less Mary Kay attitude, all framed by glinting reds, ambers, and golds of her shoulder length mane. She yanked the passenger door open. "Let's get on with it."

I preceded her to the side door which, though it had no outside handle, had been propped open. She cleared the blockage and made sure the door shut behind us.

Inside the darkened bar a single spot followed us to the stage preventing any assessment of the room. The air tasted of stale beer and cheap perfume overlaid with a hint of fresh cigar. The red glow of the lit cigar stared at me from the shadows just below the light. The glare of the spot shadowed everything and everyone else in the room. Cheap metal chairs creaked under excessive loads. I recognized the ham-handed intimidation tactics but the added stress prodded the animal behind my eyes. I tightened down my nerves.

"Get on the stage, please." Behind me Blankenship's voice had a soft, sensuous feel to it, like a wife who had planned the night's spontaneity. Under different circumstances her tone alone could calm me... or arouse.

Shielding my eyes against the light, I tried to get an idea of how big of a crowd waited for my performance. I sucked in a deep calming breath and found it laced with her perfume. "I'd rather see you up there. I bet you dance real nice."

"Maybe later, darling. Right now you need to cooperate." Her Lady Smith nudged me in my left kidney. She might not be serious about shooting me, but pistol whip my kidney and I would piss blood for a week.

I climbed the stairs at the side and strolled over to the pole. The spot light made it impossible to see anything beyond the edge of the stage. Maybe that's how the girls did it. Dancing in the light might make them feel like they were all alone.

The tension flowed out of my gut into my hands and feet. Holding the pole with one hand I leaned out to the cheap seats. My mouth disconnected from my brain. "Do I get to pick my own music? I might get in the mood with some Marvin Gaye."

Tough house. No guffaws from the crowd. I shielded my eyes against the glare. All I could make out were three vague shadows and the red coal of a cigar.

"Mr. Smiley," said a male voice, as slippery and gritty as a freshly oiled stone road, located behind the cigar. "Thank you for coming on such short notice."

"You're not welcome. This isn't how I do business." I crouched

15

down and tried to peer under the light. I hated not seeing the other guy's eyes. "Who are you? Do I know you? Is that why you're hiding?"

A fog of smoke crossed the light. My invisible host began again. "The reason I asked you here today——"

"I'm here because this lady showed me her gun. I don't like games. I talk face to face." I stood and paced away from the light, trying to break down the artificial staging of the meeting without making an overt approach. I figured the other two shadows were bodyguards for the boss, with enough muscle to make a direct confrontation not go my way.

"Mr. Smiley, please don't interrupt me again." The disembodied voice carried all the civility of a sharp knife.

A shadow detached itself from the darkness and leaped on the stage. Six-foot-four of blond, blue-eyed muscle, costumed in a three thousand dollar suit, glared at me and smacked one ham-like fist into his palm. I glared back at him.

"What's this?" I reached over and tugged the oversized jacket lapel. "I love playing dress up. I feel like Bogart. Next I expect somebody to sit at the piano and play 'As Time Goes By.'"

The muscle drove his fist into my gut. I dropped to my knees like I'd been tranquilized, and alternated between puking on the stage and trying to breathe. I lost track of my attacker. The play acting had put me off guard. Intimidation goes a long way when threats are backed up with absolute ruthlessness.

While I struggled for control, the thug stood at parade rest on the far side of the stage. When I finally got my breath, I rocked back on my heels. From this perspective the Boss became a silhouette. He looked like the Michelin man which confirmed him as Sammy "the Suit" Schwartz, the King-of-Camp from Hollywood Boulevard, Bruno's Boss. He liked to pretend to be a sophisticate, but he was just a second string mobster, not even a made-man. But just because the mob considered him a joke didn't make him less dangerous.

16

"This is a new suit," I gasped in the direction of the noxious puddle. "Can you get me a towel, at least?"

A dirty bar rag hit the floor next to the puke.

"Now Mr. Smiley, I really don't want our meeting to degenerate." I could hear the smile in the fat bastard's voice.

I wiped my mouth and dusted my clothes as I rocked back to my feet. My guts ached. "OK Sammy, you've proven you can be a tough asshole. What the hell do you want from me?"

Metal screamed as Sammy shifted his bulk in his chair. "You've shown a remarkable ability in finding people who don't want to be found. Like Jimmy the Horse. I've heard Jimmy wants to kill you. Slowly."

"If he really wants to, he can try." I threw the towel on the puke. Jimmy the Horse had run the heroin operation for the Chicago Outfit. He left a lot of dead competitors on the street. I arrested him in the famous Russian Steam Room. Sammy showing his connection to the Outfit. "Little dicks make for vicious men."

"Telling a CNN reporter he was hung like Mickey Mouse made him lose face. Of course he wants to kill you."

"Unfortunately, he'll never see the outside of Statesville until he's dead." I stood up, a little shaky but I've had worse. "Besides that was a long time ago."

"Accommodations can be made. You should watch that smart mouth, Mr. Smiley."

"My mouth isn't my only weapon, Sammy. Let's cut the crap. What do you want from me, you fat turd?" Sometimes I just have to poke the bear.

The well-dressed thug moved back towards me with his fist cocked.

"Hit me again," I said, looking upwards to make eye contact. "And I'll kill you."

"You dumb motherfucker. I saw that movie, too." He unleashed a sudden jab at my gut again. I side stepped it, driving my fingers into

17

his windpipe. For a man his size, he didn't have a lot of muscle around his throat. My fingers sank in until I felt the hard cartilage of his trachea. Sweeping his feet out from under him with my leg, I slammed him into the floor. He wasn't dead but he'd be wondering for a while.

A gun barked. My hat blew back; I dropped to the stage in case better aimed bullets followed the first.

"Stop it." Sammy's voice rose three octaves until he sounded like a train whistle.

"Mitch," An anguished cry from the shadows accompanied another well-dressed felon rushing the stage. He grabbed the choking hood on the floor. The look of sincere concern on his face made it clear they were more than best friends. Mitch rolled and thrashed on the floor choking and gasping like I'd broken his windpipe. I didn't think I had. Usually I feel the cartilage crack.

I got my feet back under me, picked up my hat and backed towards the steps.

"You cocksucker, you killed Mitch." Mitch's lover prepared to charge me. Wood splinters erupted from the stage stopping him in his tracks. The discharge of a .357 magnum round in a closed space is deafening. The gangster and I poked at our ears trying to get our hearing back. A bit of smoke drifted in the spotlight beam. Her Ladyship held the Lady Smith in a two handed grip, effectively covering both of us.

"Behave yourselves, gentlemen. This doesn't need to get out of hand." I loved the dry English understatement in her voice. So classy.

"Thank you El. Sal, you take care of Mitch and don't go shooting up the place." The red tip of Sammy's cigar bobbed into range of the spot light, followed by the rest of Sammy, dressed in a dapper, white suit with a gold trimmed vest. "So you know who I am. I admit this has been a little dramatic, but what is good drama but the truth writ large?"

"Let's cut the crap then, Mr. Schwartz. The drama got Bruno

dead, and I sort of liked him, as far as scumbags go." I dusted my hat off. My knees threatened to buckle. The bullet had creased the peak but hadn't penetrated. Good thing Mitch's friend, Sal, wasn't a dead eye shot.

"Bruno had more to do with the problem at hand than you." Sammy puffed his cigar hot and let clouds of smoke filter the lighting. "My friends in Chicago sent a courier earlier this week with some money to facilitate an exchange between a group of religious people from the Middle East and a local branch of an old Chinese trading company. In the middle of the transaction the courier from Chicago departed abruptly with the money and a special Chinese box the religious people are very anxious to get their hands on."

He took another long draw on his cigar.

"And?" His euphemisms pointed to an unholy ménage à trois of Mafia, Chinese Triads and possibly Al Qaeda. Obviously, the combination of violence, greed, and fanaticism meant something bad.

"The Chinese want the box back since they were never paid for it. The religious people want the box since the money they paid for it is gone and Chicago wants this kept as low profile as possible. We can't have these little issues interfering with business. Bruno was killed as a warning to me personally to get this fixed." Sammy the Suit shifted uncomfortably on his feet.

So, Jack triple-crossed the mob, the Triads, and a terror cell. Good man. "So you know who killed Bruno and who stole your money. What do you need from me?"

"I need you to find this courier from Chicago, this Jackie New. He's a fool to run out on the Chicago Outfit... unless he was doing what Vinnie T wanted him to do."

I nodded agreement. "You'd be some kind of stupid to fuck with Vinnie Tortelli. He has long arms."

Sammy took a step closer to me, his fat lips sucking urgently at the cigar, his little piggy eyes pleading with me. "Vinnie and I don't always get along. I need to know if Vinnie set me up. Like I said the

Chinese are involved. They want the thing Jackie took. Have you ever done business with the Chinese?"

"Just at the Golden Dragon Buffet."

"They make people like Vinnie T look like amateurs. When they send a message there isn't any answer except. . . yes, Mr. Liu."

"And you think Bruno's execution was part of the message?"

"Yes, yes. Will you find the thing Jackie took?" He grabbed my jacket as though to drag me physically into his mess. "I've got to get the Chinese off my back before they do something really bad."

I glared at Sammy the Suit until he released his grip on my jacket. Then he smoothed the wrinkles out with too much interest for my taste. I stepped away. "What's in the box? Drugs?" I couldn't imagine Jack hijacking his career for illegal dust.

"I don't know what's in the box. It's a Chinese box and they want it back. That's enough." Sammy rocked a little as he puffed his cigar. "Well?"

For all his play acting, Sammy Schwartz, a brutal, ruthless thug who had survived a merciless rise to power, begged for my help. My stomach burned like I'd drunk fire. If Jack had got in over his head, I might be at the bottom of the pool.

I needed to get away from Sammy, his thugs, and El Blankenship, so I could find out what Jack wanted me to do to stop this terror plot. Aikido shows the student that the best response to a situation is to let your opponent's momentum work against him. "If I take this job, it's five hundred a day plus expenses, two thousand in advance. I've got the picture of this Jackie character. How long ago did he skip out on you?"

"He disappeared last night in the middle of the delivery. Mr. Liu gave me until Sunday to return the money and the box. The money isn't the problem, but Mr. Liu was emphatic that he must have the box back by Sunday night." Sammy gathered his crew with a glance and stepped back into the shadows. Mitch stared death at me as his friend helped him off the stage. Sammy called out as he swept past his bodyguard. "Ms. Blankenship will provide you with what details are necessary. You should leave now."

"But..." Mitch and Sal staggered after Sammy the Suit out another side door before I framed the right way to ask my original question. Why did Sammy want to hire me? Sammy couldn't reasonably expect me to find Jack. He didn't seem to know Jack and I were connected. And he didn't seem to care Bruno was dead. Bruno had been a message and I became the reasonable response. A very expendable response.

Her Ladyship caught my arm and tugged me out the way we had arrived. The spotlight's glare left a large afterglow where the path to the door ought to be. With the spotlight turned off, the whole room became dark as midnight until my eyes could adjust. My guide apparently didn't suffer from the same problem. She walked unerringly through a maze of chairs while I crashed and stumbled my way after her.

My eyes had almost recovered when she pushed the door open and the glare from outside eradicated my vision, again. "Geeze, give me some warning next time so I can get my sunglasses on."

"Mr. Smiley, you're very foolish." She whirled around on me once we were out the door. "You were dealing with a very brutal man in there."

I pulled the Ray Bans out of my jacket pocket and adjusted them carefully. "He's a frightened man. Frightened men are always brutal. And you brought me here, don't blame me. He doesn't want an investigator, he wants a decoy."

She pursed her lips. "Our choices are limited, so please cooperate." We got into the Caddy which had superheated in the midmorning sun. Her Ladyship fired the car up and turned the AC up to 'Freeze Meat', again. She turned towards me, her face a study in seriousness and beauty. "Your participation is needed."

"Five hundred dollars a day plus expenses makes for expensive bait. The fee is payable to my office even if I don't live through the assignment." I didn't care about the money, but to these people cash meant more than blood, so hopefully, she believed I'd been bought and paid for and would give me whatever information she had on Jack before I ditched her and headed back to LA.

"We need you to find Jackie New. This operation originated in Chicago so you need to go back there to track him." She fixed her green eyes on me.

"You don't need to tell me my job. Unless you know he went back to Chicago, I need to track him from his last known location." I felt a bit of a tingle in my spine. "Besides, I'm not welcome in Chicago."

"Los Angeles has been fully investigated. Chicago is the starting point. Whatever triggered Jackie New's flight began in Chicago. You need to go there." She produced another folder and began to flick through it.

"How long was he in Cali?" So far Blankenship's briefing had setup written all over it. Maybe she wanted to find Jack, but she didn't intend me to investigate anything.

"He flew in Sunday night and stayed at the Grand in Santa Monica. He met with Bruno about 9 Monday night and the exchange was scheduled for 10. He hasn't returned to the hotel."

"Has he been seen in Chicago?" My new office manager, Lucy Diamonds, could do better. She had a knack for finding information people hid.

"No one's seen Jackie New since Monday night. If any of the interested parties had found him they would announce it. Ease the tension and so forth." Blankenship's stern business-like facade eased with the hint of a smile. "You've until Sunday to find him. How hard could it be?"

I shrugged. Away from her I could contact Lucy to track Jack's movements. "I'll need my hardware and the retainer. Hard to do a good investigation with just gum on my shoe."

"We'll get you what you need in Chicago." She smiled at me. "You've been booked on the 11:55 flight."

"I told you I can't go to Chicago. Between the Chicago PD and the Outfit I'm not welcome there. Besides this Jackie New won't be anywhere near there if he crossed Vinnie Tortelli. Chicago is unhealthy for both of us."

She turned to me and grasped my hand in both of hers. Her touch made my skin tingle. "I need you to be in Chicago this afternoon." Her voice took on sincere warmth I hadn't heard before. "Trust me."

"You were pretty sure I'd take this job, weren't you?" I eased up on the tough guy approach, and gave her a toothy smile. "This really isn't the kind of work I do. How do you know I won't just blow off the deadline and let Sammy and you take the heat from the Triads? No skin off my nose."

Her cool, professional demeanor softened with a hint of a smile returned. "You were assigned to Jack as his military liaison in Iraq, making you, I believe the Americanism is, 'Battle-Buddies.' Combine your previous police experience with Jack's current situation as an undercover policeman and I believe you'll do anything to help him. It's in your training, if not your nature."

I felt like the fish who just realized the juicy worm he ate had something hard and sharp in it. "How did you find that tidbit out?"

"I read your file after Bruno suggested you might be useful. A bit of serendipity that, since we need an operative we could persuade easily and you would never turn down the chance to help your friend." She continued to stroke my hand.

"That file is code word only. You can't see it."

The hint of a smile blossomed on her full lips. "I have connections."

"I still can't work in Chicago. If you read the file you should know why, so what do you really want from me?" Her hand had dropped to the seat between us. I slipped my hand over hers wanting to feel her electric touch again. Her eyes dilated, and the ice water on my spine turned to steam. "Who are you, Ms. Blankenship? Who are you working for? Not Sammy the Suit. What's the real story?"

"You know all you need to know, Mr. Smiley. Find your friend and the Chinese box. That's all the answer you need." Her hand stroked mine and the electricity of our connection seemed to flow up my arm and make the world spin crazily. Before I could even pull my hand away my vision tunneled to just her face. She looked a little sad, her forehead wrinkled slightly in a frown.

"I'm sorry, Jason, but I need your absolute cooperation," she purred.

The world shifted under me as I slipped into darkness.

3. SWEET HOME CHICAGO

People crowded the aisle and crouched under overhead baggage compartments waiting to disembark at Chicago's O'Hare Airport. I didn't remember much of the flight. The attractive African-American woman who had been my seat mate glared over her shoulder at me as she waited in crush rather than spend another second next to me. I could still see the spot where I drooled on her blouse. She wore the same perfume as my ex-wife Sarah, and before I awoke I had dreamed of a more intimate time, and groped the lady accordingly.

She'd slapped me hard enough to wake me up.

Once enough people exited the plane I stood up. My fedora had been stuffed in an overhead bin. Somehow Blankenship had gotten me on the plane without alerting the TSA. She must be connected.

I needed coffee and a sandwich. Then I needed to find a way out of Chicago. Blankenship didn't seem to understand how much certain people didn't want me back in Chicago, and most of them weren't as nice about it as my ex-wife. Before I reached the exit, I checked my pockets. I had my dead iPhone and a wad of cash wrapped in a piece of paper with writing on it. I hid the money in my inside jacket pocket and scanned the crowd to see if anyone noticed.

My head throbbed. Communications would be my first order of business, after coffee.

My nerves were taut as I walked up the gateway to the terminal. The beast behind my eyes woke up. This could be dangerous. I checked my pockets for weapons. Blankenship had left me the gum but took my Swiss Army knife. If someone ambushed me at the gate I'd just have to improvise. Or hope they weren't going to do anything in public.

I pushed open the door leading to the waiting area and the crowded concourse. Disappearing into a crowd doesn't take too much effort for the average sized man, even dressed in a $3000 suit.

Across the waiting room, a fat man with a ponytail, sloppy jeans and a scruffy brown fedora lounged in one of the waiting area seats, paying too much attention to me. I pulled my own hat off and stepped into the crowd, dodging a Chinese couple walking with determination towards to the central concourse with its overpriced stores. An electric cart carrying a group of old women provided good moving-cover until I couldn't see his hat.

Had he been watching for me? Were there others I hadn't seen? The wild animal clawed at the back of my eyes. I felt trapped. I needed a deep cleansing breath.

I needed coffee——with lots of sugar.

With coffee in one hand, a bagel in the other, I searched for a phone I could buy with the minimum of personal information. Blankenship's wad of cash would at least allow me some phone-anonymity. O'Hare always seemed under construction, an unfinished monument to a Chicago war hero who flew off into the night never to return. I passed three more coffee kiosks before I found a telephone store near Butch O'Hare's F4F fighter. The politicians made a hero out of old Butch, but he was just a soldier doing his job. His father, on the other hand, gave evidence against Al Capone and got assassinated for it. That's a hero.

I'm nobody's idea of a hero, just panicky for being banned by the Mob and the Chicago Police Department and now back in Chicago to find an undercover Federal cop who pissed off the Outfit. I just wanted to go back to LA and forget this business.

But Blankenship had been right, I wouldn't abandon Jack.

I bought two pre-paid cells phones at a kiosk and backtracked to see if the fat man had followed me or, if I recognized anyone in the crowd. No one stood out, and the fat man disappeared. Still, paranoia would be healthy as long as I stayed in Chicago.

I checked my watch. 3:30 P.M. California time, but the end-of-winter sky had been dark for quite a while. Lucy would still be at the office and worried about me.

The phone didn't actually ring before she picked up. "Smiley Detectives. How may I help you?"

Lucy didn't look the mother hen type. She's big boned, and blond in a Marilyn Monroe way, but that's just an act. She's a sharp operator with a lot of experiences she can't talk about from her time in the Air Force's Military intelligence branch. Her husband was a Special Forces operator 'lost in a training accident' somewhere in Afghanistan or some other 'stan no one would admit to.

"Luce, what day is it?"

"Tuesday. What sort of binge did you go on? And where are you? Mexico?" Her voice carried her disapproval of my careless ways.

Lucy came to me a few months ago. Wallowing in my own misery, I ignored daily business and the paperwork. Maybe she was putting her life back together, but she did it by holding my business together with hundred-mile-per-hour tape and zip cord, while pulling me out of the bottle I'd been hiding in.

"Some sort of tranq. Chicago. And neither were my choice." I looked over my shoulder at the crowd plowing through the airport, looking for those telltale signs of interest in an over-the-hill Private Investigator in a too-expensive suit. I pulled the Fedora down to my eyes and kept moving, another busy businessman just off the plane and on the phone. "I need you to check on a couple of people. 'L' Blankenship. She's associating with Sammy Schwartz but I don't think she's on his payroll."

"You really shouldn't be in Chicago. What's the 'L' stand for?" Lucy slipped into her controller mode, all cool professionalism. She could find things out about people they didn't know themselves.

"Dunno, just heard her addressed as 'El'. She's using the name Blankenship and she talks like she's proper English. Like a lady. Except when she gets mad."

"A woman? With a fake posh accent. Could be Ellen or Elouise." Lucy's fingers clicked across her keyboard. "Should be real easy to find out about this one. Hmmm, not really. Next?"

"The next is our client, Bruno Girodinelli, currently deceased, though I doubt more than half a dozen people are aware that he is."

"Bruno? About time. The cops don't know? What a scumbag. Did you shoot him?" Lucy hadn't liked Bruno at all for a number of very valid reasons. Not the least having to do with her brother.

"Not me. He took two small caliber sub-sonic rounds to the back of his head. Didn't ruin his face, but spoiled his day. And knocked me out cold." I slipped in with a crowd of newly arrived passengers heading towards ground transportation.

"OK. Why are you in Chicago? Isn't that a bad idea?" The mother hen came into her voice.

"Good, bad, and ugly. I need you to find out everything you can about a Jack Nesmith. He's an FBI agent, on an undercover assignment as Jackie New. Out of Chicago but last seen in LA. Current location unknown."

I could almost see Lucy readjusting her assumptions to the facts. "That's going to be dicey. Does the FBI know where he is?"

"I don't think so. Sam Schwartz hired me to find Jack. If the Feds knew his whereabouts I don't think Sammy would be looking. I'd like to know what Jack was working on."

"I don't want to blow some operative's cover." Lucy's professional veneer slipped for a moment. I had the suspicion she'd worked a few undercover operations in her career.

"He's blown already. He's either dead or not in the country. He's got something of interest to the Mob and to the Triads. I was supposed to meet him before my run-in with Bruno."

"Why did Nesmith want to meet with you?" Lucy had recovered her focus. I could hear her tapping the keyboard.

"Another good question I intend to ask Jack when I find him. First I need to know where he is." The crowd I'd been following thinned out. I felt very exposed. A businessman looked my way one too many times. I sat on a bench and tried to look inconspicuous. None of the few people passing looked my way. I kept my head down.

"And you can't ask anyone who might know, right?" Lucy's keyboard rattled in the background. "It's not going to be easy to find him if he was a ghost to start with."

"Thanks, Lucy. I've got faith in you." Lucy's question jarred me. Maybe I could call someone.

"Be careful, Boss." Lucy paused and chuckled. "Wait a second; I think Jack just sent you a message."

"How would he know I'm looking for him?"

"I don't know, but he posted on Facebook."

"I don't do Facebook. All my friends are dead and don't update their Facebook accounts."

She groaned. "I know. I put together a social media presence for the business. Jack's written on our Facebook page. He posted a picture of you with a young man, himself I suppose, over in Iraq where you served together. The caption says 'Meet me back at the hooch.'" Lucy's voice maintained a smooth monotone. "Your thoughts? Oops. Now the message is no longer available. He must have deleted it as soon as Facebook flagged that I'd seen it. And now his account is unavailable. Interesting."

I sighed. "What the hell does that mean?"

"Boss, I can only tell you what I see. I don't know jack about Jack——yet. More to follow. Have you got any money? How are you getting out of Chicago?"

"Yes, I've got money." I pulled the crumpled scrap of paper that had been wrapped around the money from my trouser pocket and read it this time. 'Union Station, locker BF567' written in a strong female hand, probably by Blankenship. She'd promised me I would get my guns back. Or she could just be setting me up. In either case I couldn't loiter around the airport. Someone would be sure to notice me, either from the Outfit or the CPD. And I wanted my guns back. I just might need some firepower.

"I assume you don't want to leave a trail. It will take a little while to pull something together." Worry had started to creep into her voice.

"You're right. No trail. Don't worry about me. I have something to do. See what you can find out about Jack. And Blankenship. And I'll call you."

"Boss, this is a bad idea. You shouldn't be in Chicago. And don't call the office line again. I'll send you another contact number. Watch your six." Her voice tightened up, suppressing emotion and getting the job done like a good soldier.

"I'll be careful. Gotta go. Thanks, Luce." I ended the call. No more random people seemed interested in me, but I didn't believe it. The Outfit banned me from Chicago, and I didn't have any friends on the CPD.

Well, maybe one.

A gaggle of passengers strode purposely past me towards the Ground Transportation. I followed them and tried to blend into the crowd even though they were dressed more casually.

I had cash. A cab to Union Station would be easy. Maybe I could figure out Jack's riddle on the way. Part of the answer involved the Outfit, but I'd been out of touch for several gangland lifetimes. I needed information about the Outfit and the CPD so I would know if I have to run for my life or just keep from annoying people.

The only person in Chicago I could trust, my old partner Mo Dombrowski, had been the catalyst for Sarah divorcing me. And now they were married. We had parted on bad terms after I pulled a gun on him at the police station. But we had been as close as brothers most of our lives, and brothers back up brothers no matter what. I punched my old house phone number into the other cell.

"Hello?" Mo answered with something between a growl and a bark.

"Dombrowski? How's it hanging, buddy?" I figured shooting at him canceled the affair with Sarah. Maybe he felt the same.

"Cocksucker. Who's this?" His voice turned to more of a bark. "Is this O'Toole's? Fucking bar pranks. I can't wait until happy hour is over."

I heard Sarah in the background asking who was on the phone just before the connection ended.

Dombrowski knew my voice like he knew my wife. Something was up.

I considered the dial tone for a minute. Maybe he didn't want Sarah to know I was in town. But he could have taken the call into the garage. Mo wouldn't just blow me off; at the very least he would lecture me on what a vagrant I was.

Unless he thought his line was tapped.

Why would Mo Dombrowski, one of the only honest cops in Chicago, be phone tapped? A bad feeling grew in my gut. Why would Mo be under surveillance the day I showed up in Chicago? I dropped the burn phone in the trash. Shit. The sense of someone watching me intensified. I pulled my hat low and headed to the cab line.

A single cabby leaned against a pillar, smoking, his blond

dreadlocks covered by a colorful knit cap. The concierge and the rest of the cabbies gathered a hundred yards down the entrance ramp under the shuttle bus sign. Not a very subtle hint that they'd been told to let this one screen the fares for someone in particular.

"Hey, mon. You need a cabby?" He asked as he swung the back door open. "Eddy D Funk is your best cabby here, mon."

Bob Marley wailed 'Get up. Stand up for your life' from the tinny car speakers. Pretty good sentiment. I needed to stand up and take charge of my life. Right after I find Jack and saved Chicago. "And conveniently, the only one," I said.

"Not the only one, mon. Plenty for other fares. You Smiley, right?" He grinned at me.

"And you were told to give me a lift. Already paid for?"

"No, mon. I'm told you're a good tipper. I'm just trying to make a living, mon." He waved me towards the back seat. "I'll take you wherever you want to go."

My options were constrained. I could blow off the cabby and grab a shuttle or try another cab, but if he worked for Blankenship I'd never shake him. "Who told you to meet me?"

"An English lady, mon. Fine red hair, don't you know. Tips well."

"Yeah, I know." I bowed to the inevitability of going where Blankenship wanted me to go. "Union Station, please."

I slid into the back seat. The dance songs of revolution flowed over me, kicking at the door that held my wild animal at bay, while Eddy snaked through traffic heading downtown. Blankenship had provided me an escort, just in case I got lost in my hometown.

Dombrowski's deception bothered me. He couldn't admit I called, but there hadn't been any hesitation. He knew my voice. He knew I would call. So instead of hanging up, he used a code, like we did when we were kids.

Mo and I grew up watching the Bulls on TV at O'Toole's Bar and Grill in our old North Center neighborhood. Happy hour was four to seven every day except Sunday. He'd be there at seven. I checked my watch. I shouldn't take the time. I needed to get out of town as fast as possible. But if Dombrowski had a plan already figured out because he expected me to call, then he had information I needed to know. I couldn't go stumbling blind around Chicago.

Jack's message had been as obscure as Dombrowski's. They both assumed I would get the clue from the out-of-place words.

Jack had said 'Meet me at the hooch,' the call we used for an off-shift evening of World of Warcraft. In theater our quarters were our 'hooch' just to remind us we weren't home.

In a sense, Jack had 'deployed' to Chicago because he was under cover. The hooch would be where he lived as Jackie New. Why would he think I would be in Chicago? Was he actually going to be there? That sounded unlikely.

Eddy D Funk pulled in front of Union Station as the Wailers started chanting Natty Dreads. Blankenship's agenda for this trip to Chicago and mine weren't necessarily in agreement, and Eddy might try to keep me on Blankenship's program.

I rapped on the partition with a hundred dollar bill clearly showing through my fingers. He turned his clear, blue eyes to me, lifted an eyebrow in question, and slowly opened the divider.

"Wait here. I'll be right back." I checked the locker directions in my pocket.

"Sure, mon, I'll be waiting." He made the c-note disappear. "Where we be going next?"

I pretended not to hear him. Depending on what I found in the locker my best option might be to ditch Eddy and find other transportation. Besides what destination could I give him? Bob Marley and the Wailers made me melancholy. I was taking the hellbound train and Eddy could just drop me off at the next station.

4. O'TOOLE'S

The locker at Union Station didn't contain an electronic message with a self-destruct sequence, a Mylar-coated map or any other directions, only a high quality back pack heavy with what felt like clothes and guns. While I stared at the locker and the backpack, the movement of a Transit Authority officer caught my attention. I avoided his stare, then an old lady stopped him with a question, breaking his eye contact and letting me ease into the crowd.

I felt like a worm on a hook. Blankenship's motives might not be the same as Sammy the Suit's. She had sent me here against my will, but had provided a supply drop and a driver. What did that mean? Despite my banishment from Chicago, why did Dombrowski expect me, at least enough to have a contact plan in place? And then Jack contacted me with coded messages on Facebook.

Too many coincidences; too many unknowns. What did

Dombrowski know? Where had Jack gone?

I stepped into a restroom stall, inventoried the back pack. Blankenship had loaded it with clothes, my guns and holsters, extra ammunition, a charger for the iPhone, and a banded stack of hundred dollar bills. I speed-changed into the mall-outlet-casual clothing; relaxed-fit jeans, sweatshirt advertising the company selling the sweatshirt, and canvas workman's jacket. It gave me a chance to conceal my guns and get out of the more conspicuous suit. I checked my watch. I had twenty minutes to get to North Center and my most immediate source of answers.

Outside the men's room the curious TSA officer conferred with a couple of CPD uniforms. The sergeant had been a rookie when I left the force for the Army. I kept my head down and strolled towards the exit.

I needed intel to justify my paranoia and Mo's clandestine meeting ought to provide it. I just needed to get to North Central.

Eddy D Funk, blond, blue-eyed, dreadlocked, funk-a-delic cabby, fit and clear eyed, had been strategically placed to pick me up at the airport. Leaning against his cab, Eddy waited for me outside Union Station, hand rolled cigarette burning for effect. He chucked it into the street and opened the back passenger door.

I could have saved the hundred.

His eyes scanned me, no doubt appreciating the loose fitting Carhartt jacket concealing my rigs. What were his orders? Eddy appeared to be more than a cab driver. I needed an ally, even an ally of convenience.

"You've been around. I don't believe you're just a cabby." I watched his eyes. The pupils constricted. "I need to go to North Center, regardless of her Ladyship's directions to the contrary. Do you have any objections?" I flashed the 10 mm Smith and Wesson I had in my shoulder holster.

Eddy smiled at me, big and toothy, then flashed a silver Desert Eagle from under his jacket twice the size of my gun. "No schedule, mon. But we best be leaving." He nodded towards the steps behind me where the two police officers descended in our direction. "Where you want to go?"

"You know O'Toole's in North Center?"

Eddy nodded. We got into the cab and pulled away from the curb.

* * *

March on the shore of Lake Michigan could be rainy or snowy; this night the rain painted the entire street with streaks of neon and midnight. Cars parked in front of O'Toole's reflected street lights and flashing beer signs. Traffic on West Addison flowed steady but not heavy. Nothing stood out as being out of place, like fogged windows in a parked car, or an idling van, but a rain-slick night conceals many details.

O'Toole's squatted in the middle of a seamless row of brick fronted buildings. A single service alley traversed the rear for access. If Dombrowski couldn't tell me in plain language to meet him here, I shouldn't go through the front door. Eddy circled the block and dropped me at the alley entrance.

The cab's meter called out $55. Apparently Blankenship wanted him to keep up the pretense of being a cabby, or maybe he really was. I tipped him with the change from another hundred. "Be cool, brother," I said.

"Eddy D Funk is always cool."

A well-used Cubs ball cap hung from Eddy's rear view mirror. "How much for the cap? I'm feeling sentimental."

"Take it, mon. It's a dark night out there." Eddy passed me the hat.

"Thanks." The ball cap would blend into the background better than the fedora. I slid out into the drizzle.

"When you need me, mon, just listen. I'll be close." The cab rumbled into the night.

O'Toole's back door opened onto an alley barely navigable by rats and shadowed from any nearby streetlight by buildings. The knob didn't turn but the door opened with a gentle pull. I popped out the piece of gum used to hold the latch back and let the door close behind me.

Nice to know Dombrowski and I still understood each other.

The door opened into a small kitchen lined with boxes of napkins and kegs of beer, and no kitchen staff. A TV blared the play by play commentary on one of the March Madness games. Two doors connected the kitchen with the rest of the establishment. Neat labels on the jambs declared the left door went to the bar and the right to the dining room.

I gently pushed the door open a crack. In the barroom, a few happy-hour die-hards crowded under the TV. O'Toole's is the kind of bar all those chain 'neighborhood' sports bars want to be. Pictures of various sports legends, from 'Machine Gun' Jack Magurn to Tom Boerwinkle, all taken with the same wizened, dark-haired Irishman, lined the walls.

A partition of aged plywood framed with pine separated the dining area from the bar. A dozen booths circled the two pool tables in the center of the room. The lighting focused on the pool tables leaving the rest of the room shadowed. If there had been a happy hour dinner crowd, it vanished. I slipped through the door. Mo Dombrowski sat in the booth in the darkest corner with a half empty mug of beer in front of him. I slid into the seat opposite, my back to the bar. "How's it going, Mo? How's Sarah?"

Since I'd last seen him Mo's jowls had gotten heavy, emphasizing his pouchy, turned-down, Basset-hound eyes. When he made detective, the guys in the squad room gave him a raincoat and fedora and dubbed him 'McGruff, the Crime Dog.'

Never taking his eyes off of his beer, he pulled the McGruff shit on me. "What the fuck are you doing, Smiley?" he growled. "You were banned from Chicago for shooting me."

"I didn't shoot you. The gun went off when you grabbed it."

"You stuck that pocket cannon of yours in my face, you ass hat." Mo's eyes flicked up from his beer. "And you fired twice."

"You fucked my wife, bro. When I asked you to take care of her, I didn't mean it that way." My head started getting very hot. Maybe this had been a bad idea.

Mo straightened up and kept eye contact. "Yeah, well, we're sorry. It shouldn't have happened but it did. The war changed you. Sarah couldn't deal with it anymore. When you came home, it's like you weren't really home. And then you went back after your brother died..."

"Can't explain it to you. Can't explain it to anyone. Sarah never needs to know what happened over there. You don't need to know." I looked over to the bar. "What does a guy need to do to get a drink around here?"

"You know you don't have any friends around here." Dombrowski pulled a couple of shot glasses and a hip flask from the pocket of his windbreaker.

"None?" I held eye contact with him until he looked back at the whiskey.

"Yeah, well, Sarah's worried sick about you. And somehow it's all my fault."

"That's a nice change." I took a couple of deep cleansing breathes. Wash away the anger. Let it go. I watched Mo fill the glasses. With us everything meant something. The liquor meant friendship. Pouring from his personal flask meant we were still brothers. It felt good to know that. "What are you into? You think you're being tapped. You haven't played the code game since we took down Jimmy the Horse."

"Not me. You." Dombrowski pushed the shot glass in front of me. "The Feds are asking around about you. Checking all your last known associates. They shut down the Organized Crime investigation I've been running." He shook his head making his cheeks and wattle shimmy. "They've been harassing Sarah, too, like you'd tell her anything."

"You finally got a lead on an investigation? That's great, bro. Anything you can tell me about?" The death creep started crawling up my spine, the same one I got on the patrol in Afghanistan right before it went to shit. I expected the Outfit to be annoyed with me, but they left families alone most of the time. The police brotherhood had cast me out, and that's fine, but they wouldn't bother Sarah. The Feds, on the other hand, showed no mercy to the innocent in their investigations.

Dombrowski looked up like I'd patted him on the head and said 'good boy'. "I've been tracking something really big. A deal between the Outfit, the Chinatown Triads and ... Wait a minute. You need to tell me what the hell is going on." He gave me that doleful, doggy-look again. "Your old buddy, Tom Rudd, is Special-Agent-in-Charge of Chicago. He says you're involved with a terrorist in California."

"Tom Rudd? Last I'd heard he was investigating Eskimo crime in Alaska." I shook my head. Tom Rudd and I went back to my days as a detective with the Chicago Police Department. We'd crossed swords on a case. I got a departmental citation; he got reprimanded and reassigned. So Rudd outlived his humiliation and returned to be Jack's boss's boss. Had he tied me to Jack already? "I haven't seen a jihadist since Abu Ghraib. And I didn't know I was 'involved' in anything until I woke up this morning. The goombahs who sent me here were no choirboys; I'm just here to pick up the trail of an old friend who needs my help."

Dombrowski shook his head. "C'mon, Jay, even I'm not dumb enough to believe that one. If your 'old friend' wasn't dirty, you wouldn't have to chase him. If you let me take you in, I'll vouch for you even if you did try to kill me."

"You slept with my wife. A lot of people would have killed both of you." I looked over my shoulder at the doorway to the bar. Still nothing happening with the basketball crowd.

Mo looked at me with those sad, McGruff eyes. "That's why Sarah hasn't wanted to see you. You don't handle change well." He leaned back and sipped his whiskey.

"You're right. I don't. Especially when it involves people I trusted." I poured the whiskey down my throat and sucked air against the sudden burn. "But, fuck it, I need your help. You're working Org Crime so you might know this name: Jackie New or Jack Nesmith?"

Dombrowski straightened noticeably but his eyes searched past me towards the bar and street door. His voice softened so I barely heard the words. "Don't know nobody named Nesmith. Neither do you."

"I was in the Army with a Jack Nesmith."

"Trust me. You don't know Nesmith." Dombrowski eyed his watch. "Jeezus, why the hell did you come here? The Feds aren't the only ones looking for you. The Outfit has got a lookout order for you. They really aren't going to want you asking questions about any Jackie New. Trust me."

"What did Jack do here to piss off the Outfit?" Did Jack know he'd been outed before he went rogue?

"Aside from being an undercover FBI agent? Rumor has it he's playing a third game that no one wants him to win." Dombrowski looked over my shoulder, again.

Mo's body language showed nerves. Trusting Mo Dombrowski came naturally to me, but he expected someone or something to come through the front door and didn't want me to know. I wanted to turn but I didn't dare take my eyes off of him. "What game?"

"I don't know. But according to my sources, there's a big business deal supposed to go down on Sunday between the Outfit and the Triads and he's fucked with it. The Feds aren't happy with him and neither is the Outfit."

"So the Feds are looking for him?"

"They're looking for you, Jay. And they are casting the Homeland net." Mo finished his whiskey in a gulp.

"Jack went missing in LA after the Outfit sent him there. Who's

40

talking for Vinnie Tortelli, now?" I got the creeping itch up my back. I could see the growing tension in his eyes, but I couldn't bolt yet.

"Jeezus, do you have a death wish? Vinnie T wanted you hit ten years ago when you took down Jimmy the Horse. You aren't going to him are you? He isn't going to want to talk about Jackie New anymore than the Feds want to talk about Nesmith."

"I just want to know who did what to whom. Someone in the Outfit sent Jack to LA. Who's Vinnie's top lieutenant? Mikey Figarello?"

"Naw. Mikey went state's evidence three years ago and never made it to the trial. Figure he's feeding the fish somewhere around Superior. Danny Shoe is the capo-in-waiting. Vinnie's on life support. He's so close to the fire he's wearing asbestos socks." Mo glanced at his watch, again.

"Funny..." Mo's tension ratcheted up another notch. Had he dimed me out to the Outfit? I couldn't reach my guns without putting Mo on alert————except for the little Walther on my ankle. I carefully extracted it from its holster and thumbed the safety off.

"Look, Jay, I don't think you're with the bad guys. You always want to be the hero but you can't play hero here. People are getting dead around here for tryin'. Remember Joey Petrocelli?" A shadow of emotion passed across Mo's face.

I nodded. "He was undercover with org crime for a long time."

"He went fishing with Danny Shoe. Never came back. Nothing to tie him to the Outfit without a body."

"I get it. They're bad people. They always have been." I slid to the edge of the booth.

"Let the system take care of the bastards. Turn yourself in and I'll make sure the rubber hose artists don't work you over."

"I've got a mission. Jack's got some bad people looking for him and he says Chicago's in danger. I can't stop to play with Tom Rudd and his friends." I pushed back to get some maneuvering room. "Or whoever you expect to come through that door."

Mo poured and drank another quick shot of the Jameson's, without taking his eyes off of me.

I got my feet under me in a way that would let me exit the booth smoothly and quickly. "I don't know what I can do about it, but I have to do something. And before you say it, I ain't nobody's idea of a hero. Learned that in Afghanistan. The real heroes are dead."

Mo raised his hand to stop me from leaving. He watched the bar room and so did I. The outside door opened with a cold gust of wind and two men entered, one with a dark yellow, rain slicker straight out of Dick Tracy. Tom Rudd. Special Asshole in Charge of Chicago. I hooked a thumb in their direction and pulled my ball cap down to shield my face. "You called them?"

Mo nodded almost imperceptibly.

"Jeezus, Mo. Did you have to?" I looked at the back door and back at my erstwhile friend's face. What did I expect to see? Guilt? Regret? Concern?

I got all three. We'd been closer than brothers before I deployed. When I came back, as far as I could see, my brothers were all dead. If the changes in me had been hard on Sarah, they'd been tougher on Mo.

But it looked like Mo was in the game and on my side now. Maybe he had to see me face to face to make up his mind. Maybe he had to ask me why I nearly killed him. The shot glasses disappeared off the table. Mo slid out of the booth and strode towards the FBI agents. His bulk provided cover while I took three long steps to the kitchen door.

5. FIONA

O'Toole's kitchen hadn't been used to cook a meal in a decade. Boxes covered most of the exposed surfaces. On my way through I grabbed a black trash bag from the supply rack. A quick slit with my pocket knife and a normal looking guy, me, turns into a homeless guy wearing a trash bag poncho. With the right shuffle in my step I'd look like a bum picking up empties to buy another bottle of Thunderbird. I killed the kitchen lights and stepped out into the darkened alley.

The lonely streetlamp at the corner did little more than spoil my night vision. The storm off the lake sucked up any ambient light like a sponge. Rain congealed into wet snow and the famous Chicago wind had knives in it, blowing a paper coffee cup down the empty alley.

I had never felt this lonely, even when Sarah told me she traded me in for Mo. Through the anger I still knew we were brothers.

At least SAIC Rudd hadn't expected a take-down, which meant my old buddy hadn't sold me out completely. With the FBI looking for me I had a snowball's chance in hell of slipping out of Chicago to find Jack. Mo's project with the Organized Crime Task Force resonated with the story Sammy Schwartz told. Jack had no safety net. If I was his backup plan he had no plan.

And Dombrowski stayed inside chatting up Rudd. Maybe Mo hoped to get his investigation back? Maybe he just figured he'd let Rudd confront me, hoping I could convince the man I got detailed to Alaska not to arrest me. But why would Rudd try to tie me to a terrorist? I'd had some questionable clients in the last three years but none on the Homeland Security watch list. I checked. I couldn't call on Mo's tapped line with my only burn phone left. I needed to contact Lucy.

I stumbled out of the alley onto an empty side street and started shuffling in the rain-soaked night. With the ball cap turned around so the bill covered my neck and my face kept down, I stepped into character.

I imagined being homeless would give me the sick, hunted feeling we lived with every day in Afghanistan where there weren't any safe zones. Where you watched every direction at the same time, because trouble came from anywhere. So I worked hard at blending in. I became one of the homeless; a target for anyone with a need to inflict pain. I watched everything but never straight on; always with my face down so I didn't attract notice. The one or two people I met on the sidewalk held their breaths as they walked by, but otherwise treated me like I wasn't there.

I kept moving, watching, and listening for Eddy's cab.

After ten minutes of shuffling away from the bar with no pursuit, and no sign of Eddy, I stepped into the dark and empty doorway of an office supply store. The rain didn't quite make it to the farthest corner of the recessed opening. I took a chance I wouldn't be spotted and called Lucy. The office burn phone rang once.

"Jason?" Her voice didn't have the same crisp professionalism in it.

"Lucy, it's me. Are you okay?" I whispered into the phone.

"Yes, I'm fine. The Feds have been here looking for you. Are you all right?" Tension put a fine edge on her voice. Had they turned her on me?

"Yeah, apparently I've gotten real popular all of a sudden." I sighed. "What did you find out about Jack?"

"Yeah, well, Jack Nesmith is a red flag." Her voice tensed some more. "I'm afraid I made things worse for you. The Feds came knocking after I began my inquiries. I must have screwed up and tripped some alert."

"Not you. Something has, though. They were looking for me before I got here. And they've been harassing Dombrowski and Sarah." I watched the rain-soaked empty street, hoping it stayed empty.

"Shoot. This is bad. I got a little on Jack before the lid slammed shut. He's been undercover for a year and a half on a terrorism investigation. His controller hasn't seen him for a week. He's not married, has at least one paycheck in his checking account untouched and his passport is missing. He has an apartment in Arlington but has it sublet for the duration of his assignment. No pets. No girlfriend in Virginia, though Jackie New seemed to have picked up some strange Goth chick in Chicago. No one knows who she is since he didn't bring her around the mob, and didn't report her to his controller."

I had to wonder how much Lucy would have discovered if the 'lid' hadn't slammed shut. Probably live drone feeds of Jack's current location. "Have you an address for Jackie New?"

"Boss, everyone's going to have his residence staked out."

"I figured out Jack's code. He's worked out a way to contact me at his apartment, or he's got a dead drop there. Don't know exactly what, but I'll have to go there to find out." I felt a little wild creature scratching behind my eyes, urging me to run as far and as fast as I could. "Don't worry the little things. If I know Jack, there's a clue in his apartment. I'll find it."

Lucy sighed. "He left you another clue on Facebook, but I don't know what it means. It shows a laptop with a wall behind it."

"Send it to my iPhone. I've got a charger for it now." Un-coded messages on public bulletin boards weren't good tradecraft. After all, if I could figure out what he meant so could someone else. I needed to be quick. "Do you have the address?"

"Jackie New rented a loft at 2201 West Wabansia, under the name Jack Newman. Apartment 3C. It's a block north of West North Avenue near the El tracks." She hesitated a half breath. "I can get you out of there without the Feds stopping you but it won't be until morning. You ought to get out of town, now."

"OK. Thanks, Lucy. But Jack needs me. I'll check in later." I put the phone back in my pocket. Lucy was right, I should get out of Chicago, not go to the one place everyone interested in Jackie New would be watching. But his apartment would be the one place he could be Jack Nesmith, even undercover. So it made sense he'd left some clue there. But on his laptop? Not very likely. If the computer had been at the apartment, I'm sure someone would have taken it by now. But unlikely or not, Jack reached out to me, and I had to reach back.

In my eagerness to avoid Tom Rudd and his minions, I'd taken the wrong way out of North Center to get to West Wabansia. I turned a corner and another corner to get on the right track. Four blocks to the mile, ten blocks to North Avenue, placed Jack's apartment at least three and half miles away and no sign of Eddy D Funk. The rain turned to sleet, slush collected on the sidewalks.

I pulled my ball cap down and tugged at the trash bag rain coat. What a damned long walk in ice-water-soaked shoes. When I stepped back onto the street a beat up Chevy cab pumping Bob Marley's 'Redemption Song' from its tinny speakers pulled up beside me. The window rolled down and a cloud of smoke drifted out.

"Hey, mon, you look like you need a ride." Eddy D Funk hooked a finger at the back seat. "It's no fit night for man nor beastly tonight."

"Eddy. How'd you find me?" I peeled off the trash bag.

"I been looking for you. You tip too good, mon. Me want some more of the easy for my woman, don'tcha know." He grinned at me and turned off the patois. "Ms. Blankenship says its time you got to work."

"Sure, mon," I said and climbed in the cab. "So where does Blankenship want me to go?"

"Where ever your heart leads you. She says you know what you're doing." He pulled away from the curb.

I gave him Jack's address and settled into the back seat to wonder if Ms. Blankenship would appreciate my efforts so far.

Eddy cruised an indirect path to Jack's apartment down North Kedzie through an area signed by every variation of the Latin Kings that had held this turf for the last thirty years. I'd had a wannabe King for a driver in Afghanistan on my second deployment.

I closed my eyes; the smell of diesel and camel shit filled my nostrils. The countryside burned green through the night vision goggles. I felt the oppressive weight of my battle-rattle, 120 pounds of armor and ammunition, and the chill of the mountains. Sitting in the front seat of our up-armored HMMWV with my driver, Pfc. Diego Zuniga, talking shit about the Latin Kings.

"Hey, Sarge. You know Chi, right? You know Humboldt Park?" He shouted over the road noise.

"Yeah. Bad lands."

"Grew up there. Wanted to be a King from the time I could walk."

"How come you didn't get made?"

"Mom didn't want me killing another mother's son. She said she couldn't stand it. I thought I'd join the Army and kill a few rag heads. It wouldn't matter then. I was gonna take a mark for each kill." The

Kings were one of those gangs that collected evidence of their crimes on their bodies, like tears for every murder.

"Yeah. How you doing with that?"

Diego shrugged. "It don't matter. I don't think I wanna be a King any more. I'm a Soldier now. I want my Momma to be proud of me."

Diego didn't find out how proud he'd made his mother. All that came back from Afghanistan of Diego was in a box. All his mother got was his bronze star and the flag that covered his coffin. He should have gotten the Medal of Honor, but the mission we were on didn't officially happen.

I blinked my eyes and saw North Kedzie again. The area slowly changed from rundown, brick-row-houses to cleaned-up, brick-row-houses. The area around Jack's address had just started undergoing gentrification. The building bore the name 'Acme Manufacturing' cast in the concrete lintel and still looked industrial except for the iron balconies on every other window. It stood three floors above the street level and a lot of personal cars parked in front. Across the street stood a playground area with its own parking lot. Old trees lined the streets, cutting down the effectiveness of the street lights.

A dark sedan inappropriately parked near the playground caught my attention. The tinted windows reflected the glare of the street lights and made it impossible to see inside the car.

"Somebody cares who goes in and out this place, mon." Eddy lifted an eyebrow to the mirror and drove past the building. Once we were out of sight he made a couple of strategic turns to arrive at the side door of the building without making it obvious we were circling around. Now trees blocked the view of the watchers by the playground, but another car's chrome gleamed in the shadows on the next block. Jack's building had been staked out.

"Thanks, Eddy." I handed him two, hundred-dollar bills, and turned my hat around backwards as I got out of the car. "Stay someplace nearby and quiet. Okay?"

He backed up and drifted away in the same direction we'd arrived.

I probably didn't have to tip him————he worked for Blankenship. Maybe she paid him well. I didn't know who she worked for.

I shambled up to the service door, with my pants sagging deeply in the crotch. I hoped I looked enough like a wannabe club kid going to his mom's apartment to not trigger an immediate reaction from the watchers. A sign next to the locked door read: RING BELL FOR ATTENDANT. The indicated button hung loosely by one of the two wires.

I banged on the service door. I would have liked to go in quiet but I had to get in and out quick. The young kid who opened the door looked like he'd just smoked a big spliff, eyes red and puffy, bit of a sloppy grin and twitchy. I couldn't imagine what sort of security the owners thought he provided their tenants. Of course that was probably why Jackie New lived here.

"You can't come in here. Go 'round t' the front," he said.

I handed the kid a bill from my declining pile of hundreds and whispered, "Danny Shoe sent me."

His eyes went wide and let me into the building. With no further direction, he showed me the service elevator. When the elevator door closed I hiked up my pants, turned my hat around and checked my hardware. The door opened to an empty hallway. I stepped out. Behind me the door closed and the cab sank back to the ground floor while the building echoed in silence. Jackie New either had some very quiet neighbors or the rest of the floor had been deserted. A little nodule of fear built up.

The door marked 3C opened onto the north end of building, at the end of the hallway away from the elevator. The location put the apartment at the front of the building with windows overlooking the street. The steel fire door had been dented hard enough to prevent the bolt from latching in the frame. Torn crime scene tape hung on either side. I wasn't the first or second visitor to Jack's apartment. Gun in hand, I pushed the door open. Chances of finding anything useful in well-searched premises were pretty slim.

Streetlights streamed through the bare windows. I used a miniature LED flashlight for illumination without risking turning on the lights and notifying the watchers.

Jack's apartment consisted of a single open space with a loft bedroom, an expensive techno kitchen in one corner, and a man-wall of electronics as the main focus. Every portable item had been thrown to the floor. Every fragile piece of equipment had been broken, judging from the glittering reflections. The furniture had been sliced open with vicious knife slashes.

Jack had really pissed someone off.

Two doors exited off of the main floor, a spiral steel stairway led to the loft bedroom. The bedroom appeared unoccupied, but the two doors concerned me. I crossed the apartment as silently as I could, weapon ready. The first door led to an empty bathroom. The second led to a ladder disappearing into darkness————probably provided roof access. I shuffled back through the debris hoping for something overlooked by the previous searchers.

Despite the mess, I didn't see single-guy junk; fast food boxes or beer cans. Jack either kept his apartment meticulously clean or he didn't actually live here. For a neat guy he'd really made a mess of things. I went up the open stairs to the loft bedroom. The bed had been tossed, sheets ripped off and drawers emptied. Jack's wardrobe consisted of white turtle necks, black jackets and black chinos all in a pile on the floor. Not a bit of color showed in any of the toss. The Jack I knew had a taste for tacky Hawaiian shirts and straw hats when off duty. I guess he never got off duty as Jackie New.

The door downstairs opened. Someone started climbing the stairs.

I eased back into the closet. From habit I pulled the 10mm from its holster, but I didn't want to get into a gunfight here. Bad guy/good guy, it didn't matter. Gun fire would bring cops and cops would bring delays and I wouldn't be able to help Jack save Chicago. I slipped the gun back into its holster. Of course this presumed I could find Jack, a real threat existed, and we really could 'save Chicago.' The phrase echoed in my head as the hard-soled footsteps came closer.

Streetlights illuminated two artificially-red pigtails on either side of a shaved head. The owner of the pigtails, a slender girl in a mini kilt and spiked platform boots with lip and nose rings. Several cat related tattoos decorated exposed portions of her skin. In the diffused light her cat-like eyes with oval irises glowed orange.

I coughed to announce myself as I casually stepped out of my hiding place.

To her credit she didn't jump when I opened the closet door. She looked up at me with those orange cat eyes. "I wondered when you were coming out. Who are you?"

I gave her a wry smile. "How'd you know I was there?"

"I could smell you. You don't smell like Jackie."

"Do you know the owner of this apartment? I wondered if he wanted to sublet." I eased to the edge of loft and checked for additional company on the floor below. The apartment remained empty.

"You weren't hiding in the closet looking for an apartment. I'm not stupid. Someone wants something from Jackie and you're one of them." She circled around me until the streetlights put her in shadow and highlighted me.

I pulled my iPhone and charger out of my pocket. I needed to retrieve Jack's last message. "Jack's a friend of mine. Do you know where he went to? When he's coming back?"

I heard jewelry rattle as she shook her head.

"Are you the girlfriend?" I jacked into a wall outlet.

"I dunno. Haven't seen Jackie in a few. He left town and didn't say where." She slouched over to a half backed lounging chair decorated with several vicious gashes and dropped into it. "Who are you?"

"Call me Smiley." I studied her profile again as the phone booted up. My first impression had been of a teenager run away from home, but on closer inspection the young lady appeared to be in her early twenties at the least, and clinging to the rebellious persona of her childhood just to avoid being an adult in an adult world. Despite all that, she didn't quite have the dissipated look I'd seen so often among disaffected youth. She had an edge and tension that didn't match her costume.

"Is that like a gang name or something?" She made a crooked smile at me.

"It's my real name. Swear to God." I looked out the window at the surveillance car in the parking lot across the street. "What's your name?"

"My name's Fiona. Is that the new iPhone?"

"I guess so." I scrolled through my messages until I found the one from Lucy with the picture attached. I paced across the bedroom and back while picture loaded, and stopped by the window again.

"What are you doing?" she asked.

"Jack sent me a message. This is the first place I could plug in." A picture came up of a laptop and what looked like a remote starter on a key fob imprinted with our unit's patch. "Christ, Jack, what the hell does that mean?"

"Oh, cool." Fiona had come over to look at the picture. She pulled the key fob out of her skirt pocket. "I think he wants me to give this to you."

"Really? And how would he know I'd be here and you would happen by?"

"He didn't know when, but he said you would come." She handed me the key fob. "I waited outside."

I shook my head and clicked the button on the remote control. A solenoid cycled in the wall beside me and the sound of wood dragging on wood. Inside the closet a drawer that hadn't been there a moment before had opened. A laptop rested inside in a foam case.

Fiona pulled the laptop from the hidden compartment and turned it on. She focused her attention on the computer. Her fingers tap-danced across the keyboard.

"Hey, what are you up to?" I reached for the computer. She wrapped her arms around it and leaned away.

"Chill. I'm talking to Jack on the computer. He wants to talk to you." She poked some more before she handed it to me.

Jack Nesmith stared at me from the computer screen.

"Jason." His voice came out tinny from the laptop's speakers. The picture jerked out of synch with his voice. With his face filling the foreground, nothing in the background distinguished location.

"Jack. Or should I say Jackie New? What's going on?" I kept an eye on Fiona. She might be his girlfriend but her attitude didn't quite match her persona.

"I'm glad you're still alive. I was afraid the Triad had taken you out with Bruno. This changes everything." Jack's face brightened with an infectious smile. He held up a brochure from a resort in Jamaica. "I need you to come here. We've got a serious problem."

"I'd say you've got lots of serious problems. Can you tell me what's going on?" I studied the brochure to make sure I knew where he intended us to meet. I hoped he'd secured this connection. It would take the NSA a little longer to recover our conversation.

"When I see you. Meet me on the nude side tomorrow. Take care of Fiona. She's the best thing that ever happened to me." Jack sounded almost chipper, looking more like the Jack I knew, and it scared me. He should have been plenty nervous from the stir he caused.

"Tom Rudd is taking a special interest in finding me in Chicago. This can't be good." I said.

"I can't tell you anything over this link. This thing is too big. I'm pretty sure there's someone inside the Bureau. Cops. Mob. Feds. Rudd... You can't believe anyone." Jack became very intense. "If we fail, Chicago, and the world, will never be the same. That's all I can tell you right now. Get here as soon as you can. We're going to need every minute to fix this."

"But if we're going to stop something in Chicago why go so far away?"

Jack scrubbed his hands through his hair. "I thought you were dead. I didn't know what else to do."

"Smiley?" Fiona had drifted to the front windows and pulled the drapes open. "Some men are coming with guns. What should we do?"

With the laptop in hand I looked out the windows. Cop cars filled the street. "Jack, we've got to split. I'll be there as soon as I can————"

"Take the roof. There's a ladder on the back side that'll get you to the alley. Hurry." Jack's voice betrayed a hint of panic. "And hit control-alt-f10 on the computer. Go."

I hit the key combination. Fiona stored the laptop back in the secret cubby. I grabbed my iPhone and cable, stuffed them in my backpack, and tried to erase any indication of where we'd been or why.

"C'mon," I grabbed her arm. The wild animal pushed me down the stairs, across the living room to the roof access. Fiona clattered beside me. The apartment door crashed open just as we hit the ladder to the roof. Fiona scampered up behind me like a cat; we climbed out the metal fire door. I slammed the illegal bolt on the outside locking the door shut.

We only had seconds. Feet pounded up the ladder. The backside of the roof had mounting rings near a tarp which concealed a light nylon line, but no actual ladder. One end of the rope had been tied to the mounting rings. I threw the rope over the edge and followed it with my arms and legs wrapped to control my descent to the roof two floors below.

"Hey, wait for me." Fiona slipped over the edge before I landed, checking herself with her leg wrapped around the rope like I had. She hit the roof lightly; we took off for the short drop to a back alley dumpster.

We were two buildings down from Jack's apartment and the CPD cruiser parked at the end of the alley. Shouts came from the roof; cop lights flickered through the neighborhood accompanied by the occasional blip of the siren. The activity seemed to be pulling back rather than following us.

I eased myself to the ground behind the dumpster; Fiona followed. I caught her to save the noise of her boots on the pavement. The streetlight on the corner had been broken, probably to facilitate illegal activities. We stayed in the shadows and moved slowly so as to not draw eyes. We followed the shadows across the alley and down a side street.

The thump of a reggae bass through cheap car speakers echoed through the dark streets. The scratching behind my eyes eased up. Things were going to work out all right. We had to find Eddy and get the hell out of Dodge.

The sleet had turned to fat snow. Fiona shivered in her skimpy jacket, her arms wrapped tight around her skinny body to ward off the icy wind blowing in from Lake Michigan. The echo of Eddy's stereo grew closer. The ancient trees in the neighborhood obscured details at any distance, even on the street. We walked a little faster to put some distance between us and the cops. Eddy couldn't be far.

Something had disrupted the rhythm of the raid. The cops should have flooded the street with sirens as more patrols raced to search for us. The silence meant something else. I dialed Lucy.

The phone picked up before it rang back on my end. "Luce, this is going to be quick. We're on the run from the cops."

"OK. Who's we?"

"My friend is at a resort on Jamaica." I repeated the name from the brochure. I didn't like doing it in the clear but she needed to know. "Can you get me there quietly with no tracks? And quick. The cops were watching Jack's apartment. They stormed the place. I did talk to Jack. Also, I may need some help stashing Jackie's girlfriend."

Lucy got very quiet for a moment on the other end. She had a way of seeing a great deal from very little information. Finally she sighed, "Okay, Boss. I'll call you back when I've got it set."

"Thanks, babe." I closed the connection.

As we came nearer to a working street light Fiona's tough act faded. One of her orange contacts had jostled loose and been lost so she had one brown and one orange eye——both glistening with unshed tears. "What's going on with Jackie? Are you going to help him?"

"Yeah. I'll help him, if I can. Right now we need to get you someplace warm, and figure out where you can stay until Jack gets back."

"No, man, I want to go with you." She shivered some more. The tears made it hard for her to see so she stopped to dig at her eyes with the hem of her tee-shirt. "You've got to take me with you."

"No." The sound of Bob Marley slowly grew louder. "I don't know who you really are. I don't believe the costume and the little girl act. Maybe you care about Jack, but I'll let him sort that out when he gets back. Until then we're parting ways."

Behind the water-works, her eyes filled with determination, and steel I'd sensed earlier. I'd do what I could to protect her because Jack asked me to, I would have anyway, but I wasn't going to put my life in her hands. Or Jack's life——either. She wasn't being honest with me, and I'd bet she wasn't honest with Jack.

Or worse, Jack wasn't being honest with me. I picked up the pace in the direction of Eddy's cab.

Just as we stepped into the faint ring of a rare working street light, a black Escalade pulled up to the curb beside us. A shotgun covered us from the back passenger window as two very ugly men with hand guns jumped out of the front seats.

Chicago had turned out to be as bad an idea as I thought it would be.

6. DANNY SHOE

Even shadowed by the rain drenched streetlights, some people are so distinctive they're instantly recognizable. From a distance, Monk Pannelli could pass for a very large baboon right down to the bowed legs, the pendulous lower lip and non-existent forehead. He waved a large bore pistol at my gut while his cousin, Tiny Tufo, who resembled a walking wall, stuck a .50 caliber, gold, Desert Eagle in Fiona's back.

Monk and I could have made a fight of it, but the guy with the shotgun in the truck and Fiona under Tiny's control presented difficulties.

Fifteen years ago I'd arrested Monk for a particularly vicious home invasion. He acted as the enforcer for the Outfit's insurance operation——the kind of insurance that guarantees you won't have vicious home invasions as long as the premium is paid. The Outfit's attorneys plead him down from extortion and attempted murder to unlawful entry, so Monk did fifteen months at the Outfit's finishing school, Joliet Correctional.

"Danny Shoe wants to talk to you," Monk growled, and pushed his pistol into my stomach.

"How do you know he wants to talk to me?" I stepped away from the pressure. "Maybe he wants to talk to some other guy."

He lowered the pistol and furrowed his hairline down to his nose in concentration. "Danny said 'Get Jason Smiley'. That's you, right?"

"Not necessarily." I took a quick look at Fiona. She showed no sign of panic, just a quick twitch as she scanned the men. Behind her, a beat-up yellow cab pulled into a tree shadowed driveway and turned around. Reggae bass faded into the night. "Maybe he meant another Jason Smiley."

"Don't be a wise guy." Life had been good to Monk while I'd been away. He'd gained fifty pounds and when he leaned forward to get in my face, his belly became uncomfortably intimate with mine and his breath reeked of garlic. "I wasn't ever going to forget you. You're the prick that sent me to prison, Mr. Smart-ass, Smiley."

"I tried to get you the electric chair. Your lawyers sent you to prison." I stepped away from him, again.

Monk scratched his head. Then he backhanded me so hard I hit the ground wondering how I got there before the pain had time to reach my brain. I shook my head and sat up. Monk pulled me up by my jacket collar. My legs wobbled as I tried to keep myself upright.

"Hey Monk," called the moving piece of wall. "What do we do with the girl?"

"She goes with us, too. Mr. Smiley's a boy scout. She'll keep him from being any more of a smart ass." He performed a quick pat down and relieved me of my 10mm Smith & Wesson and the .380 I keep in my ankle holster. The .44 dug into the small of my back and went unnoticed in his search. Then he shoved me towards the front passenger door. I licked a bit of blood off my lip and wrestled with

the wild animal inside of me that wanted to rip his throat out——
damn the consequences.

"I really hate smart ass cops," Monk said through a sloppy grin.
"Now get in the car. Remember she's insurance."

Tiny zip-tied Fiona's hands before he manhandled her into the
back seat. She tried to shrink into a corner but the walking wall hip-
checked her into the center. She looked at him like she wanted to
grow spines like a porcupine fish, but maintained a professional level
of cool. The other hood with the shotgun, a skinny, greasy fellow
with no chin, rolled up the window on the other side and made a
show of touching as much of Fiona's body as he could without using
his hands. She didn't acknowledge his existence.

Monk got in the driver's side and looked into the back. "Hey,
Nonny, show some class. Her hands are tied. She can't even slap your
weasel face."

Nonny settled down.

Fiona glared straight ahead.

My hands were free, maybe I could retrieve the .44 from my back
and shoot Monk, but with Nonny and his shotgun behind me, I
would be a dead man and no use to Fiona, not to mention Jack. I
sighed and waited while we drove through the streets of Chicago.

Monk drove straight to Little Italy, careful not to exceed the speed
limit and slowed down for every yellow light. Every once in a while
Monk looked over at me like I might be dinner. Jack must have a set
of brass balls so big he could hardly walk to go undercover with these
animals. They made Sammy's boys in LA look like fairies... well; they
were fairies, but tough ones.

"Why does Danny want to see me?" I asked.

"You wait to talk to Mr. Chourelli. He'll tell you what he wants
you to know." Spittle trickled from his lower lip.

Danny Chourelli, better known as Danny Shoe, was the Boss-in-
waiting according to Dombrowski. I didn't doubt it; Danny Shoe
waiting impatiently to take over the Outfit. Danny's brother, Jimmy

"the Horse" Chourelli got five consecutive life sentences at Statesville despite the best efforts of the FBI and Agent Rudd to screw up the investigation and the trial, because of my testimony.

We pulled in the alley behind Fiorelli's Clam and Falafel Palace. The darkened street windows said the restaurant had closed after the dinner trade. Fiorelli's used to be a classic Italian clam bar, but due to the growing ethnic diversity in the neighborhood they had to expand their menu to appeal to new clientele. It had also been an organized crime meeting place since the turn of the last century. At least two of Al Capone's rivals had been gunned down at a window table.

The crew pushed Fiona and me into the combination kitchen and storage area at the back. A walk-in freezer filled one wall and looked too large for a week's supply of meatballs and veal, but capable of keeping a few bodies on ice until they could be conveniently disposed.

A desk, a table and a couple of chairs sat as an afterthought in the back corner. A single lamp provided a halo of smoke-filled light around a sitting man. Behind him an array of security monitors showed various interior and exterior shots, including the hallway at Jack's building with cops milling around, but nothing of Jackie New's apartment. Maybe they respected his privacy? Or maybe Jack had been smart enough to disable their cameras.

"Someone turn on the fucking lights so I can see what you brought," the man growled at Monk and his crew.

Lights flicked on revealing Danny Shoe, still as lean as an alley cat and twice as pissed off. His suit hung off him like he'd bought it off the rack before he lost fifty pounds. His nose, a reminder of his northern Italian ancestors, pointed slightly to the left due to a left hook I threw many years ago.

"Hello, Smiley." He showed his teeth more in a snarl than a smile, as he got up. "Monk and his friends are going to hurt you very badly. You were warned never to come back to Chicago. And don't ever use my name like you got a right to. You do not."

"My mama did warn me no one likes a name dropper." I tried to look harmless while I thought about the .44 in the back of my pants. I couldn't afford a messy fire fight with four gunmen when I only had six shots, but these were brutal men and they were going to kill me, and Fiona, eventually.

Had Danny Shoe seen something in my eyes? He grabbed Monk by the arm. "Did you get all of his guns? Mr. Smiley has a firearms fetish."

Monk nodded, his lower lip bouncing obscenely. He held up the 10mm Smith and the .380. "See? Nice pieces, huh Boss?"

Danny looked disgusted and started patting me down himself. He quickly located the .44. I sighed. "Guess you got me now."

He stuck the gun in my face and pulled the hammer back. "Got any more, funny man?"

To be on the safe side I cringed a little, bringing me down to his eye level, and shook my head. "No, Mr. Chourelli. You got them all. Really." I shook out my coat and turned slowly around for him to see.

"Not so tough now, cop." He spat the last word out like it left a foul taste in his mouth. Personally I hoped he'd choke on it.

Tiny forced me into a straight backed wooden chair by the simple expediency of pushing me down with his weight. Monk zip-tied my hands behind my back to the slats. Nonny pushed Fiona but she set her feet and refused to move until Nonny pushed his shiny 9mm pistol into her chin. Then she shifted her weight slightly to one side, possibly preparing for a disarming maneuver.

I shook my head ever so slightly, hoping she'd catch the movement out of the corner of her eye and not start a gunfight with four killers in the room at the same time. She relaxed and let Nonny position her near Danny. We locked eyes for a moment. She knew I knew she wasn't who she pretended to be.

"Sorry, Danny. Name dropping helps me get into the clubs. I didn't think it would do any harm." The chair wobbled from loose joints. Probably too many pasta fed asses. Weakness could mean opportunity. "If you want me out of Chicago, I'm more than willing to leave."

"You ain't leaving Chicago, Smiley. Except maybe for a fishing trip." Danny smiled with some genuine enthusiasm. Must be he liked fishing. "No, you'll tell me why you're looking for Jackie New. And don't give me no bullshit. You were at his apartment and you weren't looking for a cheap rental. If you know where the little fuck is, I want to know."

"If I knew where Jack was I'd just go there. Chatting with you wasn't on my agenda."

"Don't get smart with the Boss." Monk lashed out with a vicious right cross and knocked me and the chair over onto the floor.

Bright lights flashed across my vision while I laid still trying to pull my thoughts back together. Monk hit like a freight train, slow but with a lot of force. The chair didn't feel like it would survive too many rounds like that. I wasn't sure I would.

The other two lifted the chair, and me, upright. I had no doubt I would be killed whether I talked or not, but I wouldn't take Jack with me.

"I don't care when you talk, or if. You've put your life in my hands." Danny leaned forward in his chair. "You cost me a brother. That's a debt you're going to pay."

"Don't get all upset. Jimmy's just the cost of doing business." Monk telegraphed another right. I rolled away, letting the chair take the brunt of the fall. Something on the chair, rather than my face, broke, though a glancing blow from Monk sent the room spinning. They set me upright, again. The chair wobbled even more.

I spat some blood on the floor as Danny came back into focus. "He ought to be out in another fifteen or twenty years."

"He's got AIDS. He won't make it out of there alive." Danny slapped the desk. "It would have been cleaner if you'd just shot him."

"If he has AIDS, he didn't catch it bending over in the shower to

62

pick up the soap." Jimmy the Horse enjoyed hurting people. I couldn't imagine him accepting a passive role in any sexual encounter.

Tiny and Nonny started giggling like schoolboys. Monk's deadpan cracked as he snorted something that might have been a laugh and Danny Shoe's studied toughness cracked. "Fuckin' Jimmy is dumb enough to fuck anything that walks. He shoulda' used a condom with those jail whores," Danny snorted and turned away to wipe his face.

I guess laughing with me didn't show the right family solidarity nor the appropriate seriousness for a Capo-tutti-Capo. Of course, he didn't like Jimmy any better than anyone else did. With the sudden relaxation of tension I wondered if our relationship had turned a corner.

"So are we good?" I asked with my best Irish bullshit smile.

Danny gasped for breath as he struggled with his silent laughter. When he got control of himself, he looked at me and grinned. "Fuck him up, boys," he said.

Monk cocked his arm back, telegraphing another punch. I hoped I could roll away from the worst of it but the chair leaned in the wrong direction.

The phone rang.

Danny held up his hand to stop Monk. Monk looked disappointed. The previous hit hadn't been as satisfying for him.

"Yeah, Vinnie. We'll be there in half an hour. I got a couple of things to do first." He nodded. "Yeah, he'll still be breathing." He raised his hand and gave the 'let's roll' spin of his finger.

Monk grinned and caught me with a short left hook that sent black spots dancing in front of my eyes. The chair creaked and collapsed underneath me, shattering. I tried to get my feet under me, but Nonny caught me with a kick in the ribs that took my breath away. I rolled and caught Monk across the back of the knees with the remainder of the chair slat still tie-wrapped to my arm. He hit the ground hard. Just before I could jam the board into his throat, three hammers were pulled back and Fiona sucked in a scream.

"Knock it off Smiley or the girl gets fucked up," Nonny screamed.

Danny made a disgusted face at his crew. "The only thing you guys can fuck up is a wet dream. Let's get up to the big house."

* * *

Vinnie Tortelli's mansion commanded a tree covered hill ten miles from downtown Chicago. A thousand acres of trees, and lonely, surrounded by urban sprawl. The whole community felt more like the Upper Peninsula of Michigan, except for the glimpses of the McMansions hidden behind the screening, and the fact the only way a U.P. native would get into the neighborhood would be as a groundskeeper or servant.

Fence, trees, and a mile of driveway isolated Vinnie's house. Nobody would hear a scream or a gunshot, especially not inside the massive brick and wood castle. Danny had split me up from Fiona, taking her in his black Lincoln with Nonny, while Monk and Tiny chauffeured me in the Escalade. They'd cut the chair parts off of me and hadn't restrained me in any way.

The truth is Danny Shoe knew me too well. He knew I wouldn't risk Fiona. It wouldn't matter if she'd been passing me on the street when Monk's posse grabbed us. Monk had been right; I'm a fucking Boy Scout. I really hate people who think honor is a weakness.

Danny Shoe helped Fiona out the car with my .44 pushed into her ribs. Nonny took control of the .44 and Fiona. Danny turned on his heel without a word and strode up the steps to a pair of massive carved-wood doors.

Nonny started stroking Fiona's butt with the gun barrel, trying to catch the sight on her skirt and lift it up. Monk took the gun from Nonny with a snort of disgust and pushed Fiona forward, making her stumble up the steps behind Danny. "Let's go."

I got out of the car under my own power. The raw rage burning behind my eyes filled me with energy. I bounced on the balls of my feet and focused on getting us out alive. The cousins took turns shoving me from behind as I followed Monk and Fiona. Fear is an atavistic trigger to either fight or flee, and I couldn't do either. Blood pulsed in my ears while I remained as calm and focused as a tiger. Only a conscience or a good reason prevented rape, murder and mayhem in this remote warren.

None of these men had functioning consciences.

If Danny Shoe knew my reputation, I knew Vinnie Tortelli's. We were here and alive now because Vinnie Tortelli didn't like messes. He'd polished the public image of the Outfit for the last dozen years, at least when it came to bodies in the streets. I don't think he really expected to appear respectable, but less of a public nuisance than the Mexican drug cartels. When he used violence and murder to manage his affairs, he insisted his crew be very careful not to leave any evidence, hence Danny Shoe's 'fishing trips.'

Vinnie's front doors opened onto a broad, polished limestone foyer with a winding open staircase to the second floor. Large formal rooms opened off to the right and left of the entry way, and two corridors led into the wings of the palace.

Monk guided Fiona and me into the left wing down a hallway wide enough to drive a car. I glanced at her. She radiated tension but walked with a steady pace; her eyes showed no fear. Action, for some reason I've yet to understand, controls the wild animal I'm hiding——no matter the situation. I could focus. This walk, under guard, in one of the few places untouchable by the CPD, encouraged fear. I'd be stupid not to be afraid of the most ruthless man in Chicago, but the adrenalin rush of fear was the drug of war.

My heart rate hadn't slowed by the time we arrived at the study where Vinnie Tortelli sat in a wheel chair like a king on a throne surrounded by his court of underbosses. In ten years he'd gone from a vicious, but virile, forty-something, to somewhere between a hundred, and dead. Liver spots crowded his hands, his eyes stained yellow. Age and illness should have made him weaker, but he looked as hard as a piece of jerked beef. His eyes flashed with anger and contempt.

Vinnie T's approaching mortality hadn't humbled him. It just pissed him off. I could almost understand.

"Mr. Smiley." He wheezed over the oxygen tubes trailing from his nose. "Nice of you to show up. I like respect from the young."

"Why, Vinnie T, it's always a pleasure to enjoy your hospitality." I stepped away from Monk and Fiona, my hands turned outwards in a show of submission.

"I got no hospitality for cops." Vinnie rummaged in his desk until he found a cigar. He sniffed it and started sneezing. After pushing the nasal cannular up and honking his nose until it sounded like a duck call, he dug out a couple of colored inhalers and sucked the medicine out of them. Finally he stopped wheezing and leaned back in his chair.

"You cops think we're all dumb as shit. Well, you don't know shit. I'm gonna outlive you and your buddy, Jackie the fucking hyena. Laughing and prancing around here like some big badass——"

Vinnie started wheezing again. Two more squirts from another inhaler changed the sound from a whistle to a deep rattle. Around the room a dozen minor capos looked back and forth between Vinnie T and Danny Shoe.

At last the old man regained his voice. "Doctor says I smoked too many fucking cigars. Fuck him if he outlives me by thirty minutes."

"Then you've got to tell me who your doctor is."

"Why? You ain't gonna need him." Vinnie stuffed the unlit cigar between his purple lips.

"I've got this boil... and well, hell, I'll never have to pay him, right?" I grinned like a tiger and rubbed part of my face Monk had damaged. Nobody else smiled. Maybe they didn't get it.

Vinnie glared at me over his unlit cigar.

I forced myself into nonchalance. "Anyway, this is the first time I've come back to Chicago since the war. I miss the place. California's too weird, you know?"

"That's right. You're the cop hero that went to fight the ragheads. How'd that go? Did you get any?" Vinnie rolled the cigar in his mouth.

"You've probably killed more men than I have, Vinnie. It's a lot tougher when they shoot back." I bared my teeth at him, thinking killing him would make a lot of people happy, but wouldn't get us out, alive.

"Fuck 'em. Kill all the bastards, that's what I say. They're bad for business. Too many cops looking at everything now with the Homeland security bullshit. Makes it harder for a businessman to do his business." Vinnie pulled his cigar out of his mouth and spat leaf and juice onto the floor.

"There is always sacrifice in war," I said, wondering how long he would draw out this interview before he ordered our deaths. Around the room I could see the Capos had traces of the same thought.

"War? If I was running it we'd have put those Al Qaeda shits in dirt suits and have that oil field pumping money in our pockets. That ain't no way to run an operation." Vinnie coughed wetly while his lips turned deeper purple. He sucked oxygen through the tubes in his nose two or three times before he spoke again. "What the hell you doing in Jackie New's apartment? No bullshit, either."

"He's an old war buddy. Called me and said he needed help. You'd do the same." For a cut of the action.

"Jackie New is a dead man. You don't need to fucking look for him. I heard you're a private dick now. Someone's paying you to find the fucker?" The old man pointed his cigar at me. "You workin' with the Feds?"

"No way. Sammy Schwartz from LA hired me."

"Fuck Sammy the fucking Suit. What did you find at Jackie's place?"

"Somebody'd already searched it. Probably Monk and his cousins, right, Danny?" I grinned a wise guy grin. Monk walked over to me and drove a monkey fist into my stomach. I dropped to the floor gasping like the old man. This latest abuse electrified the bruises from my earlier beating.

Vinnie waited for a couple of minutes until I started breathing again. "What were you looking for?"

I answered Vinnie with a glare from the floor. Monk's boys each grabbed an arm and lifted me to my feet. Monk drew back for a haymaker to my head.

"Not him," the old man croaked. "The girl."

Two others grabbed Fiona by the arms and Monk professionally punched her in the stomach like he had me. Her knees buckled but the strong boys held her up as she struggled to breathe and puke at the same time. I expected the horror on my face to be reflected in her's but she didn't cry out, but she had her own wild animal trying to get out through her eyes. Tough girl. She had iron in her gut.

Monk cocked his arm dramatically for another strike.

"No. Wait," I said. She might be tough, and she appeared to be experienced in the brutality of the world, but I couldn't let Monk work her over. We weren't going to be allowed to leave, but if a chance arose we both needed to be able to act. I hurt bad enough after Monk's beating, Fiona, tough or not, would be broken.

Monk looked at Vinnie, who nodded his approval. Monk dropped his fist, but stood close by her.

"So what did you find no one else did?" Vinnie growled.

"His laptop in a secret drawer. But the cops must have it. They were coming in when I left."

A knife appeared in Monk's hand, its edge against Fiona's throat. "How'd you get past them?" Vinnie asked.

"I went out on the roof and down a rope ladder to the next building."

"Real smart guy aren't you, Smiley?"

"I try." I flicked my eyes at Fiona and Monk's knife. The blade wasn't quite touching her skin now. The whites of Fiona's eyes were showing. Her breathing had steadied. "So what's up with Jack? Do you know where he is?"

The blue flushed away from Vinnie's face. "Fuck your Jackie New, hyena-motherfucker. He's as good as dead. He thought he could run an operation on me. On Vinnie-fucking-Tortelli who has lived through every change in the Outfit for the last thirty years, and those were some double-dealing fucks let me tell you. Little bitch Jackie comes here and thinks nobody's going to make him for a cop? He's a fucking FBI agent. Those straight-laced bastards don't get turned."

"So Jack went back to the FBI? Didn't know that. We've been out of touch." I wondered if they would kill us now and put us in a freezer, or take us somewhere until they could get around to our disposal. "Sammy won't be happy. Who would have thought Jackie had the stones to run an operation on the Chicago Outfit?"

"You're so full of shit. We knew your butt-buddy was a plant. That's why he was sent to LA with the ragheads' money. I figured he wouldn't hesitate to dime out a bunch of honest-to-god terrorists and we'd be shy of Jackie without touching the snitch. Either LA or the Triads or the fucking ragheads would take care of him for us."

"But nobody caught on to him? Didn't you warn LA?"

"That fat fuck Sammy? He wasn't the LA contact. Mohammed-something-the-fuck's running the operation. Figured he would've taken out Jackie-boy."

"Mohammed?" A cold shiver crawled down my spine. Jack and I had a Mohammed Abd Allah as one of our interrogation subjects at Abu Ghraib. To have Jack and a Mohammed in the same operation here didn't feel like a coincidence. I had seen Mohammed in LA a couple of months earlier.

"The ragheads give you the shakes? Real tough guy." Vinnie tried to wheeze a laugh but strangled on it. The rest of the boys shuffled restlessly while the old man caught his breath again. Danny Shoe looked out the window acting bored as hell, then back at me with a tiger's smile.

"Why are you telling me all this?" I wanted to stall the inevitable by giving the old man an excuse to vent about Jack and the FBI trying to infiltrate his operation.

"Smiley, you've been a pain in my ass for years before you shipped out. An annoyance. Then you went to kill the ragheads and I can respect a man who puts his life on the line for our country. Now you show up in town nosing around Jackie New, the Fed plant. You piss me off, but I respect you. But the Feds have their nose up my ass and I don't like it. And you draw trouble in this town like shit draws flies. If Danny had the sense god gave shit, he'd have left you and the bimbo to the Feds. But no, he had to get creative." Vinnie wheezed and struggled to catch his breath. "You're a link between Jackie and us. We can't have that."

"Hey, Vinnie. Jack's not in town. I'm just as happy to leave Chi tonight. I don't need to talk to the Feds. They're not on my agenda."

"I believe you. You always were an honest cop." The old man nodded. "Danny's going to take you on a fishing trip tonight."

People go on Danny Shoe's fishing trips and no one sees them again. "What about the girl? She hasn't got anything to do with this."

"The bimbo's here taking this all in," Vinnie cackled. "You're both going for the ride."

The old man started wheezing again. This time the inhalers didn't stop it. A nervous looking male nurse glided into the room and pushed him through a door at the back. After Vinnie left, the room lightened up.

Danny caught Monk by the arm. "Put them in the safe room in the north cellar. And don't make a mess in Vinnie's house." He smiled at me with the warmth a crocodile shows its dinner. "I'll see you later Mr. Smiley."

7. FEDEX

Monk and his crew escorted us out of Vinnie's study, through the long entry hall then down a windowless passage in the other wing. The corridor formed a perfect shooting gallery, wide enough to drive a truck through without scratching the walls, and about thirty yards long.

We scuffed along in a ragged group with Nonny pushing Fiona a little ahead of me, followed by Monk and Tiny, the walking wall, just a half step behind me, shuffling and joking to themselves. Nonny couldn't keep his eyes off of Fiona, but he missed her slipping out of the zip ties they'd used to bind her hands. Her glance suggesting this might be our best opportunity to escape, but the two of us going hand-to-hand against three armed thugs wouldn't end well.

I still had the .38. The crotch holster made it hard to spot in a pat down and after the rough handling I'd gotten from Monk and Tiny, the damned holster had shifted into an uncomfortable, more difficult to reach, position. I couldn't communicate this to Fiona I'd need a moment of privacy to retrieve it. I could only hope she wouldn't run down the hall in her platform boots and miniskirt.

Nonny's interest in Fiona bordered on the obsessive. He kept rubbing his shoulder against her and watching her skirt twitch, always jigging a little behind her and then a little closer.

"Hey, Nonny." Monk chirped from behind me. "You think she's gonna let you play before you whack her? Or you gonna wait until afterwards?"

Nonny started walking backwards, his thin lips twisted in a half grin. "Hey, knock it off. It was only that once and I didn't know she was dead until I finished."

Fiona focused a look of disgust on Nonny that should have withered his interest, but he just grinned harder and pinched her tit.

Fiona didn't miss a step. She wheeled towards him, grabbed his wrist with both hands forcing the joint up and back against its normal direction of movement. He took a stuttering step backwards then stumbled towards Fiona as the pain in his wrist grew unbearable. Stepping into his forward motion with her whole body, she kneed him in the stones.

The unhappy flirt dropped to his knees, his gun clattering across the floor out of reach. Tiny cocked his arm back to hit her but I caught his wrist, twisted it around and backwards, which held him in an awkward, painful pose. Monk put the barrel of the .44 to Fiona's head, cocked the hammer back; the sound freezing all of us like statues at the Mad Hatter's tea party.

My hand held Tiny's wrist a single moment from snapping the small bones. Fiona's laser focus watched Monk's fingers tighten on the too-light trigger of my .44. My stomach clenched; my bowels loosened. Gas released from my guts in a high pitched squeal as I tried not to mess my pants in front of God and everyone.

Monk snickered. "Jesus, Smiley."

72

In a fire fight, a thousand lethal things are happening at any given moment. A single mistake can get everyone killed. In this situation, at this moment, I knew Fiona would die if I did the wrong thing. Tiny's pistol poked out of the waistband of his chinos, within easy reach. Monk would shoot Fiona before I got the gun to bear, but the next round would kill him, then Tiny, then Nonny. I'd be free to escape but Fiona would be dead or dying.

The pressure in my guts grew intense. Monk apparently had an adolescent sense of humor to go with his psychopathic personality, so I let the pressure escape more forcibly. "We don't want to make a mess in Vinnie's nice house do we?" I struggled to keep my voice cool while Monk giggled. He relaxed the pressure on the trigger and brought the muzzle up. I released Tiny's wrist. Fiona, very reasonably, trembled as she let Nonny slip to the floor. Maybe she realized how close we came to eternity.

"The fucking whore..." Despite his injuries Nonny struggled to his feet and lunged at Fiona, pushing her back. I could see in her eyes she wanted to fight back but she let him catch her arms in his spidery fingers and pin her against the wall, his legs turned to block another kick. With his free hand he ripped her shirt, exposing her breasts. Then he grabbed the left nipple and twisted. Fiona yipped and bucked with tears running down her cheeks. The tears of pain crystallized the look of hate in her eyes.

Monk still had my gun loosely pointed in her direction. Tiny rubbed his wrist, and glared. Then he shot a round-house right at me, catching me in the shoulder as I tried to duck, knocking me against the wall. Fortunately, he'd used the hand I'd damaged; the blow lacked force and follow through.

"Fuck." Tiny tried to shake his wrist bones back in place. With his off-hand, he pulled his 9mm and pushed it in my face.

The animal in my head promised all three were dead men at the first opportunity.

Danny Shoe strode down the hallway. "What the hell is going on?

Vinnie's pissed enough already."

"The bitch kneed Nonny in the nuts." Monk gestured with the gun. His pendulous lower lip jiggled as he tried to suppress the grade school giggles. Nonny let Fiona go. She quickly tied her shirt back together, surreptitiously rubbing her injured breast while the goombas looked at Danny Shoe.

"Let her be, for now. Vinnie wants you to make sure the cop tells us what Jackie told him, before we take them fishing. Get them down in the cellar." Danny kicked Nonny's gun back towards us. "And don't let Smiley get hold of your guns."

Nonny ducked down to get his gun. Tiny grunted and pushed me towards a recessed stairwell. Fiona crashed into my back. We tumbled down to a hard darkness. I twisted to protect my head and neck from the unseen and caught Fiona. Lucky for her, my stomach cushioned her fall. Unfortunately her knee found my crotch-holstered .38 and drove it further into the uncomfortable place. The lights flashed on while I gasped for air. A raw plywood cubicle filled one corner of a large, concrete block room. A card table and folding chairs stood by the entry. The air stank of dirt and old cigarettes.

Fiona rolled to her feet with a feline aptitude, and pulled me up. Tiny covered us with his 9mm, motioning towards the wooden box. Danny and Monk clattered down the stairs, filling the room until it felt like a closet. Monk covered the room with my .44. Nonny pinned Fiona against the wall of the plywood box and Tiny pinned my arms behind my back.

"You want to tell me about Jackie New?" Danny punched me low before I could answer. Then Tiny held me up while I sagged and gasped for air. I shuddered with the effects of another punch in the stomach, but this time I'd been ready for it. Danny rubbed his fist like he might have damaged it on my guts. "It's a long time 'til tomorrow night. It ain't a question of when, just how much fun we're gonna have beforehand."

"Danny, you're gonna..." I sucked in air against the next punch.

"gonna wear yourself out. I can't tell you what I don't know. I don't know anything about Jackie New."

Before he hit me again, his phone chirped. For once I didn't mind someone ignoring me to take a call. Danny answered it with a grunt, followed by an explosive 'fuckers'. He pulled his gun. "Nonny, you and me. The cops are coming."

"What the fuck?" Monk's eyebrows pinched together as Danny and Nonny ran up the stairs. He turned to Tiny. "What the hell is he talking about?"

"I dunno. What do we do with these two?" Annoyed I'd nearly broken his wrist; Tiny grabbed me by the collar and shook me like a dog shaking a toy. But the odds had gotten a lot better, if I just got some maneuvering room.

"Throw them in the box for now. Danny'll be back as soon as he straightens out the cops."

Tiny shoved us toward the plywood room pushing Fiona in after me. I managed to stumble into a corner out of their direct sight. Immediately I had my hand down my pants fishing for the .38. He slammed the door shut but I didn't hear him slide a dead bolt or a latch.

Fiona looked at me fishing in through my open zipper and gave a snort of disgust. "Couldn't you at least turn around or something?"

"Wait a minute." My in-the-pants holster had shifted down between my legs, which is probably why I still had it. Finally I got the baby .38 I kept there, flashing just enough for Fiona to see. "That's better. Where did you learn to fight like that?"

"A girl's got to protect herself." Fiona looked at me with raised eyebrows as though to say: what were you waiting for?

"I've got five rounds and a two inch barrel. Enough———maybe— —to take out one of the goombahs, two if we're lucky, and collect more hardware. I don't suppose you know how to shoot?"

Her eyes became heavy-lidded, all expression drained from her face. She might have practiced in front of a mirror for hours on how to stymie interrogation. Whatever she knew she wasn't going to share with me. That said a lot.

Something exploded in the distance and rumbled down the hall. Fiona cocked her head to one side as dust drifted off of the raw framing. "What's that?"

The unmistakable pop-pop-pop of small arms fire answered her question. Muffled by wood, concrete, and insulation, it sounded like an infantry assault. The sound of feet pounding up the stairs gave us the best opportunity we were going to get. I kicked the door hard——it swung open. I took a low crouch to eyeball the room.

No Tiny. Monk stood by the stairs, maybe 10 feet away, looking up towards the hallway, my .44 in one hand, a big Sig Sauer in the other. He barely turned in my direction before I squeezed off a round. The bullet caught him in the throat, just below and to the right of the larynx. Blood gushed but he still managed to bring his gun up, point it in my direction. I corrected my aim putting the next two rounds in his left eye. He staggered back and slumped against the wall, leaving a bloody streak in his path. His pendulous lower lip jiggled as his one remaining eye dulled.

I recovered my .44, the 10 mm, and the .380 he had tucked in his pocket. Fiona followed me up the stairs. Gutsy girl. The gunfire had ceased. I stopped on the next to last riser, my head about knee height if I were standing in the hallway. The shadow of the doorway became as good as any camouflage.

Two troopers in full S.W.A.T. gear with FBI in blaze-yellow across their chests trotted halfway down the hall realizing what a trap it could be. A body lay halfway between the troopers and our location in the stairway. From the size of the pile I guessed Tiny hadn't made it into the fight. One of the troopers dropped to his knees to check Tiny's vitals when the stairs squeaked under Fiona's slight shifting weight. The standing gunner, trying to watch both ends of the hall at the same time, spotted me out of the corner of his eye, spun towards me and jerked three rounds of 5.65 into the door frame over my head at a standing man's chest height.

"Don't shoot," I called out. The gunner corrected his aim towards my voice as his partner reached towards him. I had both hands above my head, prepared to dive for the floor. After a long moment the gunner dropped his rifle to low alert. I drew a long, ragged breath. The Bureau had been looking for me. Looks like they found me. At least we wouldn't be going for the long boat ride tonight. On the other hand my inner animal still felt the pressure of entrapment.

"Keep your hands in the air," the shooter bawled. The team likely consisted of a Sergeant and a rookie. Probably the boy's first dance. He kept looking at his boss and waving the AR-14 with his finger in the trigger guard.

"No shit, Sherlock. I know the drill. There's two of us. We were prisoners." I urged Fiona to come out in the open with her hands up, but behind me. I didn't want to startle the kid. He acted eager to shoot again. I knew the look. All the young troops think it's great fun until they make their first kill. The good ones hate it afterwards.

We'd just stepped out of the doorway, under the watchful eyes of both troopers, when Nonny appeared at the end of the hallway with a 12 gauge pump braced on his hip. I threw Fiona to the floor and pulled my gun. Nonny caught the troopers with two quick blasts before they could react. I sent two .44s to Nonny. The slugs drove him into the wall. He slipped to the ground, the gun cradled in his lap.

I ran down the hall to check on the troopers. The FBI boys groaned. A quick check showed Nonny's aim had been center of mass and the trooper's armor had taken most of the pellets. The young one wasn't going to sit comfortably for a couple of weeks; the Sergeant would need a really good back massage. I grabbed his mic, keyed it on. "Officer down. Northwest corridor."

The sound of another shell being racked into the shotgun's chamber sent a chill down my spine. Nonny had gotten back to his feet—— his weapon in hand. Two fast rounds knocked him back to the wall where he left a bloody streak all the way to the floor. Good, quick reactive shooting saved my bacon.

Only I hadn't shot him.

Fiona held a perfect Weaver stance with Monk's Sig Sauer and my life in her hands.

I whispered to her. "Sometime you're going to have to tell me what you do for a living." And I'll be damned if she didn't blush.

The handset crackled. "Who's this?"

I brought the mic back to my lips. "Officer down. Officer down. Northwest hallway by the basement stairs."

"Damn it, who's on the net?" The voice quality of the portable radios had gotten surprisingly good. I could almost see Tom Rudd, Chicago's Special Agent in Charge for the FBI, in his yellow duster and fedora with a Tommy gun in hands. A walking, talking, crime-stopping Dick Tracy. Well, he really didn't carry a Tommy gun, just a regulation Smith and Wesson, but I'm not lying about the duster and the fedora.

"It's Jason Smiley, Tom."

"What the hell are you doing on this channel?"

"Two of your men got banged up from a shotgun and need medical help. Me and a civilian were held prisoner. The cops are alive, but Nonny's going to have a nice funeral." I waved Fiona over to give me her gun. I couldn't protect her from Tom if anyone saw her with it.

"Stay where you are. Someone will be there to take you into custody. Do not attempt to leave the building." Tom's voice had an icy edge to it. I could understand he didn't want to hear me on the radio. The last time we talked this way, I'd stepped on a sting operation he'd set up pre-9/11, which netted me Jimmy the Horse and Rudd's transfer to Anchorage.

"I'm not going anywhere, but since when did the Chicago Field Office go after Organized Crime like this was Ruby Ridge?"

"Homeland Security, Mr. Smiley. And we're not after the Outfit..." The radio crackled and went silent for a long three seconds. "We're after you."

8. GRILLED

The FBI interrogation room contrasted sharply with the grubby concrete blocks and cement floor we'd had in Iraq and Chicago. The large one-way mirror offered an excellent view of the suspect sweating for the interrogators and the video camera. A young agent guarded the only door, his coat open exposing his empty holster, as a reminder we were under prison rules, that is, no weapons allowed near the prisoners.

First Rudd had questioned my friends about me, then he lead an armed take-down of the Chicago Outfit——thanks Hostage Rescue——to bring me in for questioning. Why would the FBI risk a guns-out operation to 'capture' a two-bit detective? How did they find me so quickly? And why were shots fired? How much of this had to do with Jack?

None of this made sense. Everybody in the Chicago law-and-order establishment had Vinnie T on speed dial. Rudd could have made a trade and forgone the Rambo scene.

Something smelled very bad.

The door opened and Tom Rudd strolled into the room. He had presence; tall, rangy with the craggy face of a young Abraham Lincoln. Rudd maintained a humorless attitude so everyone saw him as deliberate and serious, which ended any resemblance to the historical Lincoln. He folded himself into the chair opposite and stared at me.

The tension of the long night——it had to be two in the morning—— ate at the lining of my stomach. Life, death, and lots of adrenalin agitated the wild animal I fought to control. And negotiations with an arrogant prick like Tom Rudd made control more difficult. One thought kept me in my seat while he tried to wilt me with his smug glare. He'd said 'Homeland Security' on the operational channel and that meant the normal rules didn't apply.

Rudd dismissed the young agent with a careless wave and placed his briefcase on the table between us. The door locked with a thud as the bolts slid home. Leaning forward he growled. "You're in deep trouble, Mr. Smiley. What the hell are you doing in Chicago?"

"Just passing through, thanks. How was Alaska?" I pushed the chair back and crossed my legs.

A slow flush crept across Rudd's features. "What were you doing at the Tortelli residence?"

"Trying not to be killed. Apparently Vinnie hasn't forgiven me, either." I grinned at him. If he'd understood the Outfit when he went after Jimmy the Horse, I wouldn't have made the arrest and broke up Rudd's sting. "Why were you there? Vinnie forget to pay for his get-out-jail-free card?"

"This is a terrorism investigation." Rudd carefully keyed in the combination and opened the briefcase. "There are no 'get-out-of-jail-free cards.'"

A lump of ice formed in my stomach. If Rudd wanted to he didn't need much evidence to make the rest of my life a living hell with a terrorism marker on my file. "I haven't been with any terrorists, just all-American gangsters."

Tom didn't blink. He should have reacted to the gangster comment at least. He pulled a set of photos from the case and slapped them on the table. A tag marked each of them 'Happy Shark', code-word-only above Top-Secret.

"Hey, I'm a civilian now. I can't see these things," I protested.

"I'm giving you special authorization." He spun the photos around. They were blurry, digitally-zoomed shots taken at low resolution, but showed, clear enough, two men standing in the doorway of a cafe near my office in LA. I was one of the men. The other man, a clean shaven gentleman in his mid-fifties, could have passed for Italian or Greek as quickly as Saudi or Syrian. In fact, he was Iraqi called Mohammed Abd Allah.

The cold, hard, sharp piece of ice in my gut sent a shiver up my spine. I wouldn't be helping Jack or Chicago in Gitmo. "You've had me under surveillance?"

"Not you. Him. Mohammed Abd Allah. He's in this country illegally. And he's a known associate of the Al-Qaeda leadership." Tom leaned back in his chair with hands still on the table. He didn't exactly look like the Lincoln on the five dollar bill but he tried for the effect.

"Oh, crap. We cleared him back in Abu Ghraib. I was there. I know." I remembered the two-minute conversation I'd had with Mohammed that day on the street. He'd come up to me at the sidewalk cafe where I had staked out the motel where Bruno's wife met her boyfriend. Mohammed said he'd come to the States to teach. I had been surprised, but pleased he had got a visa. "He's teaching at a junior college in the Los Angeles area. How can he be illegal and teach school?"

"Terror school, you asshole." Tom's phone buzzed an incoming text message. He glared at it and shoved the photos toward me. "He turned you at Abu Ghraib, didn't he?"

"Mohammed? Turned me to what?"

"A sleeper agent for Al-Qaeda," he said with an emotionless voice. He wasn't joking but he should have been.

"Do you know what sort of trouble I had when I came back from Iraq? If I was a sleeper agent I'd have been very careful not to cause trouble." I could feel any hope of reasoning my way out slipping away. All I had left was the bare truth. "When I interrogated Mohammed I found him to be an educated, peaceful man, just caught up in a crazy time. Just trying to survive. Just like the rest of us."

My mind raced. The gentle man I knew could hardly be a terrorist. He'd shown grace and intelligence under the most stressful conditions while in prison. He'd been the only case Jack and I argued over. Mohammed wasn't an innocent, but then who was over there? We played chess. I liked him.

And Jack didn't.

Tom leaned across the table at me, forcing me to sit back or go nose to nose with him. "You worked with an FBI agent over there, Jack Nesmith. You both worked Mohammed Abd Allah. We know something big is going down and there is a link between Abd Allah, the Outfit, and Jack Nesmith. What's it about?"

I sat back. Had Rudd risked dozens of agents because he thought I might know something about Mohammed? But his fishing expedition echoed Mo's investigation, and the blown gun deal Jack had run from. Except Rudd didn't mention the Chinese connection. Why?

I shrugged. "Damned if I know. No one included me in the party planning. I'm just passing through town."

Tom slammed his hand down on the table. The animal racked his hot claws behind my eyes. I half rose from my chair. Spittle flicked from Rudd's lips as he yelled at me. "Nesmith was an undercover operative, and you were at his cover-apartment last night. Why?"

Two angry men make a war. I sat back down, rubbed my eyes, and willed the animal back in his cave. I pushed out a deep sigh. Even at the risk of Gitmo, I couldn't tell Rudd I'd talked to Jack. "I can't discuss my client's business."

"Who is your client?" He leaned across the table, showing he could intrude in my space with impunity. The fire behind my eyes flared up, again.

"I can't tell you. You know that." I gripped the table, willing all of my rage into my fingers trying to break the steel tabletop. With this tenuous control, I leaned forward until we were nose to nose, and hissed, "What do you really want? Revenge for Alaska?"

Rudd pushed back, sputtering, "You should have been broken for your interference, not given a medal. I spent ten long years in that frozen wasteland. I can send you to Gitmo. We're still keeping a couple of special people there. You can join them or——"

The intercom crackled. "Agent Rudd, please come see me." The voice on the intercom flashed me back to Afghanistan. Suddenly, the air smelled of cordite, gun oil, and camel shit. I knew that voice.

Tom muttered a curse under his breath and shoved the pictures back in the briefcase. He slammed his chair into the table and pounded on the door. The bolts immediately snicked back to let him out. When the door shut and the bolts returned to their locked position the room became still except for the gentle rumble of the fan in the ceiling.

I shut my eyes hard, my gut gurgled. I could still taste the smell of camel shit in the back of my throat. The rush of anger disappeared, leaving me shaky. In the grand scheme of things I was glad not to be dead or in Afghanistan, but being on the FBI terror list could be nearly as bad.

When I'd seen Mohammed several months ago in LA, I'd seen him as a friend. We were old soldiers, done with the war. Now Mohammed and Jack were tied together, first by Vinnie T and then by Rudd. Jackie boy, what did you get into?

Someone rapped at the door to the room, a bit of politesse since I'd been reminiscing with my eyes closed and he, the anonymous interrogator, had no doubt been watching through the mirror or on the security camera. I always preferred the mirror. A small screen just doesn't catch the subtleties of body language.

"Mr. Smiley?" The gentleman who stepped into the room wore his tailored suit like a set of fatigues. A perpetual squint from too many years in the elements, leading men into truly terrible places, left the impression he saw more in you then you could see in yourself.

General Isaacson, Special Forces. The warrior king and Sun Tzu's apostle. One officer who commanded nearly universal respect. An apocryphal story had circled the campfires for years, about Isaacson briefing the Joint Chiefs, and when his bad leg started to pain him, the four-star, General-of-the-Army, himself, got up and brought Isaacson a chair. Probably not true, but believable given the man's intense presence.

I bounced to my feet and saluted before he had the door closed. "Sir. Yes, General sir."

"Relax, son. We're both ex-soldiers now. No more rank and all that between us veterans. I've seen your record. Pretty impressive. You could have been hell in the SF." He crossed the room to the chair Rudd had vacated.

"Thank you, sir." I dropped into an uneasy parade rest. My head throbbed.

"C'mon, sit down. We need to talk a bit. Do you mind if I call you Jason?" He dropped into the plastic chair and assumed the old soldier's pose, chair tilted back, legs crossed with one foot kicking the table top. I slipped back into my seat wondering what the hell happened to my brain, jumping to attention like a recruit. I wasn't so in love with the Army I had to flash back to boot camp.

"Jason, I remember you from that dustup outside of Gardiz. Your boys did a hell of a job there. I really appreciated it." He nodded.

"Yessir. Thank you." Now I remembered why I didn't like the

Army. With a single word, the General downplayed the disaster that wiped out my squad. Every day I remembered Diego eating the grenade for all of us. Too many officers talk about the glory of a warrior's death. Too few of them experience it. The heat started building again. "You retired, sir? We thought you'd stay until the end."

He smiled at me with his lips. His eyes, on the other hand, reflected a cold cynicism. "I'm working with Homeland Security now. Another great team." He nodded at me. "Jason, I need to know why you were talking with Mohammed Abd Allah. He's a bad character. Done a lot of bad things. Old Smitty should never have let him out of the hacienda."

"We're all bad men, General. We've all killed innocents. You, me, Mohammed. All in the name of our cause or our brothers' or our 'best judgment.'" If Rudd wanted to keep me for revenge, Isaacson could keep me to probe——indefinitely.

The General set his feet on the floor, leaned in close, his voice gravel on ice. "You're right, Mr. Smiley. No argument. But we didn't start the war. They did. That makes all the difference to me."

The General's deflection disgusted me, but I needed help, not honesty. The General made the animal behind my eyes edgy. "Mohammed saw me on the street in LA. We exchanged a few pleasantries and he went on his way. I didn't know he was on the list. Not my rice bowl anymore. I watch trophy wives have sex with meat puppets they pick up on the beach."

The General looked at me like he wanted to chew me a new asshole. Instead he leaned back. "There's a federal agent missing. Someone I think you know. Jack Nesmith?"

"Yeah. I know Jack's missing. He's the reason I'm in Chicago again."

"Do you know why he ran?" The General leaned forward.

The General had a reputation for talking the pitch fork out of Satan's hand. He'd certainly got through my guard. Time to shut up.

"No sir. I haven't talked to Jack since Abu Ghraib."

"Nesmith was in Los Angeles this week."

"If Jack had let me know he was in LA, I'd have bought him a beer for old times. But, according to the FBI, he was undercover. Maybe something went wrong with his operation and he went for the hills. I'm surprised the Bureau doesn't have him." If Homeland had linked me with Mohammed based on a casual encounter in the street, had they intercepted Jack's phone call to me? The walls started getting closer.

"They've got no more idea than you do. But Mohammed visited Jack's hotel room the day before he disappeared." He paused, watching my reaction.

"You guys seem to have a good eye on Mohammed. Why ask me?" The heat had melted the ice in my gut.

"Seems quite a coincidence that Mohammed is in town and seeks out the two men, you and Jack Nesmith, he knew best from his years in prison, just to chat. Smells fishy, doesn't it?" The General nodded at me like I should see the reasonableness of being made a suspect in a terrorism investigation.

I grimaced as the claws dug in. Circumstantial evidence could make me look guilty. "Makes me think he was planting a false trail, just to confuse anyone watching him. Nothing was going on."

"But you're wrong, Jason. Something is very much going on. And you're in the middle of it. Along with your old friend Jack. The sooner we bring Jack back in with the truth about what Mohammed is up to, the sooner we can all move on with our lives. You understand, don't you, Sergeant?" The honey dripping from his mouth didn't stop the simmering rage inside me.

"I understand Jack's in trouble. His investigation of the Outfit here in Chicago had been compromised. Vinnie T confirmed this intel last night. I don't know if it's in anybody's best interest to find him. Vinnie sent Jack to work the arms deal in LA. If Jack had to run, and didn't contact his controller, something must have been very wrong." Jack had warned me not to trust anyone in the FBI or Homeland Security. That would include Isaacson. "Maybe the office here is compromised?"

The General smiled and nodded. "That's why I want you to find Jack. Somebody's been leaking information to Mohammed as well as the Mob. You've had no working contacts with anyone in years and I really don't think you'd be part of a terrorist plot. I want you to bring Nesmith back to the hacienda."

The relief hit the wall of rage roiling inside me with an almost physical jolt. Once you've seen the system, you don't ever want to get caught up by the system. But the feeling of relief was a warning. I hadn't had an emotional reaction like this in years. Thirty hours of frustration, manipulation, forced sedation kicked my ass.

And now I couldn't tell if the General was attempting a trap. Was he turning the situation around so I would relax and expose Jack? "I don't even know where to begin. His trail is cold by now. And if you know where he went then all you need to do is send a team into wherever and extract him back to a rubber-hose interview."

The General shrugged. "Exactly. We have an idea, but we can't afford to piss off our neighbors by sending troops in scouring the countryside for him either. I'm hoping you'll be able to track him better than any of my other investigators. Based on your special knowledge of the man."

"So you're offering me a job?" The same job Sammy the Suit offered me, and with less reason. "I thought I was being shortlisted for Gitmo."

"That depends, doesn't it?" The General leaned back in his chair and smiled. This time it reached his eyes. I liked it less.

"I see. And all you want is Jack brought in?" The alternatives choked me. "Alive?"

"Absolutely alive. He's not going to be of any use dead. There is chatter on the net about something big going down. We've got to know what it is, who's involved, and if we're going to stop it. And

Jack is our best hope."

The General had a reputation for hidden agendas. I could work for the General like I worked for Sammy the Suit. Jack didn't trust his chain of command and I agreed with him.

"When is this thing happening?" I had the uneasy feeling I already knew the answer.

"Sunday."

"What's supposed to happen on Sunday?" I asked with no hope of a straight answer.

"We're counting on you getting that from Jack." The General eased himself to his feet and waited with some expectation that I would rise to see him out with the gentile servility expected by the powerful. Personally, after I've been screwed I like to lean back and have a cigarette.

When he saw I wasn't playing along, his expression hardened. His camouflage cracked for a moment, showing a flash of something raw and hungry before he rapped on the door. Maybe his demons were as hard to control as mine were.

The bolt clanged. The door opened. He muttered a few words to the guard then stood back while a couple of white shirt types wheeled in a portable photo ID machine. The light flashed while I stared at the lens. I take terrible pictures. They all look like mug shots, and especially when I hadn't had an un-drugged sleep in two days or shaved in three. The machine hummed, spun, and spit out a card.

A newly minted Federal ID, courtesy of the Department of Homeland Security. The fine print on the back authorized me to carry concealed weapons on airplanes, and in all fifty states——plus a few places where the rules of engagement were a little vague. With a suspiciously vague chain of command, I suspected the ID card might, under certain circumstances, vaporize or turn out to be a clever forgery. Nice.

The General nodded curtly at the techs as they rolled their equipment from the room, then he turned to me with very cold eyes.

"You can reclaim your effects at the bursar's window along with your travel package. We think he's in the Caribbean."

"I thought you said this office was compromised? Don't you think arranging travel gives us away?"

"Don't be an idiot, Smiley. You do your job. I'll do mine." He turned on his heel and followed the techs out of the room. I barely heard him say as he walked away, "And I've been doing this a long time."

9. THREE O'CLOCK IN THE MORNING

I scrawled my name on a form shoved at me by a grumpy looking HRT sergeant in return for my guns and other personal effects. The pistols and their magazines were all unloaded, the bullets returned in plastic evidence baggies. I don't think they intended to give me any of them back, but my new status as General Isaacson's boy counted for something. I reloaded and re-strapped in the elevator on the way to the ground floor. As soon as I finished, all the tension in my body evaporated, and with it the steel in my spine.

When I reached the ground floor I followed the exit signs. At the first trash can I dumped my iPhone and the burn phone. My passport, which had been in the LA office safe the last I knew, nestled in my inside jacket pocket. Tom Rudd and all his people had been conspicuously absent as I exited the building, though I suppose the quiet could be attributed to the lateness of the hour. The wall clocks said three in the morning.

Blankenship had given me the ticking clock, and General Isaacson of Homeland Security, independently, gave me the same deadline. Jack called me Monday night. Bruno died at midnight. On Tuesday, I ended up back in Chicago running from the FBI, and invited on a one-way 'fishing trip' with Danny Chourelli. So, at three o'clock Wednesday morning, Homeland Security had engaged me to find Jack and whatever he stole from the Chinese, and return it before Sunday night. To Homeland security, or the Chinese Triads, or the Mob or to L. Blankenship.

Isaacson and Blankenship had gone to extraordinary lengths to recruit me for their service.

Both wanted me to find Jack.

I'd been rolled and rolled tight, first by Blankenship and then by the general. Or had my old buddy Jack started the roll with his phone call? I'd been relatively happy chasing cheaters in sunny LA until then. Or so I told myself.

When I finally caught up with Jack the first question I'd ask: Why me? The second: What the hell is going on? The third: Who the hell is Fiona?

And where had she disappeared to? Fiona acted far cooler under pressure than any civilian had a right to act. Like she'd been trained to keep her head when threatened or abused, and to actively resist when opportunity presents. What did Jack know about her? He wanted me to protect her, but did she need the protecting or did he?

The nearest exit dumped me into a massive courtyard surrounded by skyscrapers and littered with concrete boxes holding the skeletons of trees packed dense enough to provide shadow from the double headed streetlights. Tom Rudd had brought me to an office building in downtown instead of the FBI's Chicago headquarters on Roosevelt Road. I sucked in the cold night air to clear the cobwebs from my head, and tried to understand the set up.

Question: Why would Tom Rudd operate anywhere else than his own headquarters? Answer: Tom Rudd the arrogant, officious son-of-a-bitch derived his self-importance from his place on the pile leading to the top. FBI headquarters on Roosevelt Road would be the natural place for him to interrogate a high-value, terrorism suspect. So the downtown interrogation location wasn't his choice, which put Isaacson higher up the chain of command.

Tom might bear me a grudge, but he was fanatical about the rules. The General's reputation came from his unconventional approach to missions, and the resulting body count. With the General running the op in Chicago, Tom might be having nearly as bad a day as me.

I needed to get out of Chicago without being watched by the Outfit or the FBI. If I could catch up to Jack before someone else did, maybe I could help him. First I needed a clean way to communicate with Lucy, which meant finding a pay phone, if one still existed in Chicago.

In the courtyard, a polished stone wall broke the icy wind blowing between the tall buildings. A lighter shadow detached itself from the darkness created by the trees. My 10 mm Smith and Wesson appeared in my hand before the glint of metal face-jewelry registered on my optic nerve.

"Hey, Mr. Smiley," Fiona's face resolved itself into a washed out surface of planes and shadows more in keeping with her Goth image than the softer girl-face I saw when we were captured. She wore a padded winter jacket several sizes too big for her frame.

I holstered my gun with relief, and trepidation. "I didn't get to thank you for doing Nonny. He would have ruined my day with that shotgun."

Her eyes got real wide, her breathing stuttered. "You've got to believe me when I say I never killed a man before."

I considered her for a moment. Skinny, tattooed, poked full of metal, with a command of combat skills that made an old pro nod in respect, and she'd never used them? She shot Nonny at 30 yards in the 10 ring, which was stone cold shooting for a combat vet let alone a combat virgin. Now she apologized for killing vermin? Whoever trained her hadn't considered the girl inside the armor. Must be why Jack had hooked up with her. The protective urge tugged at my good sense.

"I've killed before. It's not something I do for fun," I said.

She took a step closer to me and touched my arm. "I feel very... I don't know... good and bad at the same time. What's wrong with me?"

"Nothing a shot of Thorazine won't help." I looked her in the eye. "Just kidding. You'll be fine. How'd you get away from the cops?"

"I told them I was just walking along the street when the bad guys grabbed both of us." She nodded. "So the tall one told me to leave. I've been waiting for you."

"I'd hoped you'd gotten smart and got out."

"Jackie told me to stick with you." A flicker of a smile crossed her face. "He told you where to find him and I want to go."

Fiona's protestations of loyalty to Jack contrasted sharply with her obvious undercover status. Could she be working for Rudd? But then Rudd or the General would have known I knew how to locate Jack. So who did she work for?

"I need a clean cell phone. Do you have a cell?" I needed to get with Lucy. There were missed calls on both of the phones I ditched. She needed to know to burn her trail.

"Sure. Here." She dug through her shoulder bag and produced a scratched up LG Trac Fone and handed it to me without hesitation.

"Is this phone clean? Did anyone take this from you when you were picked up by the cops?"

"No way. I've got a couple more, just in case." Her eyes, now both bright blue, were big and round. The contrast between light and shadow brought out the sharp lines of her skull. Very spooky. One of those lighting effects that only exist in movies.

I punched in the number to the last burn phone Lucy had used.

Even after midnight, LA time, Lucy picked up on the first ring.

"Hi, Luce. Sorry I couldn't get back to you sooner. Things have been a bit crazy around here."

"What the hell are you into?" Lucy's voice had an edge like a whetted knife. "Do you have any idea what kind of people you're messing with?"

"Well, yeah. I've been chased by the FBI, kidnapped by the Outfit, rescued by HRT and threatened by the DHS with a fast trip to Guantanamo." Lucy, as the professional operational controller provided a tether to home and safety, however illusory. "And someone got my passport from the safe. I had it handed to me, tonight."

"Damn right they did. I tried to call you. They went into the office when I stepped out for dinner, tripped the alarm and nothing looked disturbed by the time the rent-a-cops got there. They took your passport." And Lucy had been sitting in the same office through the loneliest and most dangerous hours of the night waiting for a phone call——no doubt dreading the call wouldn't be from me. "Whose phone are you calling from?"

"Jack's girlfriend's. I ditched my other phones and you should, too. Did you ever meet Isaacson?" I paused for an answer. A sharp intake of breath on the other end of the line indicated she probably knew him better than I did. "He wants me to do a little job for him involving a quick extraterritorial extraction of a certain friend of mine."

"Jesus, Smiley, you've got yourself in some deep doo-doo for this friend of yours. He's on somebody's important shit list."

"The number of lists is more impressive. How's the ride out of here coming?" I glanced over to Fiona who had politely stayed where I left her.

"You've got company." Lucy's voice went flat.

"What?" I said with characteristic brilliance. I'd broken one of Lucy's cardinal rules: Don't get civilians involved in operations, and I didn't look forward to the ass chewing. She'd be right, of course. Except Fiona really wasn't a civilian. "How did you know?"

"You're talking low on the girl's phone. She's right there isn't she?"

"Yes. It's a long story but leave it with she ain't what she seems. And she's a helluva shot."

"You're sure Jack's at that resort? I couldn't find any tracks there."

"Sitting on the nude beach, probably. Apparently he thinks no one can sneak up on him with a weapon." I imagined her eye-roll. Loose cannons were the bane of controllers and Jack had definitely broken loose.

"He might have gone native and just wanted to drop out. Except his jacket at Quantico reads like a text book." Lucy snorted. "He's too perfect, so of course he has to be off the reservation."

"So do you have a flight for me? I really need to get out of this town before someone else thinks I breathe too much."

"Sure, Boss. You want a private flight down there?" Lucy's tone had returned to the calm and professional controller. She might even have been serious.

"That would be useful. Especially for getting out. Can you make it happen?"

"Sure. I work miracles every day. A friend of mine who ferries the rich and famous to their drunken orgies down in the Caribbean has to stop for gas in Chicago. He'll fly you dead-head just like you worked for the Company. Jamaica is one of his scheduled stopping points. I'll get the airport and departure time and call you back."

"Thanks, Luce. You're a lifesaver." Lucy never failed to surprise me.

"And you're a heartbreak waiting to happen, Jay. Watch your backside. Something bad is going to happen. I just feel it."

"Trust your gut. Get me that flight and make sure you aren't anywhere you usually are. Disappear. Keep the office cell phone with you." Lucy kept several burn phones, 'just in case.' "Too many people in this game with long reaches."

"I'll be fine." I could imagine Lucy looking at me like my mother, vaguely amused that I should presume to know how she should protect herself, and a little annoyed that I might be right.

"Just be safe. Do the right thing. No tracks and disappear."

"OK. I'll call you with the arrangements." She clicked off.

As soon as I lowered the phone Fiona approached me again. "Well, Mr. Smiley, do we have a way to get to Jack?"

"Not we. Me." The white light from the double-headed streetlights caught the glistening of moisture in her eyes. Face-metal and makeup faded and another persona appeared, this one tender and fragile. "Don't worry. I'll help him. But you're going to have to go someplace safe. I can't watch out for you and do what I need to do to get Jack back."

"I can take care of myself." She squinted at me. "I think you know that."

She had a point. "Where did you learn your skills?" I asked.

She looked away. When she looked back the hint of tears were gone, and with them the cocky Goth chick persona. Now she projected sensuality, not overtly, but with a slight turn of her head, and the way she leaned towards me. I felt my own primal reaction and took a step backwards. Someone had given her more than shooting skills. She might have been trained as a classic 'honey' trap, a woman who used sex to compromise her target.

Jack might trust her, but I couldn't. While Lucy worked on the flight plan, I had time to press for real answers.

"Who are you working for?" I pulled her into the circle of light so I could see her face better. "Do you really give a shit about Jack?"

Her eyes glistened with hurt or resentment or sheer acting ability. Her lip quivered. "Don't you trust me? Jack told you to bring me to him. He wouldn't ask for me if he didn't trust me."

"Hey sister, you need to turn off the water works. I'm not buying them. You ten ringed Nonny without a blink. Now you're blatting?" I brushed the tears from her face. "Besides Jack told me to take care of you, not let you tag along."

"I need to see him. He's in a lot of trouble." The seductress disappeared again, replaced with the crying girl——the tears looked more honest.

"I think you're a lot of trouble. Who do you work for?" I tried to push her away, but call me a sucker; girl's tears make me crazy. If Sarah had cried more and bitched less maybe our marriage wouldn't have exploded, but then she wouldn't have been Sarah and we wouldn't have been together anyway... and so on into the never ending nightmare of might-have-beens.

Right here, right now I had a problem. I couldn't trust Fiona, but Jack did, and Jack had put me under obligation to take care of her.

"Sorry," she whispered and dug at her eyes. "I don't work for anyone. Not anymore. I just want to help Jackie. Please take me with you. I can help."

"I'm not taking you to see Jack. But I'll make sure he gets back to see you. I promise." I lifted her chin so I could see her eyes. "You need to get out of Chicago. This isn't any place for a nice girl or a tough girl or whatever kind of girl you are. I've got a mission and a ticket for one."

Her side of the argument consisted of chewing the ring piercing her lower lip and looking longingly up into my face. This time her attraction seemed less overt, more genuine, and more in keeping with the intensity of our argument.

Temptation existed for a moment, but I have an aversion to women I can't trust. "Why don't you call a cab? Get out of town. I've got a friend in LA who could help you get settled."

Fiona came toward me, I backed into the wall. She put her arms around my neck. My hands went automatically to her hips to push her back.

"You say the sweetest things. No one has cared so much in a very long time." The light and shadow played tricks with the moment and the border of dark and light crossed her face, leaving half in shadow and half exposed to the harsh glare of the streetlight.

A flush built deep in my gut and moved slowly to my face as we stood there belly to belly. Despite my high moral position——and my distrust——long months of abstinence clouded my senses. I froze, and wondered how I could get away from her without knocking her down.

Fiona's eyes grew wide, the pressure of her arms increased on my neck, her mouth opened as if inviting a deep kiss. For a moment I wanted it, but then her eyes rolled up and she collapsed gracefully to the sidewalk.

10. LADY B IS BACK

A slender figure separated from the darkness and moved towards Fiona's still form, making the last motions of closing the breech on a gun.

I had my pistol up but didn't shoot as she crossed the sharp edges from dark to light.

Blankenship.

A black watch-cap covered her fiery hair; a flat-black pea-coat and leggings swallowed the rest of her. Standing still she became invisible. She could have been waiting in the shadows before either Fiona or I entered the courtyard. Or she could have slid up while Fiona distracted me. I waved my gun at her. "Why did you do that?"

A faint smile crossed Blankenship's lips as we faced each other with our weapons of choice. "Your girlfriend is inconvenient. She didn't need to see me."

"I don't need to see you. Consider whatever sort of deal we had is null and void. I'll take care of Jack on my own." Exhaustion sapped my reserves, which made the animal harder to control. "Just leave me alone."

She slipped her dart gun into a pocket. A cab pulled out of a nearby parking garage with faintest rumble of reggae. She shrugged. "Pick her up. We need to talk, but not out here."

"No. We're done. I'll take care of this mess. You can leave." I put my gun away. While the thought of driving her out of my life might be attractive, I didn't want to shoot her. "I'm damned tired of you jumping in and moving me like a pawn on the chessboard."

Blankenship grabbed one of Fiona's arms and started pulling her. I grabbed the other to keep Fiona's head from banging the sidewalk. We stood there in a silent tug of war with Fiona as the tie between us. The reggae beat grew louder as Eddy stepped out of his cab. He sauntered over to one side of the courtyard and flicked something towards the building behind us. The faint tinkle of glass suggested he had disabled a camera.

"Nice throw." I hadn't seen the security camera.

"Hey, mon." Eddy shrugged and scooped Fiona up without a grunt of effort.

Isaacson or Rudd would have someone watching the cameras, and now we had moments to leave before they came to investigate. I needed a quick disappearing act or Rudd would guess Fiona's connection to Jack and they would rip her apart for information. I hated myself for letting Blankenship get ahead of me again.

Eddy deposited Fiona in the back of the cab where she flowed to the floor between the seats like molasses. I crowded into the backseat trying not to step on her.

Blankenship slipped in next to me. The slight scent of her perfume caressed my nose. She rapped on the partition. "Take the loop." Eddy nodded and pulled away from the curb. She closed the partition.

"Is he actually on your payroll, or should I keep tipping him?" I eased Fiona the rest of the way to the floorboards and took her place by the door. Rude of me, but she wouldn't remember and I needed some space between Blankenship and myself. If her touch had been electric the last time we were together, her scent and body heat made me shiver. The animal wasn't always angry. "I thought you were just brokering a mission to find Jackie. Why are you in Chicago?"

Blankenship leaned against the door and used a finger by her lips to control a smile. "I've been worried about you. This was supposed to be a quiet in and out. Find Jack and then find the box. You stirred up a lot of people."

"Since you read my file, you knew sending me to Chicago would stir up the Outfit at the very least." I attributed my reaction to her close presence to the lack of food, sleep, and too much adrenalin. It couldn't be anything else.

"I might have been a little hasty." She half hid a smile with her hand as she looked out the windows at the passing blur of lights and darkness. "This wasn't supposed to be a life and death mission for you. And you ask inconvenient questions."

"And I'm finding out all sorts of interesting answers. Just not to my questions." The inevitable physical collapse from too much sustained stress started with a blinding headache.

"What do you think you know?" Her eyes reflected the night lights of Chicago.

"Well I'm pretty sure you aren't working for Vinnie T or the mob. They aren't that interested in the Chinese puzzle box." I pushed myself against the opposite door, as far from her as I could and rested my throbbing head against the glass.

"They should be." She tapped me gently on the leg. "Why did the FBI bring you in? I would've thought they would be more interested in the mobsters?"

"They asked me about someone I knew from the war," I pulled my leg away from her. "Mohammed Abd Allah."

Her eyes remained flat, but the sudden tightening of her jaw concealed a stronger reaction to the name. "You know Mohammed Abd Allah?"

"Yeah. In Abu Ghraib. You really should read the file."

She frowned. "Portions were redacted."

"Who do you work for?" I pulled myself upright, and watched her hands. I didn't want to get knocked out, again.

"I can't tell you." She smiled as she noticed my defensive moves. Then her face turned serious. "But you're right not to trust anyone."

"Interesting statement from the person who dragged me into this adventure." I watched her eyes drift out of focus and back to my face.

"My mission is to get you to take me to Jack Nesmith." She nudged Fiona gently. "We were pretty sure the girl had a way of communicating with Jack. But he'd set up a secure routing that prevented us from locating him. That's where you came in. If you hadn't found your way to Jack's place and the girlfriend, you would have been pushed in that direction. I hadn't expected the Outfit's insane hatred. You must have been a serious pain in Mr. Tortelli's ass."

"And what were you planning on doing to Jack once I took you to him?"

She frowned again and looked away. "Retrieve the box. That's all."

"Pardon me if I don't trust you. I don't even know your name or who you work for. All I know is you pretend to be English and call yourself Blankenship as a nomme-de-guerre."

"I like you." Blankenship studied me for a minute or two while Eddy eased north on Lakeshore Drive. "Blankenship will do as well as any name, but my mother named me Elouise." Her face relaxed into a smile. "I still need to find your friend."

"Elouise. A very classy name. It fits you better than Blankenship." In my sleep deprived and adrenalin depleted state she sounded convincing. I cracked the window open enough to let a jet stream of frigid air and ice sting my face until I had clarity. I turned to look at her, the icy draft keeping me sharp. "I'll find the box Jack took from the Chinese, but I won't give up Jack. Some very bad people want Jack and this Chinese box. If your bosses want you to get Jack, I'll stop you."

Elouise didn't shrink away from me, and she didn't blink as we each waited for the next move. "You're too much of a white knight to be believable."

Fiona's cellphone started ringing in my pocket. I ignored it. "I may not be a cop anymore but I'm an honest man——in my own twisted way."

After the third ring Blankenship put an edge on her voice. "Answer the phone, please. I wouldn't want anyone to worry about your health right now."

"Sure." I keyed the answer button, pausing long enough for the connection to be made. "Glad to oblige, Elouise."

I put the phone to my ear and leaned back against the door to conceal the caller from my seat mate. "Smiley here."

Lucy spoke in a tone that seared my ear. "Are you talking to ELOUISE Blankenship?"

"Yes, this is he. Do you have the flight scheduled?" I trusted Lucy to follow my misdirection like Jack had trusted me.

"I wasn't sure if the El you asked about was her. I hoped it wasn't," Lucy said in her operative, controller voice——clear, calm, and authoritative. "She's a ghost. No real history but the name has shown up quite a bit in the last three years. Mostly in the far east, and linked with drug trafficking and slavers. The people associated with her end up dead. Mostly people who need to be, but no one really knows who she works for."

"Can you get an earlier plane?" I glanced over at Elouise, now outed as an assassin for hire. I thought I could see the killer in her eyes. I could never let her get near Jack.

"All right. You can't talk. I should count my blessings no matter how small they are. Your flight leaves Midway at 6:30 AM CST. Do not go to the terminal. There is a hangar at 6302 West 63rd Street. Go through the gate and it's the first door on your left. Your pilot is Alonzo Wilson. He'll be waiting for you at the hangar. Try to ditch the witch. She's a hired gun."

"The timing of the layover might be a problem. Can you offer a guaranteed connection?" I hoped Lucy would translate my double talk.

"Can't get rid of her? Well, I've worked with Al before. He'll make it very hard for her to trace you to your destination."

"Good. That'll be fine. Thank you." I hung up. As usual she impressed me with her organizational skills and left me wondering just what sort of jobs she'd done with the Air Force Special Operations. I looked back at Elouise. "Are we done? I've got to catch a plane."

"Where to?" she asked with a pleasant lilt in her voice.

"That's privileged information. You're not getting Jack."

"Very self-righteous of you. Honor is such a rare commodity these days."

"Not much of a commodity, since it can't be bought or sold. Just lost." I looked out the window at the bright Chicago night. I used to have a firm idea of honor, but it had disappeared in the Afghan dark, but I wouldn't turn my back on Jack. All I had left was right and wrong. And helping Jack was right.

"All right, we'll drop you at the airport," Elouise said after a few minutes of quiet. She pulled open the partition; I gave Eddy the address Lucy had given me.

"Eddy, where's my backpack?" I asked through the opened partition.

He reached across the front seat and passed the bag back to me. When I closed the partition, Elouise pushed a business card into my hand bearing only an international phone number. "Call this number when you have the box. I don't care what you do with Jack and I don't want to know."

I stuffed the card in my shirt.

Elouise pushed Fiona's inert body with her toe. "What about her?"

I shrugged. "She's Jack's girlfriend."

"And what were you going to do with her? Does she know where he is?"

"No. I was trying to send her home when you knocked her out." I raised an eyebrow at her.

"She's still inconvenient. I can dispose of her for you." Expressionless features masked her intentions.

"That wouldn't be nice. She's just a kid. I wouldn't want her to wake up at the bottom of Lake Michigan."

Elouise raised an eyebrow. "And you think I'd do something like that?"

"That or put her on ice with Bruno. Either way is not in her best interest." I glanced down at Fiona who resembled a little kid curled up on the car floor while Mom and Dad drove to Grandma's house. "I guess I'll have to take her with me. She wants to go. At least she'll be more cooperative this way. Can you do something to wake her up? I certainly don't want to carry her on like luggage."

Elouise managed to look very annoyed without any overt change to her expression. "I don't have anything to counteract the knock out drug but I do have a stimulant that assists transport. She'll respond to direct orders and will walk with a little guidance. It wears off quickly so I won't use it until we're at the airport. She still won't be fully conscious for about twelve hours."

I sat back in my seat as we flowed through the lonely part of the night. The last of the adrenalin washed out of my system, I sank into half consciousness with my mind leaping through the catalog of recent events. Half of my mind wanted to believe in Elouise, half wanted to jump out of the speeding car and go running into the dark. Patience is a virtue to the hunter, and foolishness for the game. I stared at the empty streets like a hound dog, just chasing scents and trying to find the rabbit hole.

Who was Elouise? Elouise Blankenship didn't exist, a 'ghost' Lucy said. Nothing more than a name linked to events half a world away. Our agreement reached and a course of action under way, she studiously ignored me. I couldn't ignore her. Her profile, silhouetted by the lights of the city, showed something softer than the ice queen persona she typically used. Her attractiveness exceeded the superficial. She showed intelligence, resourcefulness and she wasn't intimidated by me. I frightened Sarah. Even before Afghanistan, the violence in my life disturbed her.

Elouise wouldn't shudder at a little violence.

But could she be the hired gun Lucy described? Once, I'd believed shadowy, nameless mercenaries existed only in the movies, but the dark side of the world, the place where normal people never went, was filled with names linked to faces that developed reputations and then faded into the night, or the grim reality of death. Hitman seemed likely. No rule I knew of said they had to have three-day-beards and testicles.

So I became the hound dog and she, the hunter. And not a patient one at that. I couldn't let her get to Jack. Whatever Jack's reason for running, he'd turned to me for help. And the more I learned about the people hunting him, the more I believed he deserved my help.

Exhaustion wrapped its arms around me as we cruised the loop. I closed my eyes for a moment and found myself wondering what it would be like to wake up with her pale skin pressed against me, the smell of coffee in the pot and sun shining in the window announcing another beautiful day. I traced her hip with my hand as far as I could reach and she snuggled closer. I pulled her around to kiss me and she smiled out of Bruno Girodinelli's face.

"Mr. Smiley. Wake up. We're here."

I opened my eyes, thankful for the shock ripping me from the nightmare. I blinked my eyes clear to reorient myself. Her perfume filled my nose.

We were in an open parking lot by an airplane hangar in an industrial section of Chicago, on the backside of Midway Airport. The night had begun to recede in a warm glow from the east. I rubbed my eyes. "Sorry. Haven't had a lot of sleep since the last time you knocked me out. Speaking of..." I pointed at Fiona.

Elouise took a syringe from her handbag and injected something into Fiona's arm. It only took a couple of minutes before Fiona's sleep lightened and she started to toss and turn.

"She'll respond to your voice but she won't remember a thing. Just call her name and get her to sit up."

"Fiona. Time to get up," I said.

Fiona sat up, her eyes opened but with no sign of consciousness, then slouched against the seat back like some kid's Raggedy Ann doll.

"Jason." Elouise touched my arm as I reached for the door. Her gentle touch held me just as tightly as if it were handcuffs. "Promise me you'll be careful. There is more involved in this job than I knew when I signed on. You really need to get rid of the girl. Send her home. Send her to Mars. If we aren't careful this operation can go very wrong."

"Let's be honest, Elouise. I'm not part of some operation. I'm in this to protect my interests and Jack's. Whatever you and your bad-boy friends are up to is not my business. I just want out. I can't stop the evil in the world." I freed my arm to brace Fiona against her ragdoll impersonation.

Elouise's stare softened as she caught my eye. "Jason, I'm not evil. I'm not one of the bad guys."

"You won't tell me who you work for."

"It's complicated." She looked up at me, her eyes opened wide. "I would if I could."

Elouise radiated sincerity. I didn't buy it.

"I've heard all the equivocation anyone ever wants. All the moral justifications. I don't believe any of it." I tugged at Fiona's arm. She shifted slackly. "Fiona. Get out of the car."

She moved, slowly and clumsily, and stood by the door. I climbed out behind her. I dug into the bankroll in the bottom of my backpack and handed Eddy another couple of hundreds. "Thanks for the ride."

He tried to push them back to me, but I wouldn't accept them.

Elouise stood by the back door of the cab. She reached out and touched my arm again. "Promise me you'll be careful."

I couldn't look away. Moisture glinted in her eyes. Her perfume, faded with the night and hinting of her own scent, electrified my senses. Her full, red lips tasted like strawberries when they lightly touched mine. I didn't respond, couldn't respond. The effects of the dream froze me between desire and horror. She could have killed me then and I might have thanked her.

She sat in the back seat and closed the door. I turned to Eddy. "Better take her wherever she's going. It won't do you any good to trace the plane."

Eddy grinned and turned up Marley on the stereo.

11. JAMAICA

The plane rolled out on the tarmac before I got Fiona stowed into her seat. Elouise's knockout drugs made Fiona loose-jointed, dead weight. Her seat might have been in the full, upright position but the seat belt held her like a broken rag doll. The little movements of the plane as it taxied threatened her with whiplash. I leaned the seat back and found a pillow to brace her head so she wouldn't sprain her neck.

As soon as I got myself buckled in, the pilot accelerated down the runway and rotated up like a jet fighter. I hoped he remembered he had passengers before he tried any inverted loops.

We leveled out quickly. The captain, his cracked and weathered face contrasting with his sharp white uniform, eased out of the cockpit into the passenger compartment. He filled the aisle and he wasn't smiling.

"Mr. Smiley? I'm Al Wilson. He gestured at Fiona, sprawled in her seat, drool running down her chin. Ms. Diamonds didn't mention your guest. I've been party to many things but I don't kidnap young girls."

I sighed. "I didn't drug her. It was take her and keep her safe, or leave her with someone I didn't trust. I promise you, I'm not taking Fiona anyplace against her will."

"Why should I believe you? Does Lucy know anything about this girl?" Captain Wilson looked like he wanted to kick me out of the plane in flight.

"Very little. I don't know anything about her other than she saved my life tonight." I looked into the man's eyes and realized if I'd been in his shoes I wouldn't believe me either. "Call Lucy and ask her if you can trust me. If that's not good enough, then do what you have to do."

The captain stared at me a good long while. I could feel him evaluating me against every good man and every evil man he'd met and wondered if I'd come up short. At last he nodded. "I already talked to her. Great lady. I flew with her old man in a lot of places I can't talk about. Shame what happened to him."

"Yeah. Shame what happened to a lot of them." I breathed a little easier when the captain returned to the cockpit. Lucy knew some very intense people.

Each luxury pod, which is the best description I have for the seating arrangement on this corporate jet, was equipped with a breakfast bar. I opened a chilled can of orange juice and went back to observing the sleeping, Goth girl.

Where did she fit in to the puzzle? Curled up in the seat she looked innocent; the ripped shirt, too short skirt and multiple piercings notwithstanding. The tension and pretense were gone from her face. She looked very young. But where did she learn to shoot with such a cold eye? Without hesitation she'd ten-ringed Nonny with an unfamiliar weapon. Even if she'd never killed a man before, she'd been trained to kill. Who does that to young girls?

How much did Jack know about her? Did he know what she'd been trained to do?

And what did I really know about Jack, now? The Jack Nesmith I knew had been all fresh and green, a newly minted agent from Quantico, trained in interrogation and investigative techniques to use in foreign countries. When he came to Abu Ghraib, he looked like he'd just been hatched, wet behind the ears and wide eyed, with only the cynicism of his training to protect him.

As the regular Army liaison, Jack became my assignment because of my experience as a police detective. And I hadn't been tainted with involvement in aggressive interrogation of POWs. Technically Jack was the interrogation specialist, but I'd spent many more hours discussing the nature of truth with suspects than he had. Together we worked a caseload of about two dozen detainees, and of those men, only a couple were of serious interest; a sheik who had been running guns from the Iranians to the highest bidder and Mohammed Abd Allah, a law professor caught up in a sweep of an IED manufacturing shop.

Away from the interrogation rooms, Jack's inexperience showed in the way he coped with the peculiar nature of our war as liberators turned occupiers. We lived in a secured compound adjacent to the prison, all behind protective walls and barricades. Despite the walls, safety was an illusion. We didn't go on patrols, but stray bullets, mortar rounds or missiles dropped into the compound at erratic intervals.

Specifically a mobile mortar shelled our compound by the prison almost every night. An enterprising group of insurrectionists had welded a mortar tube to the back of a ragged, Toyota pickup. The crude mount meant they couldn't adjust their aim but if they drove a particular path the rounds would drop more or less in the compound. No one had been hurt by their attacks but they did their runs in the short hours of the night. After a week of lying awake waiting for the attack, Jack began to curl up early, set his alarm so he could sit outside to watch the rounds come in. Sometimes I joined him.

One night we were dragging our lawn chairs out to the edge of the impact zone. Jack wasn't his usual chipper self.

"Jackie boy, what's up with you?" I asked as we set up at the minimum safe distance.

"Nothing," he said and opened the cooler for a couple of Cokes. "I know you've got a lot more experience interrogating suspects than I do. I respect that."

"Yeah, thanks. You'll pick it up. Don't worry."

"I'm not worried. It's just... Don't you think you're getting too close to Mohammed? You're spending more time talking to him than anyone else and he's giving us nothing. You play chess with him nearly every day."

"What are you worried about? Mohammed isn't a fanatic." I'd played chess with Mohammed every day for the last month on a handmade chess set I'd found in the bazaar. One night he had laid a very sophisticated gambit on me which would have worked if I hadn't moved my knight and checkmated him with my bishop at the apparent risk of my queen. He had been truly shocked and had required several days of contemplation before he would play me again. "He's an educated man caught in a shit storm. If Canada attacked Chicago, I'd be called an insurrectionist and a terrorist."

"You'd target innocents? Children in a school room, their mothers at the market?" While he didn't do much interviewing, he did a lot of listening. "Your friend has been instrumental in several bombings according to intel."

"That's just people trying to save their own ass by dime-ing out someone else." A surrealistic quiet stalked the night broken with only sporadic gunfire and the faint roar of a helicopter in the distance. "Most of these guys are just regular joes who don't want us here."

"You're too close to Mohammed... wait a second," Jack cocked his head like a dog. The sound of a small truck engine with a bad muffler grew louder. Each gear shift caused an echoing hiccup. The hum of the engine steadied and the first round fired. We sipped our sodas as the rounds dropped a hundred yards away sending rocks and dirt into the night sky. The quick response team began chugging away with .50 caliber machine guns. They ranged the truck while three more rounds dropped in the field, walking the usual path in front of us. The timing had a regular beat, a solid ten count from the initial ignition of the mortar round to impact. The sounds of metal torn by the heavy fifty cal. rounds interrupted the launch timing but two beats later the muffled launch detonation echoed against the nearby barriers.

Something had changed the trajectory of the incoming round. I grabbed Jack and pulled him out of his chair. We ran for the bunker and dove behind the berm as the ground erupted behind us. The last round had landed in front of our chairs peppering them and the cooler with shrapnel.

The truck still sputtered on the other side of the wall and limped away to fight another day.

As we gathered up the damaged chairs and cooler, Jack turned to me, eyes wide, skin hot with the adrenalin rush. "You need to be more objective with Abd Allah. If you let him get under your skin, you're a risk to our interrogation program."

I hadn't told Jack about my brother, about Diego and my squad in Afghanistan, and about all the Afghan fighters I'd killed. I knew who my enemies were. I just didn't believe Mohammed was one of them. "I can't be turned, can you?"

* * *

Lucy's friend landed us at a private airport near Jamaica's north shore on the evening of the day Jack asked me to meet him on the beach. This made finding him problematic since operational security should stop him from showing up at a possibly compromised meeting place. But I had no way to contact him. I'd check the beach in the morning in case he broke OPSEC, then start hunting for him if he didn't appear.

The resort Jack picked had a whimsical air to it with many areas of festival lights, toga clad residents and pools lit with underwater lights. A cool breeze blew in off the ocean stirring the fronds of the many tropical trees surrounding the resort buildings. No doubt it looked less colorful in the harsh light of day. I guided Fiona through the winding pathways toward the largest collection of vacation suites, suitably located on the 'nude not prude' side of the beach.

The walkways were well lit but the deep shadows around the buildings could easily conceal observers or assailants. I'd stowed my guns and their rigs in the backpack. The nature of the resort and vacation clothing didn't support my usual methods of concealment. Our room was farthest away from the main building, also closest to the nude beach according to the map the front desk provided.

Fiona stumbled into the room and crashed on the bed giving every indication the drugs still had her knocked out. I knew she wasn't. She'd managed to get past the customs agents showing her passport without raising any questions. I fished some Tylenol out of my bag, poured a glass of water and sat on the bed next to her.

"Great acting job." I said.

She cracked an eyelid.

"Here. Take these. My head nearly exploded when the drugs wore off me." I held the water glass and pills out to her.

She rolled to a sitting position with a rueful grin and took the pills. "Why'd you knock me out?"

"I didn't. Blankenship did. You were inconvenient."

She didn't blink. No doubt she had been inconvenient on purpose. "Who's Blankenship? Where are we?" She tried to give me her wide-eyed innocent look but winced from the narcotic hangover.

"We're at the resort in Jamaica that Jack showed me on the video chat." I sighed. "I was supposed to meet him this morning."

"And you're working with this Blankenship?" Some twinge of emotion swept across her face.

"Do you know Elouise?"

"No, of course not. How could I know somebody like that?" She protested with her mouth but her eyes calculated the effect the truth might have on me, should she choose to share any of it.

Her reticence wore on my nerves. "Your cover's been blown since you flat lined Nonny. You're an operator. I don't know who trained you or who you're working for, but I'd like to know. You probably owe me your life since Blankenship wanted to get rid of you. You wouldn't have had a fighting chance."

She went round eyed as that thought penetrated the drug induced apathy. "Thank you," she said in a whisper as she sipped the water. "It's the only weapon I've got."

"What?"

"Why I acted all weak and drunk when we got here." Her eyes unfocused as if she were delving into some old memory. "If a man thinks a woman is weak, then he underestimates the woman."

"Like Nonny did? Though in fairness I probably owe you my life. Nonny's scattergun would have chewed me up. That was very nice shooting. Where'd you learn that?"

"From my father. He taught me to shoot two quick; one to the heart, one to the head." She looked down and away from me.

"Hell of an old man. What was he? Special Forces?"

"No." She paused and turned back to look at me, her eyes red from the strain of holding back tears. "He and Mom belonged to the Branch Davidians. They were killed at Waco." Her eyes drifted towards the window as though she saw back through time and space to the FBI's greatest failure. Finally, tears streamed down her cheeks but her face remained passive. "They'd sent me away with the first wave of kids. Mom insisted on staying. She wanted to load Daddy's guns while he fought. I don't know what happened, but they never got out of the fire. Neither did my baby brother."

"Waco? That was a long time ago. Could you even lift a gun, let alone learn to double tap?"

"I was eight. I would've fought if they'd let me stay." She smiled and wiped her face. "You know how kids believe whatever their parents believe? My parents believed they were chosen by God so I ended up living with my Aunt and Uncle in Oklahoma City.

"Uncle Marty worked at the Murrah Federal building." She looked at me and hesitated a moment. "Then some guy blew it up. The house rattled like it was an earthquake and the smoke could be seen ten miles away. I never understood that one. One day Uncle Marty is smiling and going off to work." Fiona's voice became a whisper. "Then Aunt Lou is crying and Uncle Marty never comes back. Aunt Lou blamed my parents for his death because the man who made the bomb retaliated for Waco."

Fiona sat straight on the bed, holding herself with arms wrapped around her shoulders, with her head held high. She stared at some point over my shoulder. "My aunt sent me away. I was ten years old and bounced through a series of foster homes. I went to college as soon as I could get accepted and out on my own. I never had a home before I met Jack." She looked back at me with a faint smile. "I never killed a man before I met you."

She flowed off the bed and wrapped her arms around me. She shivered in my arms, warm tears soaked my shirt. I could feel every curve of her body and her scent, stale perfume and a little musk from travel, spiraled into my brain through my sinuses. With my eyes closed I pictured her as the lonely lost little girl torn from the world she understood by horrific events, even as my body began to respond to the soft curves of the 25-year-old woman she'd become. The dichotomy made me feel predatory and I didn't much like the feeling. I pushed her away. "You haven't told me who trained you."

She shrugged her shoulders and stepped out of my arms. She started pulling at the ring piercing her lip until it came out, then she unscrewed the rest of her barbells. In a few moments her naked face became different; less angry as though a mask had been stripped away. She studied herself in the mirror.

"It's a good thing we're at a clothing optional resort. I don't have a thing to wear." Fiona let the school girl mini kilt drop to the floor and tugged at the rubber bands holding her pigtails up. "I need a shower. How about you?"

For the first time I considered the obvious problem of meeting Jack at a nude beach, that is being naked in front of a crowd of strangers, not to mention Jack's soon-to-be-naked girlfriend. My better judgment told me to move fast away from her, but our conversation wasn't finished. She'd told me a lot of her personal story, but she'd left out some dark details.

"You didn't just pick Jack at random." I watched her watch me in the mirror. "Did you?"

Her lips were full and pouty. She hadn't been honest when she'd said she had only one weapon, she carried another with her all the time. She dropped her shirt next to the skirt, exposing the rest of her slender, athletic body, not painfully skinny, but lots of lean muscle softened with girl. When Nonny had exposed her she'd seemed so vulnerable, but now she was positively feral. "I needed someone. Jack is a nice guy."

"And you're here to find Jack because you're worried about him?"

She stepped close to me wearing nothing but a black thong and her platform boots. She put her arms around my neck, and focused her soft brown eyes on me. "Absolutely. I love Jack. I'm so glad you brought me to him. I was all alone before I met him. I need him." She kissed me gently on the lips, her nearly nude body vibrating against mine. "I just want to thank you."

I'm many things, but I'm not a saint and it had been a long time since I'd been with a woman. Maybe Fiona meant nothing by her actions but I needed some time and distance. Hormones made my brain think stupid thoughts. I gently disengaged her arms. She dropped her hands to her side as I took a quick step backwards.

"I, uh, haven't eaten in so long my teeth have forgotten what they're for." I edged towards the door, thankful that the restaurants here weren't clothing optional. "Want to get something to eat?"

"I'll order from room service after I shower." She sat on the bed and pulled off her boots. "Okay?"

"Sure." I hesitated at the door. I felt like I should apologize but I couldn't quite think what for.

She kicked off her boots and stood back up, thumbs hooked in her panties. "Did you change your mind about the shower?" She said with a smile as she pulled down her underwear.

I left without seeing them hit the floor.

12. JACKIE NEW

Outside of the hotel room, the warm, moist Caribbean night air wrapped around me like a lover's arms. I rubbed my face. A door opened to my right with a flash of light, then shut. I stared like a deer caught in the middle of a road as an inebriated middle-aged couple in their natural state sauntered toward the pool area.

I'd made the most basic mistake I could make on a mission. I'd lost my focus. Find Jack. Expect trouble from the bad people chasing him. Just like in Afghanistan, I had to see, hear, and smell trouble. I stepped into the shadows cast by the trees.

I put my back to a trunk and hoped my clothes were dark enough to conceal me from casual observation while I prepared myself. First, I breathed in slowly through my mouth and out through my nose, tasting the air. Mostly I smelled the sea, but with a strong overlay of chlorine. Another breath got me a taste of cigarette smoke, old tanning lotion and sweat. A third breath and I could start to distinguish distinct sounds other than the frat-party noise of the nightclubs and outdoor restaurants.

My search for Jack had been jeopardized by the detour through mob land. I'd missed the meeting. Reconnecting would take more time than we had. Maybe Fiona could still reach him on the Internet, but her motivations were murky. Jack had made the decision to trust her, but could I trust his judgment? After tonight, could I trust my own judgment?

Fiona told a good story. She'd hooked me when she'd lost her parents and her uncle to anti-government madness. My better nature wanted to shelter the sad little girl, which made my reaction to her sexuality feel dirty.

When integrity is all you have left, the thought of giving it away is like standing on a cliff and imagining the sickening fall if you just made that next step.

I breathed deeply.

To my left a couple spoke in low voices as they walked towards the sounds of a hot tub with its jets running. Awareness of your surroundings is not magic, but most people think it is when you tell them all the details they miss. They aren't aware of anything farther away than their feet. They insulate themselves from the harshness of the world by ignoring input. Survival requires noticing everything.

Couples moved all around me, each going their own way, but still in the general direction of the main facilities, where I could find food and learn the general lay of the facilities before morning.

I walked toward the main buildings with careful nonchalance, but staying in the shadows still aware of everything. Blending is the first rule of concealment, but I didn't match the demographic. Even in the dark, or maybe because of it, the resort resembled a giant, out-of-control, frat-party for the over-the-hill crowd. Groups of toga-clad, soon-to-be-senior-citizens sloshed their way toward the pools, beaches, restaurants, or their rooms. The smell, and sound, of sex wafted through the air like aerobic Viagra. Nothing unnatural to the environment, except me.

A single man stood out in the predominant pattern of couples. The going age for the guests appeared to be late forties or early fifties, though a few younger people could be seen. On the beach, in the morning, Jack and I would be wolves in with chickens. Jack would be too easy to spot. I could use Fiona for camouflage even if she was a civilian. But what would Jack do to keep from being a clear target?

The other part of surveillance is to find out if anyone is watching you. I drifted out of the shadows and made my way to the resort's gift shop, where I picked out shorts and a couple of print vacation shirts for myself and a nice dress and a swim suit for Fiona. Fiona's wardrobe would make a stripper blush and my clothes came right out of a Midwest winter.

First I changed into the colorful shirt. Then I walked back the way I came, despite the gnawing emptiness in my stomach, and window shopped while I watched the crowd. I saw the same mix of couples but no one showed any interest in me. No one looked more out of place than I did.

Finally I sauntered to the main restaurant where I showed them my room key and grabbed a sandwich and a plate of cold potato salad from the buffet. I sat at a table with my back against the wall where I could see the whole room without being in everyone's focus. I wolfed down the potato salad and chased it with some ice tea.

There weren't many men in the room younger than me, and I'm pushing 40, but there were several young women dressed in strategically draped bed sheets accompanied by their grandfathers. Something to look forward to if I lived to be old and rich.

A slightly overweight, forty-something, want-to-be diva caught my eye over the shoulder of her gray-to-balding husband. She adjusted her toga to provide me a view of her overripe mammillaries. I smiled in appreciation and continued to scan the room.

Despite the obvious couple's theme, I wasn't the only single man in the place. A group of soft-looking men in their mid-thirties, wearing togas, stood with their backs to the bar like hunters on the Serengeti looking for lions and wildebeests.

At a little table in the back of the room another man stuck out like ham at a Bar Mitzvah. He'd colored his hair a messy blond which made him appear younger and wilder, but nothing concealed the hunted look.

Jack Nesmith spotted me almost as soon as I saw him. He shot to his feet, tipping his table and bumping into a dark skinned waitress. He nodded his recognition of me and disappeared around a potted plant.

I took another bite of my sandwich, curbing my own urge to chase the rabbit. Jack's abrupt departure from the room had drawn some attention. The waitress mouthed curses and the couple at the nearest table watched the door to the kitchen. I finished my sandwich and washed it down with ice tea. Then I walked out the front door.

I followed shadows to the left of the entrance allowing a covert approach to the back of the building. The loading area stank of refuse exposed to too much heat during the day overlaid with the sweet smell of ganja. Apparently someone was adjusting their spirituality before returning to the mind numbing work in the kitchen.

Off the paths, nature had a way of returning with a vengeance. Branches and leaves crackled under my feet despite my best efforts at silence. I wished Jack had better operational training. A brush pass would have been an easy method to set up a meeting location we could both find, without me stumbling through the Jamaican night.

I worked my way through the brush until I found a trail leading away from the kitchen door. The weak ambient light of the resort showed only different shades of darkness. I stepped onto the path and caught a whiff of gun oil. Something sharp, unyielding pressed against my side.

"Jason, is that you?" The words came as a thin whisper in my ear

"Yeah, it's me, Jack. Have you got a gun stuck in my ribs?" I kept real still in case a sudden movement might spook him more.

"Well, yeah. I had to be sure it was you. I think someone is following me," he hissed in my ear.

"And you're giving them a good trail. Didn't the FBI give you any field training? Didn't you read Le Carré? People noticed you at the restaurant."

Jack withdrew the pistol. "I'm sorry, Jason. I'm doing my best but I don't know what to do. I wasn't supposed to go undercover. I'm not a field agent."

"Tell me what happened?" I turned to face him. Even in the trees, enough ambient light carried to make out his features from the darker shadows.

"First, you have to promise not to discuss what I'm going to tell you with anyone who isn't cleared to hear it."

"Jack. I'm not cleared to hear it. What the hell are you playing at?" I pulled him back from the path and pushed him up against a tree. This back way into the kitchen might well be the ganja man's highway.

"Never mind, Jay. Just don't tell anyone." Jack continued at a loud whisper. "About a year ago I was assigned to the Chicago Field Office just before the new SAIC came. My assignment was to review the financials of the various organized crime families in the Chicago area. Then, the new SAIC, Tom Rudd, placed me in an undercover assignment with the Outfit. I got two weeks of training and became Jackie New, get it? Last week, Vinnie T sent me on a courier run to LA to be his broker on a gun deal between the Chinese Triads and a terrorist cell. I knew something was wrong, because Vinnie doesn't like me. I think the old man had me made as an undercover agent."

"Yeah. Vinnie knew you were a cop."

"You talked to Vinnie?"

"After the cops got to your apartment. I'll tell you later."

Jack hesitated a moment, then took a breath. "When I got to LA,

Mohammed Abd Allah approached me."

"Why you? You weren't his friend in Iraq." The disturbing associations I'd made earlier hardened. The FBI had pictures. Jack and I tied to Mohammed.

"And I'm not his friend now, but I smuggled him into the country." Jack took a deep breath. "My controller used Mohammed's insertion as my mission-ready test. I brought him in from Canada without official entry because he needed his bona fides to infiltrate some known sleeper cells. But he didn't come to me Monday night with information about sleeper cells. He gave me money to pay for another package at the arms deal."

"And? Did you call your control officer?"

"I did, but that's when it went wrong. He'd been evasive when I told him Vinnie had sent me to LA. After Mohammed contacted me, I used my burn phone to call control. My emergency contact numbers didn't answer. I called Roosevelt Road but no one knew my controller." Jack glistened with sweat even in the cool night air.

"Is that when you called me?" I asked.

"No." He shrugged and looked over my left shoulder. "I went to the meet. Mohammed's reasons for involving me were very murky. He just said he didn't trust the others with the transaction. But when I saw what was in the package the Chinese boss gave me for the money, I realized someone very high in the chain of command, FBI or Homeland Security, was using me as a mule for Mohammed. And they didn't know or didn't care what Mohammed was up to." His voice began to shake.

"What did you pick up?" I asked.

"You have to understand just how complicated this deal was. I acted as broker between the Triads and a terror cell who wanted weapons. While the customers examined the merchandise, the Triad broker pulled me to one side to complete Mohammed's deal. A scuffle broke out. I grabbed the box of parts and the bag of cash and ran. That's when I called you."

"But what were the parts?"

"Circuit boards. I don't know what they do. But the Triad's broker did. He wanted me to tell him where we were getting the bombs."

"What bombs?"

"Nuclear bombs." Jack paused for a moment. "He said he knew we were getting nukes and taking them to Chicago."

"That's when you decided to call me and tell me I had to help you save the world?" I groaned. The weight on my shoulders got a lot heavier. Someone had to be informed, and if Jack couldn't reach them what could I do?

"Soon after that. I don't know who to trust. Someone very high up has cut me off." Jack pulled up some of the local flora and began tearing it to pieces.

"Rudd?" I couldn't see Tom Rudd involved with the bad guys, but I could see him doing something stupid to impress his bosses.

"I don't know. At least him. And Mohammed is going to want his circuit boards." Jack looked back at the restaurant. A door had opened and closed. The wind had shifted and brought the scent of roasting meat.

"Where are they? Do you have them with you?"

"I stashed them before I left the states. I only brought one to study. It has a DOD part number on it, but there are some clear modifications to the board, and something that looks like a short range antenna. I——" Jack jerked to attention, and stared into the night. "Did you hear that?"

I could hear the party in the distance. We were still deep in the grove of trees. Listening, I could hear the night animals scurrying in the undergrowth. High above came a rustling sound that might have been a bird on its roost. Behind us, and to my right, a twig snapped. Something or someone moved in the darkness. "Maybe we ought to get out of here. Come with me to the room. Fiona's there."

"You brought Fiona?" Jack broke into a smile. "Thank you. But I need you to protect her. I'll meet you on the beach in the morning around 9, and bring Fiona. I've got a boat but I can't get you to it, tonight."

"Stay with us." That would get me off the hook with Fiona and I didn't want to let Jack get away. A branch snapped behind us. I grabbed Jack's gun out of his hand and pushed him behind me. The woods were quiet. I sniffed, listened, tried to see through the darkness.

Jack's gun had a tactical flashlight on it. I thumbed the switch on. It helped break up the shadows but it also spoiled my night vision. Suddenly I heard another snap in front of me. I dropped to a crouch with the gun up, scanning for my target. The flashlight's glare reflected eyes on the ground in front of me. A creature like a cross between a squirrel and a giant guinea pig gnawed on a piece of fruit rind.

"Nothing to worry about; just a rat, Jack."

But Jack wasn't behind me. Had his nerves got the better of him? Or had someone got to him? I scanned the ground where we had been walking, there weren't any other prints but his and mine. And Jack's led back down the trail to the resort.

The trail disappeared when pavement appeared.

* * *

The salt air blowing in off the ocean tasted of seaweed, fish, and salt brine. I wandered dark paths back to the room looking for Jack, but he had gone into the wind. The lusty party roiled around me, but I remained invisible. If Jack's terse phone call had hinted of trouble, he confirmed he was in deep shit. And so was I.

Nuclear weapons. And no one to trust.

Who knew about this? Did Rudd know? Is this what Isaacson wanted me to find out from Jack? My nerves jangled. What if something happened to Jack tonight and he wasn't on the beach tomorrow?

There were three of us, me, Jack and Fiona, against vast unknown forces. I didn't trust Fiona and I didn't know how far I could count on Jack. He'd run off on me when I might have needed backup. The stakes had gotten very high. Who else had Jack tried to tell his story to?

Without Jack, the best I could do was to get some rest——and deal with Fiona.

On the ocean side sliding glass doors opened onto the room's Jacuzzi terrace. I climbed up from the beach. Fiona had the lights on and lay stomach down on the king size bed wearing nothing but a smile. She watched me as I entered the room. No matter her intentions, I wasn't letting the situation get unprofessional again.

"Practicing for tomorrow?" I said, and unwrapped my packages. "I brought you some fresh clothes, in case you might need them, and some sunscreen."

"Well, I'll definitely need the sunscreen." She propped herself up on her elbows and smirked at me as I tried not to look at the belt of flowers tattooed around her waist. "Did you find Jack?"

"Yeah. We'll meet him tomorrow on the beach."

"Why didn't you bring him back here? I want to see him." She sounded like a little kid asking for her puppy.

"Jack had to do something. He'll meet us in the morning." I made a job of unpacking the parcels.

"OK. Why don't you get comfortable?" She sat up in bed grinning at me, the bed sheet pooled around her waist. "I could get used to this whole nudist thing. Did you know there's a grill by the pool where you can eat in the nude?"

I tried not to picture her biting into a juicy hamburger and having the grease and ketchup dripping on her breasts and sliding down her body.

Her eyes perked up when I unfolded the pale yellow, dress silk screened with a jungle theme in a darker yellow. "What's that?"

"Mostly it's a toga party in the restaurant, but there are places here you might need clothes." The gift shop hadn't appeared to sell underwear so I'd purchased Fiona a skimpy yellow bikini. She picked up the dress and smiled at me again, but didn't show any interest in trying it on. Instead she folded it neatly and placed it on the dresser. Then she stretched like a cat and strolled over to me. She wrapped her arms around me, and kissed me on the cheek.

"Thank you, Mr. Smiley," she whispered in my ear.

The tension in my pants made it hard to move gracefully but I backed away into the bathroom. I might not know how we were going to get off this island, or who we could trust, or how we were going save Chicago from getting nuked, but I had one thing I could do.

Take a cold shower.

13. THE BEACH

I woke to sunshine and the hiss of the shower. My back cramped from sleeping in the suite chair. I picked up my 10 mm from the floor where it had fallen from my sleep-numb grip. I'd thought to stand guard, but stress exhaustion caught up with me. Steam billowed from the open bathroom door. I went out in shorts, shirt and 10 mm to do a perimeter search for coffee and a couple of egg and bacon sandwiches.

Returning to the room, I hesitated at the door. The shower had stopped. When I was married, Sarah would walk out of the shower in the morning with nothing on but a towel in her hair and I'd give her a peck on the cheek when she passed me. We were comfortable in our skins.

But that was a long time ago.

Fiona stepped out of the bathroom and casually dried herself. She dropped the towel on the bed and tied her hair up in pigtails in front of the mirror, pinning the braids together with a dragon headed hairpin. I ignored the tattooed belt of flowers and leaves around her waist trailing down one hip to a spray of butterflies and up her back into a dragon. Fixing my eyes firmly on her face, I said, "Jack's got one hell of a problem."

Fiona stopped fiddling with her hair and looked at me. I studied the little red marks where her barbells had been inserted in her eyebrows.

"You said you saw him last night before you ran into the shower. . . for an hour." Some emotions flickered across her face too fast for me to understand. "What's going on?"

"He thinks we're all in danger." I realized as I spoke that Jack's whole story sounded more like a spy novel than the real world. Maybe Jack had snapped. Maybe Blankenship was an undercover cop. And maybe the problems I had with the Outfit and the Feds in Chicago were all about testosterone. "He says he needs our help to stop a thing from happening."

Her lips tightened and her forehead wrinkled. "What can I do to help him?"

"I don't know. It depends on who you're working for." I considered Fiona. She didn't really fit the Jack-went-off-the-deep-end, story unless she led him there. "You didn't learn your skills watching movies."

Her initial concern shifted to a storm front; eyebrows arched, eyelids a slit, fists clenched. "I love Jack. I want to help him, no matter what I have to do."

"Jack thinks this guy we knew from Iraq is going to set a bomb off in Chicago." I watched Fiona pinch off a reaction. She knew much more than she let me know. "But there's a problem with who he can tell. The only people he trusts are you and me. I know he can trust me. I don't think he should trust you."

"Jack trusts me?" She said in a little girl voice, soft and in a higher

131

register than normal. "He said that?"

"He's looking forward to seeing you." I studied the sudden innocence on her face. She hadn't reacted to my distrust.

Fiona's smile trembled inward. "I want to see him. Get undressed. We should go."

"Take it easy, Fiona. He said he wouldn't be there until 9. We've got time to finish our coffee." Taking her to Jack might be a bad move but the whole idea of a conspiracy seemed ridiculous in the bright Caribbean morning. The wild animal hadn't woken up, except for a primal reaction to naked girl.

"OK, and let me put some sunscreen on you." She smiled. "Then you can put some on me."

Jack had trusted her enough to make contact with me. That said a lot about his faith in her.

I went into the bathroom to undress. Time to grin and 'bare' it. I came out, naked except for a towel around my waist. No need in pushing my luck any farther. She had already spread sunscreen over as much of her skin as she could easily reach. I started to do the same for myself, when she squeezed sunscreen on my back. The cream might have been cold out of the tube but her hands were electric on my skin. My towel had almost slipped from my hips but found firm support a bit lower while her hands traced down my spine and across my buttocks. I shivered as she rubbed the cream up and down the backs of my legs.

I cinched the towel back in place. She stood and put the tube of cream in my hand. "Now you do me."

Her pale skin provided a pure canvass for the black ink dragon emerging from the belt of flowers around her waist. The flowers flowed down one cheek and the dragon grew up her back until its wings touched her arms. Her skin felt cool, despite the morning heat, as I smeared lotion across the dragon and its birth rose. The towel may have provided concealment for my reaction, but it could conceal other things on the beach.

"We've gotta go." I handed her the lotion and retrieved Jack's pistol from my backpack. I wrapped it loosely in my towel. I felt ready to start the day.

We passed an older couple on the path, in nut brown birthday suits that had seen too many birthdays. I smiled a good morning to them. The woman's gaze lingered a little longer on my salute than was comfortable.

Fiona skipped beside me. "Let's go find Jack."

* * *

Sand, hot already from the morning sun, burned my feet. The sea air, flavored with melting suntan oil, greeted my nose. Fiona and I worked our way through the early sunburn crowd. She drew a few appreciative glances, but less attention than I anticipated.

The beach felt crowded, more because of its small size, less than a hundred yards long, than the number of people. Still there were enough naked bodies to make it tough to pick out an individual threat. I scanned the tree line which crowded the north side. Good cover.

"Let's find Jack and get out of here," I muttered to Fiona.

"There he is," Fiona poked me in the arm and pointed to Jack sitting in a beach chair with a black ditty bag. Jack broke out in a big smile when Fiona and I plodded over to him. "Give us a minute," she said as she straddled the chair and kissed a very happy looking Jack.

I turned to watch the crowd as she settled onto his lap.

If Jack thought the nude side prevented concealed weapons, he was wrong. I hid a pistol in the beach towel I carried. A gun or knife or poison dart could be hidden anywhere. A major assault would be difficult, but by that point the only option would be to scamper naked into the woods like a squirrel. Or a sniper could sit in the woods. OPSEC, operational security, is what keeps you alive when bad people want you dead. At that moment it seemed like Jack had stayed alive because no one really wanted to kill him.

The morning breeze blew cool in from the ocean, tainted with the ever-present aroma of salt and sea-life, and tinged this morning with some diesel from the yachts anchored out from the shore. The people moved——when they moved——with a slow deliberation in part from the relaxed nature of a vacation but mostly because the loose sand offered no traction.

The ocean, or at least this sheltered cove, was calm. The morning sun over the palms caused any disturbance in the bay to glitter like a million diamonds. Suddenly a mermaid burst to the surface in a shower of gems. The reflected sunlight glistened off water streaming from perfect curves, and her legs seemed to go forever as she walked out of the ocean. I wasn't the only dog staring but she seemed unaware of the attention she drew. She strode across the beach, oblivious to the sands shifting under her feet.

The sun at her back shadowed her face and silhouetted the legs rising to her extremely attractive torso. The water had darkened and straightened her hair, concealing the thousand shades of red and gold. She took another step closer, barely five yards separated us. Her features sharpened as a cloud passed across the sky. Elouise Blankenship. Suddenly the blank mission focus on her face changed to determination and she started to sprint across the sand.

Lucy's warning echoed in my head. Blankenship, the international assassin, here to kill Jack. She didn't have a weapon in her hands but that meant nothing to a woman who used narcotics on her victims as freely as she did. I moved to my left to intercept her, fighting the slippery sand. She was so focused on her target, she didn't see me until I stepped in front of her brandishing the towel with the gun in it.

"Elouise——"

Her eyes flashed wide in recognition as she straight-armed me in the shoulder and spun me around. The gun towel spun out of reach. Before she could get by me I caught her and pulled her backwards.

"Get out of my way." She stepped out of my grip, faked to the left and jigged right but I caught her again with my arm just under her breasts. Her skin felt ocean cool but her eyes flickered with her inner heat. Grabbing my wrist she spun me around like a punk kid, bringing me to my knees facing Fiona still straddling a twitching Jack.

"Fiona," I called in warning. She looked over her shoulder at us, her face distorted with fear.

Elouise released my arm and pushed past me. I got my feet under me, grabbed her around the waist, doubling her over as she fought for her balance. She slipped and dug her hands into the sand. I grabbed her hips for balance and held her tight to me. She used my grip for leverage to stand upright again.

"You bloody fool." Elouise shot an elbow into my ribs hard enough to make me release my hold on her hips. Fiona shot off of Jack's lap and ran toward the hotel, the ditty bag in her hand. Elouise scrambled after her. The loose sand made all out running difficult so neither had an advantage.

Why had Fiona run? Why had Elouise pursued her? I looked back at Jack for answers, but his sunglasses had fallen off, and his eyes had dulled.

Jack was dead. The animal raged. I had let my guard down and it had cost Jack his life.

Fiona killed him? I didn't want to believe it.

People stared after the two girls, probably anticipating a cat fight. I knelt down by Jack. Blood dripped from the back of his head.

"Jack-o what have I done?" I replaced his sunglasses and lifted his arms onto the chair so he looked asleep. A police response right now wouldn't help me find his boat, or the circuit board, or get back to stop Mohammed, or whoever wanted to nuke Chicago. "I'm sorry, brother."

The wild animal scratched at the back of my eyes. I wanted to lash out at Jack's killer, at Elouise, at Fiona. I wanted to beat Jack for being so damn trusting. I'd kick his ass, if I could, for having faith in a burned-out, gum-shoe, nobody.

Who saw us? Fiona and Elouise had disappeared up the trail. Before I got tied to Jack's murder I needed to disappear, too. "Sorry buddy, but I have to go. Do you have anything to tell me before I leave?"

He had a wrist band with keys on it. One was an ignition key, another appeared to be a locker key with a number on it, and the third opened a padlock. I slipped the plastic spring off his arm and onto my own. "I'll get us even, somehow."

I rose and sauntered after Elouise and Fiona, just a guy on vacation with two excitable females.

The easy-going atmosphere of the beach party had lost interest in the girls and the cat fight that didn't happen. Eventually someone would notice Jack's body. Maybe they'd remember the girl riding him, or the couple struggling in the sand or me talking to him after the girls ran off. But right now, no one seemed to care.

But I cared. Walking away from the man who trusted me, the animal gouged hot fire behind my eyes. Jack asked me to help him, and all I did was deliver an assassin.

Elouise should have caught up with Fiona by this time. Fiona needed to grab clothes in the room before she could get away, otherwise she'd draw too much attention to herself. Plenty of opportunity for Elouise Blankenship, lady of mystery, to catch and restrain the girl. I hoped she wouldn't kill her; I needed to know why Jack was dead.

The path twitched around some blind corners made by leafy bushes. Elouise lay in the trail, blood trickling down her neck from a scalp wound. I rolled her over. Assassin or not she hadn't killed Jack and she might really be on my side.

Elouise opened her eyes and muttered some improbable Scots curses.

"She hit me with a rock." Elouise glared at me and rolled to her knees. "I'm a bloody fool. I should 'a seen her."

I brushed some matted hair from her face. "She's been trained. She's not a civilian."

"No shite, choob. And why would you bring her to your mate if y' knew the hoor was evil?" Elouise pulled herself to her feet and knocked some of the mulch off her legs. "Where is she? Did she...?"

"Fiona has to be at the room." My stomach lurched with the thought of Jack's dead eyes, but in battle you let the dead be dead and do your job. "Let's go." We raced up the hill to the hotel.

I crashed into the room from the sauna side the same time Elouise rushed in the front door. We couldn't have coordinated it any better if we'd practiced the takedown drill a hundred times, even unarmed and naked.

Fiona must have hit the room at a dead run. She'd taken the dress but left her underwear and jewelry on the dresser. She'd scattered the contents of the ditty bag and the bag itself on the bed, consisting mostly of cash and a change of men's clothes.

Blankenship glared at me. "This could have been prevented if you'd called me like you were supposed to. Where's your girlfriend?" She struggled to maintain the posh accent she normally affected with such ease.

"I don't know, but I need to find her." I did a quick assessment of the room. "The only thing missing is the dress and her bag."

Elouise raised an eyebrow at me. I pointed at the forgotten pile of clothes on the dresser. Not much there but the little bit Fiona had on her when I met her and the bathing suit.

Elouise nodded. "She had an escape plan."

"The only way out is by boat or by air. She'd have to catch a cab to the airport at the concierge desk," I suggested.

Elouise darted out the door without another word and across the inner courtyards to the 'Prude' side and the concierge stand. I pulled on my pants, filled my backpack with the contents of the ditty bag, Fiona's possessions, including the swimsuit, and followed Elouise. One other thing I noticed gone was Fiona's phone. The same one I'd called Lucy on.

Elouise had turned heads on the prude side standing next to a sign indicating the minimum clothing required in this area, and making it clear she didn't have it. There was no sign of Fiona. Security came over to escort Elouise back to the nude side until I passed Fiona's unused swimsuit to her. She dressed at the desk while I questioned the concierge. Yes he remembered the girl with the pigtails. She'd caught a cab to the airstrip on the other side of the main road. Elouise had barely got herself covered with the suit top before she ran for the front doors. I followed. No sooner did we get out the front door but a private jet roared overhead.

Elouise turned her back on me and flicked the strings from her bikini top back at me. I tied them without comment.

"I need to get out of here," she said over her shoulder. "Your job's over. You found Jack. I'll make sure your account gets credited with the correct fees."

"Sure. Thanks. I'll give your condolences to his mother." I pulled her away from the front door to a quiet corner of the lobby. "What the hell are you doing here?"

Elouise whipped around. Blood mixed with sweat on her neck and her red hair matted down on her skull. Her appearance still attracted attention even covered with the yellow bikini. Her posh accent slipped dangerously close to the broad Scots she'd used earlier. "This is not on me, Jason Smiley. You brought her. Do you know if she got the Chinese box from Jack?"

"I don't know what she got from Jack. You and I were wrestling."

"Is that what you call it? I thought you were trying to shag me, you numpty basturt."

"We have to disappear. Somebody is going to notice Jack soon. And you have attracted far too much attention to us."

"So you don't know anything about the Chinese box? And you let Jack get killed?" Her eyes flashed with anger. "It was a mistake involving you in any of this. You're an idiot."

Elouise spun on her heel and disappeared across the lobby. I couldn't tell if she was punishing me or doing me a favor. In either case I still needed to find out where Jack stashed the rest of the circuits. If Fiona had one she would know he hid the rest and she, or whoever she worked for, would be looking for them.

Fiona had an exit strategy. She'd come here to kill Jack and she'd called for a ride as soon as she could. The waiting plane gave her away and more. Someone paid for the ride out of Jamaica.

What was Jack's exit strategy?

I dug into my backpack and found the brochures I'd picked up off the floor. A color aerial photograph showed several sandy coves, including the beach where Jack had died. From the aerial view an obvious trail led through the hedge to another resort property. The other folded paper mapped a route across the Caribbean between Jamaica and Cuba. The aerial photo had a spot circled in the cove belonging to the other resort with the notation 'Lucky Strike' and an anchor. This had to be where Jack had docked his boat.

I needed to disappear. Elouise had gone her own way and before she left she made sure we would be memorable. The only exit strategy I had was to call Lucy and ask for a ride, which I couldn't do without a phone, not to mention I'd compromised her communications by using Fiona's phone.

I used a house phone to make an out of country call on my room number. It didn't matter if it compromised Lucy's burn phone. It was dirty now and she needed to know it. As soon as the call went through, it went to voice mail. This wasn't a good sign. "Lucy, ditch this phone. I'll find a way to get to you later."

I clicked off, not satisfied. What if I'd led killers to Lucy as well? I pushed Lucy into the same box Jack and the rest of them resided. Something to cope with later. Now I needed to get off this island by myself.

The 'Lucky Strike' might be Jack's plan, and maybe more than an exit. It might be the key to the whole mess. The Chinese box had contained circuit boards that enabled nuclear weapons. He'd kept one and stashed the rest. Jack's OPSEC had been terrible. The location of the main package might be compromised if Fiona knew he hid it before he left the states. I had to find it. Maybe keeping that package from Fiona would save the world. Or maybe finding Mohammed would save the world from something terrible. Whatever it took, I would get us even.

I grabbed my backpack and cut across the hotel's grounds.

14. BOAT RIDE

Sirens sounded as an ambulance and two police cars crowded through the grounds to the nude beach. The map marked Jack's boat on the other side of the thick privacy hedge. I followed a worn path past the crowd gathering to gawk at Jack and traversed behind another beach with far fewer, and younger, occupants. I met a couple coming the other way, apparently drawn by the noise and the lights.

"What's happening?" the man asked.

I shrugged. "Heart attack?"

They nodded and pushed past me. I walked purposefully towards a rocky promontory. Sheltering on the far side of the little cove and hidden by a wilder piece of waterfront, a cigarette boat rocked at the end of a floating pier. Her transom bore the name Lucky Strike. A siren whooped, it's call deadened by the foliage. The dock bobbed with the rising tide as I scurried across and jumped onto the boat

141

deck.

The Lucky Strike had seen better days when I was still a virgin. The 50 foot cigarette boat that might have been new on the set of Miami Vice hadn't aged very well. Salt water cracks marred her fiberglass finish already faded by the Caribbean sun. I hoped part of Jack's exit strategy included paying someone to do serious refitting.

The aged interior of the Lucky Strike brought on a sudden surge of fire behind my eyes.

The boat wasn't anything special, a seat for the pilot, and three passengers. One seat beside the pilot and two facing forward in the aft cockpit with space for a missing cooler. The cracked Naugahyde seats had been repaired with duct tape. A series of fiberglass patches in the superstructure looked suspiciously like bullet holes from automatic weapon fire. But this boat had been the last thing Jack and I talked about. Tears I couldn't shed burned in my eyes.

I found half a dozen secret storage spots in the cockpit area, all with broken locks and signs of older repairs. Apparently this boat had been searched brutally more than once. The hull cabin had the only lockable compartment. A rough eye-and-hasp had been screwed into the fiberglass and fitted with a high quality padlock which opened with the third key on the ring.

The high-speed racer didn't have much of a cabin since most of the hull was buoyancy and fuel tanks. I duck-walked into the below decks space furnished with a sleeping bag on one of the two benches, a cooler and a head meant only for sitting. No place could I stand upright.

I searched the sleeping bag and the storage compartments under the bunks. I found some clothes and a picture of Fiona and Jack, but nothing else. The picture showed Fiona smiling in stark contrast to her Goth jewelry and makeup, and leaning on Jack dressed as the tough Jackie New, black suit and punked hair, but a big, dumb smile on his face.

He must have loved her, and she'd killed him. I hoped he hadn't noticed her doing it.

The back of the photo had a series of numbers and Saturday's date. I stuffed this cryptic bit of information in my pocket. I'd searched every other part of the boat and found nothing. Sweat dripped into my eyes. The late morning sun beat down on the boat; the cabin had only a deck hatch for circulation. I opened the cooler, fished out a bottle of beer and some ice to cool myself. Digging through the ice I found a plastic baggie.

Not a bad trick, but an old one. Jack had a hidden a box in a plastic baggie under the ice in the beer chest. I sipped the Red Stripe and opened the bag to retrieve the cardboard, olive drab box printed with Chinese ideographs.

Empty, except for a folded set of instructions written in what looked like Arabic and more of the symbols like the box itself. I can't tell the difference between Japanese, Chinese or Korean but this wasn't printed in Sandusky. I'd found Jack's Chinese box, but not the trigger circuit.

The boat rocked again from the weight of a person stepping on the gunwale. I dropped the box in my backpack, and pulled my pistol as I pushed the cabin door open.

Blankenship, still wearing nothing but the yellow bikini, leaned over the gunwale to shove the boat away from the dock. A black backpack nearly identical to mine rested on the deck.

"Did you take the keys?" she asked as she neatly coiled the aft line. Her strong shove didn't get us much momentum. Only the ebb tide kept us in motion.

"Are we going someplace?" On the shore, flashing lights and the telltale wail of police pursuit vehicles suggested someone had found Jack's body.

"Away from pursuit, I should think." She stared hard at the police scrambling from their vehicles. "Let's go before they decide we're easier to catch dead than alive."

I passed her the bottle and slipped into the pilot's chair. The second key on Jack's ring lit up the controls. I pulled the throttles to start and pushed the ignition button. The engines gave a half-hearted groan, barely turning past center, then spun and fired. Behind us the cops must have decided we were worth pursuing and pulled their service automatics. As soon as the engines came up to speed I jammed the throttles open.

The props briefly cavitated and the engines over-revved as I found the optimal setting for acceleration. The boat leapt forward. The officers behind us pointed guns and fired but we were out of easy range for their subsonic rounds. I thanked Jack's spirit for making sure the engines worked.

Elouise tapped me on the shoulder. "Better turn." Behind us one of the cops shouldered a rifle. I yanked the wheel hard and slewed around the promontory as a hole appeared in the windscreen in front of me. I clenched my ass cheeks tight and jammed the throttles to their stops. In moments we were skimming the light chop at 80 miles-per-hour according to gauges bouncing on the dash.

"Reminds me of Afghanistan, except with water and no camel shit." The vegetation on the promontory hid us from the cops in the bay. Without an idea where the shoals were I took a wild guess and pointed the boat out to sea.

"We need to get into international waters." Elouise called from the passenger's seat. "They'll be in pursuit soon."

"Better if we'd quietly slipped out from the airport. Drawing a crowd really wasn't a good idea." I found the chart plotter in the controls and got it working. I had to ease off the throttle until I knew what my hazards were.

She frowned at me. "The police weren't following me. They're following you."

"Why would they be following me?" The GPS showed us heading towards a sand bar so I zigged out into a deeper channel before I risked pushing the throttles up again.

"They think you killed Jack."

She had my undivided attention. I throttled back to an idle. "Why would they think I killed Jack? Did you set me up?"

She took a long pull on her Red Stripe, watching me over the bottle. "You're a fool, Mr. Smiley. A fool for women and a fool to think you can involve yourself in things you know nothing about."

"You came to me."

"We know you were involved. There is no such thing as a coincidence in this business, and you're full of coincidences, Mr. Smiley." She looked back towards shore.

"So you told them I killed Jack?" A murder warrant could add to my difficulties. There was no sign of official pursuit yet.

A hint of pain crossed her face as though somehow I'd hurt her. "No. You left a gun on the beach with your fingerprints. I heard the police report."

I glared at her as I eased the throttles up again so we were in motion. The hot angry monster built behind my eyes in a blink. With Jack dead, and Fiona beyond immediate reach, I wanted to lash out, and Elouise's cool manipulation made her a good target. I slammed my fists against the fiberglass cowling until bits of the sunburnt finish spalled off.

Elouise leaned against the passenger seat, watching me as I struggled for control. Why had she come to me again, with the cops in pursuit? She could have let them take me in for questioning. Why would she take the risk?

As we cleared the little off-shore island where the resorts brought their guests for private orgies, I eased the throttles all the way forward again. The boat lifted on plane and skittered across the glass sea. The wind caught Elouise's hair and blew it like fire behind her head. The skimpy bathing suit exposed a lot of creamy skin, as you might expect from a red head. An evil scar traced across her ribs looking very much like a knife strike. Time and surgery had narrowed the mark to a thin, white, jagged line. Farther down her abdomen she carried a thick red pucker like a misplaced belly button.

145

Elouise caught me looking and twisted so I could see the full extent of the scar. "Machete. Sudan." She pointed at the bullet wound. "Pimp."

I considered the depth of the stories she had to tell and nodded. "I've got a couple of those, too."

"I saw." She swigged on the Red Stripe. "No pursuit, so far."

"Good." Jamaica disappeared behind us. For the moment the horizon seemed as empty as my options. The empty box in my backpack meant Fiona had the circuit board. It hadn't been with the detritus on the bed and it hadn't been anywhere else on the Lucky Strike. The picture of Fiona with the numbers on the back might lead someone to the remaining circuits, and that would be a bad thing.

I had to stop Mohammed and his friends from acquiring nuclear weapons with or without an easy means to trigger them. The only place I knew I could find Mohammed was in Chicago. I couldn't keep running. Jack must have had a plan. He had prepared the boat for travel, but where to?

Among the contents of the ditty bag had been a chart. I dug into my backpack one-handed.

"What do you have there, Mr. Smiley?" Elouise leaned across the companionway to look at the map.

"I wanted to see where we were going." I shifted the stiff paper to my other hand, blocking her view. "We need to go someplace and our choices are pretty limited."

"Did you find the Chinese box Jack hid? Or does Fiona have it?" she asked.

I shrugged. "All I know about Fiona is that she's cold hearted. Jack loved her."

"Jack was a fool. He should have known better. I knew she was a problem when I first met her." Elouise's skin rippled with gooseflesh from the cool breeze blowing around the windscreen. "I need to change."

"You do that often." Elouise raised a whole other set of questions.

146

My emotions were on a peak because of Jack and Fiona. Death by breach of trust is the most dehumanizing thing people do. Fiona had me believing in her and then she used my trust to kill Jack. I didn't want to trust her, but I had. Jack had. Fiona had to answer for her betrayal.

Elouise evaluated me silently for another few moments then she drained the Red Stripe like a college student, hoisted the bottle in my direction and asked, "Would you like another?" She pushed open the cabin door without waiting for my answer. No doubt intent upon searching the cabin in case I hadn't done a good enough job.

She reached back through the door and tried to snag my backpack. "Almost forgot my clothes."

"Hold on, Elouise," I stepped on the straps of my backpack and handed over hers. No doubt she wanted to search my gear as well. "Here you go."

"Oh, sorry." I caught the ghost of a smile as she slipped back into the cabin.

As soon as she closed the door I pulled my rigs from the pack. I kept the 10 mm outside my shirt but the others went into appropriate concealed locations. Then I unfolded Jack's chart.

The chart showed the area between Jamaica, Cuba and Haiti. Jack had marked several carefully drafted paths between the resort's bay on Jamaica's northwest coast to Guantanamo Bay, Cuba, and to the coast of Haiti. Each route had a four digit decimal number, presumably miles, and two other numbers. The Haitian route had a red circle around it with the annotation 'bingo.' I didn't think it meant we would get lucky. Other notes indicated he'd calculated the maximum range of the boat at just about the same as the distance between Jamaica and Haiti. We'd get there but be out of gas. Big risk.

We could reach Guantanamo Bay with a larger margin of fuel, but nothing begs trouble like arriving unannounced at the most sensitive military base America has in the Caribbean. Jack had a good idea. We might have better luck with the Haitians, especially since I had inherited a bucket load of cash from Jack. Now all I had to do was not run out of gas.

With the speed boat on full plane I edged the throttles back to Jack's estimated speed so we were bouncing along about 55 knots on a smooth sea. Smooth is relative on the water. Every so often the hull would slap the surface with teeth rattling force and I could feel Elouise shifting suddenly in the compartment. When she emerged at last, all dressed in black jump gear with a Glock strapped on her thigh, but sweaty and disheveled from the cramped quarters, she glared at me. "You did that on purpose."

"Did what?" I grinned back at her.

"Made the boat rock back and forth. I had some trouble maneuvering in the cabin." She twisted her hair and wrapped it into a tight bun.

"You could have dressed out here," I leered at her. I had a plan. I didn't need her help. We could part ways in Haiti. "Nothing I haven't seen before."

"I can knock you out, you know," she gave me a half grin as she finished pinning her hair.

"You remembered to pack your poison darts?" I watched her hands as she brought them down.

Her eyes narrowed. "Do you have any idea where you're going?"

The sun had sunk low toward the horizon on my left. Like Fiona, Elouise hadn't been very forthcoming about who she worked for. Without a way to trust her I couldn't share a bit of what Jack told me. I had trusted Fiona a little and got Jack killed. "North."

"So you mean no." She looked at me with surprise. "Nothing on the chart?"

I suppose I should feel complimented she expected me to have a plan. "I was going to take a plane. But someone had other ideas."

"I need to get back to the States as fast as possible," she said. Another wave tossed the boat and slammed it down again. She stumbled into the passenger seat.

"I'm pretty sure we're going to run out of gas before that happens. I thought about calling someone on the radio, but there isn't one. I figure we're pretty much screwed." I lifted my shoulders in an exaggerated shrug. "Is there a hurry, now? Jack's dead. Fiona's gone. What can we do?"

"My bosses believe it is important for me to return, immediately. So I've made some alternative arrangements." She leaned over and pulled the throttles back to neutral. As we came off plane and coasted to a stop our wake caught us. Elouise stood up and fell across my lap. With one deft twist she pulled the keys from the ignition and killed the engines. She rolled gracefully to her feet and showed better sea legs than she had a minute before. "Jason, I've made arrangements to evacuate. Someone is coming for me."

I grabbed for the keys, but she danced backwards out of my immediate reach. As I levered myself to my feet the Glock appeared in her hand. "Stand down, Mr. Smiley. I've got to get back to the mainland quickly, and your job is done."

The Glock looked more evil than the Lady Smith she'd pulled on me earlier and the desperation in her eyes made me think her situation made mine far more tenuous than it had been in California. Clearly we weren't on the same team.

I kept my hands far away from my guns and backed up against the dash. "I'm not sure the job you hired me for is done. The Chinese puzzle box everyone is so hot for is still missing." I tried not to think about the empty box in my back pack, the picture with the location of the circuits, and the mysterious locker key in my pocket. "Or is the box even a concern of yours, now that Jack's dead?"

"If your friend had the box I couldn't find it." She glanced at my backpack. "I'm under the assumption Fiona took it from Jack on the beach. It would be better for you if you didn't have the box. That object is very dangerous."

"What is so important about a box?" I asked but her eyes flicked to a point over my shoulders. I shifted so I could look where she looked without turning my back on her. A black dot had appeared in the pristine blue skies and grew larger by the seconds until I could make out the shape of a helicopter. "Catching a ride?"

"Yes. As I said, I need to get back to the mainland." She touched the side of her head where her hair might have covered an earpiece and bone-conductor microphone. "Raid one. I have visual."

She nodded at a voice only she could hear.

"Well, give me back the keys so I can make shore someplace. I'd rather not drift all the way to Cuba." I leaned against the bulkhead trying to act non-threatening, in case I had an opportunity to turn the situation around before the helicopter arrived.

"You won't need these." She tossed the keys into the water and holstered her gun. She touched her head again and said something I couldn't hear. When she turned back to me she said. "You're coming with us."

Suddenly, blade noise made it hard to talk and the boat lurched as a whirlwind churned the water. "I don't need you to rescue me."

She pointed at a blacked out UH-60 with a rocket pod on one side and a 20 mm Gatling gun on the other, "They're not here to rescue you."

15. RESCUE

I hate hanging from a helicopter retrieval device, what they call the horse collar, and being treated like a piece of luggage. Elouise jumped onto the cable and rode up, holding on like a monkey. As soon as she could reach the door she grabbed the edge and flipped herself into the cabin.

The lifting rig stopped, leaving me dangling. A large, unsmiling man in a black, paramilitary uniform hauled me into the plane and pushed me toward an empty jump seat.

Aside from the crew chief and the pilots, two serious looking men with AR-14s sat silently in the seats across from me. No one wore insignia, but they were hard men with eyes focused on something no one else could see, yet they seemed to see everything. Old soldiers call this the 'thousand-yard-stare.' Warriors learn it in battle, on patrol and in the jungle. You have to see everything, focus on nothing, because the one thing you see will distract you from what you need to see.

I was willing to bet their names, should anyone ask, were on tombstones in their home countries. In the Army, I'd done business with Special Forces operatives who had hollowed out eyes that seemed to see battles fought long ago and friends they'd buried. They were scary people in a scary place but they were still held accountable for their actions. The men in front of me had no accountability except to the highest bidder.

These boys lived in an alternate reality. Lucy had called Elouise a ghost; these men were part of the ghost world. No rules, no boundaries and no name on your grave should they decide you're inconvenient.

They looked at me as though I might be inconvenient.

Elouise eased herself into the jump seat next to mine. The crew chief, the man who had pulled me in, handed us helmets and flotation vests, which would keep us in good position for the sharks to feed on our feet if it came to a crash in the ocean. The helmets had boom mikes and earphones, but Elouise didn't ask me anything and I didn't feel like making small talk. The iron-faced men maintained a clear zone around her, even in the cramped spaces on the helicopter.

As soon as we were strapped in, Elouise tapped the pilot on the shoulder and pointed. He banked into a sharp turn until the Lucky Strike showed in the front windscreen. The airframe vibrated as the mini-gun lit off——a trail of tracers ripped across Jack's tough little boat. A second burst set off an explosion; the Lucky Strike disappeared beneath the waves.

The brutality of the sinking struck me hard. Apparently Elouise's orders were for the boat, and any inconvenient evidence, to be 'lost at sea.'

I could just as easily be 'lost at sea.'

The troops in the jump seat across from me took turns looking at the spot just behind my head. The complete lack of emotion on their faces had the effect of dehumanizing the subject of their investigation.

Their attempt at intimidation had the unintended consequence of distracting me from thinking about flying in helicopters. As a rule I don't mind flying, big planes or small, but a helicopter isn't a plane. It's a boxcar with a propeller on top like some cartoon kid's hat. There is nothing reasonable about its ability to fly. In fact it looked and felt a lot like Peter Pan telling Wendy to just think happy thoughts.

These people didn't look like they had happy thoughts.

A storm front appeared; heading south and west, sea water reached each horizon. We'd flown for over an hour. As we skirted the heavy weather, the animal started scratching fuel consumption calculations on the back of my eyes. The pilot finally spoke. "ETA LZ 5 Mikes. Bingo fuel 10 Mikes."

"Roger that. Plenty of margin." Elouise smiled and patted my knee. I groaned. Every joe knows 'Mikes' meant minutes and 'bingo fuel' means empty and dry, so the pilot's statement that he expected to land in five minutes with only an estimated five minutes of fuel left didn't sound particularly optimistic.

Running out of gas in something that falls when the engine stops makes five minutes feel like thirty. The sudden flare to arrest our forward momentum and the elevator drop of the approach to the landing zone locked my stomach in a knot, but we landed without any real problem. The engines were still running when the crew disembarked in a controlled rush. Elouise urged me out of the cabin onto an LZ lit only by the stars.

Starlight in a clear sky on a moonless night is enough to throw shadows, but not to resolve details clearly at any distance. Feathery dark shadows reaching into the glowing sky suggested a wood-line in front of us. Behind us, the ocean rippled, black as obsidian glittering with starlight. The serious men became shadows maneuvering a blacked-out fuel bowser over to the helicopter.

"Come with me," Elouise grabbed my hand and propelled me into the darkness. "They don't like being watched."

"Nice friends you've got there. Do they have names or do you just number them?"

"Don't you ever take anything seriously?" Elouise whispered, "They weren't supposed to pick you up." She didn't let go of my hand even though I matched her stride into the darkness.

"Why? What makes me dangerous?"

She shook her head. The light red streaks in her hair had turned silver in the starlight. "You aren't dangerous, but you're more involved in this thing than anyone realized. That makes you a problem."

"But——"

"Shut up. They can still hear us."

We walked, still holding hands like a couple of kids on a first date, towards a rough structure barely distinguishable from the surrounding jungle.

She let go of my hand at the building. Inside, Elouise used a pocket-flashlight to find an oil lantern. Once lit, the lantern's flickering light brought the cabin into softer focus. The only accoutrements besides the lantern consisted of a rough wooden table, and two battered desk chairs with cracked vinyl seats. She set a couple of liter-sized water bottles on the table. "You can stay here until morning. I apologize for dropping you off like this, but it's really safer for you."

The animal had been growling for a while, now he flared hot and angry. I shoved one of the battered chairs against the wall. "Fuck."

I rubbed my hands through my hair wanting to force the animal back inside. I needed control. I needed information. I needed... "Why the fuck is Jack dead? With your black ops and access to classified shit you should never see, why the fuck is Jack dead on a beach in fucking Jamaica? Really?"

Elouise took a step back. "I'm sorry about your friend. I had

Fiona investigated after you insisted on dragging her along. She's a very scary little girl. Her parents were killed at the incident in Waco, Texas..." Elouise ran an impatient hand through her hair, loosening streamers from the severe bun.

"I know. She told me." Shame touched me for the sympathy I'd felt for Fiona.

Elouise's expression softened. Her hand brushed my arm. "That childhood trauma made her very unstable."

"So she's a serial killer?" I leaned against the rough, wood wall and watched Elouise pace in the flickering shadows of the oil lamp.

"No. Worse. She's a zealot. Her God abandoned her with the death of her father and mother. She searched until she found another. When you mentioned Mohammed Abd Allah, you named the connection." She nodded at me and waited for my answer.

"Mohammed?" The knot in my stomach tightened. Jack had been crossed up so many ways he never had a chance.

"You're surprised? She's a top agent. Surely you noticed? She had to be working for somebody," Elouise paced around the room like her own wild animal didn't want to stay in its cage.

"But how do you know?" I watched her, staying carefully out of her way.

Elouise stopped. "We didn't know until you brought her to us and I could get her fingerprints. INTERPOL matched them to some unknown fingerprints from a training site Mohammed used last year in Kenya. And we think she ran Jack as an intelligence asset for Mohammed."

"Wait a minute. I'm a little slow. Who is 'we'? Who are you working for?"

"I'm not at liberty to say." She focused a hard stare at me.

"What are you at liberty to say?" I glared at her. "Don't you think a fair warning might have been in order?"

"Don't you get it, Jason?" Her eyes flared. "You're the Judas goat. You're the bait. I needed you to flush Jack so I could get the Chinese box. Mohammed needed you for the same purpose."

"Thanks for the vote of confidence." Anger, betrayal, and grief boiled up with a twist of understanding. I gripped one of the ratty office chairs just to hold something that wouldn't break.

"Didn't she give anything away? You must have seen something."

"Fiona's reflexes showed professional training so I assumed she worked for CIA or Homeland Security. And Jack asked for her. He wasn't turned, I know it."

Elouise put her hand on my shoulder and whispered, "How do you know it?"

Her touch fed the fire in my gut. It burned. And made me feel alive at the same time. I shrugged her arm away ashamed at the betrayal of my gut. Trusting her could leave me to wake up twelve hours later in the Haitian jungle.

"Jack and I talked last night. Someone compromised his chain of command. Jack had brought Mohammed into the country under the assumption he was a double agent, but when Mohammed approached Jack in LA about a special shipment from the arms dealers, Jack decided to seek help outside the system. I didn't get more details. Jack rabbited last night when he heard something in the woods. This morning he's dead."

"You're lucky she didn't kill you, too. You're too trusting." Elouise ran her fingers through my four-day-old beard. The intimacy of the gesture surprised me, and shocked me a little out of my anger. I couldn't remember Sarah doing anything so tender, even before we were married.

"She saved my life." I gripped her wrist, and examined her hand for a drug delivery device. I might be too trusting, but I'm a quick study.

Elouise sighed and pulled away. "For her own motives. Not because she gave a damn personally whether you lived or died."

Still, Fiona seemed to care, in her own twisted, messed up way. She'd opened up to me, except she hadn't told me dick. But an evil mastermind could twist and manipulate a damaged child to do things she wouldn't do otherwise. She couldn't help herself. Or maybe she was a sick sociopath. Either way it seemed she killed Jack for Mohammed.

"Your job is finished, Jason. You can go home, now." Elouise laid her hand on my arm.

The warm pressure reached through shirt to skin to bone like lightning. I shook my head. "The job wasn't to get Jack killed. The job was always to find Jack and save Chicago."

Elouise's gaze softened. "Fiona has the Chinese box and whatever it contains. We're looking for her. When we find her we'll take it away from her."

"But will the world be a safer place?" I twisted away from her gentle touch. "Who's 'we'? I don't think you're working for organized crime, but who do you work for? Are you with the good guys?"
She didn't break off eye-contact, but neither did she answer. Actions speak loudly about character, and she had defied her orders. Maybe it mattered less who she worked for than who she was.
I picked up my backpack and dumped it on the table. Money and underwear fell in a pile with the Chinese box on top like a candle on a birthday cake. Elouise picked it up and raised an eyebrow at me in inquiry.

I shrugged. "Found it in the ice chest on the boat." She opened it and retrieved the paper written in Chinese and Arabic.

"What do you make of it? I don't read Chinese."

She examined the sheet and the empty box. The lantern light exaggerated the furrows of concentration on her face. "It's not here. Damn it."

"What's not there?" I asked, feigning innocence.

Elouise looked at me for a long moment. "A circuit board. If you don't have it and it wasn't on the boat, she must have it... Damn it."

"What does it do?"

"It's a radio controlled trigger," she said distractedly. "I really hoped you were hiding it from me. That trigger would be less of a problem in your hands than in hers."

"What's it a trigger for?" With Elouise's concentration broken for the moment, I probed for confirmation.

"A bomb. A nuclear warhead." Elouise stuffed the box and the paper in her jacket as she turned to the door. I caught her arm.

"Wait..." I'd seen real fear in her face for just a moment; a strong emotion breaking her control.

"I have to go. You did your job. You found Jack and the box. Not your fault the box is empty." The cynical professional disappeared from her eyes, but the fear stayed, along with something more visceral. "You're a decent man. I'm glad we met." Then she drew my head down and kissed me on the lips.

It's trite to say she took my breath away. Certainly a deep and passionate kiss is the last thing I expected from her, but she brought back the moment on the beach with a rush. We held each other in a timeless moment, then she slipped out of my arms and opened the door. "You should be able to catch a ride to Port au Prince in the morning. You've got enough money to stay there, and maybe do some good. These people need help."

The helicopter had cycled up to a roar as she turned to go. I caught her arm again. "Wait... Where are the nukes coming from?"

She shrugged out of my grasp and ran out the door into the darkness. She had confirmed Jack's story. Whatever else Elouise concealed, she didn't hide her fear of loose nuclear weapons and the people who had them.

And she left the wild animal behind my eyes scratching and clawing with some other emotion besides rage.

* * *

The soft music of the Caribbean night accentuated the silence at the landing field. I'd made it to Haiti. The passing storm left a fresh taste in the air. Elouise had left a different taste in my mouth.

Inside the rough, cinder block cabin, I reloaded my backpack. I might be stuck until morning, or longer, if I didn't find a phone. If I could reach Lucy, she could extract me. The heat, even in the middle of the night, left me sticky with sweat. In the middle of a long swig from one of the water bottles, the door opened.

I breathed in the water as a dark-skinned man jumped into the room waving a machete. "Ki moun ki lanfè a ou ye?" he yelled. "Ki sa ki lanfè a ou ap fè isit la?"

Choking, I couldn't answer, though he clearly wanted to know who I was and what the hell I was doing there. Conversation would have to wait until I could get air into my lungs. I pulled the automatic from my shoulder holster and indicated he should drop the machete. He hesitated as I wheezed but surrendered the weapon when I cocked the hammer.

He glared at me across the room until I finally got my voice. "Do you speak English?"

"Angla? Pa gen." He shook his head, and crossed his arms. I might have the gun but he had stubbornness.

I made the universal sign for making a telephone call with my thumb and pinky with a raised eyebrow beckoning an answer. He looked pointedly at my pistol. I holstered the gun and waited. He nodded ever so slightly.

I tossed him the other bottle of water as a peace offering. He immediately opened the bottle and drank deeply. I fished in my backpack for some cash. I didn't want him to think I'd be a better prospect dead than alive. I crumpled a few bills up, like they were the last ones in my possession and handed them to him.

His eyes widened and he smiled with this amazing array of ivory teeth. He pulled out a new iPhone out of his tattered shirt and tossed it to me. I nodded and checked the GPS to see where on Haiti they'd left me. The GPS app located me near the Jeremie Airport. Elouise's friends must have had special arrangements with the local authorities to land and refuel. The phone had five bars on the signal meter. I dialed my office number back in LA. Either Lucy would be sitting at the office against my specific instructions or she would have rigged up call forwarding to transfer the call to a new burn phone.

If nothing had happened to her.

The ring skipped and hesitated as it transferred through a series of relays. I hoped Lucy had gone into hiding, but instead of ringing through on the last relay the line went dead.

The animal gnawed at the back of my eyes again. Lucy should have answered the phone. That she didn't answer indicated she couldn't, and that meant something bad had happened. First Jack and now Lucy. I needed to get out of Haiti. I wouldn't get any answers in the jungle.

I dialed the number on the back of my special ID card.

Isaacson answered the call himself. "Sgt. Smiley. Report?"

"Just call me Smiley, General. I don't have stripes tattooed on my arm." I could feel Isaacson's glare through the phone. Rumor had it that he'd had general's stars tattooed on his shoulders before he made Colonel. I answered his silence. "Jack's dead. The killer apparently worked for Mohammed."

"Did you interview him... Smiley?"

"We talked. He wasn't rogue. I think he was under orders until LA when he realized the orders were bad." I paused, waiting for the reaction, wishing we were sitting across an interview table so I could look in Isaacson's steely-gray eyes.

"Very well, sergeant. Make your way back as best you can. We'll take it from here."

Damn him. Isaacson was going to abandon me, too. "I found the Chinese box, empty. I believe Mohammed's agent has the contents."

"Did you find anything else?" he growled into the phone.

What Jack told me, and what I'd learned from the Lucky Strike, gave me leverage of a sort. "Yes, but, I need extraction."

The General's breathing carried over the airwaves with digital clarity. I could almost see him figuring angles and casualty lists, after the operation went bad. Finally he spoke. "Stay where you are. A helicopter will arrive at your coordinates for extraction at first light. Further transportation will be arranged. Report to my office 1800." The line went dead.

I handed the phone back to my new friend now wreathed in smiles. He grabbed the lantern off the table and motioned me to the door.

"I can't go with you... damn it... I have to wait for someone." I tried to pantomime waiting since he spoke something sounding a little like French but without any words I knew. I didn't want to offend him and have him run off to get all his brothers and sons to come back and teach me better manners.

He grinned at my efforts. "You pretty good, boss. I get it you want to wait for your friends to come and get your ass." His words were sonorous with French consonants and a Caribbean lilt.

"Um, yeah. How come you didn't say you spoke English?"

"How come you point gun at me, eh, Boss?" My friend kept grinning but with hurt and suspicion in his gaze.

"OK, sorry about that. Thought I was all alone out here."

"Yeah, you Americans big chicken shit." He laughed this time and slapped his leg. "Want some breakfast while you wait?"

"I could eat something, but I don't dare wander too far from here. Much as I appreciate your hospitality I don't want to get stranded again."

"No problem, boss." He whistled loud and a young girl appeared at the door. He rattled off some instructions in Creole to her and she scampered out of sight.

"You don't need to..."

"You OK, boss. You give me lot of money and better, you shared your water. Better men than you, done less with me so I think I like you, chicken shit American."

"I'll go with that. My name is Smiley." I reached out with an open hand to him.

"JeanJac, Monsieur Smiley. C'mon outside. The air is better."

We dragged the chairs outside with the lantern. JeanJac smiled as I sucked in the sweet breeze off the ocean. The stress of the day caught me as the jungle sang me to sleep. My eyelids bounced open when the young girl reappeared out of the darkness with a huge wicker basket.

"Angelic, say hello to Monsieur Smiley. And I thank you for bringing us breakfast."

"Hallo, Monsieur Smiley. Very happy you can share our table. Au 'voir." She bobbed something between a bow and a curtsy and disappeared into the shadows.

"She learn French so she can go school in Port Au Prince. I am very proud of her." JeanJac opened the basket, passed me a bowl with rice and a spicy meat that might have been chicken. Cold leftovers from dinner no doubt, but they smelled delicious.

As the sun rose over the mountains, JeanJac and I shared a companionable beer. "Thanks for the meal, my friend. I don't actually remember the last time I sat down to eat. It's been a crazy week."

"Man's got to eat. All things happen, except food ain't always when you want it." JeanJac grinned at me and I grinned back. It almost felt like a good day.

Over the sound of the wind in the trees I heard the steady beat of a helicopter. Good to his word the General had a Huey drop into the field where Elouise's chopper had landed last night. I drained the beer and turned to say goodbye to JeanJac but he'd vanished with his basket before the helicopter flared to a landing.

So I got in another chopper with another bunch of serious men, though these wore the insignia of the Special Operations Command. By noon I strapped into a C-130 jump seat on an unmarked cargo flight to Washington, with some good guesses about where they'd taken me and no entry or exit stamps on my passport.

I didn't think I could sleep on the transport, but beer, food and stress-overload overtook me before we left the ground. Dreams are supposed to be the mind clearing itself of the detritus left over from the day's work, but my dreams repeated the same scenes of horror over and over again. To the usual collection of exploding body parts and screams of pain and machine gun chatter I now added a confused collection of images: Mohammed in his traditional thobe, arms outstretched in brotherhood, Fiona dancing in a formal dress and corset made entirely of transparent material with Jack leading her. I could see Jack's dead eyes looking at me, pleading with me to not let him be dead.

Then Jack shook me. "Smiley? We're here."

"Go on," I grumbled, wondering why he sounded like a girl. "You're dead."

"Mr. Smiley." He shook me again. "We're here."

I opened my eyes to the confused stare of the female copilot. The jet engines wound down to silence. Doors slammed open and the plane jerked as various connections were made to it.

"Where?"

"At Reagan International Airport, in DC. Time to get off the plane."

I struggled back to consciousness. The copilot left me to gather myself. The remnants of my dream still seemed more real than the plane or the concrete apron it rested on. I stripped off my guns and holsters so I wouldn't attract too much attention going through the airport and exchanged them for the scuffed and crushed fedora in my backpack. The hat still had enough character to offer some concealment from the face recognition cameras.

Had the confused and uncomfortable images been a warning from my subconscious? I'd asked for help from General Isaccson, who ran more black operations than anyone since Vietnam, used deception as a tool, and whose mission goal was murky.

I needed intelligence on the movement of loose nukes and asking the question would tell the people behind the action that I knew too much. Jack had been right. Trust no one. The wild animal behind my eyes growled and clawed.

But I still had one person I could trust. The organized crime operation Mo had told me about back in O'Toole's sounded like the same operation Jack had stumbled on, only without the Mohammed factor. Maybe Mo knew more about Mohammed's connections than he had said.

So, trust the General or not, I needed his help to get to Chicago. And I needed to get there fast. The Sunday deadline was less than 48 hours away.

Where was Lucy?

16. SECRETS

The C-130 transport had parked on the tarmac near Gate 1 at Reagan National Airport about fifty yards from the jet way. The crew chief dropped the ramp at the back of the aircraft. Every other time I'd been in a C-130 there had been others with me, members of my unit, fellow soldiers coming home, and once——my brother in his coffin.

Exiting alone felt very strange. I had expected an escort of the General's men. Now, I felt like a target.

The afternoon sun set up sharp contrasts of light and shadow on the apron and the terminal. A headphone-equipped ramp-worker waved me toward a glassed-in staircase, his eyes covered with sunglasses against the late afternoon glare, and mouth pinched in a humorless line. I crossed the tarmac to the gate area feeling the weight of the man's hidden eyes on my back at the point between my shoulder blades, just where a sniper would aim.

The top of the staircase opened onto the gate area. Two hard men, cut of the same mold as the troopers who picked me up from Haiti, but with the thick-waisted look of active men who got lazy in retirement, waited by the door. I walked between them, with a glance in both directions. They fell in step on either side. The one on my right shaved bald, the one on my left with a dirty blond haircut that met or exceeded the regulation 'high and tight.' The bald one gripped my upper arm with enough force to suggest he still worked with free-weights regularly. "Sgt. Smiley? The General wants to see you."

I didn't like the strong arm feel of this escort. I did a quick twist, stepped out of his grip. "You can knock off the tough guy act. I asked to be brought in."

"It ain't no act, is it, Butch?" growled the bald one.

"Nope. Like Sam says, Sgt. Smiley, we're the genuine article." Butch put a heavy hand on my shoulder making me stumble.

"Just making sure you come along quietly and don't get lost on the way to the office," Butch said.

"And why wouldn't I?" I showed him my teeth and slapped him on the shoulder. I felt like I'd hit stone. Despite their attitude, I felt easy with these old troopers. I just didn't understand why they acted like hard cases. Had the General told them I might run? Why? More questions for Isaacson when I met with him.

We swept through the terminal building in a tight phalanx until we reached the revolving exit door. Butch pushed through first, then Sam guided me through.

The late afternoon Virginia breeze gusted with the smell of jet fuel and the Potomac. At the curb a Black GMC Expedition with dark tinted windows idled in the no parking zone. Butch beeped the car unlocked and walked around the back out of sight. Sam hustled me to the passenger's door.

Butch pulled us out of the airport smooth and fast, and the warm comradery I felt suddenly flashed back to the dust-choked roads in the Afghan mountains. Darkness. Ambush. We were cut off from our support team. I blinked hard to see the city streets.

* * *

Little things trigger memories. Butch's tactical driving through the late afternoon DC traffic brought back the patrols around Kandahar, not because of the traffic or the scenery, but because of the wariness both men showed. Butch scanned approaching vehicles. A screen, hung by the rearview mirror, collected license plate information and beeped occasionally when something interesting caught its attention.

Sam had another screen going in the back seat which he watched only a fraction of the time. Otherwise he scanned where Butch wasn't looking.

We made good time despite the heavy traffic. The destination turned out to be a warehouse marked GSA 2028. Gotta love the GSA. They convert a lot of warehouses into offices. After all what's the difference between storing files or people? Butch wheeled us into an underground parking garage.

Butch set himself on rear guard at the elevator, while Sam escorted me through the institutional beige hallways, following signs with obscure acronyms etched in three-layer plastic. Without a guide I doubted I could have found my way through the maze before morning.

At last we came to a door marked 'Director of Operations.' Sam went to parade rest in the hallway. I walked through the open door and the dark, outer office. The setting sun shining through the fly speckled windows lit the main office. Apparently even the Director of Operations could expect minimal cleaning service during sequestration.

General Isaacson stood by the window, looking out on the Potomac. "What the hell is going on?" he growled, shoulders square and back ramrod stiff as he inspected the growing dusk.

I stopped at the desk, and waited for him to look at me before I answered. "You've got two experienced troopers on guard detail making sure I get here, and then doing security. I assumed you knew. Sir."

The General ran his expressionless gaze` over me, and my rumpled clothes. "I asked you to find a Federal agent. Now, he's dead. Why is that?"

Isaacson looked a little worse for wear, himself. The fatigue shadows burned dark around his eyes, the creases in his face cut deeper.

"I know what happened, but I'm damned if I know why." I took a deep breath. "Jack asked for this girl, who appears to be an operator. Jack vouched for her. I thought she might be his controller. Obviously, if I had better intel on her, I would have reacted differently."

The General sat down, leaned back and put his feet on the edge of the desk. His face didn't show much. Did he know who Fiona worked for? "I shared all pertinent information with you," he said.

"Really? So, I have better intel than Homeland Security? You don't know there are loose nukes involved with this operation?" A slight widening of his eyes suggested surprise, though whether from the revelation, or because I knew about it, I couldn't tell.

"There aren't any loose nukes." The General paused for extra emphasis. "We track our entire nuclear arsenal very carefully from cradle to grave."

"According to Jack, the Chinese sold Mohammed electronic triggers for nuclear bombs." I watched the General's eyes for any sort of tell. He had to know more about this operation than I'd learned, but stone would blink more.

"Do you have any idea how complex a nuclear trigger is? Warheads are never armed until they're ready to be deployed. When nukes are transported they are rendered harmless." The General let an indulgent smile touch his lips. "Keeps the oh-shit factor down."

"The girl took a circuit board intended to activate a nuclear weapon. She killed Jack for this device. Someone thinks there are usable nukes rolling around. You're the Homeland Security guy now. You must know where and when nukes are moving."

"I could if I needed to. It wouldn't matter because they aren't deployable when they're shipped." The General frowned. "The only way to have armed nukes moving, outside of a strike force, would be for people at the depot to arm the weapons and then arrange to ship them. That can't happen."

Isaccson's deflection confirmed my suspicion that he knew far more than he had shared. "General, we both know everyone has a price."

Isaacson sat upright, tightening up in little ways suggesting he considered the idea of nuclear weapons wandering around without proper safeguards sloppy soldiering.

"Smiley, you're a pain in the ass. Our joes wouldn't sell our nukes. Unless they're moles." The General's eyes focused on a point a thousand miles away. "Unless a sleeper cell activated and went to work in one of our nuclear weapons facilities."

"A sleeper cell? The background checks for nuclear weapons work should be above top secret. They couldn't have any ties to terror networks." Such a complete subversion of national security seemed impossible without collusion by senior people.

"There're sleeper cells from the USSR still in place. Iran has sleeper cells, and so does Saudi Arabia, Yemen and China." Wrinkles furrowed the General's normally unworried forehead. "And Al Qaeda."

"Then you know where they are?"

"We know some. Do we know them all? No." The General looked away again. "Your friend, Mohammed, is a dangerous man. Suppose he knew of a sleeper cell working at one of our Air Force bases with members responsible for transporting old warheads to be destroyed, he might conceivably arrange the shipment of live weapons."

"And with mob and triad support, he has access to ports and shipping across the country. That's a big haystack to search." I said. "Should you call some people?"

The General focused his empty eyes on me. "He would also need someone inside the FBI or Homeland Security, and very high up in command. We're just speculating. You haven't brought me enough proof to take to highest authority. We need Mohammed or the girl, if she's working for him. Any idea where to look?"

The General smiled his empty smile of camaraderie at me. I returned the same. He wanted me to chase Mohammed and I wanted to chase Mohammed. I dropped my cards. "Chicago. According to Jack the trail leads back to Chicago."

He sighed. "I can't send you back to Chicago. Intel from the Chicago Field Office says the Outfit has an execution contract out on you."

"I've been on the bad side of the Outfit for quite a while," I said. "Why would they put a hit on me, now?"

"Apparently, Danny Chourelli is the new boss of Chicago. Rumor has it he wants you dead, but the reasons are a little vague. Something to do with a horse?" Isaacson shrugged. He pulled a bottle of black labeled Scotch out a desk drawer and splashed some in his coffee mug.

"Jimmy the Horse is his brother. I helped put Jimmy in jail. Jimmy's got AIDS now. The Chourellis don't like me real well." I tried to relax the tension in my gut. "Sure, Vinnie looked almost dead when I last saw him alive wired up to a heart-lung machine or something. What happened?"

"He died after the raid." The General smiled with the warmth of a rattlesnake. "The doctors said the shock killed him."

"Shock? That old sociopath never blinked at murder, rape or other assorted mayhem." The General's interest in the Chicago Outfit felt a little off. Had he known Vinnie T? "The shock of a raid? I doubt it. More likely, Danny decided to hurry up Vinnie's departure. Besides, wasn't Chourelli swept up in the raid? There was a fire fight and most of his crew died."

"The Outfit hadn't been the target of the raid, you were. But regardless, Chourelli has decided you need to be an object lesson." He sipped at the Scotch.

'Object lesson' had a special meaning in Chicago. Object Lesson could mean a beating at the docks or your mother's ring finger in the mail. It also meant there was nothing sacred. "I need to get to Chicago, quietly, before something happens to my people back there. Can you get me a charter flight?"

Isaacson gave me the same look my father gave me when I asked for the car keys. "Son, I can get a lot done very quietly, but I can't quietly get you to Chicago, tonight. We can get you there in the morning on a commercial flight."

"The FBI will know if I hit O'Hare again. The SAIC might be part of the problem."

"Then you better go. Take one of the vehicles, make your own arrangements. The less we know, the safer you'll be." Isaacson reached into his desk and pulled out a set of keys and a brown bag. "How are you fixed for traveling money?" He spilled stacked-and-banded twenties on the desk.

The General's offer looked like an organized crime payoff. I might whore myself out to spy on someone's wife, but I took an oath to protect and defend. Besides, I had the money Jack stole from Mohammed. I shook my head and picked up the keys. "I'm good."

"Good luck then, and be careful." The General stayed seated when I got up to leave. "Chorellie sounds like a real asshole."

The animal clawed at its cage as I hurried out of the office. As a capo, Danny Shoe might kill me to make a reputation, but as boss of the Outfit, why bother? Especially after an FBI raid that expedited his promotion? And why would Isaacson know, or care, that an organized crime family wanted to kill a no name PI?

171

Jack connected all the players. Did they think I had some secret Jack shared with me before his demise, like the locations of the triggers? I touched the photograph in my pocket with the numbers on the back. Jack had stashed the triggers on his way out of the country and I had the key to unlock his secrets. If that's the case, the trail led right through Fiona to Mohammed.

17. STRIKE THREE

I took the stairs down to the garage of the GSA office/warehouse three at a time. The act of doing something quieted the animal. I banged open the door on the last level expecting to see Butch still standing watch instead of laying on the pavement in a dark puddle. The elevator doors opened. From the shadows, something flashed and echoed like a tin can getting kicked. Sam tumbled out of the elevator doors.

My brain registered: Silencer. Shooter. Cover! before Sam hit the ground. Instinctively I went to help the fallen, but the shooter reacted nearly as fast. Shadows hid his face; the arm motion swinging his pistol in my direction got my attention. Dropping to the floor, I rolled as a silenced bullet ricocheted off the concrete behind me. Two more rounds followed me as I scurried behind the GMC Expedition.

I dug my Walther PPK .380 out of the ankle holster and looked for feet under the cars. I had six rounds in the magazine, one in the chamber. The spare magazines were in my backpack, along with my .10 mm and my .44.

The silencer said hitman. Hitman confirmed Isaacson's assertion Danny Chourelli wanted me dead. Luck had been with me, the hitman had been watching the elevator——not the stairs. Sam would have called Butch to give me authorization to take a vehicle. When Butch didn't answer, Sam must have taken the elevator. Bad luck for Sam. Butch appeared dead in a pool of blood. Sam must have fallen back onto the elevator. I couldn't see him from my location but the cycled through closing until they hit an obstruction and opened again.

The backpack rested by the stairwell door, about fifteen feet behind me. The shooter had taken cover somewhere in the bowels of the parking garage. If I moved quickly, I might snag the pack which would give me a distinct survival advantage. Keeping at a crouch, I edged backwards. At about fifteen feet the SUV no longer covered my back.

A flash registered; concrete chips struck me from a ricochet to my right. I launched myself to the right, just as two quick rounds whistled through the space I'd just left and punctured the steel door guarding the stairway behind the backpack. I sprinted back to the cover of the truck.

I didn't have enough ammo for a prolonged gunfight. Plan B required me getting closer to the hitman to take him out. I could guarantee a ten ring with the Walther .380 at fifteen feet——any farther I might not stop him. I needed to be sure with this guy.

I slid back along the side of the truck to get closer to the elevator. Danny Shoe's hitman would be warned I wasn't a soft target. He would be patient, make sure of his kill. I took the fedora Elouise had provided me and held it an angle as bait while I snuck around the truck.

After two crouching steps a silenced bullet tore the hat from my hand. I slapped the concrete to make some noise and raise some dust. Now he had to check his kill. The capos liked evidence, photos with an ear or a finger for proof of death. This guy needed to hurry. He couldn't know if there were other guards on duty besides Butch and Sam.

The hum of the electric lights filled the hollow silence of the underground garage area. Sam groaned each time the elevator door tried to close on him. This guy showed a lot of caution. I strained to hear the sound of his movements. Finally, I heard a scrape from the other side of the SUV.

Gun first, I held my breath and peered around the front fender of the truck. The gunman crouched at the rear fender, looking right at me.

We each fired a round and dove for cover. The front tire hissed where his shot went wide. I heard him scrambling away. I hoped I'd at least surprised him as much as he startled me. I scurried for new cover and a better position. My backpack rested peacefully in plain sight, completely out of reach. I had six rounds left.

I couldn't hear his footsteps, but he had to be moving. While I took cover in the first row of cars across from the elevator, I held my breath and strained for any sound, until whispers and taps echoed in my mind. My peripheral vision caught a flicker of movement near an SUV on my left. I stood, fired two rounds at long range, with no hope of hitting him. He dove for cover.

Four rounds left.

A fire engine roared outside with its siren wailing. The Doppler shifting wail destroyed the silence. I scurried counter-clockwise around the truck providing me cover, pistol at the ready. The same echoing siren covered the shooter's own tactical repositioning. I spun a discarded cigarette box away from me between a pair of cars. A shot dusted concrete in the area of the box. Just at the left edge of my vision something moved. I fired, dove to the right and scuttled around another car as a bullet shattered a window behind me.

Three rounds.

Again I moved to my right. He couldn't have been too close or he wouldn't have missed. Where was he? Twenty yards? The silencer on his gun would hamper his aim so his kill shot would be close, seven yards or less. I did a low approach around the back of a Chevy Impala, stopped at the tail light by the mere sense of a human presence. I couldn't hear him, or smell anything but grease, exhaust and the faint tang of gunsmoke. I crab-walked backwards on the lane between the two cars, took a quick look to my left before I jumped to the right, only to crack my head against something coming the other way.

"Fuck..." yelled the obstacle.

I landed on my butt, my gun skittering across the concrete, my head ringing from sharp contact with something hard. In front of me a skinny, rat-faced man with a heavy, dark mustache held his hand over his eye while madly feeling the concrete with the other. A small caliber automatic with a screwed-on silencer rested near my left foot. A quick kick sent it skittering under a car. He scrambled after the gun. I got my feet under me and dove after him.

The man not only looked like a rodent but he must have been raised in a rat pack. He slid under the car and out the other side with his pistol like an orphan getting a second helping at the dinner table. I checked my pursuit, and slid across the hood of a Cadillac just ahead of two window-splintering hits. I landed on my Walther.

I heard the metallic sounds of a magazine being changed and the action charged. I checked the magazine in the .380. Two rounds left and one in the chamber. The hitman held the ground between me and my spare ammunition and guns.

"Hey, Smiley. You got a head like a rock," the hitman called out. "C'mon out and let me make it easy on you. Trust me, you won't feel a thing."

I worked my way into the shadows until I got to an inner wall of the parking ramp. The cars parked here bumper-touching the wall. He couldn't come at me from behind; I couldn't leave without being a target.

Detritus gathered there in little piles. I found a couple of small rocks and a Pepsi bottle with some soda still in it. I added some battlefield liquid of my own to the mix in the bottle to make a stable mass for throwing.

"C'mon out Smiley. You got no place to go. Danny says when this is over no one else gets hurt." The shooter's voice echoed from a point nearer the elevator and about six car widths away.

I chucked the stones across the parking garage. My stalker stepped into view, lured by the scraping sound of the rocks. I lobbed the warm bottle of piss at his head. Then I rolled out into the clear, exposing myself but getting a clean sight picture on my assailant.

The shooter turned back towards me and shot the hurtling bottle of piss, I fired the Walther but my shot went wide, the assassin clutched his neck and collapsed to the parking deck. I kept my pistol at high alert and approached him carefully. A dart protruded from his neck. We weren't alone.

Somewhere in the silence a stereo thumped reggae with a passion. A single shadow detached itself from the collection of shadows. Blankenship, dressed in her black combat gear with her red hair tucked under a black watch cap swaggered across the garage.

I pointed my gun in a safe direction. "I almost had him."

"I thought with your firearm fetish you would be a better shot." She slipped a gun shaped object into her jacket and sniffed the air. "Did you throw a bottle of urine at him?"

"I needed mass." I shrugged. Elouise's sudden appearance had me reacting on a number of levels. How did she and the hitman know where to find me? "What brings you here?"

"I left you perfectly safe in Haiti. No one knew you were there. This..." She kicked the hired killer. "...wouldn't have had a way to find you. But you had to come back."

"The job isn't finished." The sound of reggae blasting grew louder.

"We need to get out of here, Mr. Smiley. You're right. The job isn't finished and if you're going to insist on participating we might as well work together." Her lips twisted in a ghost of a smile.

"There are a couple of troops down at the elevator. I think one of them is still alive. We need to help them, first."

"Eddy checked them. One's dead and the other has a scalp wound. Nothing we can do, save leave before the police arrive. They've been called."

"Wait a second. What do you want? This is the third time you've showed up when things are going to crap and I don't believe in coincidences." I said. "Who do you work for?"

Eddy pulled up next to us in a very nice Jaguar and popped the trunk. He handed me my backpack before he picked up the assassin and dropped him in.

"My employers want me to look after you. . .for the moment. We understand you need to go back to Chicago, and you need backup." She handed Eddy duct tape and tools from a kidnapper's kit. Eddy expertly bound the unconscious assassin.

"Who are your employers, again?" I asked.

"You've got other problems. You remember Samuel Schwartz?" She shut the trunk and opened the back door of the sedan. "The fat man who brought you into this?"

"Yeah. Sammy the Suit. Low level Mafia wannabe. Joke of the mob. He's the least of my problems right now."

"Well, he's more of a problem catalyst." Elouise patted the roof, indicating I should get in the car. "The Triads are not patient. They want their merchandise. He gave them you, instead."

The meaning of the words hung between us like a snake on Chinese New Year. The Triads made Danny Shoe's idea of vengeance sound like sandbox playtime. They would be relentless in their search for the pound of flesh closest to my heart. I clicked the key fob to find the car Isaacson had given me. The lights flickered on a plain Dodge sedan with a shattered windshield.

"Can you give me a ride to the airport? I need to rent a car." The wail of police sirens caught my attention.

"We'll get you to Chicago," Elouise said. "Don't worry. We're on the same side."

"Have you got an airplane?" While our mission goals might not align, I needed a lift and I'd take what I could get.

"We can drive you. I think Eddy is anxious to get home to his wife."

"Hey, my friends. Let's get in the car and be going. The cops be coming," Eddy said. The sirens had grown significantly louder.

Once more circumstances pushed me to take the unknown-Blankenship's assistance. Without an organization backing me, stopping a terrorist plot seemed insane. I couldn't trust her, but I would fail without help. I slid into the back seat next to Elouise. Eddy eased out of the parking garage as the ambulance rolled in.

"I need to make a call," I said. Mo's investigation into some deal between the Outfit, the Triads and the Jihadists had been shut down. He blamed me, but what if he'd gotten too close to the truth and the link to law enforcement?

Elouise passed me her cell phone. I called Sarah's number. It rang busy, but funny like the wires had a short in them. Like someone had cut the phone line. I dialed Dombrowski's cell phone but it went straight to voice mail. Not a good sign.

I tried to tell the animal behind my eyes that they were enjoying private time, but I knew better. The Triads would know about Mo's investigation, and would tie him to me. We'd seen their methods in the old days; I never wanted to see a human hurt like that again. If I could get a flight I might make Chicago in an hour and a half and maybe do some good if I could get past the airport. But at a quarter to midnight there wouldn't be a commercial plane in the air for hours and without Lucy to work her magic, I had no access to private flights.

I called the office number. It made the skip ring of a forwarded call but then it went to generic voice mail. Again. First Lucy, then Mo and Sarah. Too many people important to me had gone missing at the same time.

There are no coincidences.

Elouise had been watching me call and not getting answers, with a carefully neutral expression. How much could I tell her? I only knew she didn't exist and people died around her. She worked for someone she couldn't name and I felt a stirring of emotion other than anger which I hadn't felt in a long time.

"I'm pretty sure somebody's gotten to my ex-wife and ex-partner. Can you get me on one of your black ops flights to Chicago? Or do you have anyone in place to back up Dombrowski until I can get there?"

Elouise looked away for a moment then met my gaze. Some of the English starch washed out of her. "I don't have assets I can call on like that. Not in this country. Not close enough to do us any real good." She traded a long silent look with Eddy.

"Mon," He nodded to the music's beat. "If we hurry now, we might make it to Chicago just after the morning rush hour."

"You can make this thing fly that fast?" I asked.

Eddy nodded. "No problem, mon."

"Chicago, it is. Let's go." The acceleration pushed me back in the soft leather seat.

As we came up to speed, I called Sarah's number again. Just in case.

18. GOING BACK TO CHICAGO

Eddy D Funk eased the Jaguar out of DC with a minimum of effort and a maximum of speed. At a signal from Elouise, Eddy jacked a set of headphones into the center console cutting off Peter Tosh in mid wail. Elouise opened up a cheap throw away phone as we sped west on the George Washington Parkway. The number she dialed rang once.

"Hello." The metallic voice carried over the little bit of road noise.

"Authorization Blankenship Midlands." She spoke with great precision. "Request high-speed pass to Chicago. Please expedite as we are en-route."

"Roger," answered the anonymous voice. Something clicked in the background. "Clear with warning. Drive carefully. Out here."

"Out here." She clicked the phone off, pulled the battery out of the back, and wiped it clean before dropping it into a black plastic bag.

Looking over Eddy's shoulder, the speedometer, reflected as a heads-up display just below the windshield, indicated a number greatly in excess of 100 mph and climbing. Late night traffic looked stalled as we overtook them in a kind of Doppler Effect at close to twice their speed. Elouise looked at me and smiled. "We're on our way, Jason."

"Does Eddy have his pilot's license? I've flown in slower airplanes." I tried not to watch the collapsing distance as we approached two drag racing semis. The trucks moved so slowly they appeared to be stopped in the roadway. Eddy flashed his headlights. A hole suddenly opened between the trucks and we slid through to clear highway.

"Eddy's very good." She smiled at me and settled in to watch the night flow past us.

Without access to Lucy's intelligence network I had only a tenuous trail to follow, the single burn phone Fiona let me use to call Lucy. I didn't know her phone number, but I knew the one I called. "Can you get a list of numbers that called a particular phone with dates?"

She looked at me with wide-eyed curiosity and a hint of a grin. "You want to know if I can access the NSA's phone data?"

"You've got connections."

"Maybe not as good as they were."

I gave Elouise the number I'd called from Fiona's cell. She typed it into an app on her smart phone. Maybe I'd catch a break. And maybe Mo and Sarah had slipped away for some private time. Maybe Lucy had misdirected the call forwarding and was waiting for my call. Maybe Fiona hadn't really killed Jack and I was still on the plane heading to Jamaica. Maybes could drive you crazy.

"You're in luck," she said and passed me her phone.

Only one call had been made to Lucy's burn phone at three in the morning. That had to be Fiona's cell phone. I memorized the number. When I had a moment of privacy I'd call and try to arrange a meeting. She might agree if she knew I had the key to the rest of the triggers. Exposing that piece of Pandora's Box to the world would focus more immediate attention in my direction, and the enemies of my enemies were not necessarily on my side.

Outside the metropolitan areas, random strings of lights broke the darkness, not like the true dark of a moonless night in Afghanistan. The unforgiving mountains taught me that nothing is the way you hope it is. "Do you want to tell me what's really going on?"

"What do you mean?" Her voice sounded tired.

"You stranded me last night in Haiti and ran off like you were going to save the world. Today you show up out of nowhere and abduct the hitman hired to kill me, just before I solved the problem on my own. Now you and Eddy are taking me to Chicago, by car, because you don't 'have the assets', but you can access NSA data to get a phone number." I sighed and focused on the slight scent of classic perfume still clinging to her. "Who do you work for? What's the mission? What's the ultimate goal?"

She looked as though she were seeing something or someone else. I studied her in the dim glow of the dash lights. The reds in her hair glinted various shades of black and green. The scent of a very retro Channel No. 5 teased my nostrils, overlaying just a hint of a stronger musk. Her day had been as long as mine at least and we were now flying across country six inches off the ground.

"You bother me, Mr. Smiley. You really aren't what you seem to be."

"And you aren't what you pretend to be. You're not a mob fixer. I don't think you're really a female James Bond." I shrugged. "You're something, I just don't know what. I don't even know your real name."

"I'd be deeply disturbed if you had known. I'm not sure I

remember anymore. I've been whoever I needed to be for the mission."

"So what is the mission?" I felt her reserve breaking down. The absolute confidence she'd had when we first met wasn't there anymore. We met each other's stare for several long seconds before she looked away.

"I'm really not sure, now," she said. "Yesterday, on the beach, I had a clear mission. Find Jack. Find the damn Chinese box and defuse a tense situation between some unsavory people. But that's changed now."

The road noise passed for silence, as we sat in the fast moving darkness. What could have changed in her world between yesterday and today to make such a difference in her attitudes?

"I may be a whore," she pronounced it 'hoor', "because I sell myself to anyone that meets my price, but I am not a murderer. I facilitate. I make arrangements. I ensure mission completion, and sometimes people don't live through the completion of the mission. But I draw the line at global terrorism. The Chinese can't be trusted. Mohammed Abd Allah can't be trusted. The Mafia is very much not to be trusted. The people who hired me cannot be trusted with nuclear weapons, especially not ones that can be detonated. You're the only person in this situation I trust."

"Trust me to do what? Jack trusted me and he's dead. Others have made the same mistake and they're dead." I'd stumped her. Elouise turned to her window and I looked out mine into the darkness blurred by the vague reflection of the dash lights.

I'd been in a lonely place after the Army, after Sarah and Mo. An angry place where nothing made the anger go away, only put a lid on the seething pit. California had been enough of a distraction so I didn't eat one of my guns, and living day to day got easier. Nothing got better, but if I didn't look, then I didn't have to feel it. But the last few days had lifted the lid off of the boiling, roiling vat of emotions. I'd brought Jack's death to him. Evil forces wanted the circuits guarded by the key in my pocket to bring a reign of terror on the world.

And this beautiful woman at my side says she trusts me? To do what?

The lack of speech isn't silence. Despite the noise isolation of the Jaguar, at over a hundred miles an hour, the road and wind-noise still formed a constant drone. Eddy bobbed to music only he could hear. From the beginning he never fit the role he played, at least physically; pale skinned, blond, blue eyes and profoundly northern European in descent, though he might well be a Rastafarian in his soul. Eddy had already showed several different layers and I suspected he guarded many more. I couldn't trust what I saw.

"And trust, once deceived, is very hard to regain." I looked at her. "My step-father used to say that to me. I suppose I deserved it, then. So you trust me. Why should I trust you?"

Elouise looked my way. Her face relaxed, becoming less stern in the soft light, younger and more vulnerable. Her eyes glittered.

"I really was a whore." Her posh English accent slipped into a broader Scots. "Barely sixteen and kerb-crawling in Edinburgh when a strange wanker from Her Majesty's Secret Intelligence Service called me over to his Mini and invited me to serve her Majesty." She snorted. "I told him 20 quid. 30 if he was going to wear a crown.

"He didn't laugh, just handed me some money and invited me into his car. Young and stupid, I got in with him. He knocked me out with the same concoction I used on you. I came to in a featureless room with a couple of doctor-ish-looking people staring at me. They offered me a choice. Either be an undercover agent or disappear. I did their mission and, in the end, I was damn near disappeared anyway." She looked away into the night. I recognized her gaze; the look of a soldier when he sees the war he can't leave. I had one of my own just like it.

She paused to breathe with great deliberation as some strong emotion washed over her. "Now I freelance. But I'm not that stupid little girl. They taught me many things, but they didn't mean for me to learn to respect the person I see in the mirror. I won't sell myself so completely ever again."

My weak spot is a woman with a sad story, and maybe Elouise recognized that in me. Or maybe she wanted to be as honest with me as she could. I'm a guy. I'll never know. In the end it doesn't matter. "Why are you helping me?"

"It's my job. But that's not all." This time she risked a glance my way. "I like you. You're just idealistic enough to make me believe again."

I let the night flow past me at more than twice the speed limit. The Jason Smiley that believed in right and wrong, in Truth, Justice, and the American Way, had died piece by piece in Afghanistan. A grin found its way to my lips. Her hand slipped over mine for a moment. Elouise the 'ghost' believed in the ghost of who I used to be.

* * *

The night beyond the glass gave way grudgingly to the Jag's headlights. Eddy's unwavering concentration brought back, with great force, night patrol in Afghanistan. Even without the NVGs I could see the world in a greenish hologram. Always scanning for the blur of heat or a well of darkness that might be a depression in the ground hiding an RPG team or the location of a buried bomb, set and waiting for us. We had the technology but we didn't understand the enemy.

Jihadists would expose themselves for a moment, fire a rocket-propelled grenade or hip-shoot a mortar then run for cover. We'd rain fire on their last known location as their weapons exploded around or near us. When we were blinded by muzzle glare, they'd attack with AK-47s and RPGs. Sometimes the firefights lasted until we ran out of ammunition, sometimes the enemy ran out of fighters.

The same thing happened in Iraq. According to Mohammed, the insurrectionists accomplished their mission whether or not they took life. They wanted to make America blink. Angry young men, egged on by cynical manipulators, attacked us with rifles and rockets. We responded with bombs and artillery, destroying where they had been but rarely where they were. And they succeeded in their mission. If they could make us react to them, they were the stronger and we were the fools. Our destruction was ensured. All they had to do was wait us out.

Sometimes they didn't wait as hard as others, like the night of fire and death when Diego lost his life.

"I'm sorry." I whispered to the ghosts out in the impenetrable darkness. To the rush of the night air over the glass. To the others I didn't want to carry as ghosts. "A right turn instead of a left and my team would have made it home. Now I've put Sarah and Dombrowski in the crosshairs."

The night didn't answer me nor did Elouise. Maybe I hadn't spoken out loud, only heard the voices echoing in my head, the terse calls on the radio net and the nervous whispers of soldiers in dangerous country. Only the roar of the engine and the rush of the wind tethered me to reality.

The war animal woke in his den and stretched, pulling me into the Afghan night, clear and cold in the mountains above Kandahar. What passed for Army intelligence had sent my platoon to a village where 'Senior Al Qaeda leadership' was supposed to be meeting with the local elders. Our mission sent us behind the village. We convoyed up a narrow path marked on the map, but when the path jogged left to avoid a serious rock outcropping, I knew we were lost.

Headlights flickered ahead of us. A convoy of mujahidin in Toyota pickups slid to a stop in front of us. Surprise on all sides allowed us to live through the initial encounter. Every one of my men got rounds off before we started taking RPGs. Specialist Chambers operated the MK 19 Automatic Grenade Launcher mounted on the roof of my Humvee. "Keep your head down, Chambers," I yelled.

The launcher barked off a three round burst and explosions followed seconds later. The AK 47 fire quieted for a moment.

"RPG team," the radio net crackled. "Three o'clock and on the rocks."

Chambers rotated, fired a burst, and then the delay as the slow moving rounds made their way to target. "RPG incoming," echoed off the net, then fire and explosion ripped the gunner's perch off the top of the HMMWV. The 40MMs that Chambers sent were air burst. The grenades chewed up the rocketeers who got him, and their ammunition bearers.

Diego and I fell out of the HMMWV with our ears ringing. The shredded, armored gunner's mount on top glowed in the NVGs with Chambers' rapidly cooling blood splashed all over it. I called out on the net. "Mayday. Need air support ..." Closer examination of the map showed the outcroppings and the faintest line for the trail we were on. I read out the coordinates.

"Fast movers inbound. Move to safety circle." The voice of the controller sounded cool and professional. I suppose I would have been cooler if my team wasn't dying.

I keyed my radio. "Everyone. Get your IFF going. We're getting air support."

The ragged call out showed too many holes in the ranks already. "Grenades," someone called out. The fast movers started their strafing run. Diego threw himself on the grenade rolling at our feet. The whole world turned upside down as the 500 pounders landed on the Afghans and the grenade exploded under Diego. The night became all blackness and pain and screaming.

"Jason." A woman's voice called me. Something hit me again. I opened my eyes to the darkness.

"Jason. You're having a nightmare. Wake up." I recognized Elouise's posh tones.

I blinked my eyes.

"You were dreaming."

"Yeah. Afghanistan." My mouth tasted like a camel's ass.

"Bad?" She handed me a bottle of water.

I drank it greedily. "Yeah."

They told me at the hospital everyone but me had been chopped up by the crossfire from the jihadist convoy we ran into and entrenched guard positions who had apparently mistaken us for the convoy as we passed their position. The call to bring in the air support, too late to save my team, likely killed the leadership target as well as his guards. With all the death and destruction around me, I hadn't even earned a purple heart but I put everyone on my team in for a medal before I let the hospital send me home.

Home to Sarah, but I never really 'came home.' I returned to Afghanistan with vengeance in my heart until the Army wisely redeployed and retrained me.

I'd lost more than friends and a wife. I'd been a police officer before I went into the Army. I'd sworn to serve and protect, but the Army changed me. As a cop in Chicago, I'd never killed a man. But as a soldier, I lost count, and it doesn't matter. We fight to protect ourselves. To save a buddy's life.

In combat friends are your greatest resource and greatest vulnerability. Jack was a friend. Mo and Sarah were more than friends, and Lucy, well, Lucy was a special woman. These people mattered to me. Chicago mattered to me. And if I couldn't save my friends, then the people responsible were going to die.

Leaning back down against the door, I finished the bottle of water. "Thanks."

Elouise shifted closer to me, settling herself under my arm and against my shoulder. I resented her intrusion into my space, but it had been a long time since I'd felt a warm, breathing body snuggled against mine. I searched for a non-awkward place to rest my arm until she dragged my hand onto her stomach.

I shut my eyes and tried to think of her naked in the Caribbean morning and her lips hot on mine in the Caribbean night, while I dragged the war animal back into his cave.

* * *

On the Ohio Turnpike, just south of Toledo, we made our second pit stop of the night. Eddy filled the Jag's gas tank while Elouise and I stretched. Eddy leaned against the Jag with a loose-jointed loiter like he hadn't been piloting a car for hours faster than most small planes fly. I paid the attendant in cash for the gas and a couple of prepaid cell phones. We'd leave a trail but not an easy one; especially since I had no idea who would be looking for me next.

Things aren't always what you want them to be. I called Mo and Sarah again, and got the same burned out ring. I called my office again, just in case Lucy had been in the little girl's room when I'd called earlier. The phone skipped from one forwarded number to another before the line went dead. Someone had gotten to the only soft points I had left. Chicago had to hold the answer.

Finally, I called Fiona. The call went immediately to voice mail. At the very least she had taken the battery out of her phone. I left a brief message and returned to the car.

One thing made sense in the mess of conflicting obligations and desires: someone knew I'd talked to Jack before he died. Fiona knew, so she might tell Mohammed. But would he call up the Chinese and chat with them about my conversations, or would he take more direct action? Elouise wanted me to think Sammy the Suit had told the Chinese of my involvement, setting me up as a patsy, but why?

Elouise's story about being recruited by MI6 notwithstanding, I still didn't trust her. Driving me to Chicago smelled of bait. In the end, despite the warmth I felt for her, Elouise did things for her own, very convoluted, reasons. I had to table my distrust, at least long enough to find Mo and Sarah. Then I could look for Fiona. And the nukes. And Lucy. All while I'm watching my back in case Elouise, lady of mystery, decided to inoculate me again.

I watched her carefully as she got into the car. I wanted to trust her, but I couldn't.

She looked me straight in the eye, and relaxed her face, releasing tension on her jaw. "Elouise is my real name."

"Somehow it fits you." Trust or not, I really didn't have a choice.

Traffic had gotten heavier with the truckers who like to move in the early morning hours. As we neared heavy population centers, traffic forced Eddy to slow from space shuttle speeds. I don't think he could go much over a hundred and twenty. As we approached Chicago with the horizon just turning red, she spoke again. "I'm sorry, Jason. I shouldn't have pulled you into this."

"What is it I'm pulled into?"

She hesitated for a long moment, then her voice dropped to a husky whisper. "I'm not sure, now. I thought it was a simple arms deal. Stealing obsolete weapons and selling them to third world dictators and terror cells."

"Not a very honorable business..."

"But one I could live with. I've acted as a double agent on these sorts of deals. A very effective way to limit the activities of certain organizations."

"And what was different here?"

"Fiona has the trigger. Now there are terrorists with the ability to ignite a nuclear bomb."

"Are you sure about Fiona? You traced her to an Al Qaeda training site in Kenya," I grumbled. "But her training is not typical of terrorists. And how would they recruit her?"

"Don't be naive, Jason. The Russians are training agents for Al Qaeda. The old KGB really only had one marketable skill. They could turn ordinary people into agents. And remember it's in the Russian Federation's interest to keep the West off balance and hunting Arabs. Keeps us from watching what they're doing." Elouise shook her head. "You Americans just don't understand how the world works."

"What makes you so sure?"

"The Russians trained me. MI6 doubled me as a junior terrorist, sending me for special training in the Russian Federation. They taught me things the British agents never thought of. Fiona bears all the marks of that training."

"What do you mean? Using sex as a way to get next to a target? That's an old, old trick."

"There are new twists like using self-hypnosis to keep an agent from slipping on the old rocks. The Russians are very good at it."

"So who are you working for?"

"It's complicated. Suffice it to say I have no official existence in this country. England will not admit to me if something goes wrong. And I have limited resources here to call on."

"Don't your masters have an arrangement with the CIA?"

"I don't have masters. I have people I do work for. I can use some of my old contacts but there is a quid pro quo. Extracting me is not something they would relish." She grimaced. "I'm expected to be self-sufficient."

"You certainly called in the reinforcements when we left Jamaica. You're working closely with somebody who has resources."

"Our rescue cost me."

"How so?"

"I was supposed to kill you."

"Who———?"

"We don't have time to get into that." She cut me off as Eddy stared weaving through the increasingly dense early morning traffic. "We're nearly to Chicago. Please tell Eddy where we are going."

19. HOMECOMING

Eddy drove us by the house Sarah and I had owned on North Seeley Avenue at 8:10, Saturday morning. It's a nice neighborhood of people who work too much and don't have time for their neighbors. Lots of single-family homes with a few apartment buildings on a tree lined street. The kind of neighborhood you felt safe in, even in Chicago. The storms blowing across the lake left less than an inch of snow, not enough to get anyone out of bed to snow blow driveways.

The scene looked too peaceful for anything horrifying to be happening to Mo and Sarah. Maybe I'd catch them having coffee at the kitchen counter.

I could use a cup of coffee.

But Dombrowski's ancient Honda Civic sat in front of the house, next to the NO PARKING BETWEEN OCTOBER AND APRIL, sign. Every house on the street had a garage accessed by an alley.

Snow dusted the car and road alike, indicating the car had been parked all night.

Behind the Civic sat a dirty, white van from the 'Happy Dragon Restaurant.' A dusting of loose snow rested on the windshield wipers. The van hadn't moved all night, either.

I called Mo's cell, as we circled around the block. When it went to voicemail I called the house phone and listened to the broken-wire ring. We passed the wide open garage in the back alley. The phone continued to ring. Elouise lifted an eyebrow in enquiry. I hung up.

"Someone's got Sarah and Mo. I'm betting it's the Triads," I said as I checked the loads on my guns.

"My instructors taught me to accept field losses. You can't save everyone. The best you can hope for them is a clean death."

Elouise's words sent a cold creep slithering down my spine and into my guts. She spoke truth. You can't save a dead man. But I didn't know if Mo and Sarah were dead, or if they were going to get a clean death. The Happy Dragon van said Triads, and Triads showed no mercy.

I tapped Eddy on the shoulder to stop three houses before Sarah's. The abductors expected me and might recognize a car passing by too many times. Both Eddy and Elouise looked at me for direction.

My operation, my risk. I had to go in guns-out without any tactical information, and the bad guys knew I would do it. There would be no time to be subtle. No time for Chicago's finest to go all SWATS on the perpetrators. I couldn't give Mo and Sarah's captors time to make a decision.

Besides, if I could take one of them alive, they might be convinced to tell me how nukes and Mohammed were related to Chicago. I needed a distraction to breech the trap but I couldn't ask for a sacrifice.

I sighed. Just the facts, ma'am. "Well, I believe the bad guys are using my ex-wife and her husband as bait to catch me and force me to give them the rest of the triggers."

Elouise blinked at me, her face carefully emotionless. "Mr. Smiley, what do mean, 'the rest of the triggers?'"

"Jack took delivery of several circuits like the one Fiona stole. He only brought the one with him to show me."

"And where are the others?"

"I honestly don't know." I looked at my old home. "It doesn't matter where they are, it only matters that no one gets their hands on them."

"And going in after your ex-wife and ex-partner helps us how?" Elouise settled in the far corner of the back seat, her gaze sharp and free of emotion.

"It doesn't matter if it helps the mission. I'm going after my friends." I inspected the rounds in the .44, locked its cylinder in place, seated it in my holster. "You can leave me, here"

Elouise hesitated for a long moment, then sighed deeply. "Eddy, keep a low profile. We're getting out here and might need you back very quickly."

Eddy nodded in acknowledgment.

I chambered a round in my 10 mm, engaged the safety and topped off the magazine. "Here's the situation. This is a trap and I need you to rattle it while I take it apart. You knock on the door like you did at the motel, real polite and insistent. Distract whoever is in the house. I'm going through the back door."

Elouise nodded. She produced a sporty, dark yellow blazer from another compartment and transfigured from black-ops specialist to real-estate lady. She slipped the Lady Smith into her pocket as she stepped out of the car. "Coming?"

I scrambled out to meet her. An engine started behind the houses. A door slammed shut. Any noise would attract the neighbor's attention.

"Interesting plan. Not much fun if they left a crew there. Won't they hear you break in?" She strolled up the street toward my old house as though we belonged here.

"I only need one prisoner and I know where the key to the back door is." We split at the corner of the lot where I followed overblown tracks in the snow around the back of the house. I checked for the key behind the trellis but didn't need it. The metal clad kitchen door had been kicked with a heavy boot, ripping the deadbolt from the frame. The bent door roughly closed. Elouise started ringing the doorbell and pounding on the front door as I pushed into the empty kitchen.

From the kitchen I could see the dining and living room with the central core of stairwells and closets blocking the front door. The drawn drapes left the rooms in shadow.

An unfamiliar stainless steel refrigerator provided me cover. Sarah apparently got something else new out of the marriage.

Elouise pounded at the door. "Hello? Mr. Dombrowski?" she called in her best 'I'm the Queen' voice.

Nothing happened. Elouise hit the door harder. "Mr. Dombrowski? Are you all right?" she cried loud enough to be heard down the block.

From the living room something wooden creaked, followed by heavy footsteps and the sound of the front door opening. A brief flash of snow-amplified daylight silhouetted a short, stocky man.

As soon as the door opened, a gurgling, gasping sound came from the living room. The noise didn't really sound human, but I'd heard noises like it before, from things that used to be men before they were destroyed. The animal behind my eyes scratched hard.

"Good Morning," Elouise chimed in her best British good-fellow voice. "Would you be Mr. Dombrowski? I'm with the Fairway Real Estate Agency. Can I come in to discuss your property?"

"What you want, lady? You make too much noise. Go way now." The voice that answered certainly wasn't Mo's, not unless he was practicing his offensive Chinese act for the next Police Department mixer.

I swept through the empty dining room and the downstairs lavatory to clear my back. The stocky man blocked my view of Elouise in the doorway, but the door itself blocked my access to the man. I circled back into the kitchen. Angry grunting erupted from the closet under the stairs reminding me of Sarah on a rampage, which gave me a good idea where to find her.

Elouise continued to harass the guard with some vapid patter about how wonderfully the housing market had recovered and how it was a seller's market. His grunts grew angrier. I slipped into the living room and scanned for other guards.

Tied to a kitchen chair set in the middle of the living room was something that might have been Dombrowski. He'd been beaten with vicious intent. His whole face was swollen, distorted, eyes bloody and closed, ooze on his face bubbling as he tried to breathe through a broken nose and possibly a broken jaw. Yet, he still tried to call a warning.

I choked back some bile and scanned the room again. The man at the door had been the only guard. If they had intended a trap there would have been more men. Maybe Dombrowski was a message and not bait. I gripped the Smith and Wesson 10 mm a little tighter.

The guard grabbed Elouise by the yellow jacket and threw her into the house. She bounced hard off the newel post. He slammed the door shut and pulled a wicked looking knife with the clear intent to cut Elouise's throat.

I shot him.

I wanted him alive. I needed hard intel on the situation. So I aimed for his leg and fired.

The FBI retired the 10 mm Smith and Wesson as a standard sidearm because of its penetrating power. Instead of collapsing from a destroyed femur, the man turned towards me with a vaguely surprised expression on his massive face.

He did drop Elouise, uncut, on the floor, then a joyful smile on his face split his face. Although obviously Asian, he reminded me more of Monk's cousin Tiny. This guy might have been five-five but had to turn sideways to get through doors. He grinned through red lips as he brought his knife up.

His knife, maybe a foot of steel with a guard at the grip, looked more like a short sword. Perfect for knife fighting. Normally I'd just smile and pull the trigger, but if I wanted him alive I'd have to be careful about my shot placement. I stepped back while he squared off against me. Elouise lay dazed on the floor. The man had barely three strides to reach me. My second shot destroyed the shoulder joint of his sword arm. He stopped, reached over with his good hand and grabbed the blade from his own lifeless fingers.

Maybe he thought I'd panic. Maybe he knew I wanted him alive. Maybe he thought he was immortal. Maybe he just had to die. He rushed me. My third shot missed his other arm and the fourth one exploded between us as I wrestled the knife away from my heart. He stiffened and staggered backwards with a look of amazement on his face as blood leaked from his chest. It didn't gush. The 10 mm hollow point slug would have separated as it hit his sternum and punched through to his pericardial cavity. The shrapnel from the bullet turned his heart to hamburger. When he collapsed to the floor his angry pig eyes stared blankly at the ceiling.

"Fuck." Elouise struggled to her feet, rubbing her head.

"Yeah. I wanted to know who he worked for." Blood soaked my clothes. I looked like a serial killer after a night of fun.

"Somebody might have heard that cannon of yours and called the police." She pulled her Lady Smith from her pocket. "I'll check upstairs."

"I've got to see about Mo." I could feel the cold sweats coming on me. I didn't want to look at him. He grunted and struggled against his bonds like a mouse caught in a trap. With lights on, the damage to Mo's face showed the effort and time put into injuring him as much as possible. "Wh-wh-who's there?" he mumbled through his ruined mouth.

"Christ, Mo. It's me, Jason." I choked on fire which had moved from behind my eyes to the back of my throat. Here comes Jason Smiley, bringer of death and destruction.

"Oh, Christ no, Jason." He struggled in the chair, his words blurred by the damage to his mouth. "You've got to get out of here," he mumbled. The ropes they'd tied him with had cut off circulation and were lost in the black misshapen sacs that had been his hands.

"Don't talk. Let me help you."

"They're coming after you and you can't let them get you." The words had become a soggy whisper.

I unfolded my Swiss Army knife with its ever-sharp blade. "Who's coming after me? Who did this? The Triads? Chourelli?" I cut at the ropes, trying not to cut the stretched and violated skin. The knife slipped; black blood oozed. Mo just grunted. Tears ran down my face. "Fuck, I'm sorry man. I'm so sorry."

"Danny Shoe? No man. No. The Chinese fuckers, oh my God." His arms, released from their unnatural position, hung limp and useless. He sobbed but the tears couldn't find an exit through the ruined flesh.

I cut a strip of cloth from my shirt tail and bandaged the oozing gash, not sure it would do him good but not wanting to let him just bleed. "Why did they come after you, Mo? What do you know?" I didn't want to grill him, but we had bare moments for me to get any answers.

He looked up at me through swollen slits. "Something big. Triads... bringing in a ship. Sunday. Taiwanese container ship running under a Liberian flag. Ming something..." Mo choked. Some fresh blood dribbled from his lips.

"What's going on with the ship on Sunday?"

"Don't know. Big... deal." Mo tried to look around the room through the swollen slits of his eyes. "Where's Sarah? Did they hurt Sarah? Oh God, Jason, you've got to find Sarah." He wiggled his broken body and shook his ravaged head like he could somehow will himself to take care of her.

I nodded back at Dombrowski "Christ I hope they didn't do that to her. I don't think I could stand it." I puked in the antique vase Sarah's mother had given us.

The animal clawed at the back of my eyes, but I needed clarity, now. Mission first. "I heard her in the hall closet. I'll look."

Elouise walked back in the room cool and professional despite the horror sitting in the kitchen chair. "No one upstairs."

Everything moved with horror-show slowness. I opened the closet door. Underneath the neat array of winter coats, surrounded by boots, Sarah lay naked with a rag stuffed in her mouth and bound up with the cloth belt from Mo's overcoat. She had a wild look in her eye and a couple of bruises but nothing like Mo. I undid her gag.

She smiled at me for the first time in a long, long time, but her eyes had the vacant look of someone with a loose grip on reality. "Smiley? Did you kill those motherfuckers? They walked in our house like they had a right to and started beating up Mo. He was so brave, where is he? I want to see him..."

She stopped talking long enough to use me to climb to her feet. Her eyes didn't meet mine but seemed to see some place else. I'd seen the same look in the faces of men pulled from exploded trucks, unaware they were missing parts of their body and believing nothing terrible had happened.

She staggered. I caught her in my arms, careful to shield her from the mess in the living room.

I kissed her forehead. "I don't think you want to see him right now. I'll call the paramedics and we'll let them fix him up. Did you get a look at the people who did this?"

She dug her nails into my arms. Her eyes focused on me, suddenly wild as she strained in my arms. "Damn right. They were Chinese like at the Flaming Wok. Bunch of young guys with an old man telling them what to do. And a big guy. He was mean. He hit me." The look in her eyes said she saw the horror she'd endured for who knows how long. Her voice cracked. "They made Mo scream and cry. I never heard him cry before..."

I wrapped Mo's trench coat around her shoulders. "The big Chinese guy's dead, so you're even there. What was special about the old man?"
I didn't know how long I could keep her attention on me and away from Mo. She might be in shock herself but if she saw him like this now, she'd never see him any other way.

"He walked like his back hurt him and he wore a padded purple coat." She struggled in my arms. Her voice climbed in pitch as she fought against me. "Let me go. I can feel my feet now. I want to see him."

"You really don't want to." I pushed her back towards the closet.

"Don't tell me what to do Mr. Sergeant-Jason-you're-not-my-fucking-husband-anymore-Smiley." Her voice reached a hysterical pitch. She relaxed suddenly in my arms and I guided her to the floor. Elouise stood behind Sarah with a needle in her hands.

"That's going to be hard to explain to the cops," I said as I covered Sarah with the coat.

"The police will respond to the gunshots. Much as I want to help you I can't be detained." She indicated the dead killer. "We have to look elsewhere for information."

"You'd better go, then. I've got this. They're the only family I've got left. I can't leave them here." I dialed 911 on the burn phone.

"Family is a weakness, Jason." Elouise dropped the needle gun into one pocket of her blazer, her Lady Smith into the other. She slid on her Ray Bans and strode out the door. "I'll find you later."

* * *

The responding CPD portables reached the door within a minute of Elouise's exit, making her estimation of their response spot on. I opened the door to their knock.

"Jimmy Mulligan," I grinned at a familiar face. "Haven't seen you in a while."

Mulligan's eyes opened wide and he took a quick step back while he pulled his service piece. "Jeezus, Smiley did you butcher someone in there?"

The fresh air contrasted with the stench of fresh blood and gunpowder. I stepped back into the living room to allow them access.

Mulligan pushed through the door, gun trembling in his hand. "What are you doing here, Smiley? If you've got a piece put it on the deck, right now." Mulligan said as his rookie partner tried to hold his gun on me and retrieve his handcuffs at the same time. I took a deep breath to calm the animal when the kid slipped his finger through the trigger guard.

I put my hands up. "Will you get your puppy under control?"

"Wilson, point your gun at the floor. Go check the house." Mulligan nodded at me to back up. "Smiley here will be a good boy. Right, Jason?"

"Sure. My pistol is under my arm and I have an ID card in my wallet you need to see."

Wilson screeched from the living room. "Jesus Christ, Sarge you gotta see what he did to Dombrowski."

"I didn't do it. You might want to investigate the dead man on the floor first," I dropped the 10 mm on the table. "And you might ask Mo what happened. He looks like shit but he's still living. For now. Where the hell are the EMTs?"

"They're coming." Mulligan walked over to Mo, side-stepping Sarah, trying to watch me and check on Mo, until he finally waved me in front of him. "You made the 911 call?"

"Yeah. I tried to reach Mo last night, but I got no answer. I had a bad feeling so I came over." I carefully pulled my wallet from my inside jacket pocket. "I'm working on a special project for Homeland Security."

Mulligan frowned at the card. "I dunno. You shot the guy on the

202

floor?"

"Yeah. Self-defense. He tried to kill me with a knife."

"Huh. Never bring a knife to a gun fight." Mulligan relaxed as he viewed the dead Chinese.

"He almost won." I handed him the General's ID card. It didn't burst into flames.

Mulligan glanced at the card, but didn't look impressed as he passed it back to me. "Well the Chief will want to talk to you. And your right to carry in Chicago was permanently cancelled, so..." he snapped out his handcuffs. "Turn around. You know the drill."

"Hold on, Officer." Tom Rudd strode into the house with his yellow duster swirling like an Old West sheriff. He flipped his identification at Mulligan. "FBI," he said, and did a fast scan of the room. Dead Triad member, Mo staring blindly and hooting "Who, who...", and Sarah out cold on the floor. "I'm to take custody of this man. Is this his weapon?" He pocketed the 10 mm, thereby contaminating the evidence.

Mulligan stepped back to call in for guidance. The EMT's arrived with their organized confusion. A female tech dragged Sarah out of the way. The wild animal started scratching to get out as I followed Tom Rudd out the front door.

* * *

Rudd clamped his fingers on my arm and pulled. I tried to shrug him off. He held on and nodded at the gathering crowd. Despite the spitting snow and bitter wind coming in off of the lake people gathered at the yellow police line. "You just get in more shit, don't you, Smiley." He guided me down the street.

Rudd parted the police lines without comment. We strode down the block to his federal cop car with only minimal attention. He pulled my pistol from his pocket and handed it to me. "Isaacson seems to think you're important to Homeland Security. He has you flagged for expeditious extraction in case you got into trouble. It didn't take you long."

"Really? It's nice to feel the love." I slipped the 10 mm back into its holster. I scanned the crowd. A young Asian face stared in our direction. I waved at him. He disappeared into the crowd. "Triads have a spotter here."

"So do we. You and Mohammed really got something stirred up." Rudd stepped in front of me. "You smell like a butcher."

My dark clothes hid the blood but the stench still gagged me. "I'll try not to get so close the next time I kill a man."

"So you're planning on killing more people? I'd lock you up, except Isaacson wants you out of custody." Rudd cocked his head back and to one side. "Personally, I think you're bait. Homeland Security wouldn't need a washout like you for any other reason."

"Bait sounds about right. The General wants me to flush out Mohammed, and if I'm collateral damage, that'll be just too bad." I looked at Rudd carefully. Too many ruthless people were looking for me now. "I need someone I can trust, just like Jack did."

"He shouldn't have run away." Rudd studied me through squinted eyes. "He could have come to me."

"Somebody's dirty around here. It could be you for all I know." I leaned against his car and scanned the crowd for any more spotters.

"Fuck you, Smiley. I take the oath seriously." Rudd frowned. "Why do you think there's corruption in my office?"

"Someone ordered Jack to escort Mohammed into the country without checking at customs." One or two people in the crowd glanced our way, but no one else paid particular attention.

"And Jack told you this?" Rudd said. "His behavior might suggest he was the dirty one."

"Jack didn't know who to trust so he bugged out." I took a deep breath. Rudd might be an officious, arrogant, obnoxious bastard but he'd been out of town, and in disgrace. Not the position of power needed to pull off an illegal infiltration. But maybe in a position to

204

protect Chicago if he knew about the threat. "I didn't get to have all the conversation with him I wanted. He was on the run. But he told me the Chinese had sold Mohammed a trigger to re-arm disarmed nuclear warheads. Mohammed intended an attack centered in Chicago."

"Nuclear warheads? What? How could he get nukes?" Rudd gripped my arm. "Why would the Triads tell Nesmith?"

"Jack said they wanted the nukes. I'm pretty sure the Triads think blowing up Chicago would be bad for their business interests,"

"This is a lot of information to keep to yourself, Smiley. Whose side are you on?" Rudd's grip tightened.

"I didn't keep it to myself. Isaacson knows. He might know a lot more. All I know is the Chinese are asking me where the triggers are." I caught myself fingering the locker key in my pocket. "I'm pretty sure Mo is the question mark."

"So the Dombrowskis were attacked because of you?" Rudd dropped my arm. He searched his pockets until he pulled a silver case from his coat, extracted a cigarette and lit it. "What does Isaacson think about all this?"

"He really didn't share more with me than what it took to get me to Chicago."

"So why are you telling me, if you already briefed Isaacson?" Rudd looked disgusted and annoyed.

"I'm going to find Mohammed and stop him, if I can." I straightened up. The ambulance pulled out of Sarah's driveway. "If I can't, I'm counting on your self-interest to protect Chicago. You can't afford another screw up."

"Fuck you, Smiley. What are you going to do? I don't want to clean up any more of your messes," Rudd dragged at his cigarette and threw it into the street.

A strong reggae beat blew our way on the cold March wind. "Start asking questions and shaking people loose, I suppose. Time is running out." My phone rang. I stepped back from him. "Excuse me

I have to get this. My assistant has been looking for me." I checked the number. It wasn't Lucy.

"Hello, Jason?" Fiona's voice wavered on the verge of tears or terror, or both. "Thank God, you called me. I need your help. Can you come to Meigs Field tonight? Please, Jason. I'm in real trouble."

Alarms went off. I expected to coax Fiona into meeting me. I smiled. Fresh bait had been put in the trap. "What's the matter? What can I do to help?"

"Eight o'clock. Please. Meet me at the old Terminal Building." The connection closed.

I turned to find Tom Rudd looking over my shoulder. "Who was that?" He said.

"A potential contact." Eddy's cab pulled up to the curb. "I believe my ride is here." I opened the back door. Rudd glared at me. "Tonight at eight. I need backup at Meigs Field, but I don't know what to expect. And be careful who you tell. Remember, there's a serious security leak in your chain of command."

The offended look on Rudd's face would have been priceless as he hooted "Who, who?" except he sounded just like Mo, beaten blind because of my friendship.

"Just be careful who you trust." I tapped the seat for Eddy to get us out of there.

Trust no one, or trust people to operate in their own self-interest. Trust a snake to be a snake. I could trust Mo to be loyal to his friends, and his bloodied face proved it. I could trust Rudd to showboat for attention. And Fiona trusted me to come and get her out of trouble even after killing Jack.

With Fiona as the new piece of bait, she would be considered disposable by the Triads if that's who had her. I needed to get in early and quietly. And trust Rudd to distract the bad guys at the right time.

I needed Fiona to locate Mohammed. I didn't want to care what happened to her afterwards, but I couldn't shake the sincerity of her story or make sense of her actions. She'd killed Nonny and felt shock, at least, at the taking of a life. And then she'd killed Jack with the ruthlessness of a serial killer. It didn't add up.

As an intelligence asset, she had dubious value because of her unpredictability. But she led to Mohammed. If she was the cheese in this mouse trap, I needed to be the smart mouse, and not spring the trap when I grabbed the bait.

20. MEIGS FIELD

Eddy took me to a safe house where I got to wash up and sleep. Like a ghost in daylight, Elouise wasn't to be seen, but I felt her presence. I woke to the smell of food and found fresh clothes laid out.

Eddy didn't require any explanation when I asked him to drop me behind Soldier Field just across the boat docks from Northerly Island; he just slipped his cab down the Lakeshore Trail until I told him to stop.

"Thanks." I watched Eddy drive away. I would have preferred company in the cold and empty night, but no one else needed to be staked out as bait for the tiger.

Meigs Field doesn't exist anymore and hasn't for a lot longer than Fiona had been in Chicago. Northerly Island Park used to be an airport called Meigs Field until Mayor Daley had it bulldozed early one morning. The man-made island is reached by a causeway across a harbor right off of South Lake Shore Drive by the Planetarium. The runways had been torn out and replaced with concert facilities and grass. The only remaining ghost of the airport is the Terminal Building. It's a very busy place.

In the summer.

On a cold spring night with the wind blowing in off of the lake it became a ghostly fairy land of light and shadow, ice and snow with the area lighting concentrated on the roadways. The lights of the city faded quickly near the shoreline, leaving long arching shadows across the abandoned marina basin.

I kept to the shadows far from the edge of the causeway until I spotted the slight gleam from a well-oiled gun barrel in the hands of a guard by the tree line. Without the easy route onto the island, I slid down the embankment to the little shallow bay covered by ice that might still hold my weight.

The city glow, made erratic by buildings and trees increased the difficulty of a stealthy crossing by illuminating random portions of the marina, but I found a path shadowed well enough to hide a man-sized dot. I did a slow crawl across the rough ice. Slow because the human eye is attracted to rapid movement in the dark. Crawl because the ice thawed in the day and froze at night leaving it more fragile after each cycle.

By the time I crossed the bay, my legs and arms were numb from the cold. I clambered up a short, rock embankment and followed a stoned path. The north wind blasted cold, whistling in trees and scaffolding left over from work in progress. The noise concealed my footsteps in the loose gravel. The old Terminal Building rose from the half dark of shadows and poorly maintained security lighting.

The contrast between bright points of light and darkness made progress difficult, but provided cover. It also hid the sentries I knew were watching the approaches. The jitters started. I tried to see and hear everything at once, but the first rule of night patrol is to pay attention to what's in front of you.

The sentry patrolling the back corner hadn't followed the rule. He looked the wrong way as he cleared the edge of the building. I dug my fingers into his larynx and swept his feet out from under him, driving his head into a raised shadow attached to the building. His neck hit with a sharp crack; as life flowed out of him he went limp. My stomach wrenched. Killing a man trying to kill you is survival. Killing a man for convenience takes a special kind of coldness I don't want.

I relieved the dead man of his MAC-10 and extra magazines, his wallet, cell phone, switchblade and a lighter. Cupping the lighter in my hands I checked his license. Joseph Wong of Chicago. Young Chinese man with an illegal machine pistol in Chicago meant Triads.

The animal clawed at the back of my eyes. This man had aided and abetted the torture of my friend. And they were using Fiona, willing or unwilling, as bait.

The guard meant the main party had to be close. Security lights lit the open field, but their illumination did nothing to help me see the courtyard in front of me. I hugged the diminishing shadows at the edge of the building and followed them towards the front. Near the corner of the terminal where the security lighting lit the area, casting harsh shadows, I caught movement and the glint of metal. Not real black operators since they didn't keep the bluing of their weapons from reflecting stray light, but bad enough to have their MAC-10 machine pistols at the ready. What the hell were they expecting? The Marines?

To my right a cell phone chirped. I froze.

"Yes, Mohammed." Fiona's tones were hushed but I heard clearly her side of the conversation.

A pause. Fiona and a stooped Chinese man in a purple quilted winter coat moved closer to the light and out of the wind. The man turned his back to me and began to pace while Fiona talked.

"He'll be here. Jason keeps his word."

The phone rattled with a tinny voice I couldn't understand.

"Yes. Mr. Chin does not like dealing with women. He wants to talk to you." She turned away from Chin. "Yes, he insists. Otherwise he won't return the circuit board."

She looked relieved and nodded at Mohammed's response. "OK just a moment." The phone beeped. "You're on speaker phone. Mr. Chin? Mohammed will speak with you."

The cell phone squawked with a familiar voice, "Chin my old friend. Can you hear me?"

"Certainly. Peace be with you, my brother." Chin stood close to Fiona while she held the phone. The pair of them weren't two feet from my hidden position. I pulled the switchblade but left it retracted for fear Chin would hear it spring open. The phone shook noticeably in Fiona's hand. She'd been cool enough to kill Jack in plain sight, but the Chinese gangsters seemed to terrify her.

"Peace be unto you as well," Mohammed said. "I understand you have some reluctance to complete our deal?"

"Not reluctance, my friend, but I will incur great costs re-acquiring that which your courier has taken; assuming this person you have sent me has the location. Certainly, just compensation is in order." Chin touched Fiona's cheek with the back of his hand. She shrank from him.

"So my brother, I should take money from the cause to pay you twice for the same items?"

Chin let his hand drift from her cheek to her jacket. He pulled the zipper down very slowly. "I never received the first monies, so you would be just paying once, although a greater price since there has been additional costs."

"Yet my agent has arranged for you to acquire the information from the source."

"And I will have to pry it, no doubt, from this Smiley's cold, dead hand. We know Jason Smiley. He won't give it up easily." Chin spread Fiona's jacket and started groping her breasts through her sweater. She trembled but didn't flinch as he rolled and pinched her

211

nipples. She wasn't the same cool, tough chick who had kneed Nonny in the stones or walked up to her boyfriend and killed him in public. What ever happened had at least made her docile.

With the old man's attention firmly divided between negotiating with Mohammed and groping Fiona, I eased the knife's blade fully open.

"I will give you another hundred thousand for your efforts."

"But what about the money your courier stole?" Chin continued to grope Fiona.

"Smiley has it. Get it back from him."

"Not good enough. Five hundred thousand and your girl here. She has nice attributes." Chin's accent thickened as he moved into haggle mode. The guard's cell phone vibrated in my pocket. A missing guard would alarm the Triads. I didn't have much time.

"I'd prefer you didn't molest my servant——"

An explosion rocked the island; the exterior lights extinguished. Gunfire erupted from the causeway near the planetarium. Chin barked sharp orders in Mandarin. The lights of Chicago, now the only illumination, throwing long shadows from any object close to the shore.

A line of cars rolled toward our position from the causeway with gouts of flame flickering at random from their windows, SAIC Rudd and his boys coming in fast and hot. Across the island individual flashes showed the guards' response to the incoming invasion. The gaggle in front of the old Terminal Building returned fire as the convoy spread out. One incoming vehicle overturned and caught fire. Return fire blew chips of concrete from the wall over our heads.

Chin grabbed Fiona and shoved her in front of him as a shield. His soldiers provided further protection standing in front and firing blindly. With no one looking in my direction, I slid up behind Chin and drove the knife into his neck. Preemptive self-defense, or murder, I really didn't care. The old man had ordered Mo and Sarah abused as a tactic to draw me out. Well, he got me out.

212

Fiona followed the old man to the ground, running her hands through his pockets as his life blood pumped out, cool and professionally without a sign of her earlier timidity. Return fire from the opposing force threw stone chips our way.

I pulled Fiona into relative safety behind the Terminal Building as another stray burst slammed the nearby wall.

"Jason," she cried in a breathy whisper. "I knew you'd come."

Gripping her arm I urged her to a run away from the fight. "What the hell were you doing back there?"

"He took the circuit board from me. I had to get it back."

We skittered down the wall until we reached the back, where I pulled her to a stop while I checked for others. We raced to a storage building by the little bay, hid behind it where the city lights let me make out some details. "You set me up. Do you know what those animals did to my friend?"

She shook her head and tried to hold on to me, but I disentangled myself. "I'm sorry, Jason, I had to do it. But I knew you would be too suspicious to just walk into the trap."

"We're not out of it——yet. Maybe we can keep a low profile until the good guys get here." I charged the MAC-10 and checked the two spare magazines, then double checked the load on my 10 mm.

The action seemed focused on the caravan of SUV's stopped in front of the old Terminal Building. Our position down range of the fire fight kept us safe from the short range subsonic rounds of the MAC-10 but fire from Rudd's agents kicked up stones that whistled by our ears.

"Jason... I'm sorry." She pulled at my arm. "We'd better go."

"It's all right. The other guys are friends of mine. We'll wait out the fire fight. No way are these gangsters going to hold the island." Behind me automatic weapons fire sounded a whole lot closer. Some subsonic rounds whizzed past us.

"Smiley, the Triads have people dedicated to finding you. We've got to get out of here. It won't help if your friends find us dead, will it?" She tugged at my arm. Behind us a path lead to the ice covered harbor.

Angry Chinese voices shouted at each other in the dark. They must have found Chin's body. Another ricochet came our way from the fire fight. The guard's cell phone vibrated again. I threw it towards the harbor. More rounds landed in our direction, but heavier like the .45s from the MAC-10s. The Chinese appeared to be regrouping and clearing the back of the terminal for a rally point. Or they knew we were back here and wanted to kill us.

"I can take you to Mohammed. He wants to talk to you," she pleaded.

"Was killing Jack Mohammed's idea or yours?" I guided her around the back of the building.

"I didn't kill Jack." She pushed back against a wall as though she needed its strength to hold her up. The lights caught a look of desolation on her face I wouldn't have seen except for a quirk of the shadows. "We were... and then he wasn't... They used me to find Jack and kill him."

The deep rattle of the MAC-10s had changed to the less frequent metallic cycling of an AK-47 mixed with the sharp barks of M-4s. Memories of Afghanistan crowded against the night until I could almost smell the camel shit. Dark figures, backing towards us, fired at the FBI.

I looked for the best escape route to the ice.

Cries in Chinese came closer. The remainders of the Triad ambush were retreating our way. I pulled Fiona and slid down the ice-covered embankment.

Shooting behind them as they retreated, the gangsters closed on our location. Angry voices called for blood. The language didn't confuse the sentiment. A Blackhawk with a spotlight focused on the Terminal Building. The remaining Triad soldiers fired up at it. The agents in the chopper fired down. The pilot jinked up and to the right as a sustained burst from the AK-47 stitched his fuselage. The spot jerked across the ground until it found us.

When it did, so did the Triads.

21. THE ICE FLOES

One Triad soldier saw us and yelled. I emptied the MAC-10's magazine in his general direction. He fell——the others sprayed bullets across the waterfront. I changed magazines and fired several more bursts at muzzle flashes and hints of movement. We picked a path across icy, slick rocks and barren scrub to the shore

Fiona slipped the last couple of feet into darkness. The ice banged and popped.

"C'mon Jason," she called from the shadows. "Let's get out of here."

The helicopter pulled up and away, to be out of easy bullet range, eliminating the spot light, but leaving haloed afterimages to spoil night vision. Voices cursing the brush and icy rock carried; so did the sound of scuffing feet as our pursuers closed in. I slid the last magazine into the MAC and sent three round bursts along the path.

Cries from wounded men confirmed contact.

The MAC's bolt closed on an empty chamber, so I tossed it and slipped over the bank to the ice of the bay.

"Jason," Fiona hissed from my right. She'd found a convergence of shadows that made her invisible.

"You OK?" I whispered. In the lee of the island voices carried. The sounds of combat behind us, the curses and cries of the wounded, got closer.

"Yeah." "How do we get out of here?"

"We'll go across the bay. It's the quickest way away from the fighting."

"But we'll show up against the skyline." Her frown showed in the ambient light. Even the shadows weren't dark enough for real concealment.

"We'll have to belly crawl. The ice isn't very thick and we won't be silhouetted on our bellies." The wind blew across Lake Michigan carrying a damp cold right into my soul as we started crawling across the ice.

I'd been cold before. The insertion across the ice had chilled me but the adrenalin rush kept me from feeling cold. This time on the ice, my adrenalin bled off. I began to shake. The ice, melted and refrozen through a hundred cycles during the past winter, had decayed to the consistency of course sandpaper ready to rip frozen, unprotected flesh or scour the skin through thin clothing. With no gloves or winter clothes we were both making quick progress to hypothermia, which prevented us leaving a bloody trail on the ice.

The shooting ceased behind us. Nothing moved in the less-dark shadows behind the Terminal Building. Lights and activity spilled from around front but nothing in our direction. I couldn't hear the chopper in the air, but that didn't mean it wasn't there. We were about halfway across. The nexus of shadow we'd been following gave out.

We had to run for the cover of the shore. On our bellies or on our feet we'd be excellent targets, but running we'd be harder to hit. Carefully, I got to my feet. My muscles were already rigid from the cold. I tried to stretch them into usefulness.

I could barely feel my ankles let alone my feet. Another fire fight had erupted near the shoreline behind us. "We're going to run for it from here."

Fiona remained crouched. "They'll see us."

I dropped next to her. "We're going to be visible. Just have to move fast."

"I'm sorry I lied to you, Jason." The faint light from the shoreline reflected off her tears. "You're the most decent man I've known. I wish we'd met under other circumstances. If we don't make it..."

"If we don't make it I want to know who used you to kill Jack. Who killed Jack?" I whispered.

"I don't know who killed him. Mohammed asked me to steal his bag and catch the plane. We were kissing and then he was dead." Fiona sobbed quietly.

I wanted to believe her, because then I wouldn't have sent Jack's killer to him, but without a good reason I couldn't pass on the responsibility. "We haven't got time for this. We'll sort it out on the shore. Right now we've got to run for it. But don't run; skate like you're on ice skates. That ought to keep the ice from cracking under you."

I looked back. Light reflected from a rifle barrel or optics. We were well beyond the effective range of a MAC-10, but too late to worry about a longer range rifle. We were forty feet from the nearest dock.

"Move. Let's get going." We dashed out into the light trying to skate on ice without ice skates. No sooner were we silhouetted by the Chicago skyline then an AK-47 spoke behind us, shooting high. The AK had the range to hit us if not the absolute accuracy. I grabbed Fiona and pulled her as we ran for the shore. The smoky ice below our feet spider-webbed with fractures. Water sloshed to our left.

With the next rounds, gouts of ice erupted around us. I couldn't hear the ice cracking because of the blood roaring in my ears. Fiona sprawled on the ice in the clear spill from a dock light. One eye stared blankly at the world, while the snow covered ice turned dark by her head. We'd almost made it.

I took a step toward where she lay when the ice buckled under me. I fell backwards and hit my head on something hard. The cold water of Lake Michigan swallowed me as the blue eyed spot from the helo came back over the harbor.

I held my breath despite being stunned, but I hadn't sucked in enough air. My lungs screamed for a breath.

Cold swept over me, through my clothes, freezing, numbing. I tumbled and fell until the difference between up and down disappeared. My lungs screamed, and the cold water burned. If I could touch the bottom of the shallow bay with my feet, I could launch myself to the surface. But the fall seemed to go on forever.

Panic kills. I let the burn in my lungs remind me I wasn't dead yet and tried to make myself sink faster. Spots flashed across my eyes.

Something stroked my face like a lover's touch. She kissed me long and hard.

It's time, baby. It's time, she said in Fiona's voice.

My lungs burned, aching to breathe anything, even fish water. I heard Fiona's voice in my head and she was dead. The dark spot on the ice had been her blood. She'd been dead before I went into the water.

No more struggles, Jason, Fiona spoke again, her voice unchanged by the depth. *You don't have to worry about Mohammed or Elouise or Sarah or Mo. Let others worry about them. We can just go. Be together forever. You and me and Jack.*

Her words warmed me. The only spot of warmth in the deep, dark cold. Give it all up. Let go. Go with her.

Hey, Jason, I'm already here. Jack's voice echoed in my head. *She doesn't need you. The world does. You have to save the world.*

219

Why did you run, Jack? Why didn't you stay with me? I asked the ghost.

He disappeared. My numb feet struck the bottom sending the shock through my legs. I wanted to let the horrible empty air out of my lungs and suck in anything. Fish breathe water so there might be some oxygen in the water for me, too. I clamped my jaw shut against such stupidity. My focus narrowed to a single spot of light above my head. I pushed off the bottom with the last of my strength aiming for the light. Fiona floated above me, beckoning me forward, begging me to follow her into the tunnel, into the light. I knew we were dead.

Mohammed would destroy the world. The man I knew believed in the beauty of grand gestures, whether meaningless vanities or the death of martyrs, he classed them all the same. He wanted the trigger. The circuit board to some nuclear system. He would explode a nuclear device in the United States.

Closer to the light, I saw angels coming for me. If they took me I wouldn't be able to stop Mohammed. I turned away from the light. I tried to swim but my arms and legs didn't respond. I couldn't get away. They caught me and dragged me into the light. I had failed Jack.

The world would die.

22. RESURRECTION

Life is supposed to exist between the gates of heaven and the gates of hell. Since neither heaven nor hell could have left me shivering with a bone-deep chill in every joint and made my teeth ache, I had to be alive.

Fiona lay in a dark pool of her own blood. I closed Jack's lifeless eyes on the sunny Caribbean beach. I followed the light. Followed Fiona into the light. We should be on the other side of this place of pain and fear, but I remained, hurt, and damned, damned cold.

Something held me tight, binding me with warmth in the cold dark pit, but I struggled against it, fighting towards the surface.

"Is he going to live?" Tom Rudd's nasal twang pulled me through the mental hole I'd fallen into. He had something I needed, but I couldn't remember what.

"Mr. Smiley is a lucky man, Agent Rudd. He managed not to

breathe any water while he was under. He has mild hypothermia. He should be fine in a couple of hours."

"When's he going to wake up?" Rudd asked.

"Anytime. I can wait," the medico said.

"No, you look after my men," Rudd said. "I'll stay with Mr. Smiley."

"Yes, sir." The medico's footsteps echoed as he walked away.

"Smiley, wake up," Rudd growled at me. The professional detachment in his voice disappeared with the witness.

I cracked an eyeball at him. "I'm not sure I want to. This dream is too much fun."

"I'm not kidding, Smiley. You've got some explaining to do."

"About what? Being alive?" I struggled to sit up. "I'm not sure I can explain that one."

A thermal blanket wrapped me like a burrito. I shivered and felt like I'd run two iron man triathlons back to back. Temporary screens had been erected, like a portable hospital. Above the screens I could see the unique interior architecture of the Meigs Field Terminal Building

"You asked me to back you up and now I've got six dead agents to explain." Rudd waved at something beyond the screens. "And another three seriously injured. What the hell setup did you get me into? And where is Mohammed Abd Allah? I thought you were going to meet with him."

"Jeezus, Tommy, don't you do any of your own homework? I went in soft, because I had no intel." I wriggled my arms out of the blanket. Once again someone had left me naked and unconscious. "Do you have any spare clothes around here?"

"Listen Smiley, you've got to give me something. I can't tell the Attorney General we lost six men on a bad hunch." Rudd paced between the partitions, scratching the back of his head every three steps.

"Fiona is the key to finding Mohammed. Where is she?" I could see Rudd coming apart in front of my eyes.

"She'd dead. Or didn't you know that?" Rudd looked down his nose at me. His hand flitted to the back of his head.

"I know she's dead, but she talked to Mohammed before all hell broke loose." A pair of white coveralls had been left on the foot of the gurney. I pushed off the thermal blanket. "I'm betting Mohammed's waiting for her to call back after you interrupted his negotiations with the Triads. All we have to do is locate her phone, and then I'll have a line on Mohammed."

"What? It'll take hours to get a warrant for the phone records." Rudd's cell buzzed in his pocket. He jammed it to his ear and growled, "What?"

I took his moment of distraction to get dressed. I stepped into the too large garment and zipped it closed. I pulled a pair of rubber soled slippers from the pocket. They fit pretty well.

Rudd's expression clouded with impatience. "Fine..." He ended his conversation and turned to me. "So where is Mohammed?"

"I need Fiona's phone, Tommy. Where is it?"

"How should I know? What can you do with it? Call him?" Rudd snorted and started pacing again.

"Yes, I'll call him. Fiona tried to recruit me while we were on the ice. I'm pretty sure he wants to talk to me." I took a couple of tentative steps away from the gurney. Despite stiff muscles I could still move and keep my balance. After I established my balance, I explored the opening between the folding partitions.

"Hey, where are you going?" Rudd called out as I limped away.

* * *

I walked up an alley made by rolling partitions delineating temporary morgue/triage facilities under the terminal's soaring glass. Rolling curtain walls gave some pretense of respect for the grim business of the coroners filling body bags. Twenty sheet covered cadavers lay on gurneys and half a dozen filled body bags.

"This didn't turn out well," I said. Rudd glared at me.

The raid on Vinnie T had smelled bad, and this smelled worse. Some responsibility for the deaths of the Federal agents was mine, but nothing about this operation displayed the careful planning the FBI's HRT was known for.

It reeked of Isaacson. Only someone like Isaacson could get the Federal boy scouts to walk into a shootout. But why?

I scanned the field of dead. At least two of the men under the sheets, had died by my hand, maybe more. "I don't want to do an autopsy on the operation. Maybe we both made mistakes. Where's Fiona?"

Rudd shrugged and pointed to a single gurney slightly apart from the others.

I'd seen a lot of dead people; friends, enemies, and collateral damage. Grief, horror and remorse have no place on a battlefield if you're going to survive so you hide them away. Some hiding places keep their secrets well, some let them out in the middle of the night. I wasn't sure which place Fiona would end up, yet. I wanted to believe she hadn't killed Jack. If she wasn't his killer then Jack and I weren't complete fools.

She lay naked under her sheet looking more like a little girl than she had in her Lolita costume. The bullet had made a neat hole just above her left ear and left a jagged crater on the right side of her head where bone and brain had been blown out onto the ice.

I didn't want to see the horror of her death. I wanted a clue.

A plastic evidence bag with her personal effects hung from the side of the gurney. I spilled these out on the table next to her; travel size tampons, wallet with a driver's license for Fiona Smalls and a picture of her with all her face jewelry, a circuit board, and a steel hair pin with a dragon carved handle and a point like an ice pick that could kill a man. I'd seen her pin her pony tails together with it.

Rudd watched me with his arms crossed and his hands tucked

under his elbows. His face maintained a rigid neutrality but his head sank into his shoulders. The inward focus and the rigidity of his appearance yanked me back hard to the days after my squad died.

"You've never lost troops before, have you?" I said.

"I've seen agents injured before. And killed." Rudd whispered. "We were ordered to go in fast and deploy at the Terminal Building to wait for you and Mohammed. I reported Triad involvement in your wife's abduction, but Isaacson discounted the information as irrelevant."

"Why would his opinion matter?" I asked.

"Homeland is running this operation." Rudd drew a deep ragged breath. "He'll be here in an hour to take over the ground operation. And I'll end up back in Anchorage."

"It doesn't make sense for Isaacson to advise you to use bad tactics." I picked up the steel hairpin. "Has Jack been autopsied?"

"Yes." Rudd grunted. "Why?"

"What killed him?"

"What does that have to do with finding Mohammed?" Rudd sighed. He pulled out his Blackberry and scrolled through it. "Two .22 caliber bullets in the back of his head. Fired from long range. Didn't you hear the gun?"

"Must have been silenced. I heard nothing. But there were no powder burns?" I looked back at Fiona.

"Not according to the coroner's report." Rudd dropped his phone back in his pocket. "What's this got to do with Mohammed? I thought you said the girl killed Nesmith."

"She couldn't have. Even if she'd had a gun tucked away someplace hard to see on a nude beach, she was sitting on his lap when he was killed. I saw her." I felt just a little sadder about the dead girl in front of me. She really hadn't been the cold-blooded killer. And maybe I wasn't a complete fool. I put Fiona in the dead-too-soon place. "And if she didn't kill Jack, then Mohammed didn't order Jack killed."

Rudd squinted suspiciously. "So, Nesmith worked for Mohammed? Is that why he ran?"

"No, Jack ran because there is an inside man, and he didn't know who to trust." I slipped the circuit board into my pocket. I couldn't leave this key to death and destruction laying around for anyone to pick up. "I still need the phone. It's not in her effects?"

Rudd straightened his back and lifted his nose before he stalked away, as though to say he wouldn't run errands for me. He disappeared around one of the rolling partitions. Moments later a familiar looking agent appeared with a cell phone in another evidence bag.

"Here it is, Mr. Smiley." He passed me the bag with his left hand and offered his right for a handshake. "Zechariah Davidson. Just wanted to thank you for saving my life during the raid at Vinnie Tortelli's house. That goombah would've finished us off."

I registered the face of the sergeant Nonny shot in the back. "Thanks for bringing the phone, Sarge."

"Call me Zech."

"Yeah." I peeled the phone out of the evidence bag and slid the battery back in the phone. "How's the back? You took a heck of a load at the Tortelli raid," I asked while the phone powered up.

He shifted slightly. "It hurts a little. Thanks for stopping him."

"I didn't stop Nonny for good. Fiona did." I nodded at her body. "She killed him. Saved my life. I tried to return the favor tonight, but no luck."

"I didn't know she was armed." Davidson frowned. "Yeah. You guys almost made the marina. Tough."

"How's the other agent? The kid?" I asked. Davidson reminded me of the cops I knew when I joined the force.

He nodded towards the array of corpses. "He's over there."

"I'm sorry——"

"No... Shit... He's on light duty so he's helping the coroners."

I grinned with relief. I didn't think I could stand another death

226

weighing on my soul. "That's good. Hey, do you know where my guns are?"

"The armorer collected them. You really like to go with some artillery don't you?" Davidson looked over his shoulder as Rudd stalked into my little alcove.

Tom Rudd's glare included us both. "Don't you have something to do, Sergeant?" he growled.

Davidson nodded and shot me a wink before he escaped, leaving me in his boss' company.

23. MOHAMMED AND THE MOUNTAIN

Rudd circled me and Fiona's gurney with slow, deliberate strides, his eyes focused on me all of the time.

I stepped out of his circle. "I'd like to get my guns back. I might need to shoot someone."

Rudd stopped abruptly and tapped his fingers, one after another, on the metal instrument tray. "You've got the phone. Are you going to call?"

"In a minute." I opened the recent-calls list. The last number had an LA area code. I wrapped my fingers around the circuit board in my pocket. I would need bait to catch Mohammed. If the gentle man I thought I knew had really been a ruthless terrorist, what better bait than the trigger for Armageddon?

Rudd stared at me across Fiona's body, fingers dancing on metal with a maddeningly monotonous rhythm. "Well, are you going to call?"

Rudd's cold arrogance had earned him hatred from half the Chicago Police Department before he landed the Alaska assignment. Yet he showed real passion about his men, and a willingness to go a little farther to stop the bad guys. Maybe I could trust him.

Maybe.

"Maybe you should have your tech guys trace this call and listen in?" I turned my back on him, pressed send and put the phone to my ear.

The phone rang.

Mohammed's timetable drove the ticking clock Sammy Schultz had handed me five days ago. I gripped the circuit board. She retrieved it from the old man after I killed him and in the middle of a fire fight. Her submissive act had been a well-played tool to retrieve the triggers for Mohammed.

The second ring. One trigger let him nuke Chicago. Multiple triggers brought a nightmare down for the whole world. I couldn't let that happen. I had the best chance of anyone to get close to the wily, old bastard.

The target phone connected on the third ring but instead of answering I heard the sound of a vehicle door opening and someone speaking, though I couldn't understand the words. Mohammed answered in Arabic telling the person to mind his own business.

"Assalaam alaikum." I said. "Hello, Mohammed."

The air hung silent except for the sounds of vehicles on a roadway. This would be the second time I had surprised Mohammed.

"Wa alaikum assalaam." Mohammed spoke in a whisper just barely audible over the background noise. "Jason Smiley? Why do you have Fiona's phone?"

"Fiona called you on it earlier this evening, so I figured you would be ready to answer the call." I spoke with the same civil tone we used in Abu Ghraib. I wanted Mohammed to remember in his gut I had held a position of power, but I didn't want him angry about it.

"Where is Fiona? May I speak with her?" Mohammed's voice showed strain, but deep control.

"Fiona isn't available. Your friends, the Chinese, got into a firefight with the FBI HRT." Outside the morgue area, Rudd had a little command post set up. His tech pounded on the keyboard while Rudd looked nervously in my direction.

"That is terrible. So the FBI has Fiona? Or is it your bosses at your Department of Homeland Security?"

"I'm not big on bosses. You should know that, my old friend. That's why you found me in LA chasing adulterers." I heard his breathing clearly over the phone until a large vehicle rolled. He had to be standing at the side of an interstate. "How is your teaching assignment? What college did you tell me you were working at?"

"Jason, my friend, I truly wish I was teaching. This thing I am doing lacks the same rewards." Mohammed sighed deeply.

"This thing... I talked to Jack. He told me about this 'thing' of yours."

"Jack didn't know what I'm doing, Jason. He had no concept. You have less knowledge than a flea." His voice had risen in tension as he spewed some of the old, tired arrogance, then he slipped once more into a more concerned tone. "Is the FBI interrogating her roughly? I'd hate to see her go through one of their 'terrorist' interviews. They can be quite as vindictive as the CIA."

Mohammed's voice carried the tone of some philosophical disagreement, instead of death and mass destruction. "Fiona is dead. Did you know your friend Chin molested her while you negotiated my death? They shot her as I tried to lead her away from the firefight."

The line went quiet. He hadn't disconnected. I could still hear the rush of trucks and breathing, and the deep sigh of a man in grief. I hadn't imagined he cared that much about a woman.

"Inshallah. She liked you, Jason," he said, in a whisper. "If it means anything to you, she thought you were a good man. Did she tell you I wanted to talk to you?"

"Yes, before she died." I sighed. Maybe we were all monsters with soft underbellies. "What do you want from me?"

"I need your assistance." Mohammed whispered.

"I've heard about the plan to nuke Chicago, and I don't approve."

"You shouldn't believe everything you hear. I don't want to nuke Chicago." He said, followed by crunching sounds of feet on loose gravel or rocky dirt.

"Then why the triggers? You raised a red flag with Jack when you asked him to procure circuits to set off nuclear warheads. Especially since that implied you had access to deployable nuclear weapons."

"You should be more concerned with where the triggers came from." More voices, their words unintelligible, grew louder in the background. He dropped his voice so low I could barely understand. "I don't have time to fence with you. In a moment I'm going to make a very real threat to make you deliver the triggers to me, but you must not deliver them no matter what I tell you."

What sort of game was Mohammed playing? "Why would I do that? Even if I had the triggers." I rocked back on the gurney.

"The people I am with thought you might need persuasion. If you don't show up your office girl will die, and these animals are eager to hurt her." Mohammed's voice dropped again. "I'm sorry. She's alive, but I can't save her. These men mustn't get any of those circuit boards."

I let the connection go quiet for a moment. "Tell me where to meet you. And know this, if Lucy is injured or molested in any way I will send the perpetrator to Hell personally, and when I join him there I will hunt him down and make the demons blanch with what I do to him."

"You're very colorful, Jason. I understand your concerns, but I don't control these people. I am only a technical advisor."

"Then why did you have Fiona working for you?" I asked.

"That's a story for another time. Your friends should have located this phone by now so I will have to dispose of it. Meet me in Rugby, North Dakota at 6PM, tonight. Don't bring any FBI or DHS or whoever else." Mohammed's voice held a twinge of remorse. "If they show up, the woman is dead. Goodbye. "

"Sure. I'll be there." As soon as the phone clicked off I knew I wouldn't see Mohammed in Rugby. He'd just baited them with a location. I needed to find a way to contact him without Rudd's people knowing. I couldn't risk their ham-handed interference when I rescued Lucy.

My fingers gripped the edge of Fiona's gurney. Tough, resourceful Lucy imprisoned by a terrorist cell. When we shared war stories, hers made mine seem like kindergarten playtime. She'd worked communications on a hundred operations. She'd watched teams she'd trained get swallowed by a flaw in the plan and no one ever heard about their sacrifice. Only a few hot rescues worked out well. Most left a litter of bodies.

In the end, all the high minded ideals and rationalizations came down to saving one life. I would risk Chicago and the world just to not have one more person I cared about, dead.

Not one more.

But Mohammed had warned me off. 'Don't bring the circuit boards no matter what I say', he'd said. No matter what he threatened? First, it bothered me that he thought I had the circuit boards, or had access to them. Second, why warn me off?

Especially since he'd told Mr. Chin they were going to have to get the information from me. So Mohammed hadn't told his people the triggers were lost, but why?

Because if they couldn't get the triggers from me, Lucy became disposable.

I had to get to where ever Mohammed intended to meet me at 6 PM, and I needed to do it without the help of the FBI or Homeland Security, by whatever means necessary.

* * *

"I might have been wrong about you, Smiley. You're not a complete fuck-up," Rudd said.

Zech Davidson came over, cell phone in hand, and whispered something in Rudd's ear. The SAIC nodded. "We got the whole conversation on tape and a trace on the burn phone he used. We'll fly a team into Rugby and take him down as soon as he rolls into town. I'd like to bring you along on the take down, but I don't think I want to risk a civilian."

"He ain't going to Rugby. Have a team check it out, but Mohammed won't be there." I watched Davidson for a reaction. He shrugged.

I nodded. "Where are my guns? I need to go."

"I don't think so." Rudd drew himself up to his full beanstalk 6'3". "The General wants to talk to you."

"All the more reason for me to leave. I need to figure some things out and I don't need the General telling me what to do."

Davidson put down his cell phone and handed me a backpack. "Here are your guns, Mr. Smiley. They've been cleaned and oiled, and we replaced the ammunition where we could. We have .380 ACP, .38 special and 10 mm but no .44 Magnum I'm afraid. Why are you carrying a Dirty Harry special?"

"I like to stop what I'm shooting at." I looked in the backpack. Davidson had found me some clothes. "Thanks, Sarge. I appreciate it." Then I looked down at her face, turned slightly away so the damage from the bullet wasn't so visible. I felt the fire monster growing behind my eyes once more. The world exploded in colored lights. I hurled Fiona's cell phone at the floor and kicked the nearest table scattering the autopsy equipment across the floor. "Fuck..." came out in a roar.

Davidson grabbed my arm. "Are you all right?"

I started seeing again. Davidson looked at me. He knew what happened. I nodded at him. "All I need is a ride out of here."

"There's a taxi waiting out front," Davidson said. "The cabby asked for you."

"Great. Then I'll see you guys." I shouldered the backpack, the hot monster still simmering. I turned to Rudd, who had started pacing again. His face had frozen in a sneer, but his eyes focused on me. "Look, I'm giving it to you straight. I don't know where he is, or where he's going except he's got a hostage. If you guys show up, she's dead."

"Why does he want you?" Rudd frowned at me. "Are you in collusion with him?"

"Not unless he's trying to stop Chicago from getting nuked or Lucy from getting killed." I hitched the backpack up. The anger wanted out again, and I needed icy control. "I gotta go. Gotta card? I'll call you when I have something."

"Where are you going?" Rudd reflexively gave me one of his business cards.

"To look for answers. I'm not going to let anyone else die because of me." I stopped to shake Davidson's hand. Something flickered behind his eyes. A frown creased his pleasant face, then he nodded and released my hand.

Maybe he held the same monster at bay.

Outside the terminal, Eddy's ratty looking cab idled, thumping out Bob Marley's 'No Woman, No Cry.' Eddy leaned against the cab, moving just enough to open the trunk as I approached.

"Give me the backpack, boss," he said as he produced an electronic instrument from the dark recesses and waved it over me first, and then the bag. He dumped the contents in the trunk and did a quick survey with his device. Holding up a black turtle neck sweater, the device beeped loudly. "Looks like they put a tracking device on you. Good thing I brought you clothes."

I gathered up my guns and rigs, while Eddy stuffed the

contaminated gear into the backpack and deposited it in a nearby trash can. In the back seat of the cab I found my backpack stuffed with clothes, ammo, burn phones and a little package I'd left in case I didn't make it back with the picture of Jack and Fiona and the locker key.

While Eddy eased away from the Terminal Building, I sent a text ':)' to the last number Mohammed answered.

My new burn phone rang back in less than ten seconds, but from another number.

"Assalaam 'alaikam, Jason. You are resourceful. We will meet tonight at the Clearwater truck stop off I-94. Be there." He clicked off. I pulled the battery out of my burn phone. By the time Rudd's guys got a tap on this number it would be in the garbage.

24. THE QUEEN'S GAMBIT

Eddy drove off Northerly Island, with the sun rising in a cold, clear dawn behind us. "Eddy, are you ready for another run? I need a ride."

"I can't go, boss." Eddy grinned in the rearview mirror and turned down Peter Tosh. "Sorry."

"I can pay the fare." According to the mapping app on my phone I had to cover 462 miles to the Clearwater rendezvous. I could be there in 7.7 hours. "And I tip well."

Eddy turned his usually smiling blue eyes at my reflection in his rearview mirror. "No, mon. She said something has gone wrong with the operation. She doesn't think it will end well and I need to get my family out of Chicago for a little while."

A shiver traced up my spine. "What changed her mind?"

"I don't know, mon. She just called me up to get you." He shook his head. "And then she started cursing in Scots again. She's scary when she does that."

"I need wheels then. Where can I borrow a car?" I thought about

Mo's Civic, but his house would be watched. But with Jack dead and the circuits lost at sea no one needed to watch his place. "Let's go back to the building on West Wabansia. There might be a car there I could borrow."

"Sure, mon. Anything you say." Eddy turned up Peter Tosh on the stereo. I let the sounds of funky revolution lull the wild animal stirring behind my eyes.

While Peter Tosh and Bob Marley sang songs of freedom. I found my last speed loader for the .44 in my backpack. My nerves took on a pre-mission hum as I checked my guns, packed spare magazines into my cargo pants and generally got myself right for trouble.

Elouise's loss of her cool reserve raised my tension level. She might have confirmed loose nuclear weapons. I watched the peaceful city streets roll by. No families scrambling for their cars. No frenzied evacuation in process. Just families getting ready for church or breakfast. "Eddy, any news on the radio?"

"Nothing special, Boss. Supposed to warm up today."

"So what's going on?"

"Dunno, boss. You have to talk to her." Eddy turned up the radio effectively ending the conversation.

When Eddy pulled into the parking lot across the street from Jack's apartment building where the surveillance had been set up I knew I'd been had. Elouise's Jaguar now sporting Michigan plates, sat in the shadows at the back of the lot. Elouise stood by her front fender waiting for us.

"You called her?" I watched his eyes in the mirror. I almost trusted Eddy, but maybe I shouldn't.

"No, mon. I bring you where you say," he said, reverting to his patois. "So be it, she want you to meet her here, too. I figure, it's all good, eh, mon?" Eddy watched my eyes as carefully as I watched his. I nodded and dropped another hundred on the front seat.

I dragged my backpack out of the cab. As soon the door shut, Eddy pulled away, his arm raised out the window, fingers spread, palm facing the wind. I waved back.

The animal growled a little as I approached Elouise. Whatever she knew or didn't know would be a secret between her and her boss. I couldn't trust her to tell me the truth. "Hello, Elouise. What's up?"

"I believe you might need some assistance. You're after Mohammed Abd Allah, correct?"

"Yes, but I don't want company, just your car." I dropped the backpack at my feet and waited for her move.

Elouise pulled a shipping box out of her oversized handbag and tossed it to me. "I thought you might want to get your hands on this."

"What is it?" I said as I examined the address: Fiona Small at 2201 West Wabansia apartment 3C. 'Confirmation Requested.' The return address was a PO Box in Los Angeles. "How did you get this?"

"The picture in your backpack of Jack and Fiona? The number on the back tracks the location of a parcel held for pickup, so I picked it up."

"As Fiona?"

She shrugged.

I opened the box to confirm what I guessed. Eleven circuits, identical to the one in my pocket nested in notched foam packing material with only one empty place. I had hoped these were safely forgotten in a locker somewhere. Now I had one more problem to deal with. "Why did you give them to me?"

"Good faith. My job is to deliver those to my employer, but I don't trust his motivations." Elouise looked up at me. Her hair, loose from her severe bun this morning, stirred gently as she moved closer. "I trust you, Mr. Smiley."

She got close enough for me to smell her perfume. She seemed to tremble a little as she looked up at me. It occurred to me she wanted me to kiss her. As I leaned forward, I caught a sense of a shadow moving in the front seat of her Jaguar. I drew my 10 mm.

"Who the hell is that?" I stepped back to cover her and the car.

"Put your gun down." Elouise rapped on the roof and beckoned at the shadow. "He's safe."

The contract killer I'd last seen stuffed unconscious in Elouise's trunk, a slightly built man with a receding chin and an enormous black moustache, emerged from the passenger side. I had him in my site picture before his hands could clear the roof of the car. "Don't move. Elouise, what the hell is this?"

"Jason, I'd like you to meet Tommy 'The Fisherman' Gonnati. He's really not a bad sort, and I thought we might need another gun."

Aside from the moustache Tommy wasn't particularly noteworthy. He had a slight build, almost emaciated. His face had an unremarkable appearance with a plain nose performing its function without ostentation over a pair of thin, bloodless lips. Even his eyes lacked the hard darkness of a career killer. Instead they were a soft brown, round with a bit of downward slant making this attack dog look more like a lost puppy.

"He's got a contract to kill me." I said.

"Well, Tommy and I have a deal. He behaves himself and the recordings I have of him making arrangements to turn state's evidence won't show up on Danny Shoe's inbox. Anything happens to you or I, and Danny finds he's got a rat."

"Where's your gun?" I asked 'The Fisherman.'

"She's got it." He shrugged. "It's like she said. But she cheated. I was drugged up when I was recorded. That can't be legal."

"I'm sure Danny won't be so concerned about the legalities," Elouise opened the back door for Tommy. "Now be a good boy and get in the back seat."

"No way," I said. "I don't want you on this adventure and I damned sure don't want him. Mohammed has my office manager, Lucy, as a hostage. My luck with hostages is fifty-fifty right now with a lot of collateral damage. I'm not getting anyone else killed if I can help it."

"You're right, of course. This isn't a lark. I've been making some

239

arrangements since the last time we talked." She clicked a button on her key ring and pushed by me.

I followed her to the back of the car where she opened the trunk revealing a small arsenal. "Been shopping have you?"

"I thought we could use some things. The next logical step is to find Mohammed and stop him." She said. The trunk contained six M-4 carbines, ammunition, three set of Dragon-Skin body armor, and a box of flash bang grenades, next to her kidnapping kit of duct tape and zip ties.

I picked up one of the grenades. "They didn't have any M67 grenades?"

She handed me a tan canvas bag with half a dozen of the fragmentation grenades. "So where is he? Shouldn't we get going?"

"I appreciate the shopping you did, and picking up the mail." I shoved the box of triggers into my backpack. "But I'm not bringing anyone with me on this mission. I won't get anyone else killed."

"I'm afraid that's not your choice."

We stared at each other. The vulnerability I saw in her earlier had fled. "I suppose I could zip-tie the both of you to a tree and take your car."

"You could try," she smiled pleasantly at me. "But I'd prefer that you weren't recovering from the knock out drug when we have to deal with you friend Mohammed."

"I can still walk away," I said.

"And I can hit you with a dart at 25 yards."

"I could shoot you and your little friend," I said as I pulled the 10mm's slide back to check the charge.

"But you won't." She smiled again, this time it felt more genuine. "Because you like me."

"Am I that obvious? Damn." I put the pistol away. "I still don't trust Tommy. You secure him before we go. Where is his weapon?"

"In the glove compartment." Elouise opened up her kidnapping kit and gathered some zip-tie cuffs. "He's not going to like this."

"He'll like the alternative less." I put my hand back on my pistol.

Elouise tied the Fisherman up with half-a-dozen cuffs tied together binding his hands to his left ankle but allowing him to sit up straight and have enough flexibility to scratch himself where it might itch.

Tommy the Fisherman sat with stoic indifference while Elouise trussed him. When she finished he could sit up comfortably in the back seat, but didn't have the freedom of movement to threaten us in the front seat.

"Thank you." He leaned back, resting his head on the window and closed his eyes. "If you can't do anything else, you can sleep."

* * *

I'd like to say we sped through the dark night like death and vengeance but the daytime traffic held Elouise to a moderate eighty miles per hour while Death took a nap in the back seat. I'd entered the address of the truck stop outside Clearwater, Minnesota, into my phone; it gave us a route and an ETA that put us at the diner a bare hour before the meet with Mohammed.

With both hands on the wheel Elouise expertly threaded our way through the heavy traffic. The clear skies and bright morning sunlight made her hair glow in a hundred shades of red and gold. She looked over at me, driving by instinct. "Jason, do you consider me as a friend?"

"Well, you've drugged me, stuck a gun in my ribs, and used me like a tool to your own ends. You wrestle naked like a wild cat, and hijacked me on the high seas. Now you've driven halfway across the country with me on a wild goose chase and kidnapped a paid assassin." I grunted out a bit of laughter. She'd been a better friend and partner than anyone I'd been with since Afghanistan.

"Yeah, I think you're a friend." I grinned at her with the hope she might feel less vulnerable and actually watch the traffic. Elouise frowned but turned back to the road. "What about Fiona? You certainly treated her like more than a friend."

Fiona. Another deep subject. Where was this going? "Don't know what you want to know. She was complicated. I felt sorry for her. Jack trusted her. She saved my life and fought Nonny like a wildcat. She let Chin treat her like a whore to secure Mohammed's deal. Now she's dead. Just another dead soldier in the same old stupid war."

"Is that how you think of her, as a soldier?"

"Sure... Maybe. Fiona was a sad little girl who got caught up in somebody else's game. She killed just as ruthlessly as any other soldier. And she just wanted someone to love her."

"And you loved her?"

"What? Did I say that?"

"No, but you put forth a lot of effort to protect her including a long night on a sex resort." Elouise's face showed no emotion. The pretense of disinterest implied interest.

"I slept in the chair. Why would you care?"

"I need to know who you really are. You've risked everything for people who haven't been loyal to you. Beyond the pittance we agreed to, there's no money in this for you. Why are you going after Mohammed?"

"You need to know my motivations? That's funny. Those mystery bosses that you sometimes work for and can sometimes call on for amazing things, what is their motivation? Are they the good guys or the bad guys? Do you know?"

"There are no good guys," she said. "They're all out for a pay day."

"OK. I'll tell you. I'm going to save the world like goddamn Batman. Mohammed has a friend of mine as hostage and I will get her back. Then I will stop him from blowing up Chicago and whoever gets in my way. I will not let the bad guys win." I could feel the lack of real sleep catch up with me as the crisp morning sun heated the interior of the car. I leaned my head against the cool glass of the passenger window. "Follow I-90 to I-94."

As the muffled road noise and the growl of the big supercharged V-8 lulled me to sleep, Elouise asked "Why you?"

"Mohammed could have ignored me in LA. Even when Jack called, I wouldn't have come up on anyone's radar. As it was he put a target on my back, and made me a tool of whatever conspiracy is driving this thing. And so I wonder, why? Does he want to get even with me for some perceived insult? Does he think somehow I'll direct attention away from him? Or does he want me to stop him?" It sounded stupid hearing the words out loud. "Chess was life to him. He had to win and I had beaten him. Maybe he's challenging me to play for the highest stakes?"

"But by that analogy, with Fiona dead, he's lost his Queen. He should be quite vulnerable."

"Fiona was a pawn. She could only go ahead and attack. Not enough range or freedom of movement for a queen. You're a queen. I just can't tell if you're black or white."

We drove on in silence——for a while.

Half an hour later she spoke. "But do you consider him a friend, like you consider me a friend, even though I've had to do. . .things. . . I wouldn't normally do because the ends justify the means?"

"Do the ends ever really justify the means?" It's a cliché, but the answer in real time is very slippery. Ideals have a way of becoming flexible when your life is at risk. And once you've survived and learned to live with the guilt, justification becomes easier.

"Yes," she said. "I believe they do at times. When we're trying to stop a great evil."

"But are we God to know the truth of which evil is greater, that which we fight or that which we do?"

"Jason, as my old instructor in Chechnya said, 'You think too much.'"

"You trained in Chechnya? I thought you were trained by British intelligence."

"I was. They 'recruited' me to infiltrate Al Qaeda. Chechnya is one

243

of their better training sites."

"I can't believe they would risk someone like you that way."

She laughed but it came out as a bitter snort and her voice took on a broad Scots brogue. "Like me? I told you I did blowjobs for a fiver and lived by my wits when they acquired me. I was expendable then and I'm expendable now."

Jack would say my weakness is empathy. I shuddered at the despair she must have felt to sell herself on the street. How could someone broken to that extent be the cool, ruthless woman sitting beside me? It didn't seem possible. Cop sense took over. If it wasn't possible then it likely wasn't true, but then why the legend?

After a long period of uncomfortable silence where images of her walking naked out of the Caribbean vied with the realization she played me like a cheap fiddle, she said, "Do you know what Mohammed's been doing since he left Abu Ghraib?"

"I hadn't heard anything from Mohammed until I saw him at the cafe in LA. Apparently, he wasn't completely honest with me." She raised an eyebrow at me, questioning. I continued. "He said he'd come to the U.S. because it was safer and he had a teaching job."

"Not really a lie, was it?" Elouise's impassiveness cracked with the hint of a grin. "He came here to teach the local jihadist how to fight you because you're too safe in your own country. He's been running classes in his own brand of holy war around the world for the last several years. Pakistan, Iran, Kuwait, India, China, Malaysia. Every major terrorist event since 2008 has been under his oversight by people he trained."

"All places you've been?" Finally Elouise looked surprised by something I said. Lucy's sources were very good.

After a deep breath she said, "Yes. I can't discuss the missions but I have been aware of Mohammed's activities for the last several years. He's a bad man. People around him, die——though he never seems to get caught."

"It doesn't sound like the man I knew." I held up my hand to stop her from arguing the point. "But I expect I'll know soon whether or not we were ever friends."

* * *

We stopped at a rest stop in Michigan. The facilities consisted of three picnic tables and some scrub trees. A worn path led into the trees. Tommy and I followed it. When we found some suitable bushes we stopped about half a dozen feet from each other. Rest room manners say don't talk, but I needed to know something about this man. "You tried to kill me," I said.

"No shit, Sherlock." He shook himself with vigor. "You've got more lives than a fucking cat. If that other shit hadn't gotten out of the elevator I would have taken you out with a single shot."

"You realize those were federal agents you gunned down?" I asked conversationally as I finished my own stream.

"Too bad." He shrugged. "They can only kill me once."

We walked back to the car. "So did Danny Shoe send you?"

"Yeah, sure. Danny really hates you. He blames you for his brother getting AIDS." He rolled his eyes. Nobody believed the Horse would be forced into nonconsensual sex. "Besides, it's just business."

"Business?"

"Yeah. Danny hires me out to take care of problems. His problems. Other people's problems. Doesn't matter." He looked at me with a very cold smile. "I saw you when I whacked that fat fuck in LA last week. You hang out with some strange people."

"I could have sworn I saw a Chinese guy shooting Bruno. And he used a rifle not a pistol."

"I use the tool I need. The Chinese wanted it to look like an East LA drive-by. You just got in the way." The Fisherman looked over at me again. "You ain't a cop anymore, right?"

"No, I'm not a cop, I'm not wearing a wire, and you'll probably be dead before you can turn state's evidence." Elouise's arrangement to control this sociopath seemed very tenuous. Shooting him in the back of the head as we walked back to the car would have been the prudent course of action, sort of like killing a rabid raccoon, but I'd never killed a person that wasn't an immediate threat and I wasn't ready to change.

Back at the car Elouise produced three one-liter bottles of water and passed them around. Tommy the Fisherman grimaced at the water but guzzled half the bottle in a single gulp.

"Thanks," he said and leaned against the car. He dug a cigarette from his jacket and lit it. "So what's the plan?"

"Not much of a plan right now," I said. "I've got a meet set up with Mohammed. He's got a hostage. I'm gonna free the hostage; then I'm going to stop him from blowing up Chicago."

"Chicago?" Tommy looked surprised. "This whack job wants to blow up Chicago?"

"Rumor has it." I said.

"Fuck him. Let's just kill them all and get it over with." Tommy bounced on the balls of his feet. "C'mon let's go. Let's toast these fuckers."

Tommy paced the length of the car twice and then got in the back seat. He pounded on the door. "C'mon. Let's go."

Elouise raised an eyebrow at me as a comment and got in the driver's seat. I drained my water bottle and took the passenger's seat.

Tommy rocked back and forth in the back seat, then became very still. "He ain't blowing up my town."

"Well, that's the plan. But we can't kill anyone until we know where the bombs are." I looked into the back of the car.

All the tension had flowed out of the Fisherman. He slouched with his hands behind his head. "Sure. Don't worry about a thing, boss."

"I worry about lots of things. Like when you said it was 'just business.'" I asked, "Who ordered the hit on me if it wasn't Danny

246

Chourelli?"

"I guess the same guy that wanted the dude on the nudie beach whacked. I don't ask a lot of questions. It's not healthy." Tommy settled back for another nap.

Elouise looked at me out of the corners of her eyes as she accelerated the car onto the interstate. The sudden return of her brogue said more than her words. "Let it alone, Mr. Smiley. We're going to need the wee gomeral."

I could feel the weight of every gun I owned. I could see the Fisherman die by my hands. And I could see how pointless it would be. He was a tool, a thing, not any more responsible for Jack's death than the gun that killed him. I could see a number of agendas at work here.

Mohammed's terrorists wanted to create fear by an attack in America. The Triads sold technology to the highest bidder. The mob provided services, but someone else had tied this unholy alliance together. Why and who were questions I suspected Elouise could answer if she dared.

I dug the package Elouise had given me out of my backpack. Inside were eleven circuit boards like the one in my pocket, each in its own slot. Using the screw driver blade on my ancient Swiss Army knife I pried under the largest component, cracking the chip and the board.

I destroyed ten more triggers in the same manner.

Elouise didn't take her eyes off the road, but she smiled ever so slightly.

25. WHATEVER IT TAKES

We reached the meeting place, a truck stop outside of Clearwater in rural Minnesota, late Sunday afternoon. The diner sat in a sea of asphalt with rows of big rigs lined up side-by-side and nose-to-tail in the back. The front parking lot held a dozen cars and pickups in various states of decay, spreading out from the front door.

Short scrubby trees and short scrubby houses bordered the pavement behind the restaurant. The cover wouldn't hide a rifle squad, and any suspicious group would stand out like a cat in a doghouse——yet one or two snipers and their spotters could easily be hidden near the parked semis when evening drew out the shadows. It wouldn't take much for a sniper to tag me on my approach or pick me off through the windows.

"This is the day, isn't it?" I turned to Elouise. She cocked an eyebrow. "The day the big deal is going down." Some dark thought crossed her eyes as she looked away.

"How much do you know about the deal?" I watched her scan the horizon and wondered what it was she saw, or didn't want to see.

"No more than you." She looked back at me. "Do you want me to cover you in the restaurant?"

"No, I'm going to walk in." I glanced over at the sleepy-eyed killer in the back seat. "Who's going to cover me from you and your pet assassin?"

Elouise tried hard to look offended but the darkness hovered around her edges. "We're on your side. I wouldn't be here otherwise."

"OK. I believe you, until I become 'inconvenient', again." I got out of the car and stretched. My muscles cramped from so much riding. "You guys gas up, stall around in front of the diner. I'll watch the back."
I checked the loads in my guns, careful not to flash my weapons at the few nearby homes. The walk in would limber me up a bit.

I was in mid-limber and working the battle-plan in my head when Elouise appeared at my side.

"Jeeze, don't sneak up on a guy."

She touched my arm. "Your bloody single-minded devotion towards your friends is inconvenient, but rather admirable. You don't have to go in alone. I'll watch your back."

"No. I don't want to startle him. I'll go in when I'm sure Mohammed is here." We were close enough to see the semis blowing smoke back at the truck stop.

Elouise handed me a pair of lightweight field binoculars. "I want you to be careful, Jason. Mohammed is a very dangerous man. If he learns you destroyed all those triggers he might kill you in the diner and damn the consequences."

"Mohammed isn't a martyr. Not the man I knew, but I'll say I didn't think he'd be a terrorist and a kidnapper." I watched Elouise watch me. Her whole expression had become somber. "You're not going to knock me out again? We really don't have time for that."

"You're such a fool, Jason." Then she kissed me —— deeply. I returned the kiss with enthusiasm, the heat of her body, even through clothes, reminding me of our encounter on the beach. When she let me go, she said, "Don't get yourself killed. I... You can't trust people, like you do. It will get you killed." She kissed me, again, quick and hard, then slipped into the car and drove away.

I hiked to the diner. My mind should have been on Mohammed, but Elouise had managed to muddle my thinking. Who did I trust in this? No one, not even myself, if I could be so easily distracted.

I couldn't trust Mohammed. He played a very deep game and double agent certainly could be in his repertoire.

I didn't trust Blankenship. She might even believe everything she said to me, but she had exploited my weaknesses with absolute ruthlessness, but to what end?

I sure hadn't trusted Fiona, and she had been playing a double game just like Blankenship said, but I'd trusted Jack and Jack got killed.

The taste of perfume, tinged with woman, lingered on my lips and distracted my senses as I approached the diner. The little settlement near the restaurant had more in common with rural Afghanistan than any part of America familiar to me. Small, cheap houses on tiny lots with collections of discarded engines and frames for snow machines and cars piled against garages. Thrift is a virtue of poverty. Thoughts of Afghanistan put me on high alert. I'd left the M-4 with Elouise. I needed to come in quiet and non-aggressive. Anything else might spook him or the locals, and I didn't want to scare Mohammed off. Lucy's life was at stake.

The meeting time was set for 6 PM. By 5 PM I slipped between the big rigs in the back parking lot, their engines idling while their drivers ate dinner and showered. The behemoths provided decent cover for the approach but narrowed my field of view to only the open space between two rigs. The number of cars and pickups crowded next to the diner had changed, but they were all of the same type, old rusty cars and shiny new pickups.

I found a sheltered spot where I wouldn't be too noticeable. I had time to get my game face on and rethink my plan. After all I could end Mohammed's troubles with a single bullet, but there were a lot of questions he needed to answer starting with: where were the nukes?

Two road-grimed, dry cleaning vans rolled into the parking lot from the north at about 5:30. They might as well have labeled themselves as terrorist transport services since there wasn't a dry cleaners for a hundred miles in any direction and their license plates were from Wyoming, a state in even less need of dry cleaning services. The lead van circled the lot while the trailing van pulled up close to the front door of the diner.

My cell phone vibrated. Elouise confirmed the white vans and sent a picture of a slender man, his head covered with a dark cap, stepping out of the van's side door. She caught him full face when he did a quick surveillance. Even with a blurred picture I could tell the man was Mohammed Abd Allah.

Both vans shifted around the parking lot in concentric circles until they found spots giving them nearly as good a view of the area as we had.

The rookie actions smelled wrong. Mohammed didn't improvise. He planned. In Abu Ghraib, where his freedom of action had been curtailed in every way imaginable, he planned our chess games, both moves and conversation. Now his crew barely arrived in time to cover the diner. Yet he'd chosen the meeting spot himself. If he'd picked a spot two hundred miles further west I'd have been the one winging it.

Mohammed sat in a window booth according to Elouise's text. Clearly he expected me to see him there. Mohammed had stage managed this meeting so his side would be rushed and off balance. On the chess board he would be drawing me in for checkmate, but in real life? We weren't playing chess. The end game here decided whether Chicago would be inhabitable for the next hundred years.

Time for me to go. I wasn't going to cross the parking lot without being seen by Mohammed's observers, so I turned my hat around, pulled my shirt out and generally made myself look like I needed to be comfortable after too many hours on the road. I walked purposefully away from the semis toward the diner.

A kitchen worker stepped out the back door with a bucket of something steaming and ugly. He dumped it into a dumpster then dropped the bucket upside down on the ground and relaxed in the noisome atmosphere to enjoy his smoke break. I wanted to sneak in the back of the diner, to throw Mohammed and his own watchers off balance, but I wasn't sneaking past the cook.

So I sauntered up to him, taking on the persona of just another trucker coming in from the rigs for the benefit of the watchers. The old man watched me approach, his face expressionless.

"Hey brother," I said choosing a path to the door that wasn't caked with years of spilled grease. "Can I buy a cigarette off ya?"

"Have one," he shook a Marlboro Red from his pack. The man was skinny with lean, ropy muscle and a face that might have been sixty or a hundred. Blurred tattoos reminiscent of the Marines decorated his bare arms. "They with you?" He pointed at the vans where Mohammed's men were on sentry.

I took the smoke and lit it for cover. "Not exactly, but I need to get inside the diner to talk to their boss. He's probably sitting at a booth facing the front door. I'd rather surprise him. Mind if I use the back door?"

"You a cop?" He squinted at me with eyes that had seen too much.

"No but I hope I'm one of the good guys."

"Go for it, Slick. Just don't make a mess of my diner." He made a point of looking at the bulge the 10 mm made in my jacket.

"Nothing going to happen here." I crossed my fingers around the grip of the .44 hidden under the back of my jacket and pushed open the battered back door.

The kitchen door faced a white wall separating the preparation area from the dining room with two swinging doors and a long pass-

252

thru window. The main doors blocked most of the diner from view but the pass-thru showed a good half of the patrons gathered at the counter exchanging stories over coffee and tuna specials.

Mohammed had seated himself at the far end of the diner where his view covered both of the entrance doorways. He split his attention between something in his hand and the front door. When I slipped into the seat in front of him his hand moved toward his coat as though to draw a gun, but then he smiled. "Hello Jason, my old friend."

"Assalam 'alaikam, Mohammed," I said.

He looked like any immigrant worker; brown skin, full mustache, worn Carhartt work jacket immaculately cleaned and pressed. His posture identified him something other than an itinerate laborer. He held himself as though he were ready to explain some point of philosophy or lead a prayer even though he sat in a greasy spoon a hundred miles from the nearest mosque.

"And may the blessings of the one true God be on you." He smiled at me with his lips but his eyes were cold and dark. "But we must be careful or the unbelievers will think we're Islamists."

"You've been working on your sense of humor. I like it." I slipped the .44 out of my back holster and held it between my legs, pointed at his crotch. I let him hear me pull the hammer back to full cock. "What are you thinking? You advocated peace when I knew you."

"You know there cannot be peace when there is so much evil in the world." He glanced at the table as though he could see the gun pointing at his manhood.

"I didn't think you were a jihadist. What changed you?"

"It's always jihad. The devil takes many forms. Do you know all the devils in this game?" Mohammed sighed, heavily, like a man who had carried a heavy burden for too many miles.

"I'm going out on a limb here and say no. Because if I did know all the devils you wouldn't tell me what you know."

Mohammed sat in silence as we contemplated each other. Finally he spoke. "Jack brought me into this country. Did you know that?"

"Yes. He said you were supposed to be an informant."

"He was told correctly. Put your gun away. I'm not your enemy," he hissed. "We only have a few minutes."

"Before what?"

"Before Ahkmed calls. He is a fool, but his brother, Amin, is a ruthless man. When he calls I must be someone I am not. For this moment you and I are brothers so I tell you, you should not have come." A fire burned in his eyes.

"I came for Lucy. Is she still alive?" I shifted uncomfortably in the booth aware of the doors at my back and the window at my side.

Mohammed lowered his voice to a near whisper. "The woman will be killed after they get what they want from you. Did you destroy the triggers?"

I leaned back and forced myself to relax. If jihadists stormed the diner or Mohammed decided to martyr himself, I wouldn't get out alive. I had a choice to make. Either believe him, or shoot the bastard. I de-cocked the pistol before I slipped it into my coat pocket and pulled out the last circuit board. "All but one. I figured I'd have to show good faith to get Lucy back."

"Good faith means nothing to these men. They will kill both of you as soon as they have possession of the circuit. And if they have the circuit board they will cause much horror and destruction." Mohammed hung his head.

"Do you have the nukes?"

"You know?" Mohammed nodded, paused. "No, not yet. But they are coming. Amin is bringing them."

"What game are you playing, Mohammed? You had Fiona steal this trigger from Jack. If you didn't want it, why not leave it alone?"

"This operation is not being run by one group with one goal. There are many motives. The man who had Jack killed would have taken the circuit board, just like Fiona did, and I don't know he would have destroyed it. I intended to destroy the damned thing and now you bring it here to trade for that woman? Pah. She's expendable. We are all expendable as long as those awful weapons are never used as Amin desires."

"Don't worry about the trigger. It won't be functional. But I will get Lucy back alive. Or there will be a sudden influx of martyrs into whatever after life accepts them."

"You're crazy." Mohammed looked away, and scanned the diner behind me.

The skin in the middle of my back started to crawl, but I refused to take my eyes off of him. "I'll stop you, and your friends, no matter what."

"They are not my friends. I have infiltrated a very dangerous sleeper cell with the help of your government, among others, who want these maniacs stopped. Amin is a sleeper agent and has risen to a high rank in the Air Force, specifically to steal nuclear weapons." Mohammed's face softened and his eyes showed great sadness. "Why don't you believe me?"

"Jack didn't believe you. He thought he was being tested by a mole in the FBI or Homeland Security." If I believed Jack, I couldn't believe Mohammed, but what advantage did Mohammed get from the destruction of the triggers?

"I'm sorry. Jack never liked me. But we are brothers, you and I." Mohammed glanced at his phone.

"Prove it. I want Lucy back, in one piece." The phone buzzed. "Then I'll make sure your friends don't leave the country with our toys."

Mohammed looked at me with sad, unblinking eyes and nodded. "Okay, Jason. As you want it. Remember, I am playing a role now."

Mohammed picked up the phone on the second ring and growled, "Ahkmed."

"Let him see," echoed from the tiny speakers in Arabic. Mohammed turned his phone around so I could the screen. The other phone camera focused on a shape struggling in the shadows of a small space. Ahkmed continued to speak in Arabic while Mohammed translated. "Mr. Smiley. We have your office woman. Do you have the circuit board you took from Fiona?"

"Show me it's Lucy. The picture is too dark." Or more importantly, as I stared at the struggling form on the screen, duct tape covered her mouth, arms and body duct taped to a chair. How badly had they hurt her? Would she be able to help me during her rescue? Someone uncovered a window and sunlight flooded the picture blanking her out for a moment as the camera adjusted.

The phone closed in on her. She had several bruises on her face. One eye had swollen nearly shut, but her other sparkled with an icy-blue hatred that should have frightened the man in front of her.

"As you see, this is her. She is not an obedient woman or we wouldn't have used duct tape on her. But shall we say the deal is her life for the circuit card?" Mohammed shook his head like Lucy should have been glad to let him kidnap her.

I looked hard at Lucy. She was alive. The tension in her body, the fury exuding from her good eye told me what I needed to know. I forced myself to unclench my fists. "Sure. Let's do the trade here and now."

"No, we'll do the trade where we'll attract less attention." Mohammed translated. The shadowy man on the phone nodded, apparently satisfied with the deal.

"Where?" I said. "Did you plan on taking her to dinner and a movie, first?"

"We don't have time for games. Our schedule is driven by forces beyond our control. Inshallah. We will find a less public spot for our exchange." Mohammed translated.

"You better bring Lucy, alive and walking." The animal started growling inside me. True or not, Mohammed's act convinced the animal and I didn't try to hide it in my voice. "Otherwise I will kill all of you."

"Certainly, my friend, but since we are exchanging threats, cheat me and she will die as slowly as time permits." Mohammed closed the phone connection and as he slid out of the booth, his persona shifted back. "Please wait here until I leave. I will do what I can to keep her alive. Do not let the circuit fall into their hands. Promise me?"

"I'm not going to aid and abet a nuclear holocaust, Mohammed. There will be no card. I'm not sure I believe you, but I want Lucy alive and well, whatever it takes."

"But I believe you, Sergeant Smiley. I need to tell you though, these are dangerous men. You are just one man." Mohammed shook his head.

"Inshallah," I said.

Confusion flashed across his face. I had surprised him one more time. Now all I had to do was trust Elouise the ghost, and Tommy the hitman would back my play.

26. THE LUCY TRADE

One of the road-dirt covered dry cleaning vans pulled up in front of the diner as Mohammed stepped out the front door. The van's side door opened while the vehicle did a slow roll. The driver accelerated hard as soon as Mohammed jumped inside. The second van followed the first out of the parking lot with tires smoking.

I dropped a twenty on the table by the untouched coffees and exited through the kitchen. The old cook nodded at me as I walked through. The young kids washing dishes and cutting apples ignored me. I pushed out the back door. Trust had become a rare commodity and Mohammed tried to buy up all I had. What would make me trust him? If he didn't kill Lucy and me when I brought them the circuit board? A breach of faith would be fatal.

So I couldn't give him a chance. But trusting Elouise and Tommy the Fisherman to watch my back felt very risky. Elouise might have some stake in stopping Mohammed and his playmates from blowing up the nukes and maybe she could keep the Fisherman in line.

"Jason?" Elouise stepped out of the shadows behind the dumpster. "What happened in there?"

"I'm going to trade the trigger for Lucy. Mohammed's acting schizophrenic and I don't know what his game is. If you're willing to get your hands dirty, I think I can pull this off." I looked around for the hitman. "Where's Tommy?"

"Around front, watching the main door. He'll bring the car back here." Elouise tapped on her cell. "You're not going to give them the trigger are you?"

I opened the screwdriver blade on my Swiss army knife and broke the chip on the trigger like I had on the other eleven. "Yeah, I'm going to give it to them but they aren't going to like me very much when I do. I need some things out the trunk, but I don't want to flash the war chest in public. We need to go someplace private to prepare for the trade."

Tommy pulled up with the Jag.

"Get in the front Jason. I'll access anything we need from the back seat." Elouise slid into the rear and opened a compartment into the trunk.

"Tommy, did you see which way the bad guys went?" I dropped into the passenger seat and slammed the door closed.

"Yeah. Heading east but they passed the exit for the interstate." Tommy slouched at the wheel making it very clear he had graduated from wheelman a long time ago.

"Let's follow them. Mohammed is supposed to call me with an exact location but I want time to set up before the trade." Tommy gave me a slow quizzical stare then he glanced at the rearview mirror. He relaxed again, after getting a reassuring nod from Elouise. My trust factor went down a couple of more notches. The non-verbal dialog looked an awful lot like one team member quizzing the other on legitimacy of the latest order.

"What did you require, Jason?" Elouise asked. She held up an M4 and a bandoleer of magazines.

"Yeah, I'll take one of those... and one of the fragmentation grenades, and the duct tape out of your kidnapping kit."

"It's not a kidnapping kit." She hid a smile by turning away to dig out the kit. "Just some everyday maintenance supplies."

Elouise checked the loads on the M4s while I taped the circuit to the grenade. I exposed enough to identify the component but not so much to expose the damage I done to it. "There's going to be multiple bad guys. Do you have any objections, personal or business, to eliminating these men as threats?"

Elouise raised an eyebrow with a slight upturn to the corner of her mouth. "I prefer not to use violence. That doesn't mean I haven't killed." She slapped the magazine home in the rifle, charged the weapon and engaged the safety.

"Boss," Tommy cut in. His eyes flickered to the rearview mirror. "I just saw one of their vans turn into that driveway."

"Pull off the road just out of sight. He'll be calling soon." I checked the cell phone for power and bars. Both good. I loaded the mapping application and located the driveway the van had turned into. The aerial imagery showed a group of buildings with a series of parking lots separated by tree lined medians. The edge of the business park consisted of dense forest.

Elouise leaned over the seat to consider the electronic situation map. "Tommy and I can move in and provide interdiction with the rifles. We're not going to get 300 yard kill shots with the M-4s but we should get 200 yard center of mass shots."

Tommy stared at her, mouth slightly open, as Elouise demonstrated her command of the language of professional murder.

"Tommy, can you shoot accurately at 200 yards?" she asked.

"Qualified expert on all small arms when I was in the Marines. I'd have gone to sniper school but I didn't pass the psych-eval." He grinned. "They thought I wouldn't have the patience."

"You are a little eager," I said. "Plus the up close head shot is a little bit too..."

"Personal?" He laughed out loud. "That's because I don't want the poor bastards to know they're dead until they are. And it's not as messy. Pow ping. The bullet rattles around inside their head for a second and then they're down. No fuss, no muss."

"You're such a thoughtful guy." I checked again to make sure I was carrying full loads and fresh magazines for my pistols. "Tommy, find a position in those woods where you can lay down suppressing fire as soon as Lucy is in the clear. Watch the guy with the grenade in his hands. He's going to be nervous. Elouise, I want you to stay concealed in the car and provide close back up in case this transfer goes to shit."

They both nodded.

"And one more thing. Don't kill Mohammed if you don't have to. He claims he's undercover and he's helping us save Lucy."

"Undercover?" Elouise's accent thickened. "Bloody hell. He was one of my instructors in Chechnya. He is an expert at deception. You cannae trust the bastid."

"I don't trust him. But the only way he can prove himself is by not killing me and Lucy. So please, don't put him to the test? I don't want him killed, but I don't trust him."

The burn phone rang. I picked it up. "Mohammed."

"Sgt. Smiley. I'm here with your dear friend Ms. Diamonds. Do you want to speak with her?"

"Yeah." I kept my voice even. Mohammed as the terrorist had become the most believable version.

"Jason? WHERE THE HELL ARE YOU? Don't you give these ragheaded, cocksuckers anything..." Lucy's rant was cut off by a muffled thud and a stifled cry.

"You Americans really should train your women better, Jason.

They don't know their place." More shuffling noises in the background and some high-pitched muffled curses. "Now here are the directions..." He rattled off driving instructions from the diner to the office complex parking lot I had located on the cell phone. "Be there in fifteen minutes or Miss Diamonds starts losing parts. And I might start with her tongue."

* * *

I eased the Jag into a driveway flanked with decorative rows of conifers. Mohammed had said to turn 'at the pine trees.' Elouise crouched on the back floor under a jacket in case we were stopped. Two watchers at the edge of the driveway faded into the shadows as I passed them.

More trees shielded the array of office buildings from the road. The spring sun had just slipped below the horizon and few of the offices were still lit. Two vans waited in an isolated corner, near the wood line where Tommy would be set up with his scoped rifle.

The shoebox lighting fixtures scattered across the parking lot threw more shadows than illumination. I parked the Jag under one of the light poles about thirty feet from Mohammed and on a diagonal, like a bishop on a chessboard. I had a clear view of the vans and the light behind me would spoil their night vision. The angle would let Elouise exit the car without observation and give her cover.

I flicked the headlights high-low-high to signal intentions and to blind a sniper in the trees on the right, then left the hi-beams on, but turned off the interior lights. "Try and cover me without them seeing you. I don't trust them to figure out shooting me blows up the circuit board before I tell them."

"Be careful with the grenade, Jason," Elouise whispered as she slipped her M4 into the front seat. "Leave your door open."

I checked the safety tape I had placed over the grenade's spoon. When I pulled the pin, the spring loaded spoon would fly away and act as a trigger to start the, hopefully, five second fuse. One Mississippi, two Mississippi, three Mississippi then throw it as far as you can. Except instead of throwing the grenade I would trade it and the circuit board for Lucy. So I secured the safety tape and tabbed it so it could be pulled off with ease.

I sucked in a deep breath, opened the door, raised the grenade and circuit board above my head so they could see it in the spill of the street light, and pulled the pin. "Yo, Mohammed, tell your boys to be careful. I have the circuit board taped to this grenade and I just pulled the pin." I tossed the pin towards the vans.

"Jason." Mohammed stepped out of the shadows.

A stocky man with an AK-47 stood at his side, the rifle raised and pointed in my general direction. His attitude and behavior identified him as the Ahkmed Mohammed had talked to. I pulled the .44 and pointed it in his direction.

"Why do you bring threats and weapons? This is a peaceful exchange." Mohammed's voice lacked any inflection. Had he made his peace with Allah? Did he expect to end me here?

I didn't want to believe it. "To make sure the meeting stays peaceful. The circuit board is taped to the grenade, and the pin is on the ground between us. Send Lucy over with someone to carry the package back. Your man can stop and get the pin on his return."

The man with the gun rattled off some guttural Arabic that exceeded my Rosetta Stone vocabulary but didn't sound very complimentary. Mohammed nodded, differentially, at the man and made a calm-down gesture with the palm of his hand. He turned back to me. "You're being so dramatic, Jason, like your American movies. We made a deal. There is no need for such steps. Put your pin back in and we'll get on with our business."

Behind him the other jihadists shifted around trying to keep me covered and not put their boss in the line of fire. I counted four men with AK-47s including the one standing next to Mohammed, plus Mohammed, and a driver in each of the vans, plus two guards at the entrance which left room in the vans for one to three effectives wandering around trying to get position to take me and Lucy when Ahkmed had the circuit. I heard something like a tin can getting kicked come from the woods, indicating Tommy had found one of the missing jihadists.

"Sorry, I don't have the pin. Best we get on with it. I want Lucy and I want safe passage before you get the trigger, and my hand is getting tired."

Ahkmed said something to Mohammed and waved at the vans. In a moment a wannabe terrorist appeared dragging Lucy by the duct tape around her hands. The duct tape bound her legs like shackles, enough for her to shuffle but not enough room for her to run to keep up with her jailer. She stumbled and fell as he dragged her in front of Ahkmed and Mohammed.

"Cut her free," I yelled. Mohammed didn't hesitate to cut her bonds with a swift slice of a box cutter, careless of drawing a little blood. Painfully stiff, Lucy rose awkwardly to her feet. Mohammed and Ahkmed both spoke rapidly at the guard, whose eyes grew wide. Lucy locked her eyes on me like she wanted to connect telepathically. Her training in the intelligence world had encouraged her to understand several Middle Eastern languages and she, no doubt, understood every direction. She just couldn't tell me. I had to assume they weren't discussing my future happiness.

When Ahkmed finished his instructions, he pushed Lucy and her guard forward. Lucy hesitated while she worked the kinks out of her legs, but the guard, trying to reassert some authority, pushed her. She kept her balance and with every step her stride became less crippled and more deliberate.

The guard prodded her in her back with his rifle. When they got within three paces of my position he stopped her with a hand on her shoulder. I raised the grenade and stepped close, sweeping her behind me with one hand while the guard stared open mouthed at the grenade. "Lucy, get back to the car. Mohammed, tell your boy to sling his weapon. He really ought to carry this package with both hands."

I waited. Ahkmed looked like he didn't like the odds of getting the chip before the grenade went off. I didn't blame him.

The guard apparently understood my request and sweated heavily as he looked at the bomb held over his head. Ahkmed grunted something in colloquial Arabic I couldn't understand. The man in front of me hooked the strap of his rifle around his neck and slung it out of his way. With a nervous lick of his lips he held out his hands.

Anyone would be afraid. While a man's alive, he doesn't want to die, but there's a certain fatalism that comes to those who've been in combat. This man didn't have it. The guards behind Mohammed moved nervously. These weren't seasoned mujahedeen. They were wannabes who had enjoyed the freedom from violence and sudden death our society provided while their distant cousins fought the best army in the world. They were pussy terrorists. Lots of big talk and one or two idiots who might blow themselves up to see the seventy-two virgins, but they didn't know combat. We had a big advantage.

I smiled. "Here you go." I peeled the safety tape off before placing the grenade carefully in his outstretched hands and wrapping his sweaty fingers around the spoon. The terror in his eyes and sharp stench of urine provided some comic relief after the last couple of days. "Now back up." I said. "And don't look down. The pin is over there."

He took a quick panicked look at his feet and the stain in his pants, then back at me with his eyes wide. I shooed him back with my hand and focused on the man Mohammed had deferred to. Mohammed drew a little away and watched the approach of the trigger with shrouded face. His body language warned me a line had been preset for the hidden jihadists to kill us. Ahkmed had his rifle raised and trained on me as I backed towards the car.

"Nice arsenal, boss. Who have you been hanging out with?" Lucy spoke sotto voce behind me and then I heard the sharp metallic sound of an M-4 being charged. "He's going to shoot you, as soon as he gets the thing."

"Chill, Luce. This isn't over yet." I picked a couple of competent looking terrorists as my initial targets for when the shooting started. "And don't shoot Mohammed. I promised I wouldn't kill him if I got you back."

"He's the only one I don't want to kill."

The terrified terrorist had taken about three steps backwards when another metallic cough echoed from the wood line. Tommy had worked his way in close. One of the men with Mohammed slipped to the ground. His friends started calling frantically, waving their guns at the horizon, the moon and myself. Ahkmed dropped his gun's sight line and called out what I clearly understood as: Shoot them.

When nothing happened, he yelled at the man carrying the grenade. As the man turned, his head erupted. Blood splashed silver in the parking lot lights. The spoon flew into the air as the grenade fell to the ground and bounced. I shot the poor bastard in the back with the .44 hoping he'd fall onto the grenade. Ducking behind the car door I counted "three Mississippi, four Mississip——" The exploding grenade rocked the Jag.

More bodies fell by Mohammed including Ahkmed. Mohammed stood for a moment looking at the dead man smoking in the parking lot. His mouth moved. "Inshallah." Then he ran to the first van. A three-round burst, from the woods, splattered the whole windshield with blood. Tommy the Fisherman wasn't lying when he said he could shoot a rifle. From the relative safety of the Jag I dropped one of the amateur terrorists foolish enough to stand still and shoot wildly into the night.

Mohammed backpedaled just as another burst tore the space where he'd been standing. He hit something unexpected in the shadows. Suddenly I saw Elouise slip into the second van with him. I tried a couple of shots but the first van shielded the cab of the second and any other shot might hit Elouise. The van reversed in a cloud of smoke and screeching tires.

I stood there with my face hanging open in shock. Why would she leave with Mohammed?

A poorly directed round got my attention. The two guards from the entrance ran at us spraying bullets randomly in my direction. I dropped behind the Jag and reached for an M4. Before I could shoulder a weapon, Lucy sent two, three-round bursts downrange, killing the men with brutal efficiency.

"Nice, Lucy. Thanks." I said through the open car door. "Where did you learn to shoot like that?"

"The Air Force. And John taught me to be thorough." Lucy's dead husband.

"Hell, yeah..." I looked in the direction Mohammed had gone, then back at Lucy. "Fuck me."

Duct tape had left the skin around her mouth raw, and several bruises on the left side her face swollen, but her eyes were bright. She seemed to like field work. "Nice to see you, too, Boss. I wondered how you were going to get me out of there." She threw her rifle to shoulder and looked ready to shoot. I followed her gaze behind me where Tommy the Fisherman had come in from his high cover. Sirens wailed in the distance. People cowered closer than should be considered safe, probably hoping to see some action.

"Stand down, Lucy. Tommy's on our side." I waved him in.

Tommy looked nervously at the distance where the sirens wailed. "We gotta get out of here. Cops are coming. Where is she?"

"I'm right here." Lucy stood beside me, M-4 at the ready.

"Not her. Ms. Blankenship." Tommy scanned the battlefield.

"Mohammed took her." I said

His eyes got the cold killer stare. "Well let's get her back. What are you waiting for?"

"Where are they going? I've got no clues." I kicked the door. "And she looked like she went willingly."

Lucy chimed in. "They're talking about a rendezvous in St. Paul."

"Cops are coming. We need to blow." Tommy edged towards the Jag.

"All right." I tossed the smart cell phone to Lucy. "Maybe Isaacson can keep the cops at bay. We can't waste time explaining all these dead people. But we can't leave yet. Tommy, you and I need to look for clues."

Tommy glared at me, then shrugged and started searching the dead. The driver of the first van had been luckier than his brothers. Only one of the three rounds the Fisherman threw his way had penetrated bone deep in the shoulder with no exit, leaving the man injured but conscious.

And afraid. He wanted help in the worst way. He didn't want to see Allah. Maybe he wasn't sure he'd make it across the bridge into heaven, let alone get seventy-two virgins. "Help me, for the love of your God, help me."

"Sure. Where are your friends going in such a hurry?" I poked at his injured arm. He flinched away.

"I don't know. How would I know? I'm just a little man. I'm just a driver." His eyes darted from side to side.

"And how were you getting your directions?" I asked as Tommy sidled up next to me. He looked at the terrified man with a blank faced curiosity as if humbly admiring his handiwork.

The wounded man's eyes rolled but he didn't say anything more. I leaned towards Tommy and casually said, "Nice shooting. That's a very tight group for the distance and on automatic. If he'd been sitting up straight all three would have caught him in the chest."

Our prisoner shut his eyes as though the sight of his would-be executioner would blind him. "The GPS box. It tells me how to go to the next destination. Please that's all I know. Please."

"Sure, no problem." I yanked the GPS off of the dash. "C'mon Tommy. Let's go."

"Sure, Boss. Just one second." Before I could stop him, Tommy pulled his .22 and put two silenced rounds in the man's forehead. "Rule number one. No witnesses."

I glared at the cold blooded murderer. "I'll remember that when the time comes."

27. INTERCEPT AT ST. PAUL

Lucy pulled the Jaguar up next to the van. Red lights glowed in the distance. No doubt we were getting a full-out SWAT response from the State Police. They wouldn't take very kindly to dead bodies lying around the parking lot.

"We gotta go, Boss," she said.

"I'll drive, you sit in the back," I flicked my eyes towards Tommy, staring blankly at the oncoming cop cars. She nodded slightly as I passed her the GPS. "I need you to work comms and navigate."

Lucy levitated into the back seat; I dropped into the driver's seat. "C'mon, Tommy." He eased into the passenger's seat——I had the car rolling before he got the door closed.

I eased the Jag towards the parking lot exit. "Are we going to be chased by the local responders?"

"Naw, Boss. I contacted General Isaacson, king of the spooks, on his private cell and got him to interrupt the hot pursuit of a terrorist attack on the outskirts of St. Paul." Lucy deadpanned her delivery and left the punch line hanging.

Tommy, suddenly returned to life, turned around to stare at Lucy and gushed. "Wow. You really got the cops to back-off with a phone call? Shit, even Vinnie T would have to pay big cash to make that happen. Especially after..." He hooked a finger out the window at the scattered bodies in the parking lot and the approaching crowd of interested citizens.

"You aren't kidding are you?" I said just as a wave of police and other responders pulled in. The lead vehicle held the rest so we could make our exit.

"Would I kid you, Boss?" Lucy answered with a twinkle in her eye. There were things I would never know. She examined the GPS and powered it up. "I see you got their map. You aren't going to believe what he's going to do."

"First, tell me which way to turn." The road we were on ended at a cross street.

"Left, towards Minneapolis." Lucy leaned between the seats and stuck the GPS on the dash. "I know where they're going. I heard Mohammed discussing their plans with Ahkmed." The game face slipped a bit. "Boss, they're hijacking a shipment of nuclear warheads scheduled for disposal."

"Yeah, I know." The trigger had been the smallest part of the holy grail of terrorist attacks. And with the FBI looking the other way. "Maybe he won't be able to detonate them without the circuit board. We don't ship functioning bombs for disposal, right? Maybe all we have to do is catch him and stop him from selling off the material?"

Lucy shook her head. "They're not planning on selling it. The triggers were the guarantee. It allowed them to set off multiple blasts remotely. This was always going to be a martyrship operation. They were making their final preparations while we were waiting for you."

"They didn't seem like very good martyrs."

"Mostly just kids caught up in the stories the recruiters tell at Mosque. Their parents came here to get away from people like them," she said. "There were a couple though, that were hardcore believers. I think they were sleeper agents, they spoke Farsi, but like they hadn't spoken the language in a very long time."

They had talked freely around her either because they didn't think she understood or they planned on killing her anyway. The latter I suspected, yet I caught the glint of a tear in Lucy's eye.

Tommy turned around. "Jeeze, how many languages do you speak?"

"Aside from English and Spanish? Arabic, Farsi, Kurdish, Pashto, Russian, a bit of Korean and Mandarin." Lucy smiled. "And who are you?"

"My name is Tommy the Fisherman. I kill people." Tommy smiled.

Lucy squinted, as she pushed the muzzle of the M-4 into the back of Tommy's head. "I do, too," she said in her telephone voice.

"Jeeze, lady, we hit a bump and my head goes all over the windshield." Tommy flinched back. He looked at me. "Are all of your women this tough?"

I glared back at the Fisherman, remembering the frightened driver he shot. "While we're working together I expect you to refrain from random murder."

Tommy's eyes became cold, gray marbles. He shrugged.

"Should I be watching my back?" I asked. Lucy looked up and shifted slightly in the rearview mirror, to get the M-4 into position behind Tommy's back.

The Fisherman grinned, at last. "Like I'd tell you?" He let his seat lay back and closed his eyes. "We're going to get Ms. Blankenship. Worry about the rest later."

"Yeah, sure. After we get Elouise." Assuming she wanted to be gotten. She'd left on her own and didn't look like she had been threatened. In fact, as I thought about those few moments, it almost seemed like she pushed Mohammed to flee. Obviously her job had been to find him, but why?

* * *

We flew through the night. Tommy snored in the passenger's seat with Lucy's M4 pushed against his back, one sensitive trigger release from spraying his guts on the windshield. I vibrated, and tried not to think about the men I killed.

Lucy had moved into operations mode. She made call after quick call on the cell to people on her net. The interior lights didn't show much, but she'd had a rough time at the terrorist's hand.

"All right," she crowed at the phone as she clicked off. "I got it, Boss. Nuclear warheads from Minot Air Force Base were shipped out by rail yesterday. That's got to be our target."

"I thought operational security rules mandated truck convoys?" I dredged that tidbit from a conversation with a safety officer years ago.

"Brave new world, Boss. The terrorist threat has been downgraded to nothing for the last six months." Lucy's eyes sparkled.

"Even with the FBI and Homeland Security looking for Mohammed the terror suspect?"

"Dunno, Boss. But the shipment from Minot is in the St. Paul rail yard waiting for another engine to take it to Texas and the dismantling plant. It's being made up right now and will be leaving in half an hour. This is Mohammed's opportunity to board the train." Lucy paused for a moment. "Ahkmed was supposed to meet his brother Amin at the rail yard. I don't know how many men Amin has with him."

"Aren't there federal police guarding this shipment?"

"My contacts say policy came down to keep these transfers low profile so they don't draw attention. Besides, the rail company has a very tough police force," Lucy reported. "Assuming they're on duty."

The stench of corruption surrounded this operation. "Somebody's been fiddling this job from the inside. What's our ETA?"

"10 minutes at the speed you're driving. But we're going to lose time through Minneapolis."

"Like hell we will."

* * *

Light Sunday night traffic let me keep my word. We arrived at the immense rail yard in St. Paul by Pig's Eye Lake. The GPS led us to a dirt road. A fence secured the site with lit guard houses at every access point, including the one at the end of the road we followed.

A mile ahead of us a delivery van bounced at high speed on the rough surface and slid to a stop in front of the guard house. I shut off the lights and idled down the road. If anyone looked our way we would stand out against the St. Paul skyline. I stopped about five hundred yards back and brought up the binoculars.

The guard opened the gate for the van and two shadowy forms got out, one tall and one short, probably Mohammed and Elouise. I grabbed an M4. "Lucy, wait here. Tommy and I are going in."

The Fisherman and I ran through the shadows. Mohammed appeared to be the only one to have survived the fire fight, but other shadowy figures moved around the cars as the engines attached to the rolling stock. The cars were military style vehicle transports, regular automotive carriers but with a perforated metal roof and walls like rolling Quonset huts with air holes. Kids throughout the country marked the cars with graffiti brags and gang tags. Mohammed and Elouise climbed in the third car from the end. Some creative soul had painted the whole side with a rising sun.

The airbrakes released on the train before we'd covered half of the distance. The men providing security on the ground jumped on the last car, a flatbed with a half sized container box on it.

The remaining guard walked back to the gate as the train started rolling. He climbed in the abandoned van and backed it beyond the fence so he could close the gate. Tommy and I slipped up behind him. I rocked the hammer back on my .44 just as the barrel touched the erstwhile guard's head.

"Please don't make any sudden movements. Your head will disappear if you do," I whispered in his ear. The guard froze, hands up in the air. "Very good, now do you know where that train is going?"

The man turned around to look at me. His eyes got wide as he looked down the barrel of the Smith and Wesson. Up close the .44's barrel looks like the deck gun on a battleship. I was pretty sure he'd be impressed.

"No, man. I don't know nothin', man. Put that thing away, will you." Under the light the man looked like any regular Joe from the neighborhood. A homegrown terrorist.

"Hey, I know you," he said dropping his arms a little. "You're the cop that did Vinnie T. Your face has been all over TV."

"Everybody should have their fifteen minutes of fame."

"Joey Turturro." The Fisherman slid up close like a cat examining a mouse. "You used to be on the Midtown crew. Whatcha' doin' out here?"

The man cowered against the side of the van. "Jesus Christ, Tommy. You scared the shit outta me. What're you doin' with this cop?"

"Staying alive, bro. That's the name of the game. What's up with the train? Don't look like no passenger train." Tommy cupped his hand around the gangster's head and applied pressure at a sensitive point. As the tears flowed out of the goombah's eyes, fear filled them.

The train began picking up speed as it moved out of the switch yard.

"Where is the train going?" I asked again. Tommy nodded. The gangster's eyes rolled from me to Tommy and back.

"Danny Shoe gonna kill me if I tell you shit. C'mon, man."

Tommy pulled out his .22, stuck it in the man's mouth, pulled the trigger on an empty chamber. The air stunk with urine. "Joey, the piss wad," Tommy said. "Now tell us the deal. What's Danny Shoe got to do with the train and where the fuck is it goin'?"

"Christ, Tommy, I'm fuckin' dead..."

Tommy racked a round in the chamber.

"Okay, Okay, It's going to Chicago. Danny's got a deal with the ragheads and the Triad. Lots of money selling this stuff off shore. They're gonna' take the bombs and transfer them to a ship. We run the rail yards and the trucks so we get our cut up front."

"You guys are scum." I wanted to pistol whip the cocky little bastard. "Those are nuclear warheads. Weapons of mass destruction? What are you greedy fucks thinking working with terrorists?"

"Naw. That's the fun part. I got a cousin who used to work for the Air Force. They completely disable the bombs before they ship them. No way to blow them up." Joey relaxed when Tommy lowered his gun. "We good, now?"

"So, no harm, no foul? Everyone gets a little good stuff and a glass of wine?" I de-cocked and re-cocked the hammer on the .44 just to watch him tense up with fear, again. "What else?"

"That's all I know, man." His eyes rolled between Tommy and me like he hoped someone would believe him.

Tommy shot him in the foot. Joey screamed and fell to the ground. "Why the fuck did you do that?"

"You're holding back on us. Boss man here can call the railroad and have them stop the train. You know something else."

Joey cowered on the ground. "No...n...n...no."

Tommy shot him in the ankle. Joey screamed some more. At close range the Fisherman's .22s would play hell on all those tiny bones. Even immediate medical attention would require amputation.

I suppose I should have stopped him, but I saw a double-double cross happening. The mob didn't know Amin wanted to blow up Chicago.

"Well," I said to Joey. "How's he going to keep me from stopping the train? These things are all computer operated anymore."

"They've got a guy who knows how to fix the controls," Joey whimpered.

That sounded like Mohammed. Find the simple solution to a problem and then make the problem go away. He must have had far more to do with the planning of this mission than he'd said.

"I guess that's it. Let's go."

Tommy raised his gun.

"And do you have to kill him?" Joey squirmed in the mud, in pain and pleading for his life with his eyes. I felt sad that I didn't have any sympathy left for him. "As a soldier, I try not to kill the defenseless enemy."

"This fuck would kill your mother and jerk off on her corpse," Tommy said. "Some people are just better off dead." He put two rounds in Joey's forehead and turned away.

"I suppose you have a point," I said as the last car rolled out of sight. "Now we have to catch the damn train."

28. CATCHING A TRAIN

Lucy skidded the Jag to a stop, showering Tommy and me with dust and stones.

"Boss, you got a phone call." Lucy handed me the cell through the open window. "It's Isaacson"

I took the phone with a sudden tension in my gut. He hadn't called one of the burn phones we'd been using, so it wasn't a back trace. He'd called Elouise's portable office-in-a-phone. Why would the General have Blankenship's phone number, unless he needed to communicate with her on a professional basis?

The number of people I trusted in the world just got smaller. I put on my best dumb-Joe attitude. "General, sir."

"What's the situation?" Isaacson's voice carried tension. His understanding of the situation probably eclipsed mine, but I had to play along.

278

"Subject heading east on a train. One captive. It's a Broken Arrow." I had no idea if that was the current code word for loose nuclear weapons, but the intent would be clear to anyone who had seen the John Travolta movie.

"Mohammed has boarded the train? Who is the captive?" Tension radiated through the phone.

"Elouise Blankenship."

"Okay. Good job, Sergeant." He paused, breathing deeply as he struggled for his professional distance again. "Give me your coordinates and I'll have some assets meet up with you."

I slipped into the driver's seat and indicated for Lucy to get in the front passenger's seat. "Sir, I have an opportunity to end this situation and rescue the hostage. I'm taking it."

"I want you to stay where you are, Sergeant. I'll take care of Mohammed and the train." The steel edge of command in his voice grated on me. "Now give me your location."

"I can't stand down. The terror cell is intent on setting off a nuclear weapon near Chicago." I kept my voice even and professional. An NSA recording of this conversation might be useful at the inquest.

"That's not going to happen, soldier. We've got it under control. Just stand down, and let us handle the rest. You've done a hell of a job." His tone of voice switched to the same false bonhomie he'd greeted me with in Chicago when he sent me on this long, wild chase.

Something was very wrong. He didn't ask what locomotive number, didn't ask what rail line or anything operational that might let him put assets on the train. He just wanted me to stay out of the way. I held the device out at arm's length. Elouise's phone. No doubt he already knew our location. I tossed it, with the General still talking, into the ditch. Then I blew it to hell with the .44.

Lucy looked out of the car with concern on her face. "What did you do that for?"

"The General isn't very trustworthy." I re-holstered my gun and

279

shifted the car into gear. "There is a mole very high in the Homeland security hierarchy, and I'm pretty sure Isaacson knows who it is. I don't trust him at all. Second, I need to know if you think Mohammed is undercover and working against the jihadists. You spent a lot of time with those clowns."

Lucy frowned. I gunned the car in the direction of the interstate while she fiddled with the GPS. "I'm not sure. If he was undercover, who would he work for? The only thing I can be sure of is he wasn't the cruel and abusive one."

"He said he was 'playing a role'. He promised you would be delivered to me alive."

"He did say that, but maybe so I could report it to you. It's very hard to pretend ignorance when people are arguing about when to kill you." Lucy shivered.

"What side was Mohammed on?" I wanted any clue. We had two choices. Board the train somehow and take control of the nukes or convince the Powers-That-Be they needed to blow the train up somewhere before Chicago, which would spread nuclear waste and pieces of Elouise all around the countryside.

"He insisted I would be of more use if I wasn't killed until after they killed you." Lucy lifted an eyebrow at the choice between getting killed now or later.

"Well, either he's a cynical, manipulating bastard or he has a lot of faith in my ability in staying alive." I checked the GPS it showed us paralleling the train track. "Let's see if we can get on the train. I need you to get a location. And if there is any way to make the train slow down long enough for Tommy and me to get on."

Lucy's fingers flew across the smartphone's keypad. "God, I wish we had a virtual terminal to plug into this."

Tommy leaned across the seats. "We're going to stop the train and get Ms. Blankenship off?"

"We've got get on the train. Not sure if we can keep it stopped." I said.

"We could blow up the tracks? That'd stop the train," Tommy grinned.

"Probably knock it off the tracks. Probably kill Elouise." I said. "Besides I don't think we have anything stronger in the trunk than the fragmentation grenades."

Tommy frowned. "Then we kill them all, one at a time. I'm good with that."

I looked in the rearview mirror at the Fisherman. With his mind settled on slaughter, he closed his eyes and went to sleep. The speedometer flickered at ninety-five as we swept down the back road.

Lucy yelped. "Got it."

"What've you got?" I glanced at her.

"The train that Mohammed swiped is BNSF 9999. We've got a fix on the train from their Positive Train Control monitoring." She tried to show me the screen but I couldn't see it as we jiggled down the country road at a speed not reasonable nor prudent.

"How the hell did you get into that?" I said.

Lucy threw me a knowing grin. "I've got friends. And I lie a lot."

"Tricks you learned working for the Air Force?" I said. "How far is the train?"

"It's about ten miles away." She grinned. "I think I can get them to override the local controls and stop it."

"Wait a minute. That's too easy. The goombah at the rail yard said they had a guy to disable the controls." I banged my hands against the wheel. "What're the chances Mohammed has thought about the train being bombed and derailed? Isaacson could get that done."

"Mohammed's no fool, Jason." Lucy looked up from the phone. "He knows no one will take out the train."

"He knows Isaacson won't take the train out? He could blow the engine off the track and derail the train with little real damage to the rails or the bombs."

"From what I heard, I think you're right. There is a very high placed conspiracy and they have a very detailed plan with a lot of high level players covering for them. You might not get an air strike. Certainly not in time." She returned her attention to the phone.

With Lucy navigating, we tore through the darkness. The chase wasn't as easy as catching the train and jumping on like some old western. The locomotive quickly got up to speed when it left the city and the tracks cut across country. The closest roads bent and wove around ponds and farms, sometimes running parallel to the tracks but a thousand feet away, sometimes turning away in a different direction. Even with the greater speed of the Jaguar we covered nearly seventy miles before we caught more than a glimpse of the train.

"Luce, what was Mohammed's job with the terror cell?" I asked as I slowed the car as we entered a hamlet.

"He was the operations guy. He took care of the details. He paid for gas and food. He directed the rest stops and made sure they didn't attract attention to themselves." Lucy looked up from her phone. "He made them stop at rest areas for me."

"So he's been instrumental in planning this operation? Or just in making it work?"

"I'd say planning. He and Ahkmed and Amin would be on the phone several times a day."

"I played chess with Mohammed," I said. "He used to set traps for me to lose a bishop or a queen. But there was always one way out of the trap, if I could find it. He used those traps as a teaching moment."

"Okay, genius," Lucy said. "What are you going to do?"

"Well, first I'm going to postulate Mohammed wants our help. If he does, there will be a way to stop the train," I nodded at the night. "What's that PTSD system?"

"PTC, Positive Train Control. The trains are outfitted with sensors and computers that communicate to the controlling region office. The office computer looks for critical situations and makes sure the train is doing what it's supposed to do, like stop."

"And we think this is the system they have overridden? Can we try getting the central office to stop the train?"

"I did already, Boss. They can't touch it. It isn't even showing on the grid, now."

A germ of an idea sprouted. "Safety systems are always supposed to fail safe."

Lucy keyed something into the terminal. "That's right. Backup controls are built into the train. If an obstruction is detected at a monitored crossing the train stops. The signal is separate and the control is separated from the main controls. But Mohammed might be able to override these as well."

"So we expect him to do it. Will the train stop or at least slow down?" As a double agent, Mohammed would want us on the train. I had to take the chance we could board the train.

"It should. He's going to have to restart the system and get the train running on manual. Even in a panic stop the train will still travel a mile or so."

"Guess we find a spot to block the tracks and go for the gusto."

I pushed the Jag to crazy speeds on dark back roads. We passed the train and raced to find a crossing we could block. Lucy studied the maps screen on the cell phone, flicking the pictures with her thumbs.

"Turn at the next road." She looked up. "Turn here."

I slammed the brakes on and slewed the car on a wild, greater-than-90-degree turn onto a dirt cow path. The car lurched and twisted as I fought for control. "Give a guy some warning, next time."

"Yeah right. I told you to turn. This road should run parallel to the train tracks for about a mile." And right on cue the road twisted to the left away from the railroad bed that rose up six feet in front of us.

"Stop here." Lucy commanded.

"Now what?" The car skittered to a halt. This wasn't what I'd been thinking: out in the middle of an Illinois cow pasture nowhere, with a freight train of nukes screaming down on us.

"Get out." Lucy pushed me out the driver's door. "I'll stop the train with the Jag at the next crossing. You should be able to jump the train before Mohammed gets it rolling again." She smiled. "Get going, boys."

"Not much of a plan." I grabbed my battle-rattle and stepped back from the car.

"Better than nothing. Watch out." She barely let the doors latch before she gunned the big V8 and tore down the road in a cloud of dust.

The distant vibration of the oncoming locomotive could be felt through the road bed. While the dust settled, Tommy and I did a quick equipment check. Tommy had brought the night vision goggles, the dragon skin body armor, and the M-4s. Nerves set in. We had one chance at this. The trick would never work twice.

Lucy raced for a crossing out of our sight, while we hid in a drainage ditch. The train vibrated the earth. Sharp air-horn blasts rippled into the distance as the airbrakes exploded into emergency-stop. Sparks lit the roadbed as every wheel on the train tried to halt its load. The night vision goggles flashed from green to white with the heat of the engine. I pushed them up before the light spoiled my night vision.

We waited at the foot of the embankment. We had to catch the train before Mohammed could recover. "Tommy. Run for the train on my signal."

He fingered his pistol. "You gonna rescue her no matter what, right?"

Would I make the choice between Elouise and the 3 million people in the greater Chicago area? Between her and Sarah? Fuck. Why'd he have to put it that way? Tommy watched me with the concentration of a pit bull deciding whether to eat me or cuddle.

I couldn't let his loyalty and my fear of failure become a toxic mixture. No hemming and hawing. No bullshit. He'd seen all the bullshit in the world already. "Yes. I wouldn't let anything happen to Elouise. Don't worry."

He believed me, I guess. He nodded his head, pocketed his .22, and slung his M4 into ready as we watched the train in its slow motion slide.

Lucy had judged her timing nicely using maps off the phone. The engine slid past, its drive wheels churning in reverse, sparks flying off wheels locked with full brakes applied. A figure dashed between the second locomotive and the first. I ducked in the weeds. The train had slowed to a walking pace when the airbrakes unlocked.

The fail safe on the brakes had been overridden. Next the train would start to accelerate. I unslung the M4 and dashed up the slope to the tracks as the last car, with the half sized container box, rolled up to our location. The train began to pick up speed.

The obvious had eluded me. There weren't any convenient ladders to grab onto like they showed in the movies. As we scrambled up the elevated road bed the train rolled past at a brisk pace. A funny little light hung off the back of the last flatcar and it had steps. Tommy caught a chain and pulled himself onto the deck. I caught the little platform with the light and hung on for dear life as the train gathered speed.

The container covered half of the flatcar deck. Tommy rolled into prone position when the container's door burst open and men boiled out with AK-47s. Tommy took them one-two-three with his rifle. The brave died either from his bullets or the fall off the train. Somebody inside fired 7.62 rounds at us through the open door. I tried to hide below the edge of the car as lead ricocheted off the steel. When the lone shooter stopped to change magazines, I threw one of the flash- bangs into the container and rolled onto the deck next to the Fisherman. Before the shooter could recover I fired half a dozen rounds at ankle height.

No one returned fire. The shooter might be playing possum but between the flash bang and the bullets he had the fight knocked out of him. I tapped Tommy on the shoulder. "Let's go."

My hand came away wet with blood. Part of his head was missing. Tommy the Fisherman, hitman for the Outfit, became one more in the growing crowd of ghosts I carried with me. "Good shooting, Tommy."

I dropped the NVGs back over my eyes. The dim hole of the container suddenly lit up with cooling sprays of blood. The shooter sat like a ragdoll on the floor at the very back of the container, his gun on the floor and blood spilling out of two holes in his chest. The container had been set up as crew quarters for a dozen men, judging by the bunks bolted to the walls. Possibly we had left most of those troops dead in the parking lot.

I checked Tommy again, just to make sure. At least he took his honor guard with him to hell.

I saw four men die. We'd killed six in the parking lot. Already more men than the usual terror cell and they hadn't all come from California with Mohammed. We'd only seen five get on the train, including Mohammed and Elouise. Mohammed had said a military officer named Amin had mission control. I'd killed his brother, Ahkmed, in the parking lot. So Amin had led another team and taken the train before Mohammed arrived. But how many?

And where was Elouise?

A radio crackled from the floor. "Where are you?" in Arabic. They'd come looking for their missing brothers soon. I had to get a jump on them.

The container also had doors at the end where the dead terrorist sat. I pushed him out of the way. The car ahead had an access door in the back. No doubt the men moved through the train using these doors. The radio crackled again. Between the train noise and my poor Arabic I didn't understand the words, but I bet someone was coming back to check on these guys. Too many variables to just wait, and too risky to cross into the unknown.

I don't mind taking a risk if I know what the odds are but these were real hard to calculate. The roofs of the transport cars were rounded and smooth. No way to hold on and climb across. And they were perforated. Even at night a cautious observer would see a shadow and a single round would end my rescue attempt, and a slight lightening to the east indicated dawn.

The radio crackled again. I closed the container doors and scrambled up onto its flat roof. Three more would-be terrorists appeared, crossing between cars with a clumsiness indicating lack of preparation. When the last one, apparently the leader, stopped at the door of the carrier car to observe, I put a bullet in his head in remembrance of Tommy.

I flicked two flash bang grenades into the container box. The explosions made my ears ring even outside. One terrorist pushed open the back doors and charged, firing his AK-47 blindly until he tripped over Tommy and fell off the back. I dropped off the roof onto the deck and rolled flat. Inside the container the last terrorist screamed and clawed at his eyes with one hand while he sprayed bullets into the night. Flash bangs are meant to disorient, and provide a minimal concussion, but apparently you don't want to be looking right at it when it goes off. I must have cheated using two.

"Don't kill me," he cried when the action locked open on his weapon. He dropped the empty magazine from the weapon and fumbled at his clothes. "I can't see. I can't see."

I pushed my .44 into his cheek before he could find a spare magazine. "How many more on this train?"

"I don't know what you're talking about." His bloodshot eyes rolled.

I cocked the hammer by way of explaining myself. He shuddered and collapsed to his knees. "Allahu Akbar, allahu Akbar."

"Where's the girl?" Something flashed across the living space. My eye caught it flashing by, my mind backed up and reprocessed the image as the 'spoon' or triggering handle from a fragmentation grenade. I looked down. He had two grenades, minus the spoons, in his hands while he continued to mutter.

I jumped through the forward facing doors, across the space between the flatbed car I had been on and the last covered car, and tripped over the body of the terrorist I'd shot in the doorway as the grenades exploded behind me. The container bulged, the doors flashed open, and shrapnel rained on the metal skin of the train. I wanted to say 'Allahu akbar' myself since he must have helped me get out of the car before the explosion.

I looked around. The car contained two HMMWVs fitted as box trucks. Each truck had a very noticeable nuclear hazmat symbol on the side. A radio crackled behind me as I scrambled for my feet. I looked up in time to see an Air Force major pointing his service automatic at me, and the flash from the muzzle.

29. MARTYR

My vision swirled from red to black and it hurt to breathe. The Dragon Skin body armor had caught several rounds aimed at my chest. When I finally could open my eyes the Air Force officer sneered at me and spit.

"Mohammed," he said. "Take this piece of shit into the other car and tie him next to the woman. I must finish installing the prototype."

I tried to move but the world spun and went black again. Mohammed picked me up in a fireman's carry. I felt the jostling and the wind as we crossed between the cars. He dropped me on the steel deck in a car just like the one where I'd been ambushed, with the center filled with a hard boxed 1093 Military Transport Vehicle, better known as 'truck', the cab facing the front of the train and bearing the ubiquitous nuclear transport markings.

In front of the truck, Elouise hung with her arms tied over her head to one of the roof braces, and pulled tight so she could just stand on the balls of her feet. Duct tape stretched across her mouth. The morning sun streamed through the various vent holes and a single beam illuminated her face. Her eyes were red and angry when she looked at me.

Mohammed looped duct tape around my hands and threw a rope over one of the roof braces. Then he tied the rope to the tape between my wrists and hauled on it until my arms extended over my head and my feet barely touched the floor. "I am sorry, my friend, but I must do one more thing before I can help you." Mohammed's hand slipped into my jacket and retrieved my 10mm. He stuck the gun in his inside jacket pocket and turned away.

The erstwhile Air Force major swaggered into the train, smiling. "Mr. Smiley? What a funny name." He came close enough for me to smell the garlic in his breakfast. "You killed my brother and I will enjoy killing you bit by bit before we get to Chicago."

I looked at the tape on my wrists and wondered if the whole arrangement would hold my weight while I wrapped my legs around his neck and tried to choke him. "Sorry about your brother. He shouldn't have picked a fight he couldn't win."

Amin, the major, laughed explosively. "He is an arrogant prick, isn't he, Mohammed, my brother?"

"Some people are arrogant, some people are honest. Did you finish installing the trigger?" Mohammed stood slightly behind Amin, supporting the weight of the gun in his jacket with his crossed arms.

"I like to think I'm being honest." I said, hoping Mohammed took my gun for a reason. If he planned on shooting Amin, I hoped he wouldn't let him have fun with me first.

Amin grunted. "I think I'll shoot you in the knees. I'll let you hang while I cut you. After a while you won't be able to breathe unless you stand, but you won't be able to stand because your legs are shattered." He pulled his service pistol and took a step back to get a clear shot, then his face and brains splattered on the metal wall next to me.

Mohammed held my 10 mm pistol with smoke still curling out of the barrel. "I didn't want him to kill you, Sgt. Smiley. And the only way to stop him was to kill him."

I glanced at the extra hole from the 10 mm in the metal panel beside my head surrounded by Amin's blood and brains. "I'm just glad you moved enough I didn't get the full face treatment. Will you cut me down now?"

"I'm not sure I will——just yet. You and your friend have some unsavory acquaintances." Mohammed waved the pistol between me and Elouise.

I nodded at Elouise who was struggling to stay on her toes so she could breathe. "I think she's been strung up too long. Cut her down and we can talk about unsavory acquaintances."

Elouise looked in serious distress. She tried to move from one foot to the other but her knees buckled. Mohammed stepped forward and cut the line to the roof brace. She fell to her knees.

"I apologize for leaving you in such an awkward position, Ms. Blankenship. One has to play one's part no matter what the consequences," Mohammed said.

Elouise sat on the floor rubbing her wrists for improved circulation. She tore the duct tape off of her mouth with no hesitation.

Mohammed turned to me. "You know someone is working from inside your government to steal these weapons."

"So I've been told. Do you have a name?"

"The woman knows. She works for those kinds of people and if she is with you, then, you do as well." Mohammed pushed Elouise towards me. "Woman, unloosen my old friend."

Elouise stumbled into me. I felt her hand snake into my pants and find the .38 I stored there. She slipped it out and held it close to her belly as she regained her balance. She took a step to untie the other end of the rope, but then she spun on the ball of her foot and fired three quick shots into Mohammed.

The first shot spun the gun out of his hand; the next two hit center of mass and splattered blood onto the truck. Mohammed toppled like a felled tree.

"Why the hell did you do that?" I yelled at her. "Mohammed was one of the good guys in this mess. You know that."

Tears flowed freely down her cheeks, but the gun in her hand never wavered. The barrel stared at me like an evil eye. "I have a job to do. No matter how much I hate it."

The countryside roared past. Vibrations from the steel wheels rolling on the rails echoed off the metal walls in a steady drone. The smell of gunpowder overpowered the smell of oil and blood for the moment. The ruined Smith and Wesson 10 mm slid across the metal deck.

"Which way is this double cross going?" I asked. Gullible, old Smiley, the guy who believes the best in people. I had to ask, as if she would tell me the truth.

"You weren't supposed to catch the bloody train." Her accent shifted to the broad Scots of her purported youth. "Didn't I tell you to get out while you had a chance? Now what are we going to do?"

"What the hell did you expect me to do? Leave you to Amin's tender care?" I nudged the corpse at my feet. "After what he did to Lucy?"

"Do you think it was an accident?" The pistol wavered in her hand. "I needed to follow them so I told Mohammed I was working with you."

"That wasn't such a good idea was it?"

She absently rubbed the bruises on her neck and arms. "I had a mission. I was to take control of the munitions on the train by whatever means necessary."

"You didn't look like you had the situation under control when I got here."

"If you hadn't been so bloody persistent about playing hero they would have left me a simple hostage." She glared at me over the pistol barrel. At least she had the .38 and not the .380. She only had two shots left.

"I'm nobody's idea of a hero. People I know die. Good people, bad people. Doesn't matter. Your pet hitman bought it getting on the train. Mohammed worked against Amin, and Amin wanted to blow up Chicago."

"Jason, don't you understand I might have to kill you?" She pleaded with me, like I might have some empathy with her position.

"You work for the General, don't you?" I leaned toward her pulling at the rope. "At least you could cut me down instead of shooting me like I was a side of beef."

She carefully felt around for the knife Mohammed had used to cut her down. When she found it she sawed through the rope and my arms fell like lead in front of me.

Then her cell phone rang.
"It might be better if I answered that." I watched her eyes for a tell-tale sign she was on my side, and got nothing.

She shrugged and cut my hands free. She handed the phone to me on the fourth ring. I tapped it on. "Smiley here."

"Sgt. Smiley." General Isaacson showed just a touch of surprise in his voice. "What's your situation?"

"The terrorists are dead. We have nukes. Elouise Blankenship is standing in front of me with a gun to my head and there is a remote control triggering circuit installed on one of the bombs. We just don't know which one, or how it's rigged to go off." I watched Elouise's eyes. They might show a hint if she intended to shoot me.

"Good, good. You just hang tight and we'll get that train stopped," the General said.

"Not sure that's a good idea until we get the trigger disabled. It might be programmed to go off when the train slows down," I said. It seemed like a reasonable precaution, and I didn't expect the

General to agree to it.

"Don't worry about bombs and triggers. We'll get that taken care of. Let me talk to Elouise." His voice conveyed the hearty handshake and slap on the back he'd give me in person right before he forgot my name. I was dismissed.

I handed the phone to Elouise. "It's for you."

She glared at me over the barrel of my .38 and clicked the phone to speaker. "Yes, sir."

"Good work El." The General's parade field bonhomie made me want to puke. "You've done a great job, so far. The train will be shunted to a remote siding just outside of Chicago. You will meet Danny Chourelli there. He will have his people in place to move the shipment to the Chinese freighter, the Jiahua, and you will escort the shipment. Make sure you pay Chourelli off quietly once the freight is loaded."

"What about Smiley?" Elouise caught my eye.

"Good soldier. Too bad." The voice echoed some insincere regret. "Pay him off, too."

The phone went dead. The hard knot in my stomach didn't come from being surprised, but from being right. General Isaacson, warrior king of the Special Forces, was running a heist of American nuclear warheads. He'd ordered the execution of Danny Shoe and me like he was asking for a glass of water. And his hitman——'hit-person'—— had my own gun pointed at my head.

"So you wanted me to hear the execution order? Like it would somehow make me say it's all right?" I put my hands behind my head and sat on the deck with my back against the wall. "Go ahead and shoot me. Don't let me stop you. All that bullshit about not wasting people."

Her upper lip began to tremble and snot bubbled out of one nostril. "Damn you, Smiley." Commitment to a course of action flashed in her eyes and the gun barked twice before I could move.

The bullets punched holes in the sheet steel six feet above my head. She clicked through the empty chambers, then threw the gun at the wall. "Do you have any idea about who is running this operation? These are the most powerful people in the world."

"I doubt it. I've run into the most powerful men in the world. They don't care about anything except their mission. Not even staying alive. Those men are powerful. Whoever you're working for wants something. Who are you loyal to?" I scooted closer to the next upright to make a place for her.

Elouise sat down on the deck next to me. Her voice went soft and sibilant again with the accents of her native Scotland. "Loyalty is not an option. I'm a commodity. The highest bidder gets me for whatever job they want done. If I fail, I'm disposable."

"So who bought you this time? Not Mohammed, but Isaacson?" I asked.

"Isaacson brought me into the operation. He needed me to keep track of the players. The Arabs were always a threat of going rogue."

"So when Jack bolted with the triggers, the operation got less stable?"

"There weren't supposed to be any triggers. Jack was sent out of town to keep him from nosing around the transfer. No one knew exactly why he bolted until you found that trigger."

"Someone knew about the trigger. Mohammed knew and I think we can agree he is closer to the right side of this situation than you are. He would have passed the info up his communications chain." I took a deep breath and a moment to appreciate the sunlight rippling across the car.

"Maybe. The General didn't. He's been scrambling to get control of the operation ever since."

"The General sounds awfully exposed by all these negotiations."

"No, he's got someone to manage details and the negotiations." She didn't look me in the eye.

"Who?"

She looked back, and cocked an eyebrow. "Me."

"So you've been in on this operation from the beginning?"

"Mohammed had the assets to get the bombs. The sleeper agents were twenty years getting in place. To get control of the train he needed the ultimate experts in coercion, the Mafia. In order to get the Mafia he needed to have a sweet deal for them. That's what Isaacson does. He negotiates with bad people. Mohammed offered him the idea of stealing the nukes. Isaacson has many contacts in shadowy parts of the world. He found the Triads ready to bankroll the deal with connections to get the weapons out of the country. The mob agreed to provide manpower."

"And the jihadists planned a double cross all the time?"

"They must have. I'm not sure Mohammed was the good guy you think. He set Fiona on Jack from the beginning." Lines of dirt and sweat highlighted the stress on Elouise's face.

"So why did you kill Mohammed? Just doing your job?" I got up to look again at my dead friend, only he wasn't there. "Or maybe you didn't do such a good job of killing him?

"What?" She shouldered me out of the way to examine the bloody streaks on the deck. "Christ's blood. He must have had body armor on. He could trigger the bomb. We have to find him."

"Okay, let's get looking," I squatted down to look under the truck. I couldn't see any terrorists under the chassis. Elouise found a flashlight in the cab and looked in the back.

"If you didn't know about the triggers, what was that business about finding Jack and the Chinese box?" I checked the second device in the truck for tampering.

"Trying to tamp down the situation. The Chinese were very edgy about Jack's disappearance and what he'd taken. They wouldn't tell us what though. Just a box."

"You knew it was more than a box."

"I suspected. Whatever it was disrupted the operation. Jack had no head for operations. I couldn't believe he had stumbled onto something so critical."

"So why was he cut off?"

"Mohammed. We were sure he'd been brought into the operation by Mohammed as a double agent. We thought finding Jack would lead directly to Mohammed and whatever disruption he had planned."

"Since Jack's dead you've been using me to find the triggers and Mohammed?" I asked. "Why?"

"The value of the bombs is having them, not blowing a hole in America. The General wanted me to control Mohammed's play and make sure the bombs got to Chicago without the trigger being armed. And I wanted to get you out of this mess."

"Why?" Our gazes met. Neither one blinked.

None of the warheads had been opened in the first car. Elouise turned and went out the door between the two rail cars. I followed covering her with my .380.

"I never expected you to try to save the world." She wormed her way into the back of the truck.

"I tried to help a friend, but your pet assassin killed him." Mohammed had been hit. Fresh blood splatter had hit the floors and walls.

"I didn't know anything about the hit." Her voice rumbled from the depths of the truck. "We had no reason to hurt Jack. We just wanted to know what he had done."

"You weren't going to kill him?"

Elouise popped out of the back of the second truck. "I don't kill if I have a choice. Isaacson doesn't understand that." Elouise's mouth turned up slightly.

"I like a girl with principles." I led the way this time into the third covered car. With Mohammed bleeding significantly, friend or foe, he would be a cornered rat.

"I don't have many principles left." She held up her hand to stop my advance and tapped her ear to say she heard something. The blood trail led past Amin's body where he fell by the door. "Isaacson will be getting desperate. His plan has been unraveling since he figured out the sleeper cell planned to double cross him," she whispered as we approached the door.

The train lurched to the sound of the brakes blowing off air, throwing me into her. The trailing car pounded against the coupling and the impact knocked us to the deck. Before we'd got our balance, the brakes released and the train picked up speed, again. I pushed myself to my feet and opened the back door. The last car of the train, the flat car with the living quarters in a half-size, container box, and Tommy the Fisherman's corpse on it, rolled to a stop in the rapidly fading distance. A man, Mohammed without a doubt, waved from the box.

Elouise pushed beside me and lifted my 10 mm, taking aim at Mohammed. Whether she could have made the shot or not wasn't relevant, one of her rounds had hit the slide. I pushed the gun to one side so she could see the damage. Firing the round in the chamber would have driven the slide into her head.

"You don't want to kill him, do you?"

"I have to. He's the missing piece. If that trigger is set then he can remotely detonate it." She looked worried.

Inside the car, the truck with the nukes was covered in bloody hand prints. I followed the trail to the weapon. Part of the housing had been removed exposing some complex electronics. One circuit board was brown instead of green and had loose wires soldered into it. The prototype trigger, plugged in and presumably ready to go. But the bloody hand prints hadn't touched the board.

Elouise climbed in and looked. Our eyes met across the nuclear bomb. She nodded. The trigger might be booby trapped but neither one of us could tell. Better to blow a hole in the countryside than in Chicago. I dragged my combat knife out of its scabbard and pried the circuit out of the mechanism.

Elouise noisily released her breath. I realized I needed to breathe, too. Every muscle and nerve in my body burned from the tension. I had been bruised so many times in last five days I had bruises with bruises. And every one of them hurt. I sucked a deep breath and climbed down to the deck.

"So why doesn't Isaacson call it off? Get the mob out of the deal and tell the Triads it's not happening." I helped her out of the back of the truck.

"He'd be a dead man. The mob wouldn't believe him and the Triads would be sure he was trying to double-cross them." She sagged against the fender. "I guess I'm dead, too. I've failed the contract. The consequences of failure are not pretty."

I smiled. The glimmer of a plan had come to me. "How deep is Isaacson's penetration into the DHS and the FBI?"

"As far as I know he's running a special investigations unit. Mostly liaison work which gives him the power to call in assets but the freedom from supervision." She shrugged. "He tried to recruit Rudd, but, stupid as the man acts, he seems to have a streak of sincerity that's frightening to deal with. Almost as bad as yours." She grinned.

Hard to imagine Tom Rudd as a trustworthy asset, but the situation I'd left in Chicago seemed ready to germinate. "What happens next?"

"If we get to Chicago and you're alive, then we're both dead." Elouise's body language expressed the resignation and determination I'd seen in my troops when they were given a mission they didn't believe they'd live through. A combination of resignation to the inevitable, determination, and an appreciation of the ironic nature of doing something so stupid for no better reason than they had to live up to their principles.

"Unless we change the game plan. Just because Isaacson set the rules doesn't mean we have to play by them."

Elouise's eyes brightened. "What do you mean?"

"I'm thinking out loud." I stroked her jaw with more tenderness than I'd felt in years. She'd been a survivor, and had given up the ruthlessness that had let her survive for me. I wanted to trust her, but trust is easy to lose and hard to gain. My fingers found her carotid artery. Her heartbeat pulsed steady and fast. I made an effort not to rub the raw skin. "What did you expect to gain from this job?"

Her pulse stayed steady. "It was just a job. But I wanted to live through it."

"I think we all do." Her pulse increased as I tightened my fingers on her throat. Her eyes grew a little wider as I rubbed the raw rope burn on her neck but she didn't move a hand to stop me. "Would you give up the life?"

She swallowed hard, didn't say anything for a moment. "I don't know. I don't think I can. Besides, I like the power."

"The power over what?"

"The power of life and death," she whispered.

My fingers tightened ever so little as her pulse increased.

"Would you stop that? You're making me nervous and there's no way you can tell if I'm telling the truth or not. If you want to know if you can trust me, just ask." She stroked the side of my face. "I think I love you."

I released her throat. "I'm not real sure how I feel about you just yet. But can I trust you? With my life?"

She shook her head. "You can't afford to trust anyone. Tie me up."

She hadn't given me the answer I expected. Instead she'd given me every reason to disable her until after we arrived at Chicago. She might be dead either way but if she wasn't, then the survivor couldn't blame her for whatever went wrong. Elegant thinking.

"What will you do if I don't?"

She smiled at me. "Die, I expect."

30. KING'S PAWN

We sat on the back of the train watching the tracks disappear behind us listening to the mindless rhythm of the rails as we flowed in the direction of Chicago. Isaacson had ordered Elouise to kill me, but she refused. She had forfeited her life for mine. I couldn't let her pay her forfeiture.

I felt like I was staring at a chess board after a long hard fought game. I could see we were three moves from checkmate, but I wasn't sure who would win.

Elouise and I had a date with some unsavory people, starting with General Isaacson———adding in Danny Shoe and his happy band of felons. Mohammed had taken himself off the chessboard when he broke the last rail car loose. He became irrelevant when I destroyed the last trigger.

But the General had stage-managed the hijacking of deployable nuclear weapons; whether he intended them to be operable and delivered didn't matter. He had brought the Chinese Triads, the Chicago Outfit and a terrorist sleeper cell together with explicit desire to profit from an enormous risk to national security. His orders killed Jack. His deals killed Bruno and Fiona as collateral damage, and brutalized my best friend. Isaacson couldn't be allowed to profit in any way from the weapons that had cost so very much.

I had a few pieces left but I didn't dare risk them. Lucy, could control the back field by directing information where it would do the most good. Elouise might be the queen in this analogy, but I wasn't sure whether she was white or black. That made her dangerous. Maybe I should tie her up for my own security.

I'd primed Rudd for support before I'd left Chicago, but I trusted Sergeant Davidson to deliver. He would make sure Rudd did his part. Capturing a terrorist would have been rewarding for Rudd's career, but capturing a corrupt government official selling nuclear weapons might get him elected.

In the end just getting out of this alive would be a challenge. I turned back to Elouise who had been watching me ruminate. "He'll kill us, won't he?"

"I believe so. The General is very exposed at this moment. His position could only be secured by destroying the train——and us—— — forgoing the financial part of his plan in favor of saving himself for another day. An air strike would derail the train and leave the nuclear devices relatively untouched." Elouise looked very tired. This run had been hard on her, too.

"We need help. Do we have any clean phones? I'm sure Isaacson at least is monitoring my cell calls when he can. I've been changing phones frequently," I said as I checked my pockets. I had brought two phones with me but they hadn't survived the fire fight.

"I have the phone Isaacson called me on. I'm sure he has it tapped." She said handing me her phone. "Who were you going to call?"

My choices of people I could trust had dwindled to a pathetic few. Few? One.

I dialed a number. The line buzzed through a couple of cell tower connections, then it picked up. "Lucy?"

"Smiley." I thought heard tears in her voice. "You made it. Did you find her?"

"This is an unsecure line." This phrase set the ground rules for the conversation. No personal information would change hands. No operational intelligence except what we wanted to share with other parties. Lucy had spent many more years dealing with operation security than I had. It would be second nature to her.

Lucy slipped back into her professional mode. "What's the problem?"

"Mohammed and his crew have been contained. The crew hired to kill me has been contained. The weapons have been disarmed. There is no immediate danger. However, there is the mole problem with Homeland Security. I'm going to attempt to stop this train. To allow the proper authorities to come collect the weapons." I grinned at Elouise.

"Got it, Boss."

"I'll call you later."

"All you guys say the same thing. Out here." She clicked off the phone.

"Shouldn't you have told her about Isaccson?" Elouise raised an eyebrow at me. "What are you grinning about?"

"I've been kidnapped, blackmailed, manipulated and threatened over these damn bombs; it's about time I turned the tables on the puppet master." I watched Elouise's eyes. She didn't return my grin, except a slight twinkle in her eyes and a tightening of her jaw.

"You are trying to get us killed, aren't you?"

"Lucy will be our witness. She'll make sure the right people hear what's going on; it won't get covered up."

"And that will make it harder for Isaacson to order an airstrike on the train?"

"Absolutely. Now for part two of the plan." I pulled a card out of my pocket and dialed the number shown. The phone picked up on the second ring.

"Special Agent Davidson, may I help you?"

"Zech? It's Smiley. I need a favor. There are a bunch of gangsters waiting on a siding outside of Chicago for a train with deployable nuclear weapons on it. I have control of the train, except I don't know how to stop it yet. You may want to contain Danny Chourelli's boys."

SA Davidson didn't speak for a minute. "Smiley, this is for real, correct? You're not under duress are you?"

"It's all green, Zech. Just calling in the cavalry."

"Got it. I'll let Rudd know what's up. Do you have an exact location?"

"No. But they can't be too hard to find. They'll have trucks and equipment to unload the rail cars. Probably a crane sitting at some remote siding near the port. Now I have to stop the train."

* * *

Women have never been my strong suit. I tend to see them as better than they are, or maybe I just want to see what's best in them. Rarely is the sentiment returned. Elouise watched me with one of those indefinable expressions women use when they aren't sure whether they are disgusted or delighted.

"I didn't think you were quite like this," she said, her voice even with a hint of smile.

"I've got principles and I can't trust anyone. Normally people operate in their own self-interest but you have to know what their self-interest is. There are so many layers to this situation that I don't know whose self-interest is being served. Therefore I have to serve my own self-interest." I kicked at the door of the rail car. "Shall we check to see if anyone is driving this train?"

I held the door for her.

"OK, everyone acts in their own self-interest. What's yours? What is it you want?"

I clambered across the coupling to the next car and called back to her. "I thought I knew when I went into the police academy. I wanted to protect the good people from the evil people. But in Chicago, the line between crime, corruption and civic virtue is very blurry." Elouise stumbled crossing the coupling. I caught her by the arms.

"It's the same everywhere I've been," she yelled over the wind.

Inside the door, where only some of the track noise penetrated I answered. "Nothing is ever black and white, but it should be. There's right and wrong, but the law is a thousand shades of grey. After 9/11, I thought I'd find the answer fighting the evil bastards that attacked our country."

As we came to the lead engine pair I pulled the .380, the only working gun I had left. "I fought them in Afghanistan when we went after Al-Qaeda. My kid brother was killed in Iraq by an IED." I cleared the control cab of the backup engine. "We shouldn't have been in Iraq. He died because some sick, old men wanted a war of their own."

The roar of the diesel generators made me finish my thought by yelling in her ear. "I love my country. I'd die for her in a heartbeat. But I hate her corrupters."

I pushed open the door to the cab on the front engine. Two crew members lay on the floor in a pool of their own congealed blood. A black box sat on the engineer's stool with a hoard of wires running to the control panels, more ran to a neat little pile of C4 plastic explosive. The train ran on autopilot and the autopilot was a bomb. I sighed. I could suppose that any disruption of the black box would light off the C4.

Elouise squatted next to the controller and the trigger. "At least it

305

won't set off the nukes." The tension in her voice brought out her highland lilt.

"You're sure?"

"Right then. The bomb requires a special series of shaped charges to drive the plutonium demi-spheres together in the bomb. A big boomer in the cab here will nae do more than break it." She started fingering the wires to the C4 and back to a couple of LEDS flashing in front of two large blue cans wired to the circuit board. "The bad news is this wee boomer goes off if there is any disruption to the capacitor trigger."

"I'd rather not blow it up. Do you think we can disconnect the auto-pilot without triggering the bomb?"

"No, I think that is the one thing that guarantees the bomb goes off. It's only purpose is to stop us from dismantling the autopilot."

"Can we disable the bomb?" My training in demolitions was limited to the very basics of setting up a Claymore mine.

"I don't know." Elouise looked at the trigger. "I'm afraid it will blow."

"We've got to stop the train. Otherwise it just keeps going, unless Isaacson can control it."

"This gear doesn't look like a Chinese knockoff. Maybe he arranged for Amin and his crew to get it."

"You mean you don't know?"

"Isaacson compartmentalizes information. I didn't know he had involved Mohammed Abd Allah until you told me." She studied the wires some more. "My bomb making experience goes back to the training I got in Chechnya, but I think the trigger is activated when the control wires are cut."

"But they reset the brake system after we forced the automatic train control to operate. They didn't have time to build this bomb afterwards."

"No, and Amin cursed you before he went forward to reset the controller." Elouise smiled. "Which means you can turn it off, and the capacitors hold the trigger open for a few minutes while the system resets."

"So we could turn the power off, disengage the motor controls and coast to a stop?"

Elouise shrugged.

I clicked the main power breaker to the off position. Immediately the control panels went blank and the train hesitated as its forward thrust was removed.

Elouise pulled the blasting caps out of the C4 with speed and desperation. She separated the blasting caps from the explosives as far as the wires would stretch. I grabbed her by the arm and dragged her back through the decelerating train. The blasting caps went off just as we got to the second engine, but the world didn't turn upside down like it would had the C4 blown the lead locomotive off of the tracks.

"You're a crazy bugger." Elouise breathed heavily into my jacket.

I pulled her tight. "You do good work under pressure. Thanks for not blowing us to hell."

"So what do we do now, Mr. Smiley? Wait?" Elouise looked up at me but didn't let go.

"Waiting's a good option. I expect the FBI to be rounding up the boys from the Outfit and the Triads. The General would have been there to see the deal through, but he expected you there to eliminate Chourelli. With Rudd in place and the bombs elsewhere he's not going to stick around. With the stakes as high as they are for him, he's going to want to know why the train stopped and he's going to want to shut me up."

"So, the old gomeral is coming to kill you. And when he finds me here I'll be collateral damage?" Elouise rolled her eyes at me. "I hope you have a better plan than that."

"I don't think he has a lot of trusted assets. The two guys that picked me up at the airport were it, and Tommy the Fisherman made a mess out of them. If he calls in an airstrike on the train he's going to need a damn good reason, especially after Lucy gets the word out I've got the situation under control and am waiting for the good guys." I grinned. It felt very good to be winning for a change.

The train slowed so gradually I barely noticed. The brakes had come on with the loss of power, and we were nearly stopped in the Illinois countryside. I opened the locomotive's door and looked past the rail cars with their cache of death. The sun shone bright in the east and a warm breeze blew from the south west.

"Looks like a good day," I said.

"What was it your Indians said? Today is a good day to die?" She looked out over the winter-browned fields of Western Illinois. "If I had a choice, this isn't a bad one."

31. DEADFALL

With the train stopped like a bombing run target in a farmer's field, the sun quickly warmed the inside of the cab. I leaned against the open doorway relishing the bit of a breeze blowing up the tracks. March had turned from the bitter end-of-winter cold to spring in a day. The sun and fresh air washed away the fatigue and fear with the promise of new beginnings. The sounds of trucks on the interstate and the sound of a tractor pulling cow manure through a farmer's field interrupted the pastoral quiet. The smell of fermented dung whiffed in on the breeze.

When you're in a battle zone the one thing you try not to think about——and can't escape——is the idea each day might be your last. You don't get used to the idea, but you work through it. Do what you're trained to do.

Today might be a good day to die, but I didn't intend to do so.

"We need a weapons inventory before the General shows up." I climbed into the first car. Elouise had laid out Amin and had his Beretta caught in the waistband of her pants. "He might come in and try to fast talk me or he might come in with guns blazing. Either way I want to be ready."

"Well, I have Amin's pistol. And my bag is in the last car." Elouise headed towards the back of the train.

"The 10 mm is toast." I said, following her through the interior of the train past the half dozen trucks loaded with deployable nuclear weapons. In my head I counted the guns I had left. The .38 was empty. Bullets were in the backpack with my clothes in Elouise's Jag. I had two spare magazines for the 10mm but that wouldn't do me any good. I had my .380 in my pocket. The .44 had been fastened to my utility belt, but Amin had stripped me of my equipment while I was unconscious.

In the last car Elouise opened the cab of the truck and retrieved her large purse from behind the seat. My utility belt had been tossed on the front seat. While she checked the bag's contents, I checked the dead man for weapons. He had spare magazines for an AK but the rifle was gone, probably with Mohammed.

"I've got my .357 and the needle gun." She held out two speed-loaders for her pistol.

"I've got spare magazines for my ankle gun and a speed-loader for the .44. Not enough ammo to win a gun battle. Especially if he brings rifles." I dug in the compartments on the belt. "And I have a grenade."

"That won't do us very much good, will it?"

"It gives them a reason not to shoot me," I said with a grin. "I can pull the hand grenade trick on them like I did on Ahkmed."

A helicopter coming in fast buzzed the train. I leaned out the back door. The helicopter banked sharply, flared and landed fifty yards from the train. Two men jumped out. One was lanky with the cavalier attitude fostered by military commanders to instill confidence in their men. The other man, carrying an M4 at the ready, had a bandage wrapped around his otherwise bald head. Good to know Sam had made it out alive. One less casualty of this stupid robbery. Couldn't dignify it with any other name. This was on the same level as sticking up a seven-eleven.

Sam faded to the left to flank the train and come in the back. As the General strolled across the field he pulled his service .45——pearl handled of course——and ran the slide back to load and cock it. He walked up with the gun John Wayne-d from his hip and headed to the front car of the three carrying the weapons trucks. I ran through the train to get there first.

"Hello the car." Isaacson rapped on the metal side.

I redialed the last number called. "Record everything." I said the moment the line picked up, then I dropped the phone into my shirt pocket.

Elouise had followed me and faded into the shadows.

I made myself comfortable in the far corner with a clear view of the door and both paths around the truck. "Hello yourself, General." I pulled the pin on the grenade and held the spoon tight. I'd left the safety tape on but I didn't want to bet my life on it.

"I'm coming in, Smiley." He clambered up the ladder to the front of the car and stepped in. Sunlight flashed through the door behind him like a searchlight. The door swung shut behind him making the dimness of the car, lit as it was by hundreds of perforations, dark as night.

I held the grenade in plain sight in my left hand. I held the .44 in my right hand, low to my side, non-aggressive but ready. "Be careful waving that gun around, General. You wouldn't want to scare me into dropping this."

The General blinked owlishly in the dim interior light, and shoved his pistol in my general direction. "Now, Smiley. There's no need for dramatics. We're all brothers here."

"Not sure I agree, sir. Seems like you broke faith." On my left I saw Sam moving in, the MP4 held high. "Sam, good to see you're still alive. I've pulled the pin on the grenade in my hand. You shoot me and you kill the General. Might not be a bad trade, but I'd rather you didn't, just yet."

"Smiley," Sam growled. "Where is the motherfucker that killed Butch? I want him."

"Sorry about Butch. Tommy, the hitman, didn't make it. Took a bullet to the head getting on the train." I tried to keep my eyes on both of them. The General seemed to have cleared his vision. His pistol held steady in my direction. The Dragon Skin body armor would stop the .45 from killing me. I turned my attention to Sam. "Did you know the hitman was called in to kill me, by the General?"

Sam's aim wavered momentarily. "He wouldn't do that to Butch and me."

"Oh, I'm sure it was an oversight on his part. Collateral damage." I sighed. "You guys were just collateral damage while the General stole nuclear weapons."

"Now hold on, Smiley." The General grinned. "I didn't steal anything. The ragheads stole the weapons. I always intended to recover them, and close down the sleeper-cell network. A grateful nation might even appreciate my leadership."

"And who were the Chinese going to pay for the weapons?" I asked.

The General barked out a laugh. "C'mon, Smiley. You know the way this works. We take the bad guys down. If they have money lying around, we gather it up to finance our operations. Saves the taxpayers beaucoup dollars."

"So what was the plan? Let them load the weapons on a ship in Chicago and stop them before they left the Seaway? Even after you knew they had triggers for the bombs?"

"Smiley, you've got the triggers, am I right?" the General said.

"Those are destroyed. What makes you think the Chinese sold all the ones they had?"

The General paused to consider this idea. "You might have a point, Sergeant. Good thing we're in clean-up mode now. Sam, kill him." Isaacson turned towards the door.

"Wait a second, General," Sam called out. "Is it true? Did you call in the hitman?"

The General turned back with a sigh. "Sam, I told Chourelli to take care of this problem. The hitman was Chourelli's sloppy solution to everything. Butch and you were collateral damage."

"Sorry?" Sam dropped his aim and stared at the General. "Butch and I have served with you for twenty-five years. And all we are is collateral damage? This was supposed to be a retirement operation. Easy time. A cake walk. After all the shit we've done, you just shrug Butch off?" Sam swung his rifle around to target Isaacson. The General barely reacted before Sam sagged at the knees and slipped to the floor.

Elouise stood behind Sam. Isaacson brought his gun on her, freezing her with only the dart gun in her hand. I brought up my .44 and aimed at the General.

"Don't do a thing, Smiley. I might not want to shoot you, but I can shoot her. She's a traitor. She sold out." The General's hand tightened on the gun. He was going to shoot her anyway for disobeying him.

We pulled our triggers at the same moment. Or I might have fired that split instance before he did. The roar of the .44 was deafening. Flame jumped from the barrel and the General slammed into the wall and slumped to the deck, the .45 dropping to the deck.

His shot hadn't been aimed at me. He wouldn't have missed at the distance we were from each other. I looked over at Elouise.

She lay in a pool of blood, next to the unconscious Sam. I kicked the rifle free of his hand and bent down to check Elouise. I couldn't see where she'd been hit but she was breathing and there wasn't an arterial spurt. I brushed some of her red hair out of her face.

"That looks so touching." Rudd's voice echoed behind me.

I spun around, gun at the ready. Special Agent Rudd had his service pistol in his hand, nonchalantly covering the car.

"Is she dead?" he asked.

"No." I stood up. "A little late aren't you?"

"The phone call was a nice idea. You can hang up, now." The pitch of his voice indicated he might have been talking to the people listening on the other end.

I pulled the phone. The connection had been closed. "Did you get the mob?"

"Oh, I picked off a few worker bees. The Triads are going to have a hard time restarting operations here. And you took care of the sleeper cell." He shook his head. "You leave piles of corpses where ever you go, Jason."

"I try not to. Most of them aren't mine."

The General groaned from his corner. The .44 had taken him in the chest, but he was wearing a good vest. "Rudd? You need to take Smiley out."

"Ah, General. You make a better dead conspirator than a live one." Tom Rudd shot General Isaacson twice in the head.

32. EPILOGUE

I woke up next to another inert body, but this one was neither dead nor male.

I could tell she was only sleeping because of her gentle snore.

I'm a detective. I notice those sorts of things. I also noticed she was naked, because where our skin touched we stuck together from heat and sweat. Apparently in our haste we'd forgotten to turn on the AC when we returned to my room at the Caribbean resort.

I rolled out of bed and opened the door to the hot tub patio. The Caribbean breeze tickled my skin in the most delightful way. Across the bay the rising sun lit the ocean to start another day. A better day, maybe one without dead bodies. The animal behind my eyes which had been so present for the last week had gone on vacation as well.

Elouise must have woken when I got out of bed. I hadn't heard her bare feet on the carpeted concrete. She wrapped her arms around my chest and pressed her breasts into my back. She nibbled on my shoulder.

"Do you want to tell me, now, what happened while I bled out on the floor?" She chased her nails down my back.

"I met the devil. We made a deal. You're alive. I'm alive. And Chicago didn't get blown to hell. Some of the bad guys are dead. Some are in jail. Some are enjoying linguini with clam sauce." I'd underestimated Tom Rudd. Alaska had changed the man. Where he had been driven by honor and ambition before his punishment tour in Nome, now he was only driven by raw ambition. Isaacson had approached him, and Tom Rudd had played the double agent, just without official sanction.

"That's very poetic, Jason, but it doesn't tell me a lot about our situation," she said between nibbles on various tender parts of my head and neck.

"We get a reset. General Isaacson's operation, which we both worked for, is exposed. Sam will be living a long time with some nasty people in a federal prison. You and I were a split decision from the same fate——or worse." I drew a deep breath of the salt air into my lungs. The touch of Caribbean breeze on my bare skin and the feel of naked woman at my back focused me on what was important. Survival. "I don't know that Tom Rudd is dirty. He killed Isaacson without blinking; he was going to kill you as well. He wanted to be the hero of the story."

"Rub some suntan lotion on me." Her accent was a posh mix of Scots and English. "Why did he want to be the hero? What made that important?"

"Alaska. I made him look bad early in his career and got him sent to Alaska. He thinks I ruined his career." I reached back and squeezed the first substantial bit of flesh I could reach. "Don't you want to shower first? We both stink."

"I'll shower as long as you rub the soap on me." Elouise pinched my nipples and turned back to the room.

I followed. I'm good at that. Especially following pretty women. Makes the day right. The save-the-world crap was overrated.

"So in the end no one had the right understanding of what was happening?" Elouise said.

"Rudd did. He was the puppet master. He brought Mohammed in to take down the sleeper cell. He enabled Isaacson. Rudd might have sold the operation as a sting, but then he wouldn't have had to kill the General. I think he killed the General because money changed hands and he doesn't want to give it up."

"So don't you have an obligation to turn him in for murder?" Elouise stopped her erotic ministrations and stared me in the eye. "He's the real mastermind, right?"

"True, but Rudd's logic is impeccable. I confirmed that the General reached for his gun and Special Agent Rudd saved my life. In turn, you and I didn't get charged with conspiracy to steal nuclear weapons. Rudd was very insistent. Any other response and we would end up dead." I touched her face. The sun stole into the room and lit up the thousand shades of red in her hair. "In the end I did what I intended to do. I saved Chicago from a nuclear attack and the world from non-state-sponsored, nuclear terrorism."

She laced her arms around my neck. "Thank you, Jason. Who's to say Special Agent Rudd did the wrong thing? Isaacson was a corrupt man. He might have wiggled out of an indictment."

"He's a casualty of a war he started, so I don't feel bad." I kissed Elouise on the neck. The taste of old coconut oil came off a little bitter, but the taste of woman still came through. I continued down to lower and even more sensitive regions.

"Thought you wanted to shower?" she said sinking back on the bed to accommodate my ministrations.

"Umm. Later." We could think of later now. Whatever we were was gone. Maybe I'd buy a boat, like Jack's, and we'd cruise the Caribbean. Maybe we could be a 'his and hers' detective agency. Whatever it was could wait until later.

She wrapped her fingers into my hair. "Oh-h. Yeah... We're just going to get all sweaty, anyway."

ABOUT THE AUTHOR

D.E. Osborne has been a story teller and writer since childhood, but the story of life pushed the dreams of a writer's life many years into the future.

Some of his most memorable moments in writing, at least when he was starting out, included a personalized rejection letter from the New Yorker Magazine saying 'write about what you know' and an Official Marvel 'No-Prize' signed by Stan Lee for character suggestions.

Rejections are always more instructive than praise, just not as enjoyable.

D.E. lives in rural Northern New York where the winters last too long and are separated by single season 'getting ready for Winter'. (Laugh loudly here….).

D .E.'s other passions include reading, music and his family.

Author photograph by Roseanne Osborne.